PENGUIN MODERN CLASSICS

Nostalgia

Mircea Cărtărescu was born in Bucharest in 1956. His novels and poetry are widely considered to be the best writing to emerge from post-communist Romania. His books have been translated into fourteen languages and he has received many awards, including most recently the Thomas Mann Prize and the Prix Formentor.

Julian Semilian is a translator, poet and filmmaker. He currently teaches at the North Carolina School of the Arts, after a twenty-four-year career as a film editor in Hollywood.

T0353912

MIRCEA CĂRTĂRESCU

Nostalgia

Translated by Julian Semilian

PENGUIN BOOKS

PENGUIN CLASSICS

UK | USA | Canada | Ireland | Australia
India | New Zealand | South Africa

Penguin Books is part of the Penguin Random House group of companies
whose addresses can be found at global.penguinrandomhouse.com

Penguin
Random House
UK

First published in Romanian by Editura Cartea Românească 1989
Revised edition published by Humanitas 1993
This translation first published in the United States of America by New
Directions 2005
First published in Great Britain in Penguin Classics 2021

008

Text copyright © Editura Cartea Românească, 1989
Revised text copyright © Humanitas, 1993
Translation copyright © Julian Semilian, 2005

The moral right of the author and the translator has been asserted

The epigraph on page 3, repeated on page 25, is from 'A Song for Simeon' from
Collected Poems 1909–1962 by T. S. Eliot, copyright 1936 by Harcourt, Inc., copyright
© 1964, 1963 by T. S. Eliot, reprinted by permission of the publisher. The quotation
on page 1 by Tudor Arghezi is from 'Epilog'; that on page 27, by Mihail Eminescu, is
from the sonnet 'Trecut-au anii' ('The years have passed'). The epigraph on page
303 is from Thomas Mann's Doctor Faustus, copyright 1947 by Thomas Mann.

Set in 10.5/13 pt Dante MT Std
Typeset by Jouve (UK), Milton Keynes
Printed and bound in Great Britain by Clays Ltd, Elcograf S.p.A.

The authorized representative in the EEA is Penguin Random House Ireland,
Morrison Chambers, 32 Nassau Street, Dublin D02 YH68

A CIP catalogue record for this book is available from the British Library

ISBN: 978–0–241–44891–5

www.greenpenguin.co.uk

MIX
Paper | Supporting
responsible forestry
FSC
www.fsc.org   FSC® C018179

Penguin Random House is committed to a
sustainable future for our business, our readers
and our planet. This book is made from Forest
Stewardship Council® certified paper.

Contents

A Short Pronunciation Guide for the Romanian Language

Romanian uses all twenty-six letters of the Roman alphabet, with the addition of four characters with diacritics: Ă/ă, Î/î, Ş/ş and Ţ/ţ

Ă sounds something like the *u* in *fur*. There is no English equivalent for î, but you might attempt to pronounce it if you said *brrrr* the sound you might get if you're expressing extreme cold – and then trying to recognize the very short vowel between the b and the r. Ş is pronounced as *sh*, while ţ is *tz*.

The accent falls on the first syllable in all cases. Otherwise, there is a close similarity between Italian and Romanian pronunciation; in other words, both are pronounced pretty much as written. A is always *ah*, as in *dart*, for instance, but never as in *fall* or in *pal*. U is always *oo*, as in *cool*. **Ce** is *chey*, **ci** is *chee*. **Che** is *keh*, **chi** is *kee*. For instance, **Mircea Cărtărescu** is pronounced (something like) *Méercha Cúrturescoo*. **Ştefan cel Mare** is *Shtéfahn chel Máhrey*. **Calea Moşilor** is *Cáhleah Móshilor*. **Luci** is *Lóochee*.

J.S

Prologue

I open the book, the book moans
I cast for the times, the times are gone

TUDOR ARGHEZI

The Roulette Player

Grant Israel's consolation
To the one who has eighty years and no to-morrow.

I record here (for what reason?) these verses from Eliot. In any case, not as a possible opening for one of my books, because I will never write anything else again. Yet, if I write these lines, I do not regard them as literature, not by far. I have written enough literature, for sixty years I did nothing but that, so let me permit myself now, at the end's end, one moment of lucidity: everything I wrote after the age of thirty was no more than painful imposture. I've had enough of writing without the hope that I would ever surpass myself, that I would ever be capable of leaping over my shadow. It's true, up to a certain point I have been honest with myself, in the only manner possible for an artist; that is, I wanted to say everything about myself, absolutely everything. But so much more bitter was the illusion, since literature is not the adequate means to say anything real about yourself. From the first lines with which you layer the page, the hand that holds the pen slips into a foreign, mocking hand, as though entering a glove, while your image in the page's mirror scatters all over the place like quicksilver, so that out of its disordered blobs coagulates the Spider or the Worm or the Degenerate or the Unicorn or the God, when all you wanted to do was simply speak about yourself. Literature is teratology.

For a few solid years now I've been sleeping an agitated sleep and dreaming of an old man who goes mad from loneliness. Only the dream reflects me realistically. I wake up weeping from loneliness, even though I may spend the day in the comfort of friends who are

3

still living. I can't bear to live my life any longer, but the fact that today or tomorrow I will cross into endless death forces me to try to reflect. Because of this, because I must reflect, like someone who is thrown into a labyrinth is forced to seek an exit, even through walls smeared with dung, even through a rathole; this is the only reason I still write these lines. Not particularly to prove (to myself) that God exists. Unfortunately I have never been, despite all my efforts, a believer, I have never had to endure a battle with doubt or denial. It might have been better for me to be a believer, because writing requires drama and drama is born out of the agonizing struggle between hope and despair, where faith plays a role which I imagine is essential. In my youth half the writers converted, while the other half lost faith, which for their literature produced just about the same effect. How I envied them for the fire their demons fanned under the cauldrons where they wallowed as artists! And look at me now, cradled in my nook, a bundle of rags and cartilage, whose mind or heart or faith no one would think to bet on, because there is nothing more to take from me.

I drowse here in my armchair, terrified at the thought that nothing exists outside any more other than night, solid as an infinite lump of pitch, a black fog that has slowly gnawed, in pace with the advancing years, cities, houses, streets, faces. The only sun left in the universe seems to reside in the lamp's light bulb, and the only thing illuminated by it – an old man's shrivelled face.

After I'm dead, my tomb, my cranny, will continue to float in the black fog, the solid fog, ferrying nowhere these pages which no one will read. But in them is finally . . . everything. I have written a few thousand pages of literature – powder and dust. Intrigues masterfully conducted, marionettes with electrifying grins, but how to say anything, even a little bit, in this immense convention of art? You would like to turn the reader's heart inside out, but what does he do? At three he's done with your book, at four he takes up another, no matter how great the book you placed in his hands. But these ten, fifteen pages, they are a different matter, a different game. My reader now is no one else but death. I even see his black eyes, humid, attentive like a young girl's, reading as I fill up the page, line after line. These pages contain my scheme for immortality.

I say scheme, although everything – and this is my triumph and my hope – is the truth. How strange: most of the characters populating my books are invented, but they appeared to everyone as copies of reality. Only now do I have the courage to write about someone who is real, someone who lived for a long time in my proximity, but who, according to my conventions, would appear improbable. No reader could accept that in his world, elbowing him in the same tram, breathing the same air, might live a man whose life is an actual mathematical proof of an order in which no one believes today, or believes only because it is absurd. But! – the Roulette Player is not a dream, and neither is he the hallucination of a sclerotic brain, nor an alibi. Now, thinking about him, I am convinced that I too made the acquaintance of that beggar at the end of the bridge whom Rilke wrote about, around whom the worlds rotate.

Thus, though not someone dear to me, the Roulette Player did exist. And the roulette, too, existed. You heard nothing about it, but tell me, what did you hear about Agartha, the ancient civilization at the Earth's core? I lived the roulette's unlikely times, I saw the plummeting of fortunes and the amassing of fortunes in the savage light of gunpowder. I too howled under the low ceiling of underground halls and cried from happiness when a man was carried out with scattered brains. I made the acquaintance of the great roulette magnates, the landowners and the bankers who wagered those increasingly exorbitant sums. For more than ten years, the roulette was the bread and circus of our serene inferno. There hasn't even been a whisper about something like that for the last forty years? Consider, how many thousands of years passed since the Greek mysteries? Does anyone today know what actually took place in those caverns? Where blood is the subject, everything is hush-hush. Everyone was hush-hush, or perhaps everyone in the know bequeathed after his death a few useless pages such as these, to be followed with a skeletal finger only by Death. Each one's individual Death, the dark twin born at the time of his birth.

The man whom I write about here had some name or another, which the world forgot because soon everyone called him the Roulette Player. Saying 'the Roulette Player', you were speaking about him alone, though there were many other roulette players. I remember him without difficulty. Downcast figure, triangular face on top of a long neck, thin and yellowish, desiccated skin and hair nearly scarlet. Eyes of a morose monkey, asymmetrical, uneven in size, it seems to me now. He gave an impression that suggested impurity, pollution. That is how he looked in his farmer's hand-me-downs, that is how he looked later in his tails. Lord, how tempted I am to sketch a little hagiography of him, to throw a transcendent light on his cheek, to put a fire in his eyes! But I clench my jaws and swallow these miserable tics. The Roulette Player had the dark face of a somewhat well-to-do peasant, his teeth half metal, half charcoal. From the time I met him until the day he died (by pistol, but not by bullet) he looked the same. Still, he was the only being who was fated to catch sight of the infinite mathematical God and challenge him to a wrestling match.

I claim no merit for knowing him or that I can write about him. I might be able to hoist, but with only his aspect before my eyes, an enormously ramified scaffolding, a paper Babel, a *Bildungsroman* of a thousand pages, where I, like Thomas Mann's humble Serenus Zeitblom, would follow with huffing soul the progressive demonizing of the new Adrian. But then, what? Even if by the turn of an absurd fate I could come up with what I hadn't for sixty years, a masterpiece, I ask myself, what is the good of it? . . . For my final purpose, for my grand stake (next to which all of the world's masterpieces are nothing but sand in an hourglass or dandelion down), it is enough to list in a few lines the larval life stages of a psychopath: the brutal child with darkened face who slices insects into sections and kills songbirds with stones, passionate about playing marbles and throwing horseshoes (I remember him perpetually losing, losing money, losing marbles, losing buttons then desperately getting into brawls); the adolescent with moments of epileptic fury and exacerbated erotic appetites; the jailbird sentenced for rape and burglary. I believe that the only one close to him during this last twisted stage of his life was me, perhaps because we had been somehow thrown together since childhood, our parents being neighbours. In any case, he never hit me and looked at me less suspiciously than the rest, whoever they may have been. I remember, each time I visited him – even in prison, where, in the greenish chill of the visiting room, cursing horrendously, he complained all the time of his bad luck at poker – he asked me for money. He wept from the humiliation of being perpetually cleaned out, of being incapable of even one lucky hand among the thousands he played, where he might win money from the others. He sat there on the green bench, a pint-sized man with eyes reddened by conjunctivitis.

No, it's impossible for me to speak of him in a realistic manner. How can you realistically present a living parable? Any automatic device, any stylistic trick or turn that hints even slightly at literary prose depresses me, nauseates me. Let me say that, after he was released from prison, he took up drinking and after one year hit the skids something horrible. He had no job, and the only places where you could be certain to find him were a few lowlife dives, where for that matter I believe he slept. You saw him ambling from one table to the next, attired in that unmistakable manner that drunks adopt (jacket over bare skin, seat of the trousers dragging on the ground) and bumming a mug of beer. Numerous times I saw the sinister prank, painful even for me, but at the same time amusing, that the usual customers played on him from time to time: they called him to their table and promised him his mug of beer if he could draw the long matchstick from the pair that one of them held in his fist. And they rolled around laughing hysterically when he always drew the short one. Not once, I am certain of this, did he win his beer in this way.

It was during that period that my first short stories appeared in magazines, and after a time my first short-story volume, which even today I consider the best work I have ever done. I was happy then about each line I wrote, I felt myself competing not with my contemporaries but with the great writers of the world. Slowly I gained entry to the consciousness of the public and the literary world, I was worshipped and violently censured in equal proportion. I got married for the first time and, finally, I felt I was alive. This was in fact fatal for me, because writing doesn't reconcile itself with happiness and plenty. I had forgotten of course about my friend, when, a few years later, I ran into him again in the most unlikely place: a restaurant in the centre of the city, in the low, hallucinatory halo cast by a cluster of chandeliers studded with rainbow flashing prisms. I was speaking quietly with my wife while my gaze roamed through the room, when suddenly my attention was drawn to a group of businessmen who occupied an ostentatiously stacked table. There he sat, in their midst, the centre of attention, in his gaunt lankiness, brilliantly outfitted but still displaying the vagabond appearance, his dim hollow eyes. He lounged insouciantly on a chair, while the others prattled on in a sort of uncouth mirth. I have always been repulsed by the burnished cheeks and the ill-bred undertaker garb men of that ilk affect to distinguish themselves. But I was above all perplexed by the unexpected transfiguration of my friend's material situation. I have no idea if he was happy to see me, he was impenetrable, but he invited us to join them, and, as the evening wore on, among the many banalities and stupidities which threaded our conversation, a few imprecise allusions filtered in, enigmatic phrases the businessmen flung over the baroque abundance stacking the table and to which I had no clue how to react. For the following several weeks I sensed the terror of beginning to discern, albeit subconsciously, some vistas which disappeared towards a space other than the bourgeois world which, after all, we inhabited, even if softly hued by art's posturing. More, I had on numerous occasions, on the street or in my office, the feeling that I was being watched, scrutinized by something indefinite, circumstantial, which floated and dissolved like twilight smoke in the air. Now I know for certain that I was indeed subjected to close scrutiny, because I had been chosen to begin my apprenticeship in the subterranean world of the roulette.

At times I am filled with happiness at the thought that God could not exist. What years ago seemed a bloody paradise (my life of that period flashes before me in a greenish foreshortening resembling Mantegna's Christ) appears to me now as an inferno euphemized by forgetting but no less probable and, thus, horrifying. They told me, in order to encourage me the first time I went underground, that only the first game is difficult to endure, that afterwards the roulette's anatomical side not only ceases to disgust, but you end up discovering in it the veritable, sweet charm of this game; for him whose blood comes to be infiltrated by it, they went on, it becomes a necessity, like women, like wine. That first night they blindfolded and took me from one vehicle to another over the city streets until I was no longer able to tell who I was any more, let alone where I was. Then they dragged me along some twisted and tortuous corridors and we walked down a few steps that reeked of wet stones and cat carcasses. You could hear overhead the occasional rumble of a tram. They removed the rag from my eyes: I was in a basement lit feebly by a few candles, where under the arched vault a few sardine barrels were arranged to resemble tables while small crates and thick cylinders cut from tree trunks served as chairs. It all looked like a wine cellar ostentatiously contrived to look rustic. This impression was enhanced by the metal cups and beer glasses from which some ten or fifteen jolly and well-dressed individuals were sipping their drinks, huddled around the barrels and talking among themselves. I noticed they were eyeing me.

Large cockroaches flitted across the clay floor. Some, half crushed by the kick of a heel, still stirred a claw or an antenna. I sat at a table next to my red-headed friend. The bets were already concluded and inscribed with chalk on a small blackboard, so I assumed that for now I would be only a spectator. The sums were large, larger than I had ever seen being staked on a game of chance. Suddenly the animation of the 'stockholders' – as I was to find out was the name given to those who bet on this game – abated, while the beverages, forgotten in the cups and glasses, slowly filled the brownish air with a sour smell of pure alcohol and stale beer. The gazes of the basement denizens fell, one by one, upon the tiny door. It opened after a while and a man stepped in, resembling closely my childhood friend during his period of maximum decline. The pockets of his jacket were torn, his trousers were held up by string. Not much to say about his face, except that it was the face of a drunk. He was shoved in by his 'boss' – that was the name given to those who employed the roulette players – who had the aspect of a bartender and carried under his armpit a greasy wooden box. The drunk stepped up on top of a pine crate that I had not spotted until then and stood there with his slouching shoulders, in the attitude of a grotesquely sketched Olympic winner. The stockholders stared and fidgeted, pointing to some aspect or another of the man on the crate. I caught one of them off-guard, crossing himself secretly. Another chewed furiously at the skin around his fingernails. Yet another shouted something at the skin around his fingernails. Yet another shouted something at the boss. But, as though severed by a sword, the clamour ended when the boss opened the small box. Hypnotized, they all craned their necks towards the little black object that sparkled as though studded with diamonds. It was a revolver, a well-greased six-shooter. The boss presented it to the crowd with slow, nearly ritualistic gestures, like an illusionist who displays the empty hands with which he is about to accomplish his wonders. He then passed his palm over the revolver's chamber and twirled it; it emitted a thin, cogged whine like the cackle of a gnome. He put the revolver down and from a little cardboard box took out a bullet, shiny in its brass shell, which he handed out to the nearest stockholder. The stockholder checked it carefully, focused his attention on each of its surfaces, approved it with a short nod of the head, as though dissatisfied at not finding something out of order; then he passed it to the one sitting next to him. The bullet made the rounds of the room, leaving grease tracks on everyone's fingers. I also touched it for an instant. I had expected, I don't know why, that it would be cold as ice or that it would burn, but it was lukewarm. The bullet returned to the boss, who with large and explicit gestures inserted it into one of the six openings of the barrel. Then he passed his palm again over the mobile piece of metal, which spun for a few long seconds, emitting the same sharp and squeaky whine. Finally, with an odd sort of reverence, he handed the glimmering weapon to the man standing on the crate. In a silence that turned your bones to dust, and in which you could hear – I recall now – the rustle of the cockroaches and the feeble hush of their antennae as they brushed past each other, the man lifted the pistol to his temple. Because of the horrifying tension and the weak light, my eyes began to tire, so that suddenly the beggar's silhouette dissolved into yellow and greenish phosphorescent stains. The rough plaster of the white wall behind him stood out in bold relief: I could see every dent, each grain of plaster thickened like the skin on the face of an old man, leaving bluish tracks on the wall. All at once the basement began to reek of musk and sweat. The man on the crate, eyes tightened and mouth twisted as though tasting something awful, pulled the trigger violently.

Then he smiled, naive and befuddled. The tiny click of the trigger was the only sound that was heard. Overwhelmed, he stepped down and sat on the crate. The boss rushed to him and nearly crushed him with his embrace. On the other hand, the individuals in the room began to howl like madmen, to curse bitterly. When the boss and his roulette player exited through the undersized door, they ushered them out with savage boos and catcalls, as you would only hear at a boxing match.

By chance, the first roulette player I ever saw escaped with his life. Since then, for many years in a row, I attended hundreds of roulettes, and I saw numerous times an image that cannot be described: the human brain, the only veritably divine substance, the alchemical gold which contains everything, scattered on the walls and on the floor and mixed up with splinters of the skull. Think about bullfighting or gladiators, and you will understand why this game soon infused my blood and changed my life. Roulette has in principle the geometrical simplicity and force of the spider web: a roulette player, a boss and a number of stockholders are the chief dramatis personae. In secondary roles, you have the basement's owner, the cop who makes the rounds of the neighbourhood, the common porters hired to dispose of the corpses. The relatively insignificant sums that the roulette provided them with were, from their point of view, veritable fortunes. The roulette player was most certainly the roulette's star and its reason for being. As a rule, the roulette players were recruited from the great throngs of unfortunates resembling vagabond dogs, the drunks and jailbirds fresh out on the street, ever in search of bread. Anyone, as long as he was alive and willing to place his soul on the battleground for much, much money (but what did money mean under those conditions?) could become a roulette player. It was also preferable that he was, as much as possible, without social relations: job, family, close friends. The roulette player had five chances in six to survive. He usually received about ten per cent of what the boss earned. The boss must be in possession of serious funds, because, if his roulette player died, he had to pay all the stakes the stockholders wagered against him. The stockholders in their turn had one chance in six to win, but, if the roulette player died, they could demand stakes ten times over, or even twenty times, according to prior agreement with the boss. The roulette player, however, did not have five chances out of six to live except the first time he played. Statistically speaking, if he placed the pistol once more against his temple, his chances diminished. At his sixth attempt, his chances dwindled to zero. In fact, until my friend entered the world of the roulette, becoming the Roulette Player in capitals, there were no known cases of survival after even four games. Of course, most of the roulette players played occasionally and would not repeat for anything in the world their dreadful experience. Only a few were attracted by the possibility of making money, and this usually in order to employ a roulette player themselves – and thus becoming bosses – which was actually possible after the second game.

There is no reason to continue here with further description of the game. It is, in truth, stupid and alluring like any game hallowed by the stain of blood, so pleasing to our despicable nature. I return to the one who destroyed the game by force of the fact that he played it to perfection. From what legend tells (which you could hear at the time in all of the city's taverns), he was not recruited by any boss but found out single-handedly about the roulette and sold himself. I suspect the boss who hired him was delighted to get a roulette player without any trouble, because long and exasperating transactions were usually necessary, agonizing bargains with those who assigned their souls to the auction block. At the start, any vagabond would demand the moon in the sky, and you needed consummate skill to convince him that his life and his blood were not worth the entire universe, but that, instead, they were worth a certain number of paper bills, and that number depended on the demand of the market. A roulette player to whom you didn't need to demonstrate that he was in fact a nobody, whom you didn't need to threaten with the police, was unexpected luck, all the more so when he accepted without discussion the first offer, proposed out of the corner of your mouth and with eyes askance in the usual manner of the bosses. About the first few roulette games that my friend participated in, I couldn't find out very much. I can't imagine that he was noticed by the stockholders the first and the second time he survived, or even the third. At most, he was thought of as a lucky player. After his fourth, his fifth, he had already become the central figure of the game, a veritable myth that would in fact burgeon exorbitantly in the years that followed. During a period of two years, until our encounter in the restaurant, the Roulette Player lifted the pistol to his temple eight times in various cellars throughout the filthy labyrinths underneath the foundations of our city. Each time, I was told – and later saw it for myself – on his tormented face almost without a forehead, an overwhelming terror etched itself, an animal fear that you couldn't bear to witness. It seemed as though this very fear cajoled fate and helped him escape. His emotional tension reached a peak when, tightening his eyelids and smirking, he abruptly pulled the trigger. You heard the slight click, after which his frame with its heavy bones crashed softly to the floor: he lost consciousness but was unharmed. For several days he was out cold in his bed, completely emptied of vitality, but then he quickly recovered and took up again the life he usually lived, between the cabaret and the brothel. As hard as he tried – being possessed of a limited imagination – he could not spend as much as he earned and ended up increasingly wealthier. He had long relinquished having a boss; he became his own boss. Why he continued risking his life was an enigma. You could only come up with one explanation, that he did it for a kind of glory, like an athlete who attempts to surpass himself in each race. If that in fact was the truth, it was something entirely new in the world of the roulette, which was always played exclusively for money. Who would get it into his head to become a world champion at surviving? The fact was that the Roulette Player managed to maintain for the time the demented tempo of that race which he ran against only one other competitor: death. And, just when it seemed that this clandestine cavalcade was about to tumble into monotony (those who went to witness my friend's roulettes did it only out of the desire to see him gone once and for all and not in order to bet, because they had developed the increasingly resigned feeling they were betting against the devil), the Roulette Player perpetrated his first gesture of defiance which practically liquidated the roulette, pulverizing any possibility of competition besides the one between him and everything that surpasses our unfortunate condition. In the winter of that year he announced, through the ineffable, speedy and certain network of information of the world of the roulette, that he would organize a special roulette on Christmas night: the revolver's chamber would be loaded with two bullets instead of one.

The chances of survival were now only three to one, if you didn't consider their progressive reduction after so many games. Many connoisseurs, even after the Roulette Player's death, regarded that Christmas roulette as his stroke of genius, and that everything that followed, though more spectacular, was merely a consequence of that gesture. The subterranean room belonged to a cognac factory and preserved the chemical reek of poor quality alcohol. Though it was larger than other rooms I had been in, that night it was packed. Anywhere you looked, you stared at the faces of well-known figures, officers and painters, industrialists and society women, even a few bearded priests, all of them animated by the unexpected innovation brought to the rules of the roulette. The blackboard on which two young men in shirt-sleeves wrote the odds of the betting occupied the entire wall behind the crate upon which the Roulette Player would take his place. In time he made his appearance, barely discernible through the blue smoke of the cellar. He stepped up on the crate and, after the ceremonial of the detailed verification of weapon and bullet – which lasted longer than usual, as the members of the crowd couldn't refuse themselves the pleasure of caressing, almost voluptuously, the gun's barrel – he picked up the pistol, loaded it, shoving the two bullets at random into the openings of the chamber, which he then twirled by rolling his palm over it. The tiny cogged cackle was heard again in the silence of the room, but as always the silence was not disturbed by an explosion, and no flower of blood stained the wall's plaster. The Roulette Player collapsed from the crate into the arms of those in the first rows, knocking over glasses and propelling rolls of coins over the improvised tables. I wept like a child, from relief and from despair: I had bet a sum which for me was gigantic, and lost, just like all those who had taken an obstinate stance despite the evidence that the Roulette Player's chance of winning was enormous. We left the tortuous lair, as always, in small groups; the night outside, the silence of the outskirts made us feel as we walked that we were the object of a gaze that had dissolved the entire surroundings in the layer of blinding, fluorescent snow that had fallen over everything, over the display windows adorned with Christmas trees and stars of silver paper, over the rare passers-by loaded with packages and bundled-up children, with scarfs shrouding their mouth and nose. Here and there a woman with cheeks glowing from the humid cold, wrapped in a fur coat, dragged her lover or husband in front of the boots or shawls in the shop windows casting violet and turquoise and azure shadows upon their faces. My walk home took me alongside the children's playground, where a horde of bewildered urchins smeared with candy paused before the tiny stands selling lemonade and gingerbread. A father huddled in bulky clothes, dragging after him on the thin ice a sled mounted by his little girl, winked at me. He was one of the bosses I had encountered at another roulette. Suddenly I felt horrible.

Certainly, I promised myself many times to break with the world of the roulette. But during that time I published around two or three books a year; I had the sort of success that preceded a long silence followed by forgetfulness. With each new book I recovered my roulette losses and then I would dive into it again, under the earth, where a foreboding of flesh and bones lures us while we are still alive. The one thing I wonder a great deal about now is the 'idealistic' and 'delicate' content of those books, the nauseating D'Annunzionism I indulged in. Noble reflections, royal gestures, silk lace, scintillating *mots d'esprit* and a narrator who is wise and all-knowing, who spun out of the substance without substance of his stories thousands of dainty charms. Once again lured into the roulette's conspiracy, it was impossible not to be instantly struck, as though by a wave that becomes progressively hotter and more turbulent, by the news about the new rules of the game tacitly imposed by the overwhelming personality of the Roulette Player. After repeating two more times the double-bullet roulette, he found himself so wealthy, so engaged in owning stock in so many branches of the country's big businesses, that the roulette, as a lowlife affair, as a source of existence or wealth, became an absurd idea. On the other hand, his odds tended to decline, despite the fanatics who ruined themselves by obstinately playing against him. At a single sign from the Roulette Player, the whole system of bets crumbled. It was now considered in bad taste to organize the roulettes where some miserable vagabond would place the pistol to his temple. There were no more bosses and no more stockholders, and the only one who still organized the roulettes was the Roulette Player. But everything became a spectacle involving tickets rather than bets, a show with only one performer who, from time to time, like a gladiator in the arena, confronted his destiny. The rented halls became progressively more spacious. The tradition of the underground hole was abandoned, along with the reek of blood and manure, the Rembrandtian penumbras. Now the subterranean rooms were decorated with heavy silks with a watery sheen, crystal goblets on the tables that were buried in waves of Dutch lace, furniture decorated with floral intarsia and candelabra with hundreds of prisms and quartz icicles. Instead of ordinary beer, sophisticated drinks were served in bottles contorted into odd shapes. Women in evening gowns were escorted to the tables, from where they inquisitively surveyed the stage on which an orchestra now played, bursting out in every direction with golden funnels of trumpets, curved necks of saxophones, graceful cylinders, in constant motion, of trombones. I suppose that was how the room looked when the Roulette Player loaded the revolver with three bullets. He had now as many possibilities to survive as to play this demented game for the last time. This new ambience, the ostentatious luxury that mantled the roulette's terrifying insect like a chrysalis, did nothing if not inflame the spectators' fervour for the smell of death. Everything that follows is very much the truth. The Roulette Player doused his hair with brilliantine and wore a smock with the loose trousers fashionable at the time, but the revolver was real, and so were the bullets, and the probability of the expected 'accident' – greater than ever. The weapon circulated through everybody's hands, leaving on one's fingers a subtle odour of oil. Not even the most delicate lady in the room concealed her eyes, in whose violet sparkle you could read the perverse craving to witness what many only heard about the roulette: the cranium cracking like an eggshell and the ambiguous liquid substance of the brain gushing on the gown's lap. As for me, I have always been shaken by the craving of women to be near death, their fascination with men who, almost metaphysically, smell of gunpowder. The incredible success with women of a chimpanzee, haggard and stupid, who from time to time gambles with his own life, must have its roots in this. At no other time, I believe, did they love with such zest, those women who after witnessing a man's death went home with their lovers, shedding their bloodied dresses, stained like bandages by the ashen substance and the ocular liquid. But the Roulette Player stepped up on the crate, adorned now with red brocade, lifted the pistol to his temple and, with the same expression of convulsive fright on his face, jerked the trigger. Then, in the silence that suspended everything for the space of a few seconds, all you heard was the thud of his frame hitting the floor. After a few days' delirium at the hospital, the Roulette Player resumed his usual life. It's difficult for me to forget his tortured aspect, sprawled on the Bukhara rug at the foot of the crate with his eyes staring upwards. Other times the roulette players who survived were booed and hooted by the forlorn stockholders; but, now, my friend was cheered like a movie star and his body, plunged into unconsciousness, was surrounded with veneration. Young women, hysterically weeping, swarmed towards him and were happy merely to touch him.

The roulette with three greased bullets inside the chamber fuses in my mind with the events that followed. It was as though the diabolical arrogance of the Roulette Player propelled him ever more to offend Chance's divinities. Soon, he announced a roulette with *four* bullets thrust into the chamber's alveoli, and then, with *five*. One single empty opening out of six, one single chance of survival out of six! This game ceased being a game and even the most superficial among those who occupied the velvet armchairs felt – not with their brains, but with their bones and cartilage and nerves – the theological grandeur that the roulette had achieved. After the Roulette Player loaded his weapon and twirled the chamber, unleashing again the tiny staccato cackle of well-oiled black metal, the hexagonal cylinder, heavy with bullets paused – with its single empty space – in front of the hammer. The click of the trigger, which sounded with a hollow echo, and the collapse of the Roulette Player were surrounded by a sacred silence.

I sit at my writing table with the blanket thrown over me, and yet I am horridly cold. While I wrote these lines, my room, my tomb, has whirled so quickly through the black fog outside that I got sick. I twisted and turned in my bed all night long, a helpless sack of bones steamed by sweat. Outside nothing exists any more, or will evermore. No matter how long you might journey, in whatever direction, all the way to the infinite, all you would find is the black fog, dense and solid as pitch. The Roulette Player is the stake I wager on and the kernel of dough around which the fluffy bread of the world might grow. Otherwise everything, whether it exists or not, is as flat as a biscuit. If he existed, and he did exist – that is my wager – then the world exists, and I will be no longer forced to shut my eyes; with shrivelled skin on my bones, with my flesh as my sheath like a fur of blood, I will march forth for as long as eternity lasts. From this story let me fashion myself an aquarium, the most miserable of aquariums – because I have no interest in a fancy aquarium – where he and I, guarantors of each other's reality, will attempt to survive, like a couple of semi-transparent fish whose heartbeat is on view, dragging along after them a thin strand of excrement. I am horrified at the thought that the aquarium might get punctured. For God's sake, let me keep trying, though I no longer feel my spine . . .

*

For years on end the Roulette Player had the Angel by the lapels, trying his best to throw him and shaking him all over. The evening came, however, when he grabbed him by the throat and, gathering all his strength, stared him deeply in the eye. And the Lord, towards morning, crippled the Roulette Player and changed his name . . . During that last evening, practically the entire upper crust of the city congregated in the huge refrigerated hall beneath the abattoir. The hall's décor may have appeared entirely odd to those accustomed to the parvenu's ostentatious luxury of previous halls. I can't tell whether it was someone's imagination or a reminiscence from Huysmans' *À rebours* that inspired the nostalgic hybrid – a somewhat perverse admixture of promiscuity and refinement – whose effect was far more powerful than the pomp from the previous roulettes. At first sight – with the exception of the sheer size of the hall – you had the impression that you were inside one of the old cellars from the 'prehistoric' period of the roulette. The walls were filled with obscene scribblings and inscriptions rudely scratched or traced with charcoal, but an eye with the merest of training could not help but notice right away the aesthetic refinement, the coherent and emotionally stirring manner of a great artist whose name, for obvious reasons, I prefer not to remember. The tables made of precious wood essences and golden mouldings simulated the sardine barrels of the bygone era. Crystal mugs imitated the gross aspect of those made from cheap glass, down to the greenish nuance and the artificial blemishes. Gloomy filters scattered a morbid tallow flame light, admixed with waves of bluish smoke, like the cheap stogies of old, except that now they were perfumed with musk in order to awaken a delicately nostalgic feeling. On the stage, at the front of the hall, brought in from the harbour, rested an actual orange crate inscribed with Arabic script. Inside the hall, lured by that evening's fantastic stakes, you could recognize diverse petroleum magnates in their white burnooses, movie stars and singers in current vogue, industrialists with starched shirt fronts and carnations inside their lapel buttonholes. Everyone agreed at the entrance to have a silk scarf tied around their eyes, not to be removed until they were already in the hall. I myself was a sort of star – I say this with plenty of disgust, in order not to be suspected of a lack of modesty – who attracted the stares of even the most blasé among them, even those who were sitting next to me. Never before were my books – which had grown progressively thicker and in keeping with their taste – so highly publicized: noble, yes; first and foremost, noble. Generous, first and foremost, generous. Thus sounded the commendation of the jury when I received the National Prize: 'For the noble and generous humanity of his books, for the complete mastery of an expressive language.'

When the Roulette Player made his appearance in the room, bedecked in bizarre strips of cloth that tastefully simulated rags, and when the master of ceremonies, disguised as a boss, opened the box which he had brought under his arm offering the public a superb ivory-handled Winchester with a shimmering barrel (at present in a private collection), everyone and I stopped breathing. We refused to believe that what was to follow could actually take place: the Roulette Player had announced a few weeks earlier that at the next roulette he would load the revolver *with all six bullets*! Between the progression – no matter how improbable – from one bullet to five and thence to the present insanity, there was a chasm spanning the distance from one single chance to no chance at all. The last drop of the *human* which the Roulette Player had still preserved in his attempts had evaporated now under certitude's million suns. The verification of the bullets and the weapon lasted hours on end. When they were returned to him, the Roulette Player took his place on the crate, made them clatter in his fist like dice, then inserted them, one by one, into the six openings of the chamber. With a violent jerk of his palm, he put them in motion. 'Useless,' I remember someone whispering next to me. In the terrifying silence, the tiny cogged cackle of the chamber could be heard clearly. Shaking, his face convulsing, his eyes betraying a terror that you could only witness in those in agony, he lifted the pistol to the temple. The crowd stood up.

I strained so hard to scrutinize him that I could feel the bulging of the veins in my temples. I could see the pistol's hammer lifting slowly, appearing to vibrate. And abruptly, as though this vibration propagated itself into the room, I felt the ground run from under my feet. I saw the Roulette Player crumbling from the crate and the revolver discharging with an apocalyptic blast. But the air was already filled with a deafening clamour, split by the screams of the women and the clanging of the capsizing bottles, now in splinters. Overtaken by the panic of the constricted space, we stepped on each other in order to scramble out. The tremors lasted a few good minutes, transforming entire streets into piles of debris and twisted metal. In front of the exit, a derailed tram crashed into a furniture store and smashed the windows to smithereens. After an hour, the earthquake started again, less forceful now. Who had the courage to venture into their own homes that night? I walked the streets until the morning's fog whitened the horizon and the dust of the shattered buildings settled on the sidewalks. It wasn't till then that I remembered the Roulette Player had probably been abandoned there, in the subterranean hall, and I went back to see if he was still living. I found him stretched on the floor, tended to by a few individuals. One of his legs was dislocated at the hip, and he gasped from pain. Next to him lay the revolver, reeking of gunpowder, with only five bullets in the chamber. The sixth left a blackish hole in one of the room's walls, near the ceiling. I stopped a car on the street and took my childhood friend to the hospital. He recovered quickly, but limped for the rest of the year that he still lived. That evening, he buried the roulette, soon obliterated from everyone's mind, the way we usually forget anything that we bring to perfection. The younger generations after the war never even suspected that such Mysteries ever existed. I alone bear witness – but for you, no one; but for you, nothing.

From the evening of the earthquake on, the Roulette Player absconded to his dubious quarters, leaving behind him, as usual, a series of barely hushed-up scandals. It seems he never thought about the roulette again.

I can't write even one page a day. Constant pain in the legs and vertebrae. Pain in the fingers, in the ears, along the skin on my face. What will be, what will be after death? I would like to believe – how I would! – that a new life will open up there, that our present state is larval, a period of waiting. That the ego, the I, as long as it exists, must find a means to assure its own permanence. That I will embark upon something more infinite, more complex. Otherwise everything is absurd, and I see no place for the absurd in the world's design. The billions of galaxies, the imperceptible fields and finally this world which surrounds my cranium like an aura could not exist if I were unable to know it in its entirety, possess it, be it. Last night, cradled under my blankets, I had a kind of vision. I had just been born from an elongated and bloody belly, unutterably obscene, that propelled me with an odd twirling motion, with infinite speed, leaving behind me tracks of tears, lymph and blood. I twisted myself like a screw into the night. And suddenly, out of night's edge, appeared before me a gigantic God of light, so large that my senses and understanding could not contain him. I was headed towards his enormous chest, while the traces of his severe face were shooting upwards, flattening out at the edge of my field of vision. Soon I couldn't see anything but the great yellow light of his chest, which I pierced in my twisting, and, after an endless navigation through his flesh of fire, I gushed out through the spine. Gazing behind me as I flew away, I saw this colossal Jehovah plummeting to the left with his face downwards. Little by little, he diminished in size and disappeared, once again I was alone in the limitless night. After a period impossible to appraise (but which I would name eternity), at the edge of my sight arose another enormous God, identical to the first. I pierced him as well and gushed forth into the void. Then, after a new eternity, another one appeared. The row of Gods, perused from behind, proliferated in size. There were hundreds, then thousands, plummeting with face downwards to the right and to the left like the teeth of a gigantic zipper of flames. And opening the zipper in my flight, I unveiled the chest of the true God, which I beheld in foreshortening, more grandiose than anything in the world. Twirling and incinerated by his light, I hoisted myself to such a height above him that I could view him in his entirety. How beautiful he was! With hairy chest, like a bull, he displayed a woman's bosom. His face was youthful, crowned by the flame of his locks braided in thousands of tresses; his hips wide, sheltering his powerful virile organ. In his entirety, from his brow to his soles, he was made only of light. His eyes were half-open, his smile was at once ecstatic and melancholy, while directly over his heart, underneath the left breast, he exposed a horrible wound. Between the fingers of his right hand he held, in an unbearably graceful manner, a red rose. Thus he floated, reclining in the space that strove to contain him, but which appeared soaked through, contained by him . . . I woke up amidst the cold furniture of my room, a senile man weeping dry tears. I wanted to throw away these senseless pages collected here. But what can a man who wrote literature all his life do? How can he escape the arcana of style? How, with what instruments, can you cloak the page with a pure confession, freed from the prison cell of artistic convention? Let me collect myself and have the courage to admit it: you can't. I've known this from the beginning but, in my cornered animal cunning, I concealed my game, my stake, my bet from your gaze. Because, finally, I staked my life on literature. I used, in my maso-chistic, Pascalian reasoning, everything that seemed to stand against me. This is my reasoning, everything that causes me to take this 'story' (only I know by what effort) to the end: *I knew the Roulette Player.* Of this I cannot have doubts. In spite of the fact that it was impossible for him to exist, still, he existed. But there is a place in the world where the impossible is possible, namely in fic-tion, that is, literature. There the laws of statistics can be broken, there you can have a man more powerful than the laws of chance. The Roulette Player couldn't exist in the world, which is a way of saying that the world in which he existed is fictional, is literature. I have no doubt the Roulette Player is a character. But then I, too, am a character, and so I can't stop myself from bursting with joy. Because characters never die, they live each time their world is 'read.' If he never kisses his beloved, the shepherd painted on the Grecian urn knows at least that he will forever gaze at her. Thus, my wager and my hope. I hope from the bottom of my heart and I have a forceful argument: that the Roulette Player did exist, that I am a character from a tale and that, although I am eighty years old, I will never die, because in fact I never lived. Maybe I do not live in a worthwhile tale, perhaps I am only a secondary character, but for someone at the end of his life any perspective is preferable to that of disappearing forever.

There were hundreds of speculations regarding the fantastic luck of the Roulette Player. What can I do except add one more, if not more real, at least more coherent than the majority of the others? Being familiar with the Roulette Player since childhood, I know that, in fact, what always distinguished him was not good luck, but, on the contrary, bad luck, of the darkest, I would say supernatural, bad luck. Never once did he experience the joy of winning even the most childish game where chance played a role. From the game of marbles to horse races, from throwing horseshoes to poker, it seemed that destiny used him as a clown, always peered at him with an ironic eye. The roulette was his great chance, and it's bewildering how this man, so rudimentary in his thought, found the cunning to capitalize on the only point to pierce, like a scorpion, fate's armour and to transform everlasting ridicule into eternal triumph. How? It seems to me simple now, primitive, but at the same time brilliantly simple: *the Roulette Player staked his bet against himself.* When he lifted the pistol to his temple, he divided himself. His will turned against him and condemned him to death. Each time, he was convinced with his whole being that he would die. From that, the expression of endless horror which appeared on his face. However, his bad luck being absolute, he could only fail each time in his intention to commit suicide. Maybe this explanation is foolish, but as I said, I can't see another that has a chance to stand on its own. In fact, none of this matters any more . . .

I am tired. I make the effort of a lifetime to write a single page. It will be the last, because the dice are cast and the aquarium is finished. Let me plug up the last leaking crack – and then I will rest next to it, silent and motionless. Only the tresses and veils of swimmers will pulsate from time to time. I await that moment with such voluptuousness that I can barely wait to finish the tale of the Roulette Player. His end came quickly, soon after the six-bullet roulette which he monstrously survived. Less than a year later, returning from gambling one milky morning, he was abruptly dragged into an alleyway off the abandoned path he took home. An adolescent, less than seventeen years old, put a pistol to his temple and demanded his money. He was found a few hours later, dead, with the pistol next to him, from which the unfortunate punk didn't wipe his fingerprints. The corpse had no trace of a bullet wound, and medical expertise concluded that death was caused by a heart attack. In fact, inside the revolver, which never went off, there were no bullets. The young man was found the same day, hiding at some friends' house, and everything became clear. His intention was merely to rob. The pistol was empty, and he used it only to intimidate. But the drunk he attacked was overwhelmed by a terrible fear and collapsed to the ground, while the young man lost his head, threw away the revolver, and ran. Because he had no relatives and no one seemed to know him (I myself hid for a few days, till the whole thing blew over), the Roulette Player was buried in a hurry, with a simple cross made of boards stuck on his grave.

This is how I, too, close my cross and coffin of words, under which, like Lazarus, I will await my return to life when I hear your powerful and clear voice, reader. I close – in order that the tombstone should have an epitaph, in order to complete the circle – with Eliot's verses, which I love so dearly:

Grant Israel's consolation
To the one who has eighty years and no to-morrow

Nostalgia

To wrench a sound from the past,
To cause you, Soul, once again to trill,
I glide my hand across the lyre for naught;

Now all is vanished in the Youth's horizon vast,
While time behind me grows . . . and I grow chill,
And silent is the tongue that sweet song wrought.

MIHAI EMINESCU

Mentardy

I dream enormously, in demented colours. I have sensations in my dreams I never experience in reality. I wrote down hundreds of dreams over the last ten years, some of which repeated themselves convulsively, dragging me underneath the same Caudine Forks of shame and hatred and loneliness. Of course, they say that the writer loses one reader with each chronicled dream, that dreams in a story are tiresome, being nothing but a convenient and worn-out method of plunging into the abyss. Rarely indeed is the dream significant for another. Besides, writers sometimes resort to fabrication, they construct the dream according to preordained specifications in order to both reflect and organize the random reality of the story, like placing the cap of an ink pen in the middle of an amorphous piece of scribble and seeing a naked woman reflected in it. Because I wish to begin this tale with a dream, I am now making an attempt at defending myself against the accusation of laziness and naivety which it would automatically unleash.

I am, as you well know, an occasional writer of prose. I write only for you, my dear friends, and for myself. My true occupation is commonplace, but I like it and I know its gimmicks very well. The writer's gimmicks, however, leave me cold. For a year or so since I have been attending your Sunday meetings, I could have learned much regarding the technique through which a story comes together. On the other hand, I was afraid that I didn't have a lot to say. In fact, until that night when I dreamed what I wish to tell you about, I was convinced there is nothing in my life worth being brought out into the light. Thus, I do not try to leap into the abyss but only wish to begin at the beginning, because I am convinced that, in life as in fiction, the beginning sets the tone. It is so even in madness. I recall how a friend of mine began to go astray. He came over to my studio apartment one evening in a very agitated state and recounted in an oddly coherent way what had happened to him an hour before: 'I got on a tram to go visit an acquaintance. Because of the cold outside, the windows of the tram were steamed up. On a bench in front of me sat a peasant woman in a brown, dirty parka and a green head-scarf. I hadn't even paid attention to her until she raised her hand, in a thick glove, and wiped a portion of the steamed-up window. I was staring outside through the stain, which had become transparent, when the tram entered a tunnel and the stain became black as pitch against the white background of the rest of the window. Well, the stain reproduced perfectly Goethe's profile from the well-known shadow silhouette. Everything was there: the straight nose starting directly from the oblique forehead, the wig ending in a pony tail, the firm lips, the round chin . . .'

But to get to the point and begin the story of the dream I mentioned. Two months ago I dreamed I was locked up in a jar, but one chiselled out as though of crystal rock. I was walking around inside the jar, which from time to time flashed with rainbows, and I gazed with great contentment through its walls at the fluid, flickering world around me. A bird approached from the distant mountains, paddling towards the jar, and the closer it got the larger it became, arching itself around the curved walls. When it got very close, I saw its gigantic almond eye widening as though seen through a magnifying glass and abruptly enclosing me from all sides. I covered my face with a horrified feeling of shame and pleasure. When I uncovered my eyes, I noticed that on the wall of the jar, which sparkled frantically, appeared the thin contours of a door. I rushed at it, frightened at the thought it might be open. But I was relieved: an enormous lock, soft, as though made of flesh, was suspended from the door. On the path that snaked down from the distant mountains and ended at my door walked a little girl. She looked gentle and well-mannered as she walked towards me, with wet lips and large bows tied around her pigtails. The walls of the jar had now become square and sparkling clear, and suddenly I felt an irrational fear, a terror I would never experience again. The little girl paused in front of the door and started to pound with her little mother-of-pearl fists on the thick crystal. Trembling, I flung myself to the floor, but would not let her out of my sight. When she grasped the lock, I felt that my entrails were being wrenched, that my heart was exploding. She tore the lock off and, with blood-smeared hands, pushed open the heavy quartz door. She stood frozen on the door-step in an attitude that is impossible for me to describe to you, for which there are no possible words. And suddenly I saw this same scene, but from somewhere behind the little girl: I was moving away from it, walking on the path leading to the distant mountains, so that I encompassed in my sight an increasingly larger surface of the massive walls of glass or crystal or ice of the jar, which was by no means a jar, but a giant castle, an obtuse construction, with cornices and mouldings and chevrons and gorgons and skylights and balconies and crenellations and watchtowers and drainpipes, made from a cold and transparent matter. I stood there writhing on the ground, above the thousands of chambers with translucent walls and the little girl framed by the wide-open door, while from the castle entrance to the centre chamber, hundreds of doors with bloody locks flung open against the wall.

I woke up with an uncomfortable sensation which annoyed me all morning, but I didn't remember the dream until after lunch, at first as flashes of pure emotion in the plexus, then later at school while listening to my students, as unintelligible, painful events. I needed all of the next day to reconstitute what I have told here. And I even have the impression, I don't know why, that I had remembered much more than I know now but have forgotten it in the meantime. Yes, now as I write, the thought seizes me that *I knew* what gestures the little girl made in the dream and what words she spoke but feel that I can in no way concentrate on them. I hope to remember them in the course of this telling . . .

I tried, as usual, after I wrote the dream down, to prepare an anamnesis for it. I began at random, with the intent of remembering a detail from it around which to string a sequence from the dream. After a reverie of about two hours before my coffee cup, during which time I concentrated on the dye-transfer picture glued on it – a purple butterfly with two spots like two immense blue eyes on the wings, fringed with gold and with the thorax shaped like a smooth and disgusting worm – I wrote in my journal the following text, which came to me spontaneously: 'When I dream, a little girl leaps over her bed, goes to the window and, with her cheek glued to the glass, gazes at the sun setting over the pink and yellowish houses. She turns to face the bedroom, red as blood, then cuddles again against the wet bedsheets. When I dream, something comes near my paralyzed body, holds my head in its hands, and takes a bite from it as though from a translucent fruit. I open my eyes but do not dare make a move. I jump abruptly from my bed and go to the window. I gaze outside: the entire sky is nothing but stars.' And instantly, as though having uttered a sacred formula, I began to recover a few bits. Some of them I forget, but I know that suddenly I became aware that the jar image was rooted in a discussion I had on the phone with an ex-girlfriend who told me, among other things, that she had bought a pair of hamsters which she kept in a jar, on sawdust. Then my oldest memory came to my mind: I was at most two years old, and my parents lived on Silistra Street. The owner of the house, whose name was Catana, gave me a tiny bell as a gift. I remember even today, with perfect clarity, how I came out of the courtyard of my house and walked with my baby boots into a large muddy puddle spanning the length of the street. I let my little bell fall there in the water, and though I rummaged with my tiny hands through the bottom of the puddle, which was no deeper than a few centimetres, I never found the little bell again. I recall how perplexed I was. From this memory I realized that I must situate the unfurling of the dream much deeper in the past. I concentrated on the little girl, her pigtails tied with enormous bows of starched white cloth. I noticed a resemblance to the peasant women painted by the Dutch masters, women with their heads covered by large and vaulted lace. I thought of all the Dutch bedsheets on which reclined the superbly curved nudes of Ingres, and suddenly I was cornered by a memory: the little girl's name was Iolanda. Then I had before my eyes the glass door of

Entrance One in our apartment building, which was so difficult to open, the Dambovita Mill, the toy watches, so violently and painfully coloured, and the image of Bucharest viewed from the balcony, illuminated at night by red and green billboards that flashed off and on. With an exhilaration that is difficult to describe, I disinterred from memory in a few minutes a number of things I was certain I knew nothing about any more. More, I realized that it was that period of my life which infused me with all that is original and perhaps even unusual. I can't understand how I managed to block out till now this perfect, mother-of-pearl globe, locked inside the ashen valves of my life as an unmarried and blasé teacher, who lives simply because he was born. But I felt extremely happy that I also could have after all some interesting things to write about from my own experience. I am not thinking that I will write a story, but a kind of account, a short and honest narrative of the oddest (in fact, the only odd) period of my life. And I feel the hero of this narrative, even though he was only seven during the time when 'the action took place', is worth being spoken about, because I am convinced he marked forever – though subterraneously in my case – the destiny of all the children who played behind my apartment building on Ștefan cel Mare Boulevard.

The apartment building is eight storeys high, while behind it there are now parking lots where the cars shiver next to each other in this winter's bitter cold. Twenty-one years ago, when we moved here, my mother was barely out of the maternity ward, where she had given birth to my sister. I recall how, in the middle of an absolutely white and empty room where the light splashed in through a window that had neither curtains nor curtain rods, my mother sat on a chair and suckled the baby while blindingly illuminated by the spring's white sun. My head reached exactly as far as the height of the kitchen sink, whose enamel had been chipped by time in such a manner that it displayed on the bottom the outline of a stain which reproduced precisely the contour of Africa, with its principal deserts and rivers.

The apartment building was in a stage of near-completion. It abutted on one end a building which always made me feel uneasy because of its crenellations and watchtowers, its infinite perspectives – which later I found again in de Chirico – while in the back, facing the mill (another medieval building, of sinister scarlet), it was still propped up by rusty scaffolding. Behind the apartment building the earth was ransacked by sewage ditches, which in places plummeted to the depth of two metres. This was our playing field, separated from the mill's courtyard by a concrete fence. It was a new world, strange and dirty, full of places to hide; and we, seven or eight boys, aged between five and twelve, armed with blue and pink water pistols we bought for two lei at Little Red Riding Hood, the toy store at that time in the Obor district, became every morning its masters and explorers. That was the old Obor, the true one, where it always smelled of turpentine.

Our gang was organized according to a strict hierarchy based upon the principle of physical force: who could beat up whom. I recall a few of its members: Vova and Paul Smirnoff (how disturbed I was later when I heard of a vodka bearing the same name!), Mimi and Lumpy (I don't remember their last name), Luţă, Dan from Entrance 3, Marconi and his brother Chinaman, Luci, Gimmi the Gypsy, who married a salesgirl from the candystore about two years ago, Jean from the seventh floor, my neighbour Sandu, Little Nicky from the apartment building next door. Each one, it seems to me now, was interesting in his or her own way. Paul ate tar and sucked butterfly bellies, claiming they were full of honey. His brother, Vova, was docile and bashful but obsessed by the compulsion to speak to everyone he met about the *Titanic,* which he insisted was taller than three apartment buildings placed on top of one another and had one thousand propellers. Mimi raised a hedgehog and collected boxes of foreign cigarettes, some of which were made of thin plastic. He was the biggest among us, and he could beat us all up. That's why he was our leader, despite the fact he was dark, like a Gypsy. On the other hand, his brother Lumpy was a wimp. He was the colour of tar, and his nose was always full of snot. He whined most of the time, which is why we nicknamed him Symphony in C Major. He must have been four and was sort of mentally retarded; he could barely babble a few syllables. Luci was my best friend. He and I wandered all over the place together, while I listened to him talk about horses – he only talked about horses – galloping across fields mantled in silk and shod, over their horseshoes, with slippers of flowered cashmere. As for Luță, he was sort of morbid; as a matter of fact, his older brother, after finishing high school, climbed up on the balustrade of the terrace on the roof of the building and jumped. I was in my room folding paper into different shapes when I saw his large frame diving across my window, his arms flapping with strange undulations. I heard the crash and looked out of the window: on the asphalt, next to a Pobeda automobile, sprawled the former high school graduate, his noble profile displaying its contour against a cheery stain, light purple and widening leisurely.

Certainly, the gang contained other members, less important or whom I don't remember. For instance, in an apartment off Entrance 6 lived a little boy who suffered from polio. His leg was trapped in a complicated metal mechanism, like the one Harieta, the sister of the poet Eminescu, must have worn. His grandmother took him out behind the building, where he watched us play witchbitch. But it was as though he never existed. And let me not forget Crazy Dan, to whom the thug Mimi gave an odd nickname, which even now I can't figure out where it came from or how it might have sprung up from Mimi's limited mind: he called him Mentardy. Dan would step up on the balustrade surrounding the building's terrace and shout at us from the height of eight floors, gesticulating and pretending to fall. We were scared even to approach the balustrade, let alone get on top of it.

It was understood that girls our age were not allowed to join the gang. They spent their playtime sketching on the asphalt endless landscapes with white, yellow and purplish chalk, or even with pieces of brick, or playing out ancient fairy tales with embroidered head-scarves, Prince Charmings on fiery steeds, precious stone, one alone, one alone, precious stone, all that silly girl stuff. I give you only a few names: Viorica, daughter of the deaf-mutes, the only one who could speak, but who communicated in sign language with her parents; Mona, Dan's sister, psychopathic just like him, with yellow eyes glittering with hate, the only one who was allowed to play witchbitch with us; Fiordalis, the daughter of some Greeks whose last name was Zorzon; Marinela, whom Jen mocked by singing to her to the melody of 'Marina, Marina' the words 'blonde and tall, tall and big, taller than an oil rig', and, finally, Iolanda, who appeared in my dream.

I do not wish to spend any more time with them. All these little coloured and perfumed clouds are merely a way of painting a 'picturesque' landscape, and I can't allow myself to bore you with a picturesque tale. *Background* – this is what all of us were, for him who came and changed something in us or at least left an inexplicable mark on our lives, for him who couldn't even beat up Lumpy but was for a time the focus of rapt attention and respect for Mimi himself. Everything I've reported here for you so far is but an introduction to this, let me call it a tale, but the effort is worth it, perhaps out of my practice as a Romanian language teacher who reiterates each time the opportunity comes up: each story must have a beginning (where you introduce the time, the place and the story's characters), a middle and an end. My beginning has become rather long, but, still, I can't graduate to the middle. I have to tell you about our 'amusements' before the arrival of the main character.

Most of us never ventured over the perimeter surrounding the area behind our apartment building. Glued to the Pioneer bakery, as though emerging out of it, there was an old and tortured chestnut tree, with a hollow filled up with cement and at an oblique angle a rusty stake stabbing the bark teeming with ants. We used this stake – Sandu, Luci and I – to get up the tree, where we were in our element, just like the old folks in Capote's *The Grass Harp*. Up there, the branches opened up into another hollow that we used to support our feet. At the beginning of summer we found this hollow filled with plastic pencil sharpeners from China: the richness of their pastel colours took our breath away. There were more than fifty of them, in the shape of all kinds of benign animals, squirrels with furry and twisted tails, little white rabbits, rocking horses, Disney deer, tiny frogs with blue eyes. There were also red and green tennis rackets, transparent pink midget barrels, porpoises and giraffes with long necks and mobile tails. It was morning when we found them, and the night before there was nothing there. In the days that followed we didn't see anyone besides us stalking the chestnut tree. We concluded that the pencil sharpeners grew there, they simply unfurled from the tree in a mirific inflorescence, just like the cactus or the bamboo cane that blooms once in a century. We took them home. Underneath the rabbits or the benign deer hid the firm and unforgiving steel blade. High in the chestnut tree, in the likeness of old Indian wise men, we held council. When Luci got tired of talking about horses, after he was done bedecking them in so much golden filament, rubies and heavy silks that he ran out of things to invent (he bragged that he, indeed, possessed those horses at his country house); after Sandu, who would never end up being a mathematician, bored us with his absurd affirmation that he had found an arithmetic book where addition, subtraction, multiplication and division were done with letters rather than numbers; and after I, finally, swore that I saw a ghost – we settled down to serious matters. Could it be true that the word, so short, that we found scribbled on the concrete wall, or scratched on the pitch covering the sewer pipes, signified that all adults . . . And then, all the songs we sang with so much glee: 'Round and round in their pyjamas / My old man is chasing mama,' etc., were they not referring to the same disgusting thing? It was true, declared Luci, and added cynically: 'Even my mother and my old man do this thing.' Then he began his spinning yarn: when they have to do this thing, they go to a kind of hospital, where they are given a room without windows and with the keyhole plugged up with cotton. In the middle of the room, there is sort of an operation table, where the woman lies down facing upwards. Above the woman hangs a hammock. The man climbs up a ladder and positions himself face down on the hammock. The man climbs up a ladder and positions himself face down on the hammock. Then a mechanism lowers the hammock, and the parents find themselves one on top of the other, just like in Mimi's jokes. This process lasts a long time, hours in a row, during which the woman reads a book. Then, they come back home. 'How do you know this?' – we asked him, and then got tangled in controversial scholastics. We were reasonably clear about the short word, but with other cuss words, which assured the listener that different variations were possible, we could reach no agreement. And, even with that short word, we had our doubts: hospital or not, my parents seemed too serious to engage in such acts.

I pondered those things during the long and agonizing afternoons when I was supposed to be asleep. The golden-reddish light slowly filled the bedroom, reflected itself in the wardrobe's glassy sheen, and fell on my cheeks. I lay on the bed with my eyes open and stared through the window at the bewitching clouds, rolling capriciously and glimmering across the summer skies. Sometimes I would steal out of the starched bedsheets, rigid as broken glass but light as paper, and tiptoe to the window. I watched Bucharest's skyline, frozen under the clouds, with its mist of ancient homes with tiles and transoms, with skylights and massive oak doors, and further in the distance large and ashen buildings teeming with windows, the downtown skyscraper with the Gallus billboard like a bluish globe above it, the Victoria department store, the fire watchtower to the left, the arching buildings on Ştefan cel Mare Boulevard, and off in the beyond, the hydroelectric plant, with its immense chimneys spitting out twisted strands of steam. All was filtered through the agitated foliage of the poplars and birches, whose tops, light green, emerald green, dark green, shot out intermittently between the buildings. I was never sleepy. I quickly scurried to the bed at the lightest creak, because I knew my father, a nylon stocking on his head, was coming to check if I was asleep.

Our games were sometimes cruel and barbarous. I see Luţă driving a nail, with single strike of rock, into the chest of a sleeping cat. The nail lodged itself between the cat's ribs and more than likely touched its heart, because the cat became stiff, its little back paws jerked a few times, recoiling spasmodically, and then froze still despite the fact that the story went these animals had nine lives. Then we dipped our arrows in its blood and let them fly into the air. Mimi's flew as high as the apartment building. Another time, Sandu and I found an already grown baby sparrow with the feather barbules already formed. We chased it through the ditches until we got our hands on it. Then we played doctor with it. Our game lasted for hours in a row, during which we poured down its throat all sorts of trash, rubbing alcohol, essence of almonds, urine, etc. When it couldn't even throb any more, we played tennis with it, with our primitive plastic rackets. Then we buried it, still alive, in a box for medicinal wine, over which we poured dirt, and stomped.

All day long we chased each other through the labyrinthine sewer ditches. We found our way down through certain sports, walking on top of the pipes painted with pitch and the giant faucets; the smell of dirt invaded our nostrils, of earthworms and larvae, of pitch and fresh putty. It filled us with madness. We armed ourselves with water pistols, covered our faces with masks made of corrugated cardboard we got from the furniture warehouse. In order to make them all the more frightening, we painted the masks at home with leering fangs, with bulging eyes and dilated nostrils. Then we chased each other through the tortuous ducts, while above us a thin slice of sky darkened with the passage of time. When, turning a corner, we came face to face with an enemy, we roared and charged at each other, scraping ourselves and ripping each other's T-shirts or printed blouses. No one knew who invented the game we called witchbitch. We continued playing it for years without getting tired of it, still playing it even in the eighth grade. It was a mixture of more benign games: cops-and-robbers, hawks-and-doves, hide-and-seek. At the start, there was only one witchbitch, which we picked by counting. The witchbitch alone wore a mask; 'she' also carried a stick from which the bark had been removed. She counted to ten with her face to the wall, then charged through the ditches, looking for victims. You could leave the ditches but weren't allowed to hide on the apartment buildings's stairs and jump over the fence in the mill's courtyard. The witchbitch hunted us through the evil-smelling ditches, and when she succeeded in striking one of us with the stick, she let out a horrific roar. The victim had to remain frozen in a paralyzed position. The witchbitch dragged him by the hand to the lair, where she knuckle-cuffed his head an agreed-upon number of times; thus baptized, the prisoner became a witchbitch himself. He put on a mask, and the hunt continued. Towards evening, when above the mill's giant towers the first stars glimmered on the still bluish sky, only one survivor remained, hounded by a horde of witchbitches who bellowed their sinister shrieks. The tenants awaited that moment with horror. They threw potatoes and carrots at us from their balconies, while the cleaning ladies lunged at us with their brooms, all to no avail: the witchbitches would not rest till they captured the last victim, usually a tiny child who, upon seeing the game turn to reality, became terror-stricken. At night it was terrifying to come face to face with a single masked witchbitch, let alone an entire flock. The last one to be caught was dragged to the nearest stairs, where the rest of the gang made hideous faces at him and acted like they were about to swallow him. This went on until our indignant mothers came to take us home.

When we had no taste for playing witchbitch or erasing with the thinned soles of our tennis shoes the blue houses, yellow trees, or the green mothers the girls drew on the asphalt – this just to hear them scream and run home – we would gather the gang and, sitting down on various scattered pieces of curb, begin telling each other all sorts of tales or playing 'Film Titles'. I remember how Gimmi the Gypsy told us of his escapade in the mill's courtyard: 'I jumped the fence by the little house with the skull and crossbones on it. I got very close to the mill. The miller saw me. A few more millers showed up. I turned around and started to run. They threw rocks after me. I ducked. When they ran out of rocks, they took out their pistols. They didn't get me. They shot at me with machine guns. They shot at my head, I ducked down. They shot at my legs, I jumped up. They brought cannons. I kept on running. They went after me in their tanks, I still kept on running. They sent aeroplanes and dropped bombs on me, but I reached the fence and jumped over it, there by the gate.' He was so serious when he told us the story, we almost believed him. You barely heard a skeptical, 'Yeah sure, man.' When we played Film Titles, we already knew the titles, in alphabetical order. *After the Rain* was always followed by *After the Thief,* while *Agatha, Give up Your Life of Crime* was third. Next, starting with B, the first title was always *Babette Goes to War.* When someone was stuck, we would whisper to him the wrong answer: 'Say *Cruise Ship of Iron!*' Then, when he said *Cruise Ship of Iron,* we would shout contemptuously: 'There's no such film.'

One day, a little boy and his mother moved into an apartment on the first floor of Entrance 3. I had just turned seven and was to go to grade school in the fall (Vova was already in the third grade, while Mimi had to complete the fourth year all over again). The little boy was about the same age as me, and in the beginning there was nothing about him that drew my attention. His mother, on the other hand, was extraordinary, completely different from our own, who washed and ironed all day. She was a lady and was so tall you could barely make out the features of her face, lost as though in a distant horizon. Long and thin, she almost seemed to be sleepwalking amidst the furniture that filled the hallway, giving directions to the porters who dragged their hemp straps all over the place. I never saw her except in purple. Even in the house she wore a robe of red satin. Her hair was jet black, and her face seemed haunted by a bluish shadow glinting with thin traces of rosy mother-of-pearl. The boy sat apathetically in an old easy chair, which, because of its flowered girth, made him look even thinner. He was indeed thin and delicate, with firm eyes, alert and down-cast. We came out for a time from our ditches and approached him. We asked him if he was moving into our apartment building and if the endless woman was his mother. But your father, where is he? 'My father is a carpenter,' he told us, as though he was answering the question. Eventually we left him alone, because all he did was to give us long stares and short answers. We dove again like devils into our holes and started up again our game of witchbitch.

During the following days, the little boy showed up again among us. He was very clean. He wore 'rompers', as my mother called them, short trousers shaped like bloomers and held up by long braces. He didn't utter a word. We called him to join us in the ditches, but he didn't want to. He just stared at us from the first floor. It made us lose our taste for playing, seeing that we had a spec-tator. He was watching the girls with the same interest, which made us feel contempt towards him. He even asked Mona (of all the girls!) for a piece of purple chalk. Mona, who did not stand on decorum, turned her little rump in beige shorts and slapped it with her palm. 'You sure you don't want this?' The boy stared at her absent-mindedly and left. For about a week we spotted him talking every day with the kid who had polio. He explained all sorts of things to him, with the aid of sketches which he drew on the concrete with a piece of chalk he had brought with him and with gestures which I would now call *ritualistic*. Sometimes it seemed that a translucent spider web stretched out from him. At other times, he pointed with his finger to the sky, smiling enigmatically. During the evenings wrapped in purple fog, dissolving imperceptibly into coffee-brown, we stalked them, protected by our cardboard masks: the metallic glitter of the orthopaedic mechanism worn by the first boy and the sibylline gestures of the second took on a bizarre and enigmatic air in our eyes, difficult to decipher. When they went home, always earlier than us, crooked circles and other figures remained on the blue concrete. We erased them hatefully.

The boy gave himself airs, acted above his station. That was our conclusion, so we decided – I don't recall if we deliberated upon it or whether it was spontaneous – to force him to take a position in regard to our gang. If he wanted to be our friend, fine. If not, even better, because we felt the need for a real enemy. We had made one other attempt at being heroic, not too long before, but had failed painfully. We got together behind the apartment building, by the saffron-yellow light of a fire we lit using cardboard television set boxes. We armed ourselves with long wooden slats we got from the furniture warehouse. In grave silence, we set off on an expedition to ambush the kids from the building to the right of the Circus Alley, the one with the flower shop. Our masks on, we roared and charged upon them from behind. We chased all the children who were play-ing foot-tennis or kicking a striped ball against the wall. The girls, shrieking oppressively, stampeded into their apartment buildings. We took one prisoner, a kid the size of Lumpy, whom Crazy Dan and Paul were forcing to swallow an earthworm, when three fathers in undershirts rushed out of the building. At the sight of the hairy chests and arms of the three males, we dropped everything and scattered down the alley. As the newly arrived boy had no father (or he hadn't showed up so far), he seemed like an appropriate enemy. Thus, one morning we surrounded him conspiratorially, the same way the senators surrounded Julius Caesar. We grabbed him and dragged him towards the sewer maze. We wanted to turn him into a witchbitch. The little boy rooted himself on his heels and writhed horribly. From up close, his face was completely different than any other child's I had seen until then. His hair was chestnut brown, lightly curled. Golden reflections splayed out of the loop of each curl. The strands of hair above his head were lightly ruffled, forming a reddish tangle. Under the forehead's ringlets, the thin eyebrows arched over the two large ovals of his half-open eyes. Through eyelids that were missing the lashes, hemstitched by a blackish film, the halved irises' violet discs peered out. The eye sockets seemed darker than the delicate copper of the cheeks. His nose was thin and elongated, but harmoniously so, while the furrow underneath the symmetrically sketched nostrils was unusually deep. He held his lips clenched together and almost never revealed his teeth, though he smiled sometimes with wet lips, expressing something between cunning, irony and pure kindness. Now, however, as we dragged him to the ditch, his expression was of extreme concentration. You would get tired simply from looking at him. I was holding his left arm when, having arrived at the edge of the ditch, I suddenly felt that his convulsions took on an unusual force. He began pushing his narrow chest forwards as though he wanted to heave it out of his shirt, while his shoulders tightened up with a force whose intensity so surprised us that we let go of him and, frightened, widened the circle around him. The child remained standing for a moment, convulsing and folding his spine as though he wished to fracture it, then moaning in a loud tone, he let himself fall slowly to the ground. He moaned and cried with enormous tears. We all ran away towards Entrance 3 and scaled up to the terrace, from where we gazed, shuddering, at the boy's mother who, all red pleats and folds, darted out the building's hallway. She lifted him in her arms and, darting again, disappeared inside the hallway.

I went home, where after I ate I was subjected again, as always, to the torture of an afternoon sleep, which was no sleep at all.

What was truly tormenting was that I didn't have a clock and so had no way of knowing when the two hours of forced sleep in the summer's dry heat would end. Out of the window, the blue and glittering clouds, swept by the tops of the poplars, unreeled endlessly. When I went downstairs again in the afternoon, I found the gang huddling behind the building. Their mouths wide open, the boys were staring up at something apparently sensational, something I could not see because of the building's corner. 'Come here, Mircea, man!' they shouted. 'Come here and see Mentardy number two. He's even crazier than the original!' Even Mimi and Vova, who were older and so for whom it was not appropriate to be so easily astonished, seemed hypnotized by what they saw. Luţă showed up as well, him with his dark complexion and no eyelashes. Little Nicky, fat and dressed like an aristocrat with his John Lennon glasses, joined the gawking in his perplexed and irritated myopic manner. I stepped up close to the gang and froze.

Next to the Dâmboviţa mill with its scarlet walls, beyond the concrete fence, loomed the Pioneer bakery. It was an old factory building with a zigzag roof and an odd assortment of troughs whitened by flour facing the round windows. Lumpy sat on the fence all day because the workers sent him after newspapers and cigarettes. In exchange, he got roasted buns or hot rolls, which he slobbered over for an entire hour. The bakery was dominated by a brick chimney, red and thick and taller than our building, which rose to the clouds, shooting out over the oval coin-like leaves of the acacia trees. We never saw it up close, but you could make out along its height, all the way to the top, a fire escape that looked like it was sketched with ink; it was protected by rings in the likeness of a trachea. That afternoon, three quarters of the way up, that is, about the level of the sixth floor of our building, we saw a yellow spot. It was the rompers belonging to the new boy who, slowly and heedfully, was climbing to the top of the chimney. His frame, inside a little flowered short-sleeved blouse, covered less than a quarter of the brick tower's width. The alarmed tenants came out on their pickle-jar-filled balconies and were shouting at him to come down. But, step by step, Mentardy (because eventually that's what we all ended up calling him, the other Mentardy reverting back to his old nickname of Crazy Dan) was making his way up to the top of the chimney. Finally, the boy reached the top, lifted himself up on the edge of the chimney, and squatted for a few seconds. The frightened shrieks of the women in the balconies escalated, and a few workers in white overalls and aprons darted across the courtyard towards the base of the chimney. But, as though to defy his audience's fears, Mentardy slowly stood up. As this as a nail, he remained in the upright position at that dizzy height. He was looking up but signalled with his hand in the direction of the ground, probably at us. Then he began to descend the metal steps, his frame proceeding past all the rings of the fire escape, until he disappeared into the acacia's foliage. After a short while, gawking through the rhomboid holes of the concrete fence, we spotted him running towards us. He clambered over the fence with difficulty and jumped down right in our middle. He stared at Mimi and said: 'I don't like witchbitch.'

It is possible that some of you, my prose-writing friends, for whom I have been agonizing for the last few days to translate this history, are no longer paying any attention. It may appear to you that I am walking the well-beaten path of the genre of the child-hero who sacrifices himself for an idea or a noble cause. Indeed Mentardy, in the way that I knew him, belonged to that archetype. But, fundamentally, I hope he will not be thought of as some sort of comic-book hero. His words and actions, which I now recall with a clarity that I find suspect after being submerged for more than twenty years in the tinted fogs of my subconscious, had nothing childish about them but seemed a series of rather attractive fantasies that captured us little by little in the net of their enchantment. I will put down here that I dreamed about him last night, I saw his face distinctly, and that is why a few pages back I was able to sketch a fairly accurate portrait of him. I ask myself if Mentardy really looked the way I saw him in my dream. In any case, I am obsessed by his eyes, hemstitched by a black film that looked like make-up, and his ambiguous aspect, firm but at the same time sweet.

From the very next day on, we allowed ourselves to be taken in by Mentardy's charm. In the morning, we did not descend as usual into the ditches, even though the dirt's smell still awakened our nostalgia but instead surrounded him and listened to him telling stories. He told us, I recall now, the legends of the Round Table; Charlemagne and Arthur, the horrific pagans and a sword that had a name. Then he told us about 'The Brave in the Tiger's Skin', but he paused in the middle of the story and said the place was not right for telling stories. The dirty ditches, he said, the dirt mounds, the pipes mended with putty did not allow him to concentrate. 'I know a better place,' he said, smiling, and took us there. That place was Entrance 1.

A narrow and very dark corridor between our building and the office building nearly glued to it took us there. During the nearly two months since we had all moved there, none of us had had the curiosity to explore that spooky passage. Following Mentardy we traversed the corridor's twenty-metre length, getting ourselves all scratched and dirty with plaster dust from the walls, until we emerged into an enclosure surrounded on three sides by the two buildings and on the fourth by the mill's concrete fence, through whose cracks crept in the acacia branches and leaves. It was a tiny enclosure, walled in asphalt and very clean in comparison with the lot behind the building. One side led to the glass doors of Entrance 1. A few tall steps on the other side ended in a small platform bordered by stone banisters that opened out to a doorway blocked by bricks and belonging to the office building. We named these stone stairs the Attic. Glued to the fence stood a concrete cube ending in a kind of metal pan-shaped object displaying a curious hollow. We never found out what its use was. We named this object the Throne. Finally, the third unusual aspect of Entrance 1 was the great transformer, with its curved pipes and concrete façade, which I now recall mainly as covered up with Mentardy's large and multicoloured letters. I think the transformer was broken, because it had been abandoned there for a long time.

For about two months, this was the only place where we hung out. The only thing we thought about was Mentardy's stories, whose development kept us on edge from one day to the next.

When he didn't feel like going on, we played foot-tennis, told jokes, talked about soccer. He didn't participate much in these discussions, which were natural to us. In a short period of time, we realized that this kid who was younger than most of us surpassed us all in ways we had never been aware of. At home we drove our parents crazy with stories about what Mentardy did, what he said . . . In time, from his throne of concrete and metal, he began to speak, between stories and as though in a dream, about things other than knights and swords. His voice would suddenly change in the middle of a story, his face become rigid and beyond challenge. He would then utter a few phrases whose meaning we tried in vain to decipher.

This is the place in the story that I wanted to get to. I ask myself, shuddering, how it is possible that I remember these words that I couldn't understand then and which I thought I forgot the moment I heard them. Some of his bizarre 'theories' directly contradicted what our parents had taught us or what we learned from the popular science programmes, such as *Rose of the Wind* on the radio and *Tele-Encyclopedia* on television. But, I don't know how, Mentardy filled them with significance and enchantment simply through his presence, through his voice and his gestures, even if you didn't take into consideration that what he said in itself came from another world. I believe that only a fragment of everything I've ever read can compare in spirit with what the boy had told us: the description of the Land of the Blissful from Plato's *Phaedo*. Just so that you get the idea, I enumerate here a few of the theories I remember, expounded by Mentardy during those evenings, crimson as flames, or the azure mornings, lined by the glittering-yellow walls of Entrance 1:

1. Inside my head, under my cranium's vault, there is a little man who looks exactly like me: he has the same features, dresses the same way. What he does, I do as well. When he eats, I eat. If I sleep and dream, he sleeps and dreams the same dream. When he moves his right arm, I move mine. Because he is my puppeteer.

But the vault of the sky is nothing but the cranium of a giant child, who looks exactly like me: he has the same features, dresses exactly as I do. What I do, he does as well. When I eat, he eats. If I sleep and dream, he sleeps and dreams the same dream. In order for him to move his right arm, it is enough for me to move my right arm. Because I am his puppeteer.

The surrounding world is the same for me as it is for him. And my puppeteer and my puppet are both surrounded by a Luță and a Lumpy and a Mimi, and by you, all the others, and who are the same as you. This beer bottle cap on the ground exists both in the very very small world of my puppeteer and in the very very large one of my puppet. Because everything is the same.

But in my puppeteer exists another puppeteer, who lives in his cranium and looks exactly like me, and in him another even smaller, and so on to infinity. And my puppet manoeuvres another puppet, much larger, in whose cranium he lives, and who manoeuvres as well another puppet, and so on to infinity.

I myself don't know which one I am in this line. This moment, as I tell you this story, an endless line of puppets and puppeteers speak in their own worlds, using the same words, to an endless line of children.

2. The world is an animal endowed with thought and will. But its will is much greater than ours, we who are glued to it. The birds and the butterflies, however, have an even greater will, and that is why they can fly. But if we can exert our will to the utmost, we can become light as air. (Mentardy performed for us a practical demonstration of this theory. He squatted in the hallway of Entrance 1, holding his knees in his arms and leaning his head back. Then he clenched his eyelids and tensed so hard that we got scared. His face during those moments lost all human characteristics. He shook, lips tightened and cheeks literally filled with blood, like bags furrowed by blue veins. After about a minute, Gimmi and Vova, standing on each side of him, lifted him to the ceiling with their index fingers. We played with him for about a quarter of an hour, blowing from one side to the other this live ball curled up in the foetal position that had now become as light as a balloon.)

3. Women never couple with men. They bear a cell in their womb. When they reach the right age, they want to give birth. Then they launch the birth steps. This is what these are: from the cell a flea comes out. From the flea, a beetle. From the beetle, a

frog. From the frog, a mouse. From the mouse, a hedgehog. From the hedgehog, a rabbit. From the rabbit, a cat. From the cat, a dog. From the dog, a monkey. From the monkey, a man. Women can stop at any step. Some women give birth to frogs, others to cats. But most of them long for children. They could give birth to a being far more enchanting than a child, because these degrees of birth do not end with man. (And Mentardy concluded: 'I saw such a being.')

4. People are not of the same kind. They are of four different kinds: those who have not been born, those who are living, those who have died, and those who have not been born, are not living, and have not died. They are the stars. (This very short word uttered by Mentardy was among his last, shortly before his fall. I see the scene before my eyes. It was about nine o'clock at night, and we were expecting our parents to call for us at any second. We could barely see our eyes glimmering in the dark of the evening. Above the mill, the sky was the colour of indigo. A little red star flickered somewhere very far. It was the star on top of *The Spark* newspaper building. Mentardy seemed to sense something, because I had never seen him exude so much suffering and yearning and nostalgia in his voice than at that moment when he pointed with his finger towards the slice of sky above the mill's chimneys.)

5. (He uttered the next words after he witnessed a fight between Paul and Nicky, who had just come out with a few tiny red and tricolour paper flags from a parade. 'My dad brought me ten flags from the parade,' said Paul. 'Mine brought me fifty flags,' said Nicky. 'Mine brought me five hundred flags,' said Paul. 'Then my dad brought me one million flags,' said Nicky. 'My dad brought me a billion flags from the parade,' said Paul. 'Then my dad brought me a quadrillion flags from the parade,' said Nicky. 'Mine brought me five million hundreds of quadrillions of flags,' said Paul. 'Well, my dad brought me an infinity of flags from the parade,' said Nicky. 'And mine brought me a million infinities of flags,' said Paul. 'That's impossible, my dad told me that infinity is the biggest number. There is no bigger number.') No, there isn't only one infinity. There is an infinity of infinities. Along this line, ten millimetres long,

there is an infinity of points, while on that one, one metre long, there must be even more. I define one kind of infinity as the Bull, because this little bag around my neck is embroidered with a Bull and I imagine that in the little bag I have an infinity, an entire universe where there are many worlds just like ours. But this little bag is nothing compared to me, who is made of an infinity of points. It is just a smaller infinity. And this building is an infinity greater than me. In the whole world there are nothing but infinities, some smaller, some greater: the chair is an infinity, the carnation is an infinity, this piece of chalk is an infinity. Infinities that crowd each other, infinities that eat each other. But there is an infinity that contains all other infinities. I imagine it as an endless herd of bulls.

6. After you die, you follow a very long path that rises endlessly. You go on and on and little by little your features change. Your nose and your ears retract into the flesh of the face like the little feet of an oyster. Your fingers retract into the flesh of your palm, and your arms get reabsorbed into your shoulders. In the same way, your thighs retract into your hips and you don't walk any more, you float along some walls of red brick where your shadow protracts like an elongated disc. You are now so round that you become translucent and begin to see all about you at once. When we're alive, we see only as though through the slot of a mailbox, but after death we see all around, with our whole skin. We float and stare at the ever nearing brick walls, but then, through a fleshy red brick, we get to a round place. There, in the middle, we see a cell, because we are in the womb of a mother. We get into the cell, and, as the birth steps begin, we look out through the eyes of all beings, of the flea, of the beetle, of the frog, of the mouse, of the hedgehog, of the rabbit, of the cat, of the dog, of the monkey, of man, and with a little luck, we get to see through the eyes of the enchanting being who is next in line after man. A dead man is looking at you right now through my eyes.

7. (In fact, the seventh point is not a 'theory,' but a few lines written by Mentardy with large letters, in chalk of different colours, on the smooth, slightly sloping cement surface of the transformer in the inner courtyard. It's possible he got up early one morning to

write them, because we found ourselves looking at them one day in the middle of the summer, about three weeks after his arrival. He said nothing about them. After he was convinced that all of us read these lines, he sat on his metal chair and went on with the tale he had begun the evening before, 'Tales of the Asian Peoples.')

DO NOT LAUGH AT LUMPY

DO NOT TORTURE ANIMALS

DO NOT HARASS GIRLS

DO NOT PLAY WITCHBITCH

DO NOT GET DIRTY

DO NOT TALK DIRTY

DO NOT LIE

DO NOT SQUEAL ON EACH OTHER

DO NOT ARGUE WITH EACH OTHER

DO NOT FIGHT WITH EACH OTHER

(From the moment we saw them, we realized we had to live by those words; we even realized that there was something in us that prevented us from turning away from them. For about two or three weeks, no one thought of doing any of the things prohibited on the list.)

I don't recall any other similar theories – I say 'theories' because I don't know what else to call them – but all of them were in the spirit of the ones above. They fascinated us because they were the substance of Mentardy's substance. You had to hear him speak and especially see him gesticulate, you had to feel the enchantment and the fright and the melancholy of those evenings. It was as though we were watching a strange film in muted colours, from coffee-brown to ashen-gray, the garnet-red of the mill and the greenish-black of the acacia's leaves. I don't need to say that, pausing from the telling of some tale with Arabs and caravans, he left us veiled in the pungent perfume of fiction, ready now for revelation . . .

That's how we spent an entire month that summer, huddled around Mentardy. We did nothing without asking him first – and our parents, even though puzzled on account of our clean T-shirts and blouses, were wary about our dependence which, day by day, was turning into fealty. 'Honey, what's that child doing to you, he's hypnotized all of you!' But we knew nothing but 'The Brave in the Tiger's Skin', 'Ruslan and Ludmila', 'Tristan and Isolde' and all the other heroes from Mentardy's stories. Even the girls left behind their silly games and tangled drawings of green women with blue legs and orange houses and gathered around the throne of metal and concrete. They sighed when the stories didn't have happy endings. And even Mona didn't show Mentardy her behind any more but looked at him – her eyes like two green slits – with less hatred than she looked at everyone else. But Iolanda was the closest to him, and you could see the two of them often exchanging a few words. She had gigantic bows tied around her pigtails and called everyone 'dearie', even dolls and cats. Once she amused herself by flinging gooseberries at an enormous spider, immobile in the middle of its web suspended between two trees. She was trying to hit it with the red berries, and when the little ball of claws and feet darted towards the margin of the cobweb, she called out to it: 'Wait a minute, dearie, where are you going?' But Mentardy never exceeded a certain reserve in his sporadic dealings with the girls; still, that was a lot more than the rest of us, who never talked to them at all. Certainly, we still played soccer, or brought out our chess table or button-soccer field. But they weren't the central focus of our interest any more. At that time, Mentardy went looking for the handicapped boy, and they spoke together for a long time.

About five or six years ago, around February, I was on a short recess and took a stroll through the city. I was walking out of the Sadoveanu Bookstore and passing by the Cyclops mall when something like a violent flame sent a shock through my stomach like an unbearable nostalgia. I had been staring in the small window displaying an assortment of lighters and plastic military decorations, located to the right of the tar-reeking entrance to Cyclops. The overwhelming emotion was provoked by the mere sight of a disposable lighter. The colour of this lighter, like a Proustian madeleine, elicited a memory from the time of this tale. The lighter was an odd kind of pink, more violet actually, that gave the impression, because of its wavy plastic, of soft and fleshy waters and yellowish half-moons. It was exactly the same colour as the little watch I bought for fifty bani the summer of that year, my first watch during the twenty-one years I lived in the building on Ştefan cel Mare Boulevard.

I remember distinctly the afternoon when that character in the red-checked shirt crept through the corridor which connected Entrance 1 to the rest of the building. He was crawling like an earthworm between the two buildings and almost froze by the gas metre. Finally, having reached safety, he caught his breath as though after a difficult climb and wiped off his plaster-stained elbows. He motioned us over to join him and began taking something out of his pocket. No matter how hard I try I can't recall what he looked like. I see only a white balloon. But in his open palms I make out even the smallest details: yellow and cream chewing gum wrapped in cellophane, with a tiny drawing in relief, little golden tin watches with multicolour plastic bands, whirligigs of various hues with two-bladed propellers that glided around two twisted wires until they lifted off, spinning up into the sky. We stood in a circle around him, asking the price of each and every object. Then we scattered, each of us to his own Entrance, in search of money. I bought the watch I mentioned with that uncanny pink-violet band for fifty bani. Mentardy bought a coloured whirligig. After the man left, he followed him with his eyes, the way the man slunk away through the crack of the corridor, then shifted his eyelids dreamingly towards the propeller at the base of the two nickel-plated wires twisted around each other. He stared somewhat absent-mindedly at the two cardboard blades, when suddenly they began to twirl all by themselves, faster and faster, till they lifted off into the air, even higher than a metre, and then maintained altitude, twirling for more than a few minutes. He kept staring at the propeller, but as though thinking of something else.

Before he left, the man in the red-checkered shirt had showed us something else, which he held on his palm with great care, caressing it from time to time. We closed the circle around him. The object in question was a black fountain pen. It displayed a rectangular window, framing a woman dressed in a black one-piece swimsuit. If you lifted the pen with the nib pointing up, the black of the swimsuit turned out to be a slow-draining liquid revealing first the woman's breasts, then the rest of the body, until she was completely naked: I had never imagined that a woman was like that. 'It's twenty-five lei, off-limits to snot-face kids like you,' the man laughed.

A little past nine, after everyone went home, Luci and I snuck out behind the building and crawled up the old chestnut in whose hollow we had found the pencil sharpeners. For about a quarter of an hour, we commented on what had just occurred – the arrival of the gewgaw peddler – all the while studying under the pale light of the mill courtyard's neon our little golden tin watches. Luci had just started one of his tales of lace-clad horses, when we heard Mentardy coming out of the building's stairwell and, slowly and hesitantly, heading for the sewage ditches. We couldn't believe our eyes when we saw him easing himself down into one of them. We nearly fell out of the tree from shock. Mentardy was strolling up and down the dirty labyrinth, making odd gestures that reminded us of witchbitch. He paused and took something out of his rompers' chest pocket. When he came into closer view, we saw that he had put on a frightening mask, painted with watercolours, much more primitive, much more leering, much more threatening than anything we had come up with in the realm of witchbitch masks. It wasn't till ten o'clock that he finally climbed out of the ditch and headed for the apartment building's entrance.

(I would like to interrupt the telling of the story for a moment. From time to time I feel the need to come up for air. But never so much as right now. Maybe I tried to hang on for too long with my head submerged, my hair waving, under those gelatin-thick waters of that summer, and my eyes are burning from all the gold and the reflections. But I think I am gasping for another, much deeper reason. I think that, I want to say this, I am not so sure I wish to read this text in our literary circle. It is not really literature, and it's becoming too much of something else. I have been writing for two weeks now and feel the need to put in things that have nothing to do with the history I was writing about before. What I mean is that I am beginning to notice that the act of writing is beginning to change me as a person. When I am not writing, at school or during my free time, I feel and behave like someone in a state of perpetual hallucination. I have not been able to finish correcting my students' papers this week, because pale images suddenly erupt on my brain's silver, images that afflict me even when I am listening to my students. Not to mention the fact that I have been suffering from frightening dreams, impossible to recount. And everything culminated – I hope, culminated – when a forceful and jerky sound woke me up last night. On the desk at the foot of my bed, my typewriter's keys were pounding by themselves. I woke up like a robot, turned on the light, and leaned over the page, ambling from one side to the other along the typewriter's carriage with a noise of bells and of typesetting machines. I began to read. The unseen fingers had started my tale from the beginning. They had gone as far as the dream with the glass jar and were just then writing the sentence: 'When I uncovered my eyes, I noticed that on the wall of the jar, which sparkled frantically, appeared the thin contours of a door.' As I read, I felt the sacred terror of the fulfillment of a prophecy. It expanded abruptly, aiming at the infinite, accompanied by a high-pitched noise in my temples, golden-yellow and unbearable. I felt my skull dissolving in the terror's flames. It was only then that I woke up for real, but for a long time in the bluish night till early morning I was not sure I had not crossed into another dream. So if I continue to write now, I will do so from an interior impulse only, and for myself alone.)

Immediately after the gewgaw peddler's visit, whatever closeness there was in our gang dissipated. Mimi, Lumpy, Luță, and Gimmi now barely paid any attention to Mentardy's stories; in turn, Mentardy, as I soon noticed, began to neglect his audience. He still sat on his concrete throne, but instead of telling us new stories, he would begin again with the 'Knights of the Round Table'. Many times, he would pause for entire minutes to recall a single word. Then, he would aim his vacant stare at the eyeless wall of the building, and in the painful silence you could hear the rumble of the trucks unloading wheat in the mill courtyard. I think that only Luci and I could sense that something strange was going on. And then, in the afternoon in my bed of torture, as I stared at the frozen and glittering clouds, I could only think about what I had seen the evening before: Mentardy wearing his cardboard mask, wandering and casting spells through the filth of the winding and fetid sewage ditches . . .

Summer was coming to an end, or perhaps the first days of September were already there (my parents were already fretting about buying my book bag and school supplies for the first grade). After an entire evening of, once again, 'Ruslan and Ludmila', Mentardy uttered those words that I still love: 'There are four different kinds of people: those who have not been born, those who are living, those who have died, and those who have not been born, are not living and have not died. They are the stars.' He followed with that gesture of his, tearing his arm away from the stars above the mill's tower. Walking home through the narrow tunnel, I asked him why he said those words. He was silent until we got behind the apartment building and, staring at the ditches, he said he didn't know. He asked me to come over the next day for a visit, because his mother had no idea what kinds of things she needed to buy him for school and wanted to ask me what my parents had bought for me.

I went over to his apartment about nine in the morning. His mother was dressed in a purplish robe; she was vertiginously tall. However, she spoke just like my mother and all the other mothers. She brought a plate of sliced apple pie and left us to play in Lonel's, or Vasile's, or maybe George's room, I still don't know Mentardy's name. His room was filled with a surprising number of toys, most of them disassembled. You could hardly find a car in one piece. From an ambulance only the body remained, while the engine with cogged rollers and steering wheel lay in a corner of the room. A tin frog was split in two and, like a shiny intestine, the spring had snapped out of its niche. A triggerless rifle rested underneath a chair with a pink back. There were books on the shelves but not as many as I had suspected, most of them thin and with giant letters, for very young students. I don't recall what we talked about, but I'm rushing to get to the essence. When Mentardy went out of the room for a few minutes, I slid some books out of the small library and spotted something falling from the shelf's veneer. I don't think that I was so shocked even when I saw Mentardy in the sewage ditches: behind the books was hidden the black fountain pen with the dressed–undressed woman. I replaced it, and when he returned I scrambled to tell him I had to go. While I was buckling my sandals in the hall – because his mother had asked me to take them off when I came in – I glanced at them one more time, mother and son, framed by the door, Mentardy holding her tenderly by the waist, she, foggy and immense in her purplish satin robe, pressing her hand to his shoulder. They both smiled the same smile, one that contained an infinity of meanings ranging from cunning to irony or, simply, kindness. They had matching eyelids, missing the lashes and stitched with delicate black. I was very disturbed. Outside I ran into Luci and told him all I had seen. We couldn't figure out when Mentardy had bought the pornographic pen. In the four days that had passed since we saw him last, the gewgaw peddler hadn't showed up around our building again. No, not even now do I understand how Mentardy came into the possession of the pen.

God, if only I were able to write, to describe that live and agonizing image that still lingers in my memory! Maybe then I could shed it. But no matter how badly it torments me, do I really want to shed it? Or do I wish to see it, again and again, each and every second of my life? It is only now that I arrive – and I do not know whether I am ready for it or not – at the essential scene of the present chronicle. I don't care that it will appear to lack verisimilitude. I write only for myself, and what I saw was real. This scene causes me shivers even now; it may be that translucent egg that incubated inside me, without my knowledge, for the last twenty-one years. What a monstrous fledgling it might engender! But I don't want to go on thinking about it. All I want is the ability to describe realistically this scene, though it seems next to impossible.

It was as though Mentardy had gone mad. At least, that was the opinion held by most of the members of our gang, who couldn't explain the moments, increasingly longer, of uncomfortable confusion, of the disoriented wandering of the boy in yellow rompers along the dirty walls of Entrance 1. He would barely start an Asian tale, 'The Wooden Cup and the Clay Cup' or 'The Genie from the Bottle', and then leave it unfinished. He would gaze lost in thought for an hour at a time at the odd drawings by the girls and even began conversations with them. The intimate adviser and confessor role which the crippled boy, with his orthopaedic nickel-plated boot, played for Mentardy was taken over by Iolanda, the one with the enormous bows. Mentardy talked with her often, describing odd curves in the air with his expressive arms. The evening before the morning of his ultimate fall, Mentardy, surrounded by us all and with Iolanda at his feet, told us the most beautiful story we had ever heard. It was like collective hypnosis, because we listened till ten, till we couldn't see our faces, till all that remained of the world was the square of dark blue above us, crisscrossed by the starry powder of the Milky Way. It was the tale of 'The Eleven Swans', and the child's voice rose, fell, and twirled, making us mad with melancholy. The mute girl, weaving vestments of stinging nettles for her brothers who had been changed into royal birds, their flight across the boiling green sea, the boy who was left with a swan's wing – these stories had long been in us. Mentardy only reminded us of them. When he finished the story in the quiet of the night, you could hear the hum of the trams on Ştefan cel Mare.

The next day was the last. That cold morning, I met with my friends Luci and Sandu and scooted up the chestnut tree. The tree had spawned some large and prickly fruit. We cracked the shells from the shiny chestnuts all morning. I remember Sandu's shriek of surprise. He had found under a green shell full of thorns a glimmering crystal, large and heavy. It was a glass egg through which light refracted in odd ways. It is a bad sign when a chestnut tree spawns such strange fruit.

Around noon, Mentardy still had not showed up at Entrance 1, and everything seemed to stagnate. We thought of an old game we played before witchbitch, called 'Explorers'. Halfway down the building was a sheet-metal door painted grey and studded with rivets. That was the entrance to the entrails of the basement. We opened the creaky door carefully and stepped down the spiral metal stairwell, keeping clear of the black oily walls filled with electrical panels. It got darker and darker as we went down. We paused before a long and narrow hallway that reeked of putty and rust-soaked hemp; out of the walls grew a tangled gut-work of various-sized pipes veering around corners that bristled with faucets and manometers. The humid cement below us flickered mutely under the pale light stealing in through the tiny grated window, cut far above in the ceiling. We stared in wonder at the pipes. Some were thicker than our bodies, others as thin as fingers and endlessly long. We crossed in silence this hallway of the pipes and opened another metal door that led to the hallway of the boilers. The multitude of pipes had stabbed through the walls and disappeared into an enormous womb of scarlet metal engirdled by rivets larger than fists. They looked like metal pigs sprawled out on cement pedestals. Here and there, the black-ciphered manometers glittered out threats from behind their greenish glass. We felt as though we were in the temple of a powerful and incomprehensible deity. After we cut across the womb monsters, we tiptoed to the last chamber, the one most deeply hidden in the belly of the building, the furnace stoker's room. The door between the hallway of the boilers and this room was also made of metal, but was cut by a tiny window. Rising high on the tips of our toes, we managed to peer inside. We froze.

The room was severed diagonally by a wide ray of light falling through a grated window high up. The ray scattered a luminous steam around it, so that we could see what we had never wanted to see. In the bare room, three metres by three at the most, two children were standing, facing each other without any clothes on. The filtered ray splayed across the boy's hair and sketched a delicate drawing of the girl's ankles and feet. The children were unbearably beautiful. The golden light made them look blonde. The boy's hair burned with reddish and golden curls, while his face appeared to be illuminated by the obsidian film hemstitching his eyes. The gap below his nostrils furrowed deeper than ever before. His lips were drawn and animated by an odd, inexplicable smile. His narrow body with its muscles barely traced by yellow streaks, with its frail ribs in slight relief, with its thin but firm legs, looked like a delicate and disturbing drawing. Barely shorter than him, her bows tied in white satin, her tresses twisting on her forehead, Iolanda gazed at him with a puzzled smile, that smile I later noticed on all naked women. I see her body before me as I write: it was delicate and white, with the tiny copper coins of her breasts, the sex merely a line inked between the thighs. There was almost no other difference between the two childish bodies. Below on the ground, their clothes draped the cement in an odd arrangement. I saw the way they gazed at each other, with no feeling that could be defined, because their faces did not display human expressions. They were like statues . . . but not like statues. When the girl lifted her arm and touched the boy on the shoulder with the tip of her fingers, Sandu wrenched himself from the window and dashed off, running through the hallway of the boilers. Filled with terror, me and Luci dashed off after him. Even now I shiver and sigh when I recall this scene in the furnace stoker's room. I hear even now, shattering my eardrums, Iolanda's frightened shriek at the clatter of our scampering feet, a shriek that followed us, reverberating between the boilers and pipes all the way out into the street.

We didn't stop till we got to Entrance 1, which was deserted at that hour. We couldn't even look at each other, we didn't know what to do. Luci shook like a madman and even developed a fever during the following days. At noon, we went home. During the afternoon sleep, with my head under the bedsheets, I became delirious and remained so till evening. I could see nothing but the two frail bodies facing each other in the furnace stoker's chamber. I could not understand it. Why did Mentardy change so abruptly, so absolutely, after the gewgaw peddler's visit? I didn't even know what questions to ask myself. Sandu, on the other hand, had a different reaction. He was indignant, filled with fury. That evening, when the whole gang got together next to Entrance 1, he told them everything, including a number of things he had made up. According to him, Mentardy tricked us with all his deranged concoctions, but now the cat was out of the bag. Vova and his brother bolted for the transformer and erased with their palms the multicoloured phrases that Mentardy had chalked in and which, over the weeks, we had redrawn time and again. Mimi was gloating: potbellied and swarthy, he crawled on top of Mentardy's throne and from there conducted the dispute over the punishment to be meted out to him. Of course, he couldn't come up with anything more imaginative than 'Let's rough him up.' Gimmi proposed that until we figured out what to do with him we should play a game of witchbitch, because we hadn't played it in a while. So, we scurried behind the building and swooped down the dirty ditches breathing in once again our precious reek of dirt, milky larvae, and worms, but especially the penetrating smell of fear. We covered our faces again with cardboard masks, turning ourselves into demons and monsters, giants and dragons and wild men, and chasing one another through the tangled network.

Mentardy appeared around eight. We couldn't believe our eyes when we saw him approaching the ditch's edge. We had been certain he would stay hidden in his apartment for at least a week, but the fact that he hazarded coming face to face with us was the epitome of conceit. We dropped our game and, from down there in the ditch, began leering at him. He wanted to say something, but Paul picked up a ball of dirt and threw it at him. It hit him in the leg, pretty hard. Jean followed with another, and Mentardy took off, running in the direction of Entrance 1 under a shower of dirt balls. Shouting and howling with our masks on, we charged after him, our pockets filled with dirt. Erupting out of the narrow corridor, we paused in the middle of the interior courtyard. There was no place there where he could escape. We didn't see him at first but eventually spotted him hidden behind the bridge's banister, the tiny platform leading towards the walled door. He was balled up in the dark. Shouting, we began pelting him with dirt balls again, but Mentardy shouted even louder and defended himself like a demon. He had covered his face – in the neon light of the mill courtyard, we could see his horrible mask painted with watercolours – and he threw back at us the balls that bombarded him from all sides. He was positioned higher than we were and was well protected by the two banisters, while we were out in the open; thus he defended himself for a long time, an entire hour, until a dirt ball hit him full blast in the head. We saw him, then, in the penumbra slowly lowering himself to the ground, arching his body from head to toe, and writhing with a horrific might. We moved in on him, but he appeared not to see us. His eyes were streaming with tears. He groaned and roared in short sporadic bursts in between the spasms that contorted his frame in impossible angles. We got so scared that Luţă darted to Entrance 3 and rang Mentardy's door. Hidden underneath Entrance 1, we spied the woman in red rushing in and picking up the writhing boy.

This is how everything ended. Mentardy's mother sent him off to his grandparents or to a boarding school or somewhere, because we never saw him again. The next day, it began to rain, a frozen drizzle that turned the back of the building into a mucky swamp where it was pointless to play. School started a week later, and by the next summer our gang had disintegrated. Twenty anonymous years followed. I went through high school, the army, college, and here I am, a teacher. But for the last three months, since the dream with the hamster jar, I have become a completely different man. I can't go on. Each night I have nightmares that I don't dare write down in my dream journal. I sense the approach of something, I smell the scent of poisoned ice that makes the pores of my skin shudder. Sometimes, I weep during the afternoons, tearlessly, anxiously, with a sense of imminent dissolution. I was seized by such a crisis of desperate sobbing yesterday, after I wrote the scene in the fire stoker's room. What will I do now that I am finished with this tale that sprang so miraculously from my memory? Will I roam the streets aimlessly, will I go into restaurants and shops, will I disturb the silence of movie theatres shouting Mentardy's story out loud? Because I feel I haven't told everything, because I can't keep myself from hollering this truth which is mine and mine alone, I can't control this torment, I can't . . . No, I will not read it to our literary group, because these pages are not literature but a horrible prophecy. I will take them out with me and read them in a snowstorm, on the streets, by the light of the window displays and in the trams, and I will seek out and find those who will understand and follow me, and we will rummage through the whole city and scout out Mentardy, and we will know that he exists, and we will understand him, and we will weep and sing, while he, shrouded by a fur of rays, spraying blue lightning, will stand and lift his arms, illuminating the whole city like daylight, up to the stars and beyond the stars, while we will turn into white ash, purer, purer, oh, I can't go on, I can't . . .

♦

This morning while trying to find my Scotch tape to fix a book cover, I found these typewritten pages which, by the look of them, appear to be about two years old. They were on top of the wardrobe under some mounted photos. I read them and couldn't prevent myself from adding these words about how surprised I was. There is no doubt they were written to my 'Erika' and refer to a period of my childhood. Without fail, I recognize certain coordinates from this chronicle. I did live in that building on Ştefan cel Mare. The mill, Entrance 1, the scenery are all real, and you can find them there even today, with the exception of the subterranean network, because our building never had boilers in the basement. The children are real, I retain their names, some of them I even see today, but the whole Mentardy story seems absurd. We never had such a wise child in our building. Vova Smirnoff is now an engineer, Lumpy is a waiter at Athéneé Palace, I keep seeing him there. Gimmi is something or other somewhere, Sandu is an engineer, while little Nicky is my friend Nicolae Iliescu. But where is Mentardy? Where in the world did this story come from? I would reread the text, but I confess that I am afraid. I don't want to throw it away but don't want to come upon it again either. I am going to find a good place to hide it, somewhere where it can lie hidden forever without danger of being thrown out with the newspapers or some other trash, because my wife is a specialist at things like that . . .

The Twins

Shaving takes you longer than you expected. You had shaved your armpits back then and for the last two weeks or so, that is, from that time, the beard, sporadically, but this time it is different: you must not nick your skin at any cost. That is why, holding the Gillette with pedantic awkwardness by the yellowish-white handle, you drag the blade over the hyperabundantly soaped cheek, leaving timid tracks on the pink skin, over whose surface the few hair strands sectioned just above the roots irradiate minuscule greenish-hued dots. The tracks drown instantly in the water streaming down from the wet hair. You stare in the mirror, eaten away by humidity and reflecting the mouldy wall which, who knows by what sort of whim of taste, had been painted an ultramarine, and the toilet bowl, cracked and coarsely cemented together with plaster. For shaving cream, you use a perfumed paste from a Hungarian spray can you found on the shelf next to the two or three multicoloured tubes and a few used razor blades that had been left to rust in a puddle and now clung together. The water on the chin, cold as ice, streams down the neck and chest, heavy with shaving cream. You stare with amusement at the chest in the mirror. If anyone came home now you could go and meet them as you are, jeans and bare chest, there'd be nothing to be ashamed of. While at other times ... You amuse yourself for a while, recalling there were other times, as you continue dragging the shaving instrument slowly, carefully, over each portion of the skin, stretched over the protruding bones belonging to the jaw. You curve the blade under the chin and begin to pick up the swaths of cream covering the Adam's apple. Not even the tiniest trace of hair must remain. The electric bulb is tiring to the eyes, the contours in the mirror appear to you at times attended by a glowing mauve or lilac. You drag a towel across chest and belly and wipe off the water, causing the skin to break into goose bumps. Glued to the door, bulging and blackened by humidity, is a dye-transfer print of a woman's pink profile with locks hyperbolically puffed up and sectioned by degrees into bands: a blood-red band followed by other more diluted reds, giving the impression of acrylic paint. Thin letters underneath the woman's arching bust spell out: CRISAN SHAMPOO. The beard is now off. The moustache is a more complex issue, its long strands, about two centimetres, are very thick. 'He wore a moustache, the poor bastard,' you think spitefully, then whistle: 'Screw him. That's just what he needed!' Again you press the spray can's button, filling the left hand's fingers with a thick and perfumed foam and saturate the upper lip with it. You feel the strands soften like the legs of a spider that has fallen in water. It is actually not too difficult. You just need to rinse the razor more often, shaking it in the sleek column of water flowing out of the faucet's curved pipe. The water is so silent and resolute in its fall that you have the sensation that it isn't flowing, that it is a glass column frozen between the faucet's opening and the bottom of the basin, layered with foam and strands of hair. Moustache only half shaven, you contemplate the face in the mirror. You laugh. Then abruptly, you begin to cry with hysterical sobs, your forehead resting against the cold lip of the basin. Eyes still wet with tears, you shave the other half of the moustache, then wash the face for a long time. Unfortunately, the hot water has been turned off. You wipe off the water, rubbing the face with the rough surface of the orange towel and stare in the mirror once again. Good Lord, how will you manage? Without its hair, this elongated face seems even more masculine, even more difficult to control. Before you wash the Gillette, you dry-drag it across the breastbone, sacrificing the timid spider web of a bristle that nestled itself there. This time the razor blade squeaks something horrible as though wishing to protest. It gives you the shivers. You apply the aftershave's light foam to the face, and, twisting the Gillette's swivel-base knob, its little wings open up like a drawbridge and reveal the shiny blade. You give the blade and the Gillette a thorough cleaning, making sure to follow the warning: *Do not wipe blade*. You stare at the blade for a while. How unfamiliar this object had been for you until so very recently! You squeeze it lightly between your fingers. 'London Bridge' is printed on it, and the letters seem to take on an intensity and a life of their own. An inexplicable impulse makes you kiss the blade, then glue it to the cheek; the eyes fill with tears again. You insert it back inside the Gillette and leave the bathroom.

There is no one in the apartment. The doors pushed against the walls open out into the sinister perspectives of the rooms and hallways. In the bedrooms, the beds have been left unmade, and there is something indecent in the tangle of the yellowish sheets and blankets revealing strips of the sofas' flowered tapestry. Through the giant window covering the size of the entire wall, the flaming rags of the summer sky's clouds take on the shapes, disordered in their design, of Renaissance paintings. If you were to open one of these giant transparent panels and stick your head out the window, you would notice about twenty metres below the Ştefan cel Mare Boulevard shrouded in a reddish orange light, suggesting in its detailed and yet transfigured realism, somewhat betrayed by the filtered hue, an illustration from an American magazine. Towards the left Ştefan cel Mare extends out into Mihai Bravu Boulevard and veers towards Vitan Street, while to the right it sharpens like an arrowhead, impaling the great sun, now suspended two or three centimetres above the horizon. The room itself, like a cubical and illusory parasite, sucks the bloody outside into the wide stripes on the walls.

You walk into the room. You wonder how in the world you managed to get your jeans so wet. They simply stick to your ankles. You take them off and, in your shorts now, you sit on a chair in front of the mirror above the vanity. You smile because you know the contents of the drawers in great detail. The fact that he has a sister is an unexpected good fortune. You open the first drawer, and the room fills up with the smell of powder and cream. You take out a Chinese make-up case that contains in its flat box, underneath a layer of

sponge spotted with bluish and sienna stains, a row of lipstick tubes
of different nuances, some mixed together, a few symmetrically
arranged oval cases containing mascara, some nearly used up, others untouched, a plastic stick with a piece of sponge stained a light
shade of green on one end, a large oval case containing pink powder, a tiny mascara brush, black and oily, a cheap eyeliner not
originally belonging to the case and making it difficult for the box
to close and, God knows why, a few rubber washers. You find two
small conical bottles of nail polish, one containing a viscous scarlet
liquid, the other a lustrous mother-of-pearl white goo. You place
them on the chest's macramé. You also find eyebrow tweezers. In
the second drawer, there is another bottle of nail polish with tiny
golden specks in the whitish liquid (what bad taste, you conclude)
and two or three other lipstick tubes, one of which is of good quality, a Dior. You spot it instantly, instinctively knowing it is the right
nuance to use. But you realize right away the absurdity of your
thought. You find as well at the bottom of the drawer a coquettish
powder case, French, made of plastic engraved with roses, carved
with golden sinuous lines. You open it, recalling it is available in
stores, even around here. You stare at yourself in the mirror, gri-
macing. You simply can't get used to it. The box has only two little
squares, one of a light green shade, the other a light pink, thus
making it more interesting. Still, damn it, it is too little. From these
odds and ends you must improvise the best you can an honest
make-up job. You open one of the side doors of the chest. You find
it difficult to endure the sweetish smell of locally made cheap perfume (at least it's not Bulgarian . . .) that emanates from the seven
or eight bottles of various shapes crammed inside the tiny plywood
chamber. One of them, the epitome of kitsch, is enriched with a
sort of armature of yellow metal. Another is bedecked with a top
larger than itself, fashioned like a gigantic headdress from another
century. But among them, through who knows what miracle, like
an exiled queen, you spot (who could have given it to her?) a superb
bottle of Emotion. You pick it up with love, removing it from its
unacceptable company, unscrew the top and press lightly on the
knob, pointing to the back of the left hand. You inhale the

voluptuous scent on the now ennobled skin. This is the way it should be, you think, and even say it out loud: 'OK.' You place it on the vanity and slam the door on the other perfumes. Behind the right side door you find, in a messy pile, a few AGFA cassettes and the microphone with the cable tangled around it. That's just how it is. No reason to despair, though not much of an occasion for rejoicing. As far as the clothes go, it's going to be more complicated.

You begin by voluptuously plucking the eyebrows. Each painful sting causes you a nostalgic happiness. You pick at them for half an hour and don't give up till you get (from a dog's tail, you tell yourself) two thin, perfect arches that lend the masculine face the harlequin's unbearable sadness. You paint the eyelids in a light pink, merely a hint, then dab the mascara abundantly, for contrast, on the eyelashes, fortunately unusually long for a man. You look at yourself in the mirror. Not bad. You rouge the lips, surprisingly full, handling the Dior tube with dexterity, then rub the lips together until the perfumed paste, tasting lightly of alcohol, spreads evenly. You take the time to try to correct the bitter expression of his mouth. But the bitterness remains, floating somewhere outside his facial traits, independent of them. His cheeks harbour a cadaverous aspect, the eyes, lengthened by their sparkling black, seem to extend over the entire face, while underneath, the mouth is marked by a disdain that borders on the indecent, a sensually cynical indifference. You correct that impression using powder to fill out the concave cheeks. From the depths of your soul, you regret the lack of a foundation for the complexion, but that's just how it is. You fidget in front of the mirror, staring at this unexplored head. The air in the room has turned the colour of coffee, so you turn on the lights; you contemplate in their glimmer all the colours you have bedecked yourself with. The face has evolved in beauty; it is possessed of a beauty that no woman or man ever hoped to have. You view yourself in profile, looking into the large mirror through the powder case's tiny mirror. Though you've thought about the 'secret weapon', telling yourself you will use it when you're already dressed, you lose your patience. You open the bedroom's wardrobe door and remove from an old purse a pair of clip-on, rhomboidally shaped earrings in two colours, the latest fashion. You put them on; that is not your secret weapon, but that object you happened upon a few days before, also in the wardrobe, the object whose discovery caused you to make the important decision you are carrying out tonight. You bring out, with that grateful sigh, the wonderful object. It's a blonde wig, unusually lavish, with curls that cascade majestically and in the most natural manner down along the shoulder blades. The inside lining is soft and elastic, so that after fifteen minutes you do not doubt that you are wearing your own hair. You put on the wig and linger before the mirror, drawing the comb through it for a long time. Each of the crimson comb's sweeps unfurl the locks, the hair unrolls, only to gather back into a curl a second later, a lazy and graceful motion. Because the comb crackles at each contact, you think about turning off the lights. In the nearly complete darkness that permeates the room, bluish-green sparks, unimaginably thin, shroud your hair with an ephemeral lacework, spreading for a metre around you. By this palpitating, stroboscopic light, you can see in the mirror an incredible lady with masculine shoulders, a flat chest and prominent collarbones.

You turn the lights on again, but the fascination persists, making you ill. You clench your hands over your ears, wig and cheeks, then stare at the pale, rhomboid traces left by the earrings on your palms. You sense that the entire live substance that fills the crate of your chest, your breastbone's marrow, the lungs, the heart, become rarified all at once, being replaced by a network of gelatinous emotions, a system of tiny tubes and filaments, the colour of brick and roses and violent scarlet, unspeakably painful. You stand up from your chair and start to rummage through the large wardrobe against the wall by the door. You drag out everything that looks like women's clothes. Once again, you marvel at your good luck, that he should have a sister who is as tall as he is. Thus, all her clothes will fit you. First, you find a whole set of pretty panties, not entirely mini – that would have made them unusable – but very dainty. There are seven pieces, white, each embroidered in front with a few birds sitting on a branch, and, underneath, handwritten with beautiful green letters, the days of the week in French: *Lundi,*

Mardi, Mercredi, Jeudi, Vendredi, Samedi, Dimanche. You slip off his and put on the ones with *Dimanche* on them, which become you well. You try on next a pair of black fishnet stockings, with a fine mesh, which mitigate the instinctive embarrassment at not having found anything suitable with which to remove the hair on the legs. Then, you spend a long time thinking whether or not to wear a bra. But, partly because you didn't often wear one before, and partly because it seems grotesque to stuff a bra with something like socks or cotton as in the cheap movies about vulgar drag queens, you decide against it. There are enough babes with flat chests who look as charming as you can get . . .

Now comes the moment of truth. What to wear. You don't have too many choices. You have to eliminate from the start jeans or cords, which don't go together with either the idea of uttermost femininity or bony and narrow hips. You need something sentimental, something wrapped in fog, you have to become the woman everyone dreams of, something like the dreamy blondes on the L'Oréal billboards. You try first a scarlet cashmere blouse, with puffy sleeves, fastened in the back with two beautiful mother-of-pearl buttons. It would go well with jeans, disco style, but not for this. You find an ostentatious kind of dress, with a square lace collar, tailored from retted yellow fabric, with a gold lamé belt and large pale flowers applied to the hem, probably something from a costume shop. You twist and turn in front of the mirror, then drop on the bed, freeze in a rigid position, then, lifting your head, stare at yourself once again. Not quite right . . . You need something sweeter, more sensual, but at the same time innocent. You sit up and contemplate that face, made up and framed by ringlets, beaming an ambiguous beauty. You smile oddly, thrust your head forwards a bit, guide your shoulder forwards and – for what reason? – point with your finger at the image in the mirror. You linger in that position, pointing directly towards the phantasm's chest, then get up and extend your finger till you brush the finger in the mirror. With a rushed gesture, you take off your dress and let it drop on the floor. You find in the pile of clothes a flowery summer dress of a pale lilac hue, plainly cut and sleeveless, with two thin shoulder straps. You try it on, and, though it becomes you, it doesn't work with that dignified head you constructed. You fear you will give in to the temptation of incessantly trying on all the clothes, thus losing sight of your purpose. You remove that dress as well and look for something more sophisticated. You spot on a hanger an evening dress, black and woven with silver strands, with a low neckline and ending, under the high and romantic waistline, in an explosion of ruffles. Despite the cheap material, the tailoring job is first class. You settle on it. On the other hand, the chest . . . You will decide as you go. You leave the dress on, it goes well with the stockings, which call for the right kind of shoes. You have always loved shoes. Ever since high school, not a single day went by that you didn't walk into a shoe store on the boulevard. Ankle boots, made from a tiny piece of leather, with very very high heels, causing the foot to stand at an almost vertical angle, stepping only on the tip of the toes – you went crazy over those. It didn't matter how many pairs you had at home, you still wanted more. But now you have to be content with those boat-shoes of his sister's. Elegant nonetheless. Still, it just isn't the same thing. You freeze at the thought she took the black shoes with her on the trip to the country. Of course, the idea is absurd. She never took them out of the wardrobe except for special days. You bolt at the wardrobe's third door: they are there, sitting on a wavy rabbit fur. The foot is the same size in length, but a little wider. Keeping in mind you are not going anywhere, it's fine. In any case, they fit. The heel is about seven centimetres, nothing like what you're used to. You wore thirteen, fourteen centimetres, all kinds of heels, the kind that models wear.

'Not bad,' you say out loud, while pacing back and forth before the mirror. As a last touch, you clasp around the neck a thin gold chain with tiny discs and a large, baroque pearl, unpolished, and finally press the dainty Emotion perfume bottle's golden top and spray yourself with fresh, sensual aerosol clouds. Oh Lord, you suddenly notice, you forgot to do the nails. And you still have to powder the shoulders a bit, where the muscles' veins – though he was a far cry from the athletic type – still burrowed some bothersome virile shadows. You dab neck and shoulders with the elastic and perfumed pad, then you tackle the nails, which fortunately you took good care of during the last few days when you had to move into his place. But no matter how much you clean the cuticles (he sometimes bit the skin next to his nails till he drew blood), and though his hands were thin and lanky, you still couldn't turn them into a lady's hands. The fingernails are wide rather than long. You choose mother-of-pearl. You unscrew the tall and striped top and remove the tiny brush, clotted in the thick liquid with the familiar reek of ether. You paint each nail carefully, first the left hand, then the right, waving and fanning out the fingers through the air with theatrical gestures. When you finish, you feel a slight fatigue in the spine. You stand up and stretch. What to do with the chest, there's a troublesome question. You try at random some cotton (you find one whole package and another one half used up on a shelf in the wardrobe, behind a stack of folded shirts). You roll two balls the size of apples and cram them inside the chest area. As the neckline's ribbon is stretched tight across the skin, the effect turns out unexpectedly well. They're good for something, those vulgar films about transvestites, you tell yourself, laughing. The babe in the mirror is now endowed with the sweetest pair of darling little tits!

You sit on the bed and want to cry, but can't for fear of ruining the make-up. You force yourself not to think. You start to put the room in order. Everything has to be clean and in its place. You make the bed, put the clothes back in the wardrobe, the make-up and the rest of the things in the drawers of the vanity, arrange the books and the vase on the table, draw the curtain, making sure folds are of equal size, and straighten out the drapes. From the living room you bring some jewel cases of sculpted wood, two brass candleholders and a few fanciful pillows which you use to improvise a coquettish boudoir décor. Then you bring a few little knick-knacks (in bad taste), which you place on the library shelves that occupy about half the wall.

You go into the bathroom. The ultramarine walls seem now, late at night, even more phantasmic. The yellow bulb throws dreamy lilac stripes inside the mirror. You open the medicine chest, suspended on the wall opposite the tub. You pick the bottle of meprobamate, unscrew the top, lift the cotton and empty it in your palm. There are about twenty pills, the necessary amount. In order not to fail, you know you need at least ten grams. You have about fifteen, perhaps too much. The pills are small, you are not afraid to take them. You know he has difficulties swallowing medicine, but this time it will go smoothly. You rinse the glass you find there upside down on the glass stand and fill it with water. A picture of two children holding hands, the sign of the Twins, is stamped with green paint over its transparent surface. Below the picture you read, printed in large letters: THE TWINS, May 22–June 21. You divide the pills in three little heaps and swallow them one by one. You return to the bedroom and stretch yourself on the beautiful bed with silk pillows. The next day, around lunchtime, returning from the trip to the country, they will find in the bedroom facing the street a very, very beautiful lady, pallid, breathless and with a cold heart.

'After a night of agitated sleep, a horrific insect woke up transformed into the author of these lines.' This is how I might begin – inverting the phrase at the start of Kafka's *Metamorphosis* – the story which I have thought about relating here, if I wished to publish it. It would be a dramatic beginning, which would not diminish its veracity, taking into consideration that the insect is *me*. More so, much more so than Gregor Samsa, let us say to the degree that the insect was a Hoffmann, or a Nerval, or a Novalis. Like all these Romantics, I will write not to construct a story, but to exorcise an obsession, to protect my poor soul from a monster, a monster terrifying not through hideousness but beauty. I am thinking now of Rilke's unbearably beautiful angel, and I would like to quote something from the 'First Elegy', but, since I have been here, it seems as though my memory's resources have, if not darkened, at least fogged up a bit. (I am afraid. A few moments ago, I was sitting on the sofa, staring distractedly at all those icons painted on glass with a predominance of bright red and azure, at the yellowish and shiny keys of the upright piano, at the bureau with the peeling wooden doors, painted with a sorrowful character with a dark, Byzantine face, wrapped in an ample blue toga cascading into multiple folds and holding in his hand a budding branch; behind him, the violet beyond darkens, and the red clouds leak sadly between the cypress trees. Below, written in golden letters: AMOR OMNIA VINCIT. I stared at that space, unendingly tall, bordered by the rich drapes covering the windows, and asked myself if her blood, irrigating the lobes of my brain through thousands of tiny tubes, might not, little by little, relocate her being in me; if her past, emanating from this room filled with sculpted furniture and hammered copper, would not march out in skeletal troops against my own memories, as in Brueghel's *Apocalypse*. I leaped to my feet at this thought, exactly the same way I did a week ago, when I decided never to look at myself in the mirror again. And, just as I sewed together then this rough hemp cloth that I used to cover the mirror's waters, I decided now to write, to make out of these pages another cloth, another weft, to protect me – this time not from her body but her psyche, from her sorrows, her madness, her happiness, her stupidity, her idealism and her baseness, her superb rapacity). I would like to read, but where are the books? The illiterate darling, the only good things on the three or four shelves she calls a library are the books I gave her: a gorgeous Huizinga, a Baltrusaitis on Gothic art, that's about all. As for the rest, dictionaries, folk art books, bad novels, all unreadable. Still, and this is just one of her contradictions, not only did she read, she also wrote verses. She even kept a journal where she wrote down her strange and colourful dreams, impossible to psychoanalyze, fairy tales really, of paradisiacal gardens. I think the wealth of colours and light in her dreams was caused by the fact she slept with her eyes open: I never saw anyone sleep like that before. It was frightening to watch her sleep, it was like watching a dead person. I will not attempt to explain here why I loved her, it is unexplainable, like all natural things. I don't even want to talk about what happened with us ten (eleven? twelve?) days ago. I would like only to recall my past, or to remodel my past or to invent it, or all those things at once, because the only thing that concerns me now is to have a past, a series of images to substitute for the present chaos.

Now, ever since they, those poor little old people rattled by anxiety, noticed that something very odd is going on with me (the bit with me covering the mirror and a whole bunch of other things), and ever since I exercised my new vocal chords by howling at them in a fit of hysteria, they leave me alone here in this room, which is tall as a tower. All you hear these golden and nostalgic afternoons is the rustling of a few sunlit leaves and the numbers counted out by some girl playing by herself on Venera Street's abandoned sidewalk. As before, I lie on the bed ruffled by loneliness and nerves, my mind filling up with old memory fragments, painful and heartrending, from my distant childhood. I thought I should write down a few of these violet flashes from the recurrent illuminations I experience while, with my head glued to the pillow, I stare at the thick golden stripes on the opposite wall. But not in the Proustian mode, too refined for what I am after. In fact, whether I prefer it or not, the Proustian method was familiar to me before I even knew who Proust was. It is odd, but as an adolescent I had all the experiences, unique and unrepeatable, of certain writers: I know Proust's madeleine effect – the discoidal candies, spongy, pink and excessively perfumed; or the gleaming of a badge on the chest of a passer-by that engendered in me the powerful emotion of recalling a place, of recreating an atmosphere. I know the sensation of fainting that assaulted Max Blecher on abandoned lots; I experienced the entire network of Kafkaesque symptoms: false perceptions, *jamais vu* and all the rest. And I also have sensations which are truly unique, not encountered anywhere in literature, but I won't get into that now. I want to remember – though I know that the road to remembering will lead directly to catastrophe. I feel I will not be able to write about anything incidental, not compromised by obsession, by chimeras.

Since I began writing, the little old lady poked her head two or three times through the door, peering at me with concern. Each time I waved my hand in anger to make her understand I wished to be left alone. I am afraid they will send for the doctor and I will be forced to play the farce of normality. I stare now at the hand that holds the pen. The nail polish has nearly peeled off. My handwriting is slightly different than before; still, I am in control of it.

First, a few lightning-like memories awaken, perhaps from the age of two or three. I see at the corner of an alley three men in white shirts, their profiles against the flame-red sky, smoking and chatting peacefully. In the distance, the giant red-brick walls of repair shops with windows black from soot, abandoned even then. It was somewhere near the Obor train station, because that's where we lived then, and I see railroad tracks reflecting the red sky. Not a sound, not a smell that I can associate with this enigmatic movie. I approach the three men and stare at them, leaning my head back. They seem gigantic to me, my head barely above their knees. They lean forwards over me. They have monstrous faces, made only of flesh and blood. They laugh noiselessly, while one of them lifts me by the armpits and tosses me up in the air, catching me an instant later. I begin to scream, also soundlessly, and he puts me down. I turn around and run to our gate, where my mother, tall as a tower and wearing a navy blouse, is waiting. In an instant I soak her chest and her blouse's collar with tears and saliva.

Another time, all three of us are returning from the movies. We'd gone to a summer outdoor movie theater and saw *Venice, the Moon, and You.* I remember perfectly that title, which for me was magical. I have forgotton hundreds of movie titles but I will never forget that one. Certainly, I don't remember the film itself, the same way I don't recall the book *Blue Evenings,* which I read in my first years of school and which I can't find anywhere, but whose title awakens in me a pervasive nostalgia. We walk the dim alleys, I am in the middle, my mother and father are holding my little hands. I see a street with tiny houses, with street-level shops, with minuscule balconies, whose pavement resounds sonorously under our footsteps. Before us walked the moon, fuller and larger than I had ever seen it before, yellow with brown-orange spots but still excessively bright. I say 'walked' because it seemed to move forwards in rhythm with my steps, oscillating up and down to the beat of my little shoes on the violet cobblestones. My parents, terribly tall, whispered over my head, while I gazed at the moon with fascination, mystified that we couldn't pass it, that it continued to walk ahead of us. Suddenly, I found myself inside a passage guarded by frightening cement creatures. We walked underneath the vault of the passage till we reached a room, large and very bright. We were in the home of people whom I had never met, who were happy to see my parents. I was kissed by a hefty woman with lots of make-up, green eyes and a string of green beads hanging around her neck; the beads were the size of ping-pong balls. On the walls, I saw hideous masks made of rags, and perhaps a musical instrument, a sabre . . . A dirty glass chandelier burned above us with buzzing bulbs. The table was full of dishes and sweets, but, after I munched on the corner of a piece of pie, I found myself pushed into another room, where a girl who must have been six years old and a little boy of about eight began to show me all sorts of toys. There were carousels that spun by themselves, with wires from which little tin aeroplanes were suspended, a kind of train running along tiny rails surrounding a tray, a yellow motorcyclist and two birds, all made of nothing but tin, spinning and hopping on the waxed wooden floor. There was even a toy car that turned around by itself once it reached the edge of the table. We played together for a while. One by one, they spread out a series of toys I never dreamed I would ever possess. And then they showed me a toy that took my breath away: a Chinese puppet, the figure of a mandarin with his hands crossed over his belly. The toy was made of plastic and composed of a large sphere representing the stomach and a smaller one placed on top, with Chinese facial features painted on it, fierce and at the same time benign. The object was very heavy, its bottom filled with lead, and rocked endlessly from one side to the other like a Weeble Wobble. The astonishing thing for me, however, was that, while it wobbled, the mandarin also sang, emitting a high-pitched and delicate melody that appeared to be generated by a multitude of minuscule copper gongs, clockwork music arising from the mechanical spinning of the cammed axis inside. The wobbling and the minaret music were hypnotic, and I don't recall when my parents finally took me home. Later, even though I asked them numerous times, they never knew whose house we had visited that night and did not remember *Venice, the Moon, and You,* even though the film did actually run in

Bucharest. Who was the hefty woman? Who were the two children, the boy with the swollen face, leisurely gestures and a horrible fixed gaze, and the sweet girl with lightly red hair so full of grace? Who was the spectral man who led us to the door and filled my pockets with Christmas candy, even though it was summer, and golden chocolate coins? But, twenty years later, I saw the same puppet in *her* house. It is now next to me while I write. I shake it, and, wobbling sleepily on the bureau (she always said 'bewroo), the mandarin hums his metallic, iridescent melody.

About two years ago, I was rummaging through the cupboard looking for a document. My folks kept all their receipts, ledgers and loose papers in a deteriorating old scarlet purse that belonged to my mother before she was married, when she worked as a seamstress at Donca Simo Weavers. In a partition next to the electrical fuses and a series of tiny springs for God knows what sort of contraption, I came across something wrapped in newspaper, whose pliancy piqued my curiosity. I opened it and found two blonde tresses, about fifteen centimetres long, tied with a rubber band at the severed end and with a blue ribbon at the other, where the hair strands thinned. Next to the tresses was a yellowed photograph, with a folded corner, still very clear. It portrayed a little boy, about two or three, standing buck–naked in a garden, a curl above his forehead and hair braided in two ashen-yellow pigtails falling on both sides of his head all the way down to the shoulders. He held a fist in front of his eyes, while on his face you could read a feeling of apprehension. His lips were pursed, and he looked like he was ready to burst into tears, and, like lightning, my mind suddenly filled with memories, unusually alive, colourful images seeming to spring out of the beginning of the world: gigantic beds of tulips, the sun gushing forth apocalyptically between the leaves of the bitter cherry, the black earth with unusually large clods, as though observed through a looking glass, rotted wooden boards and a woman approaching, with her skirt in flames from the sun. Then, a stranger, dark, heading directly towards me with a gleaming piece of machinery. Yes, I recall the photographer whom I confused with the doctor who gave me shots. It follows, therefore, that those were *my* pigtails. Mother told me many times she dressed me like a little girl, with little white aprons, until all the neighbours in the slums where we lived called me Andriuşa or Andrea and kissed and fondled me till I nearly suffocated. My consolation is that I was a beautiful child. After three years, I began to lose weight and rather than a colour portrait I became a charcoal sketch. And, irony of ironies, I will write here that for the last two weeks I recaptured my former beauty – in fact, I actually surpassed it. Such an overflow of beauty could only mean disaster or death for someone. It is not mirrors and copulation which are abominable, it is beauty.

One night, I dreamed of Marcela. I remembered that dream long after, in one of my afternoon reveries. I dreamed of her the way she was when she became my playmate, the year we moved into the apartment building with four floors, when I was a little older than three – in fact I was about to turn four that summer. Marcela – the way I saw her in the dream and the way I suspect she actually looked – was a tomboyish girl, a little older than I, with broken teeth that looked frightful. Her clothes were always dirty, most of the time her yellow shorts and flowery T-shirts were stained with peach juice. She had a constantly demonic grin, but she was very charming in her incessant carelessness, her jailhouse hairdo and her golden earrings with a crimson rock that shined too crassly to compete with a ruby. I loved roaming about all day with Marcela. Mornings, she knocked on our door, her lips already stained and, when Mother opened it, she never failed to ask: 'M'am, how is your little baby?' (This because my baby brother was only a few months old. A few months later, he would die of double pneumonia). We would go out together and visit the solarium, a place filled with sand. Once, scooping out the sand that got progressively wetter, we dug out some enormous scabby frogs. We dragged them through the sand till they looked like quivering cakes, but with large, limpid, human eyes. We played the wheel, catching each other by the feet and rolling across the sand, first on her back, then on mine, until we dug furrows in the sand basin and the sand got into our mouths, our nostrils, our ears. In the evening, we went exploring. Near our apartment building in Floreasca, there was a kind of a storage warehouse, a melancholy watchtower. Along its façade, the rusty remains of a fire escape hung like rags. Large clamps cast long shadows on the red bricks reddened all the more by the setting sun. She was the first to go in, through a slit in a side door missing a board. We crept in easily through that crack, so narrow that only cats could go through. Marcela, defter than I, with her twig-thin limbs, could get through in one move. Inside was a warm, amber-brown darkness where the sparkling rays of coppery light, penetrating through the cracks and nail leaks, gushed in forcefully towards the interior. We strolled through the nameless machinery, heavy metal carcasses immobilized in the black oil, cogged wheels taller than we were, leaning against workbenches shrouded by sheet metal. Marcela wanted to touch and feel everything, she wouldn't stop till she was completely smeared with fuel and discarded oil, till she hung around her neck the rusty metal necklaces, till she scaled the top of the complicated metal gearing. The ground was scattered with large nails the size of my forearm, ball bearings crusty with compacted rust, wooden boxes filled with hacksaw blades, screwdrivers, files, spokes, wires of all thicknesses. When it got completely dark, we would get frightened. One evening, Marcela took off her T-shirt and wiped the dust off one of the windows until we could stare at the dark blue sky, sprinkled with stars. After those expeditions, we would always get a spanking. At least Marcela would, who showed up the next day filled with bruises, but just as happy and ready to begin anew.

She taught me to play doctor. There was a storage area a few steps below our apartment building's first floor. Just before turning towards the door that led to the storage area, there was a niche in the wall with a bench. That's where we played. No one was allowed to know about our game. Because of this game, we found out the disturbing fact that Marcela and I were not the same, that there were odd differences on the other side of our clothes, that these differences existed between all girls and boys. I remember how difficult it was to accept the evidence. Many times we withdrew in the semidarkness of that bench and contemplated each other with sadness. The incipience of contempt insinuated itself in me, while in her, it was the beginning of humility and veneration.

In the autumn, we moved to another apartment building on Ştefan cel Mare, and a few years later school started. I don't remember much relating to the first four years of school, except for what occurred during summer camp, where I spent the summer break between my third and fourth years. We were roomed in long pavilions furnished with beds to accommodate thirty children. The entire complex was located in the middle of the woods. The forest, with its magic, with the indifference of its endless vegetation, with its thousands of trunk shapes, of roots and rotted matter, with rarefied vaults and traces of light falling through the transparent leaves, is one of the most bewitching places I have ever experienced. We roamed through the forest all day long, whittled boats out of spruce bark, fought with each other and played soccer. We were divided in detachments according to age, boys on one side, girls on the other. The girls collected lilies of the valley and other wild flowers, made crowns out of daisies, gathered wild strawberries growing in the sunlit grass. At night we, the boys, got together before the unusually large window frame, and there on the marble slab behind the drapes told each other frightening tales. We spoke about sleepwalkers who wander at night through the house with closed eyes, and if you woke them up they'd die on the spot, while you could go crazy. Among us was a boy with a strikingly mature aspect and a vocabulary like an adult, who even at that age could recite Poe's 'The Raven' by heart. His name was Traian. To this day, I still don't know who he was, what became of him or what bizarre illness he suffered from. Each night, as though reading, he would recite a chapter from the famous Hungarian children's book *The Boys from Pal Street*; he also had a gigantic praying mantis that he kept in a glass jar, about ten centimetres long, covered with furry down, and endowed with round eyes clear as rubies. When we returned from dinner and crowded into the dormitory, some of us rummaging through our bunk beds for our pyjamas while the others changed behind the huge drapes, letting the melted globe of the sun permeate the long white room, Traian would place his jar on the window frame. He always remained clothed and pensive amid the naked boys or those only half dressed in their polka-dot pyjamas, fixing the giant insect with his eyes as though intending to hypnotize it. The praying mantis would then stand up with its front claws against the glass now reddened by the setting sun and remain frozen still. This wordless dialogue went on for minutes in a row, seemingly longer and longer every evening. Traian would tell us that he was attempting to concentrate on the creature so intently that he would enter its head and look at us from inside the jar. And then the insect's mind, he said, would permeate his head. If this actually were to occur, we should run away from him just in case he decided to sink his teeth into our throats. These things filled us with terror. One night, after a pillow fight fought to exhaustion, two or three of us decided to kill the praying mantis. Traian kept it under key in the locker beneath his bunk bed and kept the key on a string around his neck. But we had another key that fit the lock and thus, with the help of a flashlight, we fumbled for the jar, which vibrated on account of the struggling inside. We took it to the lavatory and, under the bright bulb, stared for a long time at the monstrous animal within. The creature stood up at an oblique angle, propping the digging hooks of its claws against the glass wall. We didn't know what to do with the jar. We were too scared to unscrew the plastic top into which Traian had hammered some holes with a nail. In the end, we chucked it through the upper window of the lavatory into the bushes behind our pavilion. We went back to our beds, but soon after I dozed off I felt someone shaking me. The dormitory was in turmoil. By the beams of three or four flashlights wavering in each and every direction, I made out that everyone was awake and streaming in a silent rush towards the dormitory door. 'Don't wake him up, don't wake him up,' they whispered, with eyes dilated with fright. My neighbour, a tiny boy with Tartar mien, told me that Traian was a sleepwalker. For us, that was the equivalent of ghost, or something close to it. I followed the children out into the corridor and, about twenty metres ahead of us, I saw the big blond boy shuffling slowly towards the entrance door. His bare feet upset the order of the neat row of shoes lined up along the wall, the sneakers and sandals with multi-coloured socks thrust in them. He opened the door and walked out into the night. We dashed outside after him, some of us even charged ahead and were able to see his frozen face, eyes open wide and reflecting the sparkling stars in the sky. The sky's deep blue scattered into the space ahead and became a whitish trace across the horizon. The yellow stars burned brittle, the spaces between them wide, while in the distance they became denser and denser, fusing with the white fog beyond. Traian walked ahead under that carpet of stars, veering behind the pavilion, then wending his way directly through the weeds surrounding the drainpipe, finally enshrouding his frame in the bushes that choked the courtyard all the way to the wire fence, and plunged so far off into the night that even we couldn't make him out any more. Our flashlights hurled bands of light into the blue smoky sky. The boy became completely entangled in the spiny shrubs, marching stubbornly ahead in a straight line. He hesitated an instant, then turned, holding in his hands, shiny as silver, the jar with the praying mantis. He returned to the hall, crossed the corridor without paying any attention to us, unlocked the box underneath his bunk bed, placed the jar inside, and locked the box again. Then, he sat up in bed and stared off into the void for a long time. We did not dare return to our own beds until he got under the covers and we were certain he was asleep. We each had a blanket attached to the panelling at the head of the bed to protect us from the moon. Of course, we did not sleep that night. And the following nights, we kept watch in shifts in order to keep an eye on Traian, but nothing more happened.

Traian maintained that he could move pieces of paper or matchsticks with his gaze alone, and when his eyes were not set upon the praying mantis, which he fed daily with pupae and earthworms, he would fix them on one of the white, lusterless glass globes that hung from the ceiling at the end of a metal rod. We also stared at the metal rod until our eyes hurt, and at times we even had the impression that the globes were quivering a little. Only Traian succeeded in making them oscillate from side to side, the distance of about five or six centimetres. He complained often of headaches. Once, when we 'put him to sleep' as we called it – that is, we held him in our arms, pushed his head into his chest and pressed against

83

his jugular – we nearly lost him: he lay unconscious for a half an hour, until they took him to the infirmary. I saw him again when I was sixteen, in the lobby of the pharmacy of General Hospital Number 10 on Rozelor Street. I was waiting in line to get I don't remember what medicine when I saw him enter. It is rare that I have felt a more powerful fascination than at that moment. Traian had uncoiled to an incredible height, taller than are metre eighty. He was wearing a flame-red gym suit and basketball shoes, but his physical aspect disagreed with his athletic apparel. His hands and his face had developed wrinkles, and he stumbled like an old man. Only his glassy eyes gave away his identity. He was in effect a ruin. It wasn't just me. Everyone else waiting in line at the two counters or sitting on the sofa, absent-mindedly reading the booklets about prevention of the flu or venereal diseases or staring at the customary water carafe on the coffee table, directed their gaze, filled with pity and horror, towards Traian. I didn't have the guts to speak to him; in any case it had been seven years since that summer. I picked up my medicine and rushed out onto the street.

But Traian comes to mind now for another reason, for the sake of these pages in which I attempt to write down the inexpressible, to recreate a path that does not exist on any map or in anyone's memory. Because Traian had also a day personality, which was just as strange for us as his night one. Traian was interested in girls. They were the only thing on his mind, and he explained to us for the first time what love meant. Hearing him talk about such things made us leer and think about the dirty stuff. But he defended his view. He insisted that love was not just dirty things: it meant to have a beloved, to think of her and her alone, to follow her constantly, to make for her braids of daisies, to roam hand in hand with her in the woods. 'And in the woods . . . ,' we elaborated, leering even more. Because for entire nights, the only thing we talked about was how girls were made and what could be done with them. 'No, no,' replied Traian, 'to love a girl is a very beautiful thing, you write her verses, you sit across from her in the cafeteria . . .' His passionate words weakened our bravado somewhat, but they also stoked our determination to sneer at his ideas. Girls and boys

seemed to us two different species, which we delineated symboli-
cally by scratching with a twig in the dust a tiny circle crossed
diametrically by a line for boys and two tiny circles and a line for
girls. Of course, Traian found himself a girlfriend. Her name was
Livia Ante, and she was older than us, already in the fifth grade.
Her hair was cropped in the shape of a bowl, anticipating by a few
years the style of the French movie star Mireille Mathieu. After
swimming, her chestnut hair glimmered with auburn hues. She
was svelte, very graceful and had very good manners. In her favourite dress, a tasteful turquoise, she seemed like a young lady. Traian
hung out with her all day. In the spirit of emulation, a few other
boys, some of the best-looking guys of the bunch, followed suit and
also found themselves girlfriends among Livia's companions. During their free time, they went out by themselves in the woods,
roaming paths blocked by toppled tree trunks under the vault of
the trees, in the golden silence traversed by sharp bird trills and the
buzz of thousands of flies glittering in the fleeting streaks of light.
The boys adorned their heads with fir-twig crowns and armed
themselves with sturdy sticks. They girded themselves with belts
of bark and dashed around the sparse forest shouting shrill calls. At
times, they tore the bark from fallen trees, so spongy by then that
you could easily lift it, and stared at the decay inside, the insects
writhing at the end of long and narrow tiny trenches. They
squashed with their feet the mushroom nests and rummaged the
tree hollows for birds' eggs. The tiny group then crossed the creek
and plunged into the most beautiful part of the forest, till they
reached a clearing sprinkled with bellflowers and sorrel. There
they sat in a circle. What they did, what they said, oh how I wish
now that I knew! It's something I longed for with my whole being
my entire life – though I never confessed it to anyone – but it was I
alone who was to blame for being excluded from those mysteries. I
had become the leader of another group, hostile and contemptuous, and with an inexplicable hatred considered it a bona fide crime
for the boys and girls in Traian's group to be friends. We organized
ourselves in patrols that spied and tracked them, stalked them from
behind trees, and unexpectedly, shouting and wielding crooked

sticks, we charged at them, challenging the boys to battle and chasing the girls away. With our feet, we squashed their crowns of daisies, some a few metres long, destroyed the large and motley bouquets of forest flowers left behind as trophies. Our hatred was so great that, instead of eating the little heaps of wild strawberries the children had gathered for their secret meeting, we trampled them. Girded in our bark belts and crowned with leaves, we sat in their place and wondered what else we could do to wipe out any trace of contact between boys and girls in our camp. If, for example, we spotted a boy playing volleyball with the girls, he became our enemy. We even beat up those boys who gathered flowers or looked for birds' eggs, girl occupations in our opinion. Once we caught a kid who clenched in his fist a particoloured egg the size of a hazelnut. I took it from him and threw it at the ground. The shell splintered in bits, and a tiny puddle of blood widened in the grass. A nearly full-fledged chick was curled up and covered with bloody drool. For a moment, I thought that I saw its tiny hairless wings flap. I was sick all evening.

The boys from Traian's group didn't give up and confronted their persecution with fortitude. Traian concocted all sorts of romantic defences: he organized a network for the girls and the boys through which they constantly circulated notes and secret signs. From time to time, we would capture a note on which we would find the following: 'Squirrel, tell the horse to go to the castle,' and would agonize for entire hours trying to figure out who the horse was, who the squirrel and where the castle was. By and by, we began to find notes in our pockets and underneath our pillows on which it was written with large letters: REVENGE. I see them even now, these strange, rhomboid letters with red arrows drawn underneath them. Every once in a while, one of us was captured by them. A wet sheet of paper with a multicolour drawing in a felt-tip pen was applied to his forehead: it depicted a donkey or simply bore the word STUPID. When the paper was removed, a tattoo remained, impossible to erase for two or three days.

In turn, we tried to ridicule Traian in every way possible. Naturally, we found the surest means to harm him: to harass his girlfriend,

Livia Ante. We found in the cafeteria six empty truffle candy boxes made by the company FONDANTE. We cut the first part of it off, so that all that remained was ANTE. Underneath, we wrote with a felt-tip pen in black, green and mauve: AND TRAIAN. In the evening after dinner, we hid behind the cafeteria by the edge of the woods and nailed the candy cartons to six trees. The result was terrible. The camp counsellors were incensed. They gathered the whole camp in a square and called out at random a few children, some of the usual troublemakers, without guessing who the guilty ones really were. But Livia was to be sent home, and Traian went nuts, ready to start a fight with just about anyone.

Summer camp was almost over, and my involuntary hatred for any amorous relationship had not yet exhausted itself. During the last two or three days, however, I had a painful surprise. It was the beginning of August, and the brilliance of the blue sky with the fluffy white clouds crowded into dense and precise forms, the wistfulness of the sunlit forest, the sorrel's lightly sour taste and the reek of the hedgehogs dead on the forest paths, all blended into an odd feeling that began to tug at my heart. A few times, I surprised myself by staring furtively at Livia. Her amber hair, so different from all the other girls', the turquoise that her dress radiated, which I perceived out of the corner of my eye before she appeared, her walk, all those things, I now understood with horror, attracted me, made me yearn to see her. By the light of the campfire, I would spot her profile through the fir's incandescent sparks, at times yellow as saffron, at others red as porphyry, depending on the hues of the flames reflecting on her face. The heat from the tall pyre, the glitter of the butterflies' sequins and wings, the thrumming of the guitars, all descended, layer by layer, and charged upon my retinas, my mind, my skin: all I wanted was to see her. I felt ashamed, though it was a sweet and innocent shame. When we arrived home after a few hours by train, Bucharest felt deserted and our house cramped and sullen. At the dinner table, in front of my parents, I began to cry.

The following years, during the second grade-school cycle, I became frighteningly timid. I wasn't even capable of exchanging a few words with a girl. I watched with despair the boys and girls who played together along the alleys by the Circus. Every time a girl tried to joke with me, I invariably replied: 'Leave me alone.' Or I would simply turn my back and leave. It seemed to me that the most shameful thing was for someone to think I was in love. It was an absolutely unbearable thought. I was still a good-looking child. Once, the girls in my class rated all the boys in order of looks on a piece of paper during a break but then tore it up in little pieces. A few boys picked them all up out of the wastepaper basket and spent a few agonizing hours reconstituting the paper. I recall that I rated the fourth out of seventeen boys. This surprised me, but it must also be kept in mind that I was an excellent student, a fact that weighed heavily on the balance of aesthetic judgements. It still didn't change my behaviour. I could not look a girl in the eye; eventually, I couldn't even look a boy in the eye. It seemed to me that doing so would unconsciously betray my hidden feelings or cause the other to suspect me of those feelings.

I remember the heavy winters of that period, with snow mounting all the way up to the school's windows, with the twilights descending in waves of ashen-scarlet over the chestnuts in the courtyard and the nostalgic feeling I always got from the brick warehouse next to the school. The air became the colour of coffee and, in the sleet awaiting them at the end of the school day, the boys with soaked mittens and snowballs in their fists were awaiting the surge of girls flaunting their purple eyes, scintillating as birds. The early stars sprinkled the harsh air while we, at the end of the school hours under the glare of bulbs, gazed in bewilderment at the grotesque succession of chemical formulas, the odd ratios of Avogadro's number, the crooked, crystal figures of spatial geometry. At other times, the snow fell profusely while we, staring out the window during our Romanian literature hour, had the sensation that the entire room was flying obliquely and at hyperspeed like a spaceship into the air. The electric light in the classroom, contrasting with the immensity of the darkness outside, gave us an atavistic feeling of intimacy, of shelter, such as primitive man must have experienced in his cave. The world became small, and it was easy to be alive. I recall that it was during one of those evenings that I had my first hallucination, about which there isn't a lot to say and nor can I find an explanation for. It was during a break, and we were bantering about soccer or something of that sort. The girls, more studious than us, were huddled around the blackboard and looking for different cities on a map of Europe. Many were already taller than the boys, and their breasts had already begun to rise under the sleeveless dresses like charming hills. The boys, who had taken on odd totemic nicknames – Rat, Mammoth, Pig, Duck – were circling around them. In the classroom's confusion of sounds, in the yellow air tattered by silhouettes and familiar faces, an inexplicable event occurred. I looked up suddenly, as though someone was calling my name, and about a metre above and a bit before me, I saw a blue sphere. It was about sixty centimetres in diameter and glowed with an intense and phosphorescent, hypnotic blue. It waited there, frozen in the air, like a gigantic soap bubble of gelatinous consistency. Everything I thought about during those moments was subliminal, the way you think when you are, for example, in grave danger or when you have to make an instant decision. I believed at first that the sphere was a spot on my retina, some sort of a luminous impression, but switching the direction of my stare I didn't see it any more, so I turned my eyes back to the sphere and had to accept it was either a real but inexplicable object or a product not of my eyes but of my mind. The large blue globe remained in its place above me about for half a minute, during which I stared at it, incapable of tearing myself away from its enchantment. It was evident that no one else saw it, but also strange that no one noticed my absent and frozen state during that half a minute. The globe disappeared suddenly: I disengaged my eyes from it for an instant and, when I looked again, it was gone. I wasn't even scared during those few moments and only much latter returned to my senses.

It was during that time that I fell in love with Lili. This for me was equivalent to disaster. What could have happened at summer camp was really happening now – and I had no chance of escape. I saw her every day, this girl who even now seems beautiful (she appears in a photograph I still have), with her hair tied behind, bringing into relief a rounded forehead, dimpled cheeks, full lips insinuating an incessant smile and black eyes, possibly a little prominent, with a warm, somewhat ironic gaze. Actually, I never looked at her straight in the eye and avoided her as much as I possibly could. But I kept seeing her face, at times reflected in the windows or display cases of the physics or chemistry laboratories. Lili always infused the surroundings with a disturbing air. Sometimes she told her girlfriends things that troubled them. She brought with her various books in which, if you looked carefully, you would find passages of vague erotic content. Then, the more audacious girls huddled together and read, smiling oddly and discreetly, red in the face, but, in any case, not snickering like the boys. In fact, the most embarrassing subject was biology, when we began the study of reproduction. Some of the teachers even skipped it completely, because you couldn't carry on a dialogue with thirty leering faces, always ready to burst into giggles. But our own teacher was a conscientious little old lady who wasn't easily intimidated. Her problems began with the rabbits, with the inevitable lesson on multiplying. But now it was worse, because we had moved on to human beings, and she bore down even harder, almost unbearably so, upon the spiritual dams which our families had been striving to build for years. We had learned at home that it was disgraceful to broach those subjects, but now a serious female adult, and a teacher to boot, spoke to us from her desk about those matters, a fact which shattered us internally, causing our shame to grow to an unbearable tension whose only release was laughter. Three students were called to answer questions, one of whom was Lili, who never killed herself studying, though neither did she neglect school completely. The other two students refused to answer any questions, preferring instead to receive bad grades. Lili, on the other hand, began from the beginning and, with meticulous calm and a cool attitude, as though speaking about the nervous system or the digestive apparatus, went all the way to the end without omitting anything and without even the trace of a smile. Why didn't our wounded psyche react then? On the contrary, we regarded her with admiration, like a heroine.

Though it's possible she had a boyfriend outside school, Lili couldn't do without a companion in our classroom. He was Colorado, a very tall boy with a red face, the reason for his nickname. He walked her home every evening, sent her notes during classes and was careful to isolate her from other rivals. When late in the evening we played a game of forfeits (in fact, I never played; I merely hung around, forcing to the point of tears a fake smile of indifference on my face) and they happened to end up as a pair, they would clamber on top of a bench in the middle of the classroom – as punishment called for – and silhouetted in amber against the thick twilight outside the window, they held each other tight and kissed. The tenderness and languor with which she glued herself against him, recalling the sleepy motions of a little girl embracing her mother, seemed to me to have no place in reality; they were golden worlds, thick with ecstasy and emotion and suffering, worlds in which I wouldn't be able to breathe even for a second. Still, during those moments I suffered like a dog. I felt myself excluded and left behind once again, forced away from a terrifying and yet blindingly beautiful experience. I am sure it was not difficult to see that I couldn't bear it when she looked at me, that I was lost if she happened to address even a few words to me. She noticed all this and, in order to amuse herself, began finding ways to associate with me. During that period of time, the kids in our class began playing oracles, a series of questions relating to love which you could answer yes, no or maybe. There were a hundred questions about the person you were in love with, anything from the colour of their eyes and hair, their height, if the person was in your class, to their favourite actors or singers or if actual kissing had taken place. The answers were added up and thus, based on the results, the oracle made it possible to divine the feelings the person in question had towards you. For instance you could get, 'She loves you,' or, 'He finds you attractive, but doesn't love you,' or 'You are admired,' or 'She can't stand you.' When the oracle was cast on someone, we would bundle up around the person, guessing who the dream lover might be and making jokes. Each little detail gave rise to ironic comments: 'Aha! I bet she loves Tedi . . .' 'No, it's

Saşka, he's the one with blue eyes!' 'What do you mean, Saşka's not short?' Certainly, when answering the oracle, the girls weren't always thinking of the boy they liked. Sometimes, they amused themselves finding a client among the flunkies and slobs in order to entertain the crowd. In any case, the game had an insinuating and meandering quality about it and, like the game of forfeits, it was emotionally engaging. One long day, at the end of eighth grade, the oracle was cast by Petruţa, a dark and lively girl, a flirt who didn't have a boyfriend of her own but mediated encounters for others. After a few of the students answered questions, among them myself (I was actually thinking of Petruţa and got 'Finds you attractive, but doesn't love you'), it was suddenly Lili's turn. She smiled with her enchanting mouth, her crimson and glimmering full lips. Her eyes were enormous and sparkled before she spoke, her gaze impossible to bear. It had been two years since I had been in love with her. I knew every detail of her profile, the hair tight around her temples, the round breasts, the legs with powerful calves. She was answering questions and laughing. I shivered with suspicion when she was asked about the height of the boy she was thinking of. She aimed her gaze at me and answered: 'Medium.' I heard the rest of the questions as though in a dream. I knew, my exacerbated instinct would not deceive me, that she was speaking about me. I had the feeling everyone knew about this, that I was the victim of a conspiracy, and that everyone would start to ridicule me and my absurd suffering. I wanted to leave but was afraid everyone would know why. I endured everything till the end. The boys were having the time of their lives, Colorado among them. When the questions ended, the oracle was consulted. For me, the answer was bewildering: 'She loves you, but hides it.' Then, laughing uproariously, Lili pointed me out abruptly with her finger, aiming it at me for a few seconds. The students were cracking up at my expense, were teasing me in jest, and even I laughed along with them. After a few minutes, it was someone else's turn, and I crept away unseen and dashed to the bathroom. I wanted to wash my face, which was burning from shame, but ran into the smokers and gave up.

After that day my love for Lili grew even more. She never lost a chance to try to speak to me. I would give her the shortest possible answer and walk away, wobbling. At night, I would wake up unable to breathe. I would toss and turn in bed thinking of Lili, then walk to the window and glue my forehead to the cold windowpane. I knew she lived on Barbu Văcărescu Street, and I would turn in that direction and begin speaking to her. One night, I heard her replying. She pronounced my name, her voice resounded clearly in my right ear: it was not a hallucination. Even now, I am convinced that we communicated like that many evenings in a row. It was only necessary that the moon was up and that I gazed in the direction of her house. Then I would hear clearly: 'Andrei, is it you?' and then we shot the breeze for a half an hour. School began to slow down, it was the end of the year; the students as well as the teachers were bored and exhausted. Sindili, the Greek, brought a tape recorder, and we huddled by the back wall of the classroom and told stories. The day after the year-end celebration – when all the students were lined up and herded into a square, that whole absurd ceremony with the handing out of the prizes – the real celebration took place, the one for which our school rented each year the entire State Circus. The huge auditorium, with the benches stacked up at an abrupt angle, with the circular arena above which were suspended all sorts of sparkling trapezes, ropes and nets, filled up with parents and children. The little ones from the first grade bustled about, walked around the massive metal reflectors bedecked with green, yellow and red discs that twirled in front of the powerful beacon, while the older kids bundled together by grade and talked endlessly. We, the graduates, showed up brazenly out of uniform, wearing the best shirts and trousers we owned. The girls were decked out in the gaudiest attire, their skirts hung extravagantly on their waists, the blouses transparent and revealing perforated brassieres; and they wore stockings, which they borrowed from their mothers. Their hair was braided in a touchingly pathetic fantasy style, but even being vamped out like floozies kind of became them because of the freshness of their faces. Some of them had even painted their nails, and two of them, whom the school's principal sent home, decorated their faces like a circus act.

They were all on fire, saw themselves as veritable ladies. The fact they were only fourteen was humiliating to them; they felt themselves capable of turning the head of any man. With what contempt they must have viewed us, little boys still preoccupied with automobiles and fight movies.

Lili, whose arrival I awaited anxiously, showed up late, long after the programme started. It was a kind of musical, improvised after *The Enchanted Grove*, and we, the boys, were drooling over Lizuca, a tall girl in the seventh grade, incredibly well proportioned and decked out only in ballet leotards. By her side, costumed like a dog and leaping around like a clown, was a small boy named Patrocle. The stage was filled with children-butterflies, children-flowers and other things of that sort. The old speakers emitted a continuous rumble which at its source was the sweet song of children. I was probably the first to see Lili. She was dressed in a simple outfit, with a very low-cut, sleeveless white blouse and a black skirt high above the knees. If she had showed up at the beginning, they wouldn't have let her in, because you could see her thighs. She held a pale pink rose between her fingers and strolled in, flouncing through the plushy seats with her unique style of grace. She sat down at a distance from us, and sat alone for a while, sniffing the rose from time to time. Then, she changed her mind and came towards us, finding a seat two rows above me. My eyes were constantly shifting towards her. Once, when I turned to see her, pretending that I wanted to say something to one of my friends, I couldn't believe my eyes: Lili was sitting cross-legged, in an attitude which would have seemed indecent had it not been so charming. You could see her legs with their white and toned skin all the way up, and I suddenly became aware that she was staring straight at me. I don't remember when she moved next to me. She was powerfully perfumed. She smiled and stared at me from the corner of her eyes. I was staring straight at the pantomime on the stage. Then she took my hand. Astounded, I turned my head towards her and wrenched my hand away. 'Andrei, why do you avoid me?' she asked, and took my hand into hers again. 'Leave me alone,' I said, 'they'll see us,' but I wasn't strong enough to withdraw my hand again. I looked straight ahead and began to shake. There were other sections in the auditorium next to the orchestra or other places where no one sat because of the loud sound or the distance from the stage. It was towards one of those places that Lili eventually dragged me. We sat there next to one another, Lili playing with the rose while I was sweating and feeling lost. She didn't even pay too much attention to me, she knew her presence and her perfume were enough to rattle me. All the kids were turning their heads towards us and leering suggestively. When I couldn't bear it any longer, I stood up and dashed out of the first exit I found. I heard her voice ringing after me, soft and ironic, and then all the way home I chattered and shivered and ran. I threw myself on the bed, unable to even move. I developed a fever; my mother was terrified when she read the thermometer. She gave me pills and then called the doctor. For a few days, the first of summer break, I was ill, sleeping fitfully, with hallucinatory dreams. Time after time, writhing in my humid sheets, I would open my eyes and stare through the blue air of my room bleached by the moon towards the armchair by the bed. There, I would see Lili very clearly in her school uniform pinafore, with hair tied back and her glimmering lips, smiling oddly and ironically. I would get up from the bed and touch her hair, her shoulders; I was convinced she was totally real. I felt a warm fluid flowing from my chest to my finger-tips, and my hands, as if driven by an internal knowledge, attempted to undress her. But she was all of one piece, her clothes one with her body. She was no more than a statue of glassy consistency, but alive and moving. She could not be undressed.

For a moment I lifted my eyes from the multiplying pages before me and instinctively looked at myself in the mirror. I was shocked when my gaze was obstructed by that other text, made of canvas; it is the sheet thrown over the mirror. It is an occult, coded text, and nothing can penetrate it. I know that all I have to do is tear it away for the truth's rays to overwhelm me, to destroy me. There would be light, but who would profit from it? It would be the flame to consume me. And how I would like to take a look in the mirror, even once! I will not do it though, not until this story that urges me on is completed. Many times, since I have been writing, the old folks tiptoed into the room, under the pretext of feeding the goldfish in the aquarium or picking up a case with all sorts of beads and hairpins or wiping the dust off the ancient furniture and the religious icons shrouded by vine branches heavy with grapes erupting from the side of Christ. But they ended up closing in on me and, with poorly veiled worry, caressed my long hair. The old lady started crying when I explained to them in a kinder tone than before that I was all right, that I needed to write a story and once I was done she could call as many doctors as she liked. I promised them I would be ready in week. They accepted and resigned themselves to my demands, but I could hear them whispering together with the other old folks in the living room for entire afternoons. Their child had clearly changed and it filled them with fright. I can't eat in the living room because of the large Venetian mirror – I couldn't ask them to cover that one as well. So, they bring my food here to my desk and watch me while I eat in a hurry, then resume the thread of the story.

I was a difficult adolescent, with bizarre idiosyncrasies and absurd ideas. I am convinced that without her appearance in my life in the eighth grade, I would have definitely lost any contact with the real world. I read all day and most of the night, discovering – one thing leading to the next – entire families of poets (because poetry is what I read most) whom I then explored individually, borrowing books from four libraries. I easily retained all the poetry I liked, and during breaks, while my fellow students played ping-pong on the teacher's desk, I was filling the blackboard with verses by Verlaine and Eluard. In my French and Latin classes, I concocted sentences with bizarre examples. If I had to conjugate a verb in a sentence, I would write, for example 'The black flower spied on the transparent fox' or 'I strike the green with an apricot cow,' making sure that the exercise was grammatically correct. Of course, the poor teachers were aghast. But I was an excellent student and won a few prizes in creative writing competitions, and so everyone left me alone. I saw myself as damned and felt profound contempt for my fellow

students. And of course I, too, began writing verses and kept a journal which I read and reread so often that I knew its contents by
heart. With each new reading, I acquired a new life. I was by turns,
with my entire being, Camus, Sartre, Céline, Bacovia, Voronca,
Rimbaud and Valéry. I barely noticed what went on around me. The
other students always came to school bringing records, usually in
very bad shape, with the sleeves Scotch-taped together both verti-
cally and horizontally. The sleeves' luster projected dour and
grotesque figures of bearded men, eccentrically tricked out, or landscapes of melancholy factories with gigantic smokestacks and a little
winged pig on top. Mysterious vocables crossed the course of our
conversations in which I participated absent-mindedly: Inagada
Davida, Led Zeppelin, Samba Pa Ti, Imagine. The kids murmured
hypnotic refrains and recited rough-hewn verses: 'I don't believe in
Hitler/I don't believe in Zimmerman/I don't believe in the Beatles/I
only believe in me/In Yoko and me/And that's reality/The dream is
over.' They brought their reel-to-reel tape recorders to class, they
connected them to the school speakers, which emitted such shrill
guitar licks that I couldn't listen for more than five minutes. I was
indifferent to everything the kids my age loved. During the two
years that my crises lasted, I got so close to madness that even now
I feel its gelid breath girdling my cranium. The same way that the
snake's scaly skin gradually separates itself from the snake during
moulting, my world separated itself from the real world, became a
parallel world with the consistency of dreams. Since it was impossible to spend the entire day reading and, since I had nightmares and
difficulties in breathing if I didn't go out in the fresh air, I took regular walks each day before sunset. I would walk down Galați and
Princess Ruxandra Streets, cross Galați Plaza, and roam the golden
and silent alleys on the other side of Toamnei Street, towards Calea
Moşilor. I stared at the old houses, with alveolar-shaped balconies
dangerously suspended above the street, with stucco walls, cornices, grotesque figures and humid plaster Atlases under the
arcades. As the sun dropped towards the horizon, the gold of the
walls turned amber, then purple, the cheeks and noses of the gorgons on the pediments cast pointed shadows along the walls, the

windows filled up with blood, and a little girl in a blue dress, standing in a gate of forged iron decorated with lances, unsettled old memories – so old it seemed they existed before the world. Many times I walked along Venera Street, without suspecting that in one of those large houses with storefronts, with white and pink friezes, lived the girl who would end up being the most monstrously beautiful thing in my whole life. I was fascinated by the leprous aspect of some of the shops and small factories lined up along this street. Their fronts had been painted with acrylic paint, which after a few years began to peel, revealing large spaces underneath the yellow plaster that covered them before. Large strips of strident blue paint still hung in dried-up layers. Down the street, there were cottages with horses in the courtyard or tiny, charming country houses with arching vines, in whose porches retired folk, using dyes, painted on pieces of discarded cardboard marine landscapes or still lifes with lilacs. As twilight fell on Venera Street, carcasses of refrigerators, abandoned on the road next to Silvestru Elementary School, rusted in the rain and drizzle, turned an unreal pale pink, and the whole landscape became artificial. I would return home filled with sadness.

My eroticism entered a phase of aggressive inhibition. Everything was paradoxical, unsolvable. I searched through art books or catalogues for erotic passages or nudes while on the other hand something in me was against these impulses. I felt that I was inherently different from the others, that love and everything related to it was not for me, that I travelled a road which took me way beyond the banal human condition. In fact, through this tendency towards absolutism, which I experienced so intently at the time, I came to believe that it was eroticism itself which prevented man from realizing himself, that love – and thus woman – was the cause leading to trivialization, to failure. For two years, in that state of alienation which I have been attempting to explain, I created for myself a monstrous system of ideas. I had determined that I didn't have the right to get to know a girl because I had a higher mission to fulfill. I was convinced that immortality depends upon chastity and the moment you love or make love you taint yourself past all hope.

This wasn't because of any sort of lucid realization but impulses which I could not deny. Of course, I agonized by myself but couldn't do it any other way.

Woman meant monster to me. I saw in her a modified man, a crippled man. The breasts, the fat which defined parts of her body, the widened hips, the hair so different than a man's, all these seemed to me disgraceful infirmities. Feminine conduct, the grace of certain gestures, the dissimilar psychology, I took these to be a form of affectation. I viewed with hatred girls who dressed stylishly, took care of their looks and flirted with boys. For me, it meant only that they were exhibiting their erotic desires. I had read that the female spider devours the male during the process of coupling, and I had begun to write a story in the fantastic style, in which I imagined what it might be like if the female destroyed the male during sex in the world of humans. I pictured the dilemma of the male caught between two fundamental instincts. To know for certain you would be destroyed by her, and yet be unable to escape her fascination . . . Or, I was thinking of the strange case of the praying mantis, who during copulation gnaws away at her lover. Or the female scorpion, who can find in a few seconds the male's single vulnerable place, the only fissure in his chitinous armature, and pricks him there with the venomous needle in her tail . . .

If, for instance, I had seen slimy, gigantic spider webs draping the gables or cornices of buildings on Magheru Boulevard or Romană Plaza, in the middle of which naked women with their pincer-like breasts hung motionlessly lying in wait for the next victim, it would have seemed more natural to me than reality, in which women seemed like actual human beings, 'our mothers or wives, sweethearts or daughters', who lured us only into the net of their gestures, smiles or weaknesses. The more my delirium grew, the more I subjected myself to questions on this topic, plunging into all sorts of speculations. I asked myself, for instance, what kind of traits characterized femininity. For the newborn, the gender can only be discerned anatomically. Until the age of two or three, children are dressed in different colours: boys in blue, girls in red or pink. But then, during the time they learn to distinguish between friends who are boys and friends who are girls, their cheeks take on traits nearly impossible to define but which the eye catches with ever-increasing precision. Beyond the artificially created differences (longer hair for girls, specific attire: skirts, dresses, exclusive adornments such as earrings) and the secondary characteristics which appear in adolescence, there are psychological reference points, and I think they are the most powerful, because they determine the passions. We don't love a woman because she has a perfect body, but for the unique shape of her eyes or mouth, in which we recognize (when did it take shape? when did it become visible?) her profoundly and subtly erotic personality. It is easier for us to bear the thought that our lover is cheating on us than to see her smiling at another while lifting a single eyebrow, or to catch those furrows of ironic tenderness appearing on her cheeks and around her mouth, which you believed were solely the result of your influence – and thus impossible to repeat for another . . . If the female eye is not made up, it is impossible to distinguish from the male eye. Maybe girls have longer and denser eyelashes and possibly more elongated eyes, but who could explain why the eyes of the woman we love are immense, flaming in a purplish-obsidian, and only become ordinary eyes when we love her no longer? Her mouth appears more easily distinguishable from a man's mouth, but through what traits? You are certain that a mouth or the lips are feminine, but I don't believe that you can explain the distinctive elements in rational language. As we may not escape our sex, we inevitably see with a man's eye, or a woman's, these infinitesimal traits.

I was changing day by day. My face acquired ascetic features, my eyes shone with a strange, melancholy light. My mouth kept its sensual quality but agonized as though by an interior urging. A moustache began to take shape under the long and very thin nostrils, and all of the facial lines started to lengthen. I indulged in solitude, I defended myself with all my might against something which was about to happen. One evening while walking on Venera Street, I heard a high-pitched mechanical melody. I recalled instantly the childhood scene, that strange house, the children with hundreds of toys. It was the rattling melody, in an Oriental scale, of the celluloid mandarin. The sound came out of an open window, situated on the corner of a building above a multicoloured glass marquee. Sitting on the marquee, I saw in the twilight's uncertain light a golden-orange cat, curled up in a ball and gazing with a frightened look towards the interior of the room. Once the mechanical melody ended, a girl's voice with a somewhat broken timbre shouted: 'Psssst, you shameless thing, off with you!' The cat slunk away along the wall and leaped on to a large willow by the window. A girl appeared there, framed by red woollen drapes. She seemed to me unusually tiny and attenuated, her light chestnut hair was long and curly, the colour of oak bark. Two saffron eyes peeped out of her round face with its beautiful tiny rounded cheeks. I retained only vaguely, in passing, this aristocratic mien and went on with my walk till nightfall. After that, I looked up at that window above the marquee each time I took my walk on Venera Street, but for an entire half year there was no one there except, sometimes, an old lady. Through another, much larger window facing the street, I could see a globe of the earth, ostentatious and probably very expensive furniture, and a grand chandelier with crystal icicles and coppery polish. Not even in my journal, comprised of verses, reading notes, strange dreams and too few exterior events, did I write anything about this encounter. All that I noted that day in my lined notebook is that I had begun reading Nerval's *Aurélia*.

I was in my last year of high school and about to turn eighteen. I was progressively worried about my future. Only a year before I had decided to renounce, categorically and without regrets, everything pertaining to life, the 'joy of being alive'. People who seemed content with their small lives disgusted me. I saw myself as universal, ready to become the cosmos itself. But soon, it became physically impossible to endure this mode of life. Little by little, I began feeling like a failure rather than a genius. This change took place under the weight of loneliness. Before, I was content to be left alone, to lock myself in the house for weeks, to read till I couldn't see any more. I cursed if I had to answer the phone. During the first two years of high school, my fellow students would invite me to parties or birthdays, or to the discothèque in the school's auditorium, but since I never went they stopped inviting me. They viewed me with the horror mixed with the reluctant admiration reserved for the chrysalis that might someday become a butterfly but also God knows what sort of horrific vermin. Even those who took my side – because despite it all, I was being talked about – couldn't imagine themselves having a personal relationship with me. When I turned seventeen they prepared a gift for me, elegantly wrapped in paper and tied with a ribbon, but which no one had the courage to hand me: instead, they placed it on my desk. They were flustered and a little frightened of their own gesture, as though they were presenting an offering to an unearthly being. Even today, I have no idea what the contents of the box were, because I left it on the desk without touching it. I had lost all traces of humanity – I realized this – but I believed it was the only way to progress along the path to becoming superhuman. During the break between my eleventh and twelfth years, I had attained such a degree of solitude that I was frightened for my sanity. For the period of three months, I constantly sensed that my heart was heavy with an abstract love, a love for no one. I couldn't stand being home for a moment. I would go out and roam the streets of Bucharest, translucently golden from the sun, incessantly expecting to meet someone unknown. I stared with envy at the strolling couples with their arms around each other, the girls tricked out in the latest fashions, the boys my age with their LPs constantly under their arms, always trading in front of the Muzica record store: *Sticky Fingers* and 50 lei for *Deep Purple in Rock; Caravanserai* plus the single of 'My Generation' by The Who for *Ummagumma*. I would return home dead tired, but in the afternoon I would begin all over again.

I could hardly wait for school to begin again, something that had never happened to me before. Because I felt very alone, like a fallen angel, or at least one in grave danger of falling. But I knew that, in order to remain an angel, I had to ignore what I was fighting inside me, which was perhaps malignant and had progressively gained more power over me. Many times, I would wake up weeping from loneliness. Finally, I began twelfth grade, and seeing the familiar faces made me happy for the first time. In the biology lab, where we happened to meet for our first hour, I spotted Cotton, a racing cyclist with a wide jovial face and green eyes always half closed. He was marking in his notebook each time the biology teacher called us 'little children'. His collection was remarkable (over 200 check marks), but the teacher spotted him and brought him in front of the class in order to quiz him. Cotton, with an innocently disarming expression, knew his stuff about the paramecium pretty well, but got a low grade because he kept calling that tiny animal 'Paris Matchum', despite constant correction. Then, there was Dalu, over one metre eighty tall, and nicknamed Hypohippus, evidently after an ancestor of the horse, about whom we learned in biology class as well. And, to finish with this list, I also noticed Mera sitting at one of the benches with his maloccluded teeth and the dull stare of a blonde who was familiar with Mallarmé. One day, the teacher sent him to get a life-size skeleton from the laboratory and bring it back to our classroom downstairs. Mera tripped on the wide stairs and tumbled with the skeleton until the bones came off the wires and scattered across the floor in front of the faculty office, under the gaze of 'Uncle Violet', the principal. And then there was The Dead, a boy small enough to be in the eighth grade, with an incredibly pale face, and who distinguished himself – but only once – with an epic poem which he began writing – he himself couldn't tell why – during a maths class (while the teacher, the notorious Miss Twang, about whom an epic could have been written, spoke about her favourite Pekinese). The poem, which ultimately consisted of only two lines, which became famous: 'In the penumbra of a lamp/Two bearded men were holding camp.' Then there were the twins Grigoriţa and Negruţa, and another pair, Mihalache, a one metre forty wrestler who wore seven-inch heels, and Neagu, a giant with a crooked head because of the forceps that were used to bring him out and who had one single interest: electric toy locomotives. I end with Lulu, a vulgar sort of buffoon who showed up at a costume party at a summer camp we both attended dressed and made up as a woman, which made me so ill that I had to lean against a wall. As for the girls in our class, they were for me a nearly undifferentiated mass. Still, there was one, last name

Farcaş, with a cleaning-girl kind of face, very preoccupied with fashion magazines; another who was called, I still don't know why, by the male name Vasile; then another, a very peculiar girl who was a kind of slum beauty with a naive-perverse flair about her; and another yet, a kind of black swan by the name of Dialisa, who got pregnant in eleventh grade and didn't finish high school. Of course, there were nice girls also, who were good students, and others who were pretty and came from good families, just to go on with the gossip. But none of them interested me very much, and today I remember them only with great effort. There were two new girls, a blonde with a ponytail who answered to the graceful name of Pleşcoiu, and another, who had transferred from another high school, small and thin, 'a miniature diva', as someone nicknamed her during a break. There was something about her, with her aristocratic face, her loud and crackly voice like a duck's call, that was vaguely familiar to me. During breaks and for about a month during the first trimester, I kept seeing her in the hallway without really noticing her, always blabbing away with a group of friends. She dressed very stylishly, wore rings with precious stones, and was constantly changing her earrings, clip-ons probably, because her ears weren't pierced. Of course, during class hours she would remove her rings, but would keep them on if the teachers were men and tolerant, like Tom, our English teacher, who changed his ties and his suits far more often than was usual. Her name was Georgiana Vergulescu, but her girlfriends called her Gina, or Ginuţa, as she was probably called at home. Ginuţa was by no means an endearing moniker, because it was easy to see her girlfriends didn't care for her very much but were trying to cut her down to size, to view her as no more than a snobbish and spoiled brat. She outclassed them all in regard to clothes and make-up, the perfumes and soaps she used outside school. After every other word she would resort to the kind of empty vocables that had the same lack of meaning for me as those used by rock-and-roll-crazed boys. I had never heard, for instance, of Burda, Chanel, Miss Dior, Helena Rubinstein, Ella, Obao, Lancôme, Lux, Rexona; I didn't know the difference between bitter and sweet perfumes; I had no idea that not all deodorants and shampoos were equal, that it wasn't worth spending half a day looking for a pair of shoes, that blue jeans and cords, let alone jewels, are not for common mortals. Most of the other girls weren't so different from me in regard to their ignorance in that domain. They spoke with her hesitantly, fearful of saying the wrong things, in the same way they spoke to me about literature. But they hated her instinctively, for the fantasy world she inhabited, for the sophisticated arsenal she possessed. When the bell rang for the next class, she would flounce towards the door with quick, lively and haughty steps, like someone used to wearing high heels and schooled in the various manners of walks. Her various little shoes, of the smallest size, made a characteristic sound, which I recognized immediately before I even saw her, clickety-clacking down the long hallway with the red-and-white mosaic.

I ask myself when we began speaking to each other for the first time. I think that we exchanged distracted words a few times. She felt slightly attracted to me, partly because of her interest in literature, but more specifically because I was thought of highly by some of the students – 'first-rate' – which for her had a hypnotic effect. Once, I bought the literary newspaper *Luceafărul*, which, as I was walking in, got wet from large drops of autumn rain. In the classroom's ashen light, I spread out the pages the size of bedsheets across my desk and was rapt in reading a translation of Sandburg. She sat down next to me (my benchmate was out playing soccer) and grave as a cat began reading the poems along with me. 'I don't like them,' she said. 'That's not poetry. Anyone can write this.' I took on a professional air and started explaining to her that Sandburg was a great poet, but Gina argued back indignantly. Another time, I walked her home, along the grey wet walls of the houses on Taras Sevcenco Street. From time to time, shiny fruit fell from the nearly bare chestnut trees. There was a powerful, nostalgic smell of smoke in the air, wafting from the courtyards with forged iron fences. She wore a raincoat made of shiny lemon-yellow material and was engrossed in scattering the piles of dead leaves with the tips of her shoes. She told me with a half-childish, half-affected expression about her 'friend at the College of Mathematics', namely

Silviu, who would end up being my nightmare for many months. But that afternoon I smiled bemusedly, my thoughts elsewhere. I saw her defects so perfectly: her pampered bird mind, her superficially mannered gestures. Her laughter made me laugh as well, because she revealed a set of crooked little teeth, amusing as a malicious bat's, but between two gorgeous lips of a uniquely individual shape: the upper sported a kind of a vertical ridge at the point where the two lips joined, creating thus an arc in relief, full of personality. Her mouth never had a passive, 'typically' feminine expression, that is, one of gentleness or kindness; on the contrary, it displayed nervous energy, affectation, irony, childishness, but also the refinement – not entirely integrated – of a mature woman. The tip of her nose was slightly flat, which gave her an obstinate look. Only her eyes, yellow and luminous, had a conventional beauty. I wasn't yet attracted to Gina, but from the very beginning she seemed to me different from all the other girls I knew. Sheltered under my umbrella, she told me all sorts of tales whose heroes were people I knew nothing about, but who were important enough to her to talk about. Who were Maricu and Tanicu, who was Penelopa? It was only her own mother that she referred to – tenderly – as 'my mother'. She mentioned Frau Else from the kindergarten, and the group of children who grew up on her street, spoke about the amorous relationship between Fofo and Micheline, about Ilieș and Simina. It wasn't until we arrived at her house, the massive house with the marquee and willow in the courtyard, on Venera Street, that I saw the connection between Gina and the girl I had seen that evening at the draped window above the marquee. I mentioned this to her, and she replied with an indignant air that the damned cats always peed on the marquee's stained glass. She was forced to conduct permanent war with them. Then, she invited me up for a cup of coffee, 'to warm our bones a little', which surprised me. I followed her through the massive gate, with its gigantic wrought-iron knob decorated with tiny leaves growing on branches. After passing through a small and dark marble hallway, which connects me to so many memories that I feel like giving everything up, and climbing a few steps, we arrived at the door of her apartment.

The house seemed labyrinthine to me. I recall now – even better than the actual image of the house – the page from my journal where I wrote about this unexpected place. I see the notebook with a red plastic cover, and I see every line I wrote on that day:

'November 9, 197–. Moving further and further away from life. My face emaciated, wooden, weary, the eyes seeming to tumble into spirals of reed, voice black with capitals and gables, something Renaissance and a splintered and dusty youth.

'I was in a big house, old and with tall and smoky chambers (a sienna-coloured stove in each one), with walls congested with glass and metal icons, uncanny, multihued and miraculous, crucifixes and ancient furniture varnished like bronze. The house was alive with living wax figures: a few old crones, identical in aspect, an old man with absolutely white hair. Everything was painted in a contorted, unnatural manner. An old house, soaked in silence (and even the silence was viscous with music. Wajda's camera would have meandered along the cracked walls with the fallen moulding, over the faces of the horse-riding saints and the bony Christs made of wood and chalk standing above the keys of the upright piano with its artful carvings, over the macramé and the frozen crones shrouded in green and rose silk, with the luminous skin around the nose and watery eyes. Like a soft, barely felt ribbon the rooms were filled with the calm concentration of a Bach fugue). I remained silent and stared at the icons in black and rotted frames and wondered what sort of monster this seventeen-year-old must have been (the archaic aspect that I had long discovered in her, the gravelly voice, the small and bony frame, the bat's teeth – but at the same time a girl thrilled by obscenities and trifles; nothing naive-sentimental-feminine in her. She said that she cried when her 'friend' called her common and banal, but I couldn't imagine her crying, she is too dry) who moved around this sectioned space, embalmed in shadows and withered hues. The rugs on the floor had been removed, so that there was nothing to obscure the glassy and dirty polish of the chandeliers suspended from the ceilings of every room. A ferociously dead life.

'A passage worth noting, from *Royal Highness* by Th. Mann: "I must confess I had no other choice. I always felt myself completely incapable of any other human activity. It seems to me that this indisputable and unconditional lack of capacity for anything else is the single proof and the touchstone of the poetic profession, and as a matter of fact, poetry must not be seen as a profession, but the expression and refuge of this incapacity."

'Finally, something capable of giving you hope.'

Of course, now I laugh at the forced aesthetic manner I used at that time for writing any trifle. Gina's characteristics and the sense of her surroundings appear in that journal page twice deformed, because of the manner of writing as well as because of the above-mentioned psychological motives, that is, my aversion to girls, my need to protect myself against an erotic aggression. Gina was indeed a girl raised by old people, causing her to develop many of her tics and odd behaviours. But to say that she was like an old person seems to me ridiculous. It is true that in one year she suddenly matured, becoming a veritable woman, but once again it seems odd that at the beginning I thought of her as so thin. Should I attempt now, while I am writing, to concentrate on her face (and how easily I could make it appear before me, in a matter of seconds), I would see only the way it appeared in a colour slide taken last summer at the sea. She was stunningly beautiful in it. She is wearing a thin checkered men's shirt, while her long hair, straight or perhaps only very lightly curled, the colour of oak, is parted in the middle. Her face, photographed against the background of the green sea, is turned towards the viewer and bears a plaintive, longing aspect. Her eyes are large, and her bitter smile forces her mouth to wrinkle, emanating emotion. I had seen some other pictures of her, from the time she was an adolescent. They all seemed impossible for me to bear, like putting your hand on a hot plate. She didn't even know you existed when they were taken, and the fact that you didn't get to share so many precious moments with her, that she squandered so much feeling on someone other than you, even though it might have been for no one else, is beyond understanding, unbearable.

That day, when I walked her home the first time, she had me wait in her room, that is, this very room where I am right now, scribbling these lines. I stared avidly at everything around me, especially the icons. She came back with two cups of coffee and put a disc on a record player of very poor quality with a grey vinyl top, the kind that you could buy in the Fifties. Gina sketched a few tango steps as she came in, then sat next to me, and we began a literary conversation, because there was nothing else I knew how to talk about. After about half an hour, I left. In the afternoon, I didn't feel like studying for the next day. Sitting on the case next to the couch with my feet up on the cold heater, I stared out the window for a few hours. I had a feeling of predestination, I knew even then that this woman-girl would demolish my entire internal edifice. I walked her home again during the days that followed, and gradually it became our custom. I strove not to take her seriously, constantly spoke to her harshly, answered her ironically. Despite all this, I quickly noticed that her allusions to various friends, with whom she said she was spending her Sundays over a game of canasta or Saturdays over tea, began to hurt me. I had to tolerate – albeit with a condescending and ironic smile – all sorts of confessions. I was current with the great love between her and Silviu; in this matter Gina displayed an unbelievable cruelty. During classes she scrawled SILVIU in large letters on the margins of all her notebooks. Once, she took up designing the interior of a room. But then, with a few thick lines, she disfigured the framed photograph she had planned to place above the bed. Sometimes, she came to school in tears, and one day she left after the first two classes. Gina suffered, her love was not going well, and I was the one who was there to deal with her unhappiness. One evening (I think it was in the middle of November, because a trace of snow had already begun to fall and it was dark outside), she took me by the hand. We stopped in the middle of the street. She was transfigured by unhappiness. However, she converted all her despair, as she would later continue so many times, into an exalted and breathy discourse in which she nearly shouted how much she adored me. She begged me to help her, to stay with her always. She embraced me passionately, and I too put my arm around her shoulders, and we walked into her apartment holding each other. We paused in the hallway, filled with a coffee-hued air, and we kissed, uncomfortably, more on the cheeks and eyes than the mouth. Her face was wet with tears, while I, speaking her name over and over again, holding her tight in my arms, caressing her neck, caressing her breasts through her overcoat, forced myself with all my might to avoid, to postpone the words that formed themselves of their own will in my mind. For about a week, she continued being full of tenderness, but that dark melancholy on her face, her obstinate silence brought me more pain than the happiness of our moments in the hallway. I wasn't even capable of writing verses any more, I could hardly wait for the bustle at home to end, for me to get under the blankets and go to sleep. In my dreams, I had a rending feeling of loneliness. A few times, I dreamed that I was roaming the endlessly crisscrossing alleys of a park. The twilight was pink and violet like a lightly luminescent fog. In this crepuscular domain, things had no weight, they had only a grave emotional density. The air had a mother-of-pearl-like quality, the mist was painfully concentrated inside me. I knew that space was infinite and there was no hope. Suddenly, hurling its columns and carved statues to a vertiginous height, twirling its cupola the colour of faded copper towards the twilight, a colossal monument sprang up in a plaza of incommensurable size, a half-ruined construction with arches and gables creeping with lichens, with gothic chimeras, deeply fluted and leering atop the walls. Nothing was of human proportion on this edifice. I clambered to the top of the cupola on an endless spiral staircase. There are no words, even in dreams, capable of defining the feeling of someone finding himself under the arch of so gigantic a cupola. Above its centre, about a hundred metres up from the rhomboid slabs that made up the floor, a circular window opened out into the twilight flames of the floating clouds. Various degrees of darkness, coppery blue, filled the space in which one felt like an insignificant insect. And suddenly I began to grow, to dilate, to fill up the geometric space furrowed by incandescent veining. As I grew, I stared at the pale frescoes on the curved walls, the darkening air outside penetrating through the eyes of the skylights, in whose ovals, profiled by the purple, alighted a dove. Soon I was forced to bend, crawl on the ground, bring my knees to my mouth and cross my hands and legs, because I had completely filled the gigantic vault. I woke up dizzy from loneliness, with the feeling that my life had come to an end.

Snow had already began to fall, and it was dark when we went home now. We walked hand in hand, and sometimes she put her hand in the pocket of my overcoat, without letting go. She was terribly moody, sometimes happy, sometimes absent-minded, sometimes filled with an unbearable sadness. We walked slowly through the thin layer of snow illuminated by the light of the windows, happy and hopeless at the same time. As our relationship progressed, I realized that we were from different worlds, that our only tie was the irrational footbridge of unilateral feeling, a footbridge no one would cross. I was filled with despair each time she told me about her trip to Leningrad, where she had gone the previous year, the strolls on the shores and bridges of the river Neva, the dawns white as milk. I imagined her alone, dreamy, roaming with her hair ruffled by the river's current, under the forged-iron streetlamps, by the stone lions or sitting on a bench in a park devastated by twilight and autumn. She told me how, at the sea, she swam in a sunbeam reflected in the water. And she recounted endless scenes from her childhood as a little girl from a good family, and showed me a large courtyard with a fence made of lances on a street not far from hers, where a few children in blue overcoats and green felt jackets were playing in the snow, and told me she had played there many times when she was in kindergarten. She would freeze for a long time, staring through the fence bars with an expression from which I had to turn away. She didn't speak about Silviu any longer, but in everything she said, in the tone of her words, in her disposition, even in her kisses – because she would abruptly stop at times in the solitude of the snow-covered streets and, leaning against a pole, would say: 'Kiss me' – in all her whims, I sensed his presence. I knew that Gina used me to protect herself, to let her unhappiness take a breath, to avoid being alone, to have someone hold her hand when she was forced to stare at her love's agony in the face. Who was I to be her boyfriend? An ugly and bizarre boy, on the threshold of

schizophrenia, who knew nothing outside of a smattering of literature, who had no experience of life. I dressed randomly, I had never
travelled, I had no friends. All I could give her was my blind fear of
losing her. For me, Gina was much more than a girlfriend, she was
a being impossible to endure, a drug far too strong but which I
couldn't live without. I knew sooner or later that everything would
fall apart, that Gina would leave me. But in her hallway, in the darkness where we could barely make out the contours of our faces, our
love gestures were becoming more and more daring, uninhibited.
Her tiny and thin body was learning not to contract any more when
my caresses became more rash. I was learning to hold a woman in
my arms, I was learning to enjoy caressing, to become dizzy from
contact with her soft mouth, the dull taste of her lips and teeth and
tongue, the shampoo smell of her hair, her eyebrows' aroma. I was
learning, underneath her blouse, the shape of her breasts. After I left
her at home, I walked alone the distance of a few tram stops, through
the frozen snowflakes. The winter air agreed with me. My palms
preserved the smell of her skin till late into the night, when I fell
asleep.

Many odd things occurred to us during our walk to her house.
One night, clear as a crystal, we crossed Galați Plaza while staring
up at the full moon, which rose above the station where the Number 40 bus stopped and turned the tram tracks to gold. We were
speaking about the moon. She was telling me that during a trip to
the mountains with a few friends, she had felt so alone that she
wanted to eat the moon, literally. 'But do you know what I mean?
Literally!' Of course, I felt a shiver of jealousy and attempted to
parry with something of my own, but my mouth remained wide
open because, staring at the moon, I saw clearly that its sphere was
not perfect any more, that one side had changed shape and that a
shadow which could only be the earth's shadow was slowly taking
over most of its surface. Amazed, we dropped our bags and, holding each other tight, we gazed at this spectacle above the roofs.
Soon, the amber globe was half its size, while the shadow grew,
leaving only a thinning scintillating sliver. All the while, buses and
taxis drove by, pedestrians rushed along their way through the

Galaţi Plaza but no one joined us to watch the moon, which soon began to grow back until, a quarter of an hour later, it regained its former perfect global shape. Later, both of us thought of it as an inexplicable dream.

Gina didn't want us to meet on Sundays. I would telephone her, but she wasn't home. As usual, her grandmother answered the phone, told me that Gina was out. What was she doing Sunday night? What was she doing during the evenings when she didn't let me walk her home? I imagined the most unlikely scenes. For a while now, there had been a certain arrogance in her tone, that vulgar nuance that she used each time she felt herself superior to someone or the master of a situation. Her face then took on a look that drove me insane, simultaneously cynical, affected with guilt, and mysterious. Her language was spiced with erotic terms and allusions, which she smuggled compulsively into our conversation, indifferent to subject matter. I felt that she wished to brag or perhaps communicate something, and that wish was stronger than her concern to spare my feelings. 'What a great place to make love!' she said once when we passed by a house with a small tower. Then, it may have been the same evening, she implied that she knew what a naked man looked like. Of course, I would mock her or make an absurd remark, but each time I felt the full strength of the blow. Still, it helped me dominate (however illusorily) those desperate situations, because then, when I was under pressure, I became unusually eloquent. I cajoled her and then captivated her with a terrific burst of imagination. But she wanted me to feel her joy and her triumph and, eventually, after a few days, she told me she had gone back to Silviu, that she went home with him, that she let him take her clothes off but, of course, 'nothing happened'. She told me all that in the shadow of the hallway on the marble steps, painting everything in typically female fairy-tale hues: first, he took her to the restaurant Berlin, where they drank Cinzano, then he bought her a red rose and they went to his place by taxi. He had a motorcycle, and the following Sunday they would . . . I shouted at her then to stop and rushed out into the street. I began crying convulsively; I was fortunate it was dark outside. I walked by the windows displaying ski-wear, by the TV repair shops, through the viridian light of shoe stores. I knew I had lost her and couldn't understand why. It was as though someone had told me that I had died, or that Gina had died. I couldn't imagine what school would be like if she was going to be around all the time, the Gina who wasn't my Gina any more. What would it be like from then on without our walks home, what it would it be like without putting up with all her whims and affectations and cynicisms . . . I left long tracks on the snow. It was the end.

That evening, I decided to have nothing to do with her any more. I wrote in my journal: 'Gina doesn't want to, DOESN''T WANT TO be with me. I can't understand how this monstrosity can exist, the ignorance of this perverse child. I watch the dissolution, column by column, step by step, wall by wall, like sugar in water, of our edifice. In any case, there is nothing to be done, you can't fight against her animal irrationality. I have to recall who I am, to take back my previous life, whatever it might have been. I am a man who writes, I can't lose myself for the sake of a subhuman, obnubilated, unfortunate being.' And I continued on like this for about three pages, in a state of delirium in which I saw Gina as the embodiment of human vileness and depravity. Perhaps what tortured me more than the incessant obsession with her face, her voice, were the purely physiological aspects of my passion: the accelerated heart-beat to the point of palpitation, the weighty and warm pain in my chest and bones, the insomnia in which I constructed endlessly bitter monologues. The next day at school, her silhouette jumped at me right away: as usual, she chattered with her girlfriends, without worrying that anyone was listening, without paying any attention to anyone's replies. How affected seemed her rhetorical flourishes, the French and German expressions with which she carelessly spiced her conversation! It was the language of an old coquette, affected to the point of being ridiculous, peculiar and, for me, very attractive, despite my disdain for histrionics and affectation. Sometimes, I was amused to think about how well the word 'pearl' fit every expression Gina used, how well it expressed the mixture of magic and superficiality that characterized her. That day, I tried my best not to look at her at all. I found other things to do with the boys. I told jokes during breaks, talked about soccer, about the differences in the singing of Mick Jagger and Robert Plant. But it was as though I was fitted with an interior radar that detected Gina wherever she was. I saw her even when I sat with my back to her, even when I went out in the schoolyard, in the snow. I could hear her talking, indifferent to the distance. I knew what she was talking about, I knew she couldn't prevent herself from trumpeting her love affair everywhere. Her girlfriends already knew that her boyfriend from the College of Mathematics would take her out next Sunday on his motorcycle. What hurt most was that she wasn't even avoiding me, that she showed up a few times at my desk, where I was reading during a break, and drew quickly on my notebook a little flower, next to which she wrote, GINA. The vivacity of her motions was uncanny: the rhythm of her steps, the movement of her arms, the speed of her writing constantly amazed me. The fact that she thought of me merely as a friend, that I saw no change in her behaviour towards me, humiliated me, filled me with waves of hatred. Many times, she tried to start a conversation with me, but I rejected her brutally. She smiled then, with that mocking tone, that air of indifference that makes me furious even now. I had developed a kind of erotopathy, a mixture of love, hatred, disdain, admiration, idolatry and disgust. In the evenings, I returned home all by myself through that gentle flurry of snowflakes illuminated by the headlights of the passing cars, through that odd solitary turmoil of late winter twilights, the time of day when it seemed that the impending night would rule forever.

She became large while I dwindled. From a bizarre and affected little girl, a child raised by old folks, she grew little by little into an immense, hieratical being. Gina became the All. Sunday, I couldn't stay home. I wrapped myself in my scarf and winter coat and walked to the centre of the city. The morning was blinding. The snow on the boulevards' sidewalks, on the rubber banisters of the escalators, on the towers of the University and of the Institute of Architecture, put me in a state of exaltation. The frozen and glimmering air, clear as glass, dulled my interior sensors, wiped away the image that tried to cling tenaciously to the walls of my cranium: she and he, on the motorcycle, with orange helmets, Gina's trickling with a tress of chestnut hair. I went into the Danube restaurant and ordered a pastry, which I ate slowly, with long pauses. I stared outside through the yellowish glass. There were beautiful women in winter jackets or stylish overcoats; there were foreigners, Africans and Arabs, huddled in their parkas with large fur collars. I attempted uselessly to view myself objectively, from above, to struggle with this psychic illness which was my love. The inner images overwhelmed the outer ones.

Monday, Gina didn't come to school. The next day, she showed up during the first hour, but after the class began. She remained quiet and isolated till the end of the school day. I couldn't discern whether it was fatigue or sadness on her face, which I stared at constantly from the corner of my eye. After the first break, when I returned to my desk, I noticed on the corner of a notebook the four-petal flower I knew so well and next to it in capitals, GINA. I stared at her, but she wasn't paying attention to me: She was copying down in her notebook a list of irregular English verbs. It was strange the way she could change my disposition with the smallest of gestures. Abruptly, the same way a toothache disappears under the impact of a powerful painkiller, this tiny flower sketched quickly with red ink infused my entire body with a sense of calm I had not hoped to ever achieve again. This relaxation was so powerful that within seconds I felt myself immaterial. That evening, she called me on the phone. She said she was alone at home and it was dark in her room. I imagined her, tiny and made of mother-of-pearl, inside that house with heavy furniture that must have looked frightening in the dark. She asked me to forgive her, she told me that everything was over between her and *him* (but the fact itself that she avoided saying his name and used instead *him* in such a significant manner proved the contrary; the same way there existed for me only one *her*). Then, she resumed her usual, exasperating emotional discourses, in which she expressed her suffering and nostalgia in an impersonal manner, so that, though they were nothing but the censored eruptions of her unhappiness, you could almost see them as lightly veiled declarations of love. She told me that she felt more alone than ever, that she regretted our parting; she projected on me, as in a state of inebriation, her amorous phantasms which otherwise would have suffocated her. Quickly, between tears, she confessed that she liked me and didn't want us to part again. After I hung up, I paused to think for a moment. The fact that there was a minimal chance that what she said was true blinded me, made me want to believe that Gina could be mine, made me forget all about our differences, which I had ruminated about hundreds of times till then and each time seemed to me insurmountable. I had no choice. I had to believe, with my whole being, every one of her words. But somewhere in the wellsprings of my mind remained the certitude of disaster, the conviction that Gina would never love me. That feeling alternated with irrational hope, in a manner that toppled my interior equilibrium. My psyche was on its way to ruin on account of that permanent oscillation between love and hate, hope and despair, admiration and disdain. But for now I was happy, disposed to believe in the end of the story between Gina and Silviu, and felt myself liberated, as though this was the only hindrance between her and me. The next day, we walked home in a snowstorm. Winter break was near, and I was thinking with horror about the New Year celebration. Would I spend it with her? It seemed unlikely. We angled forwards as we walked through the snowfall that shot ice needles at our cheeks and penetrated behind our necks. The tangled streets, pallidly illuminated here and there in dull orange, were swept by the snowstorm until the black of the pavement came into sight, while in other, more protected places, the snow undulated in the blue shadows. She took off her glove and stuck her hand in my pocket, lined with fur. I held tight her inert little fingers, which only responded from time to time with slightly perceptible quivers. Many times, we paused to kiss, nearly falling over from the force of the wind. We pushed our fur hats against each other, tried to embrace while fighting our heavy coats, stared in each other's eyes in that frozen gloom that latched icy stars to our eyelashes. Gina was arrayed now in snow, glimmering in the light of the window displays of the self-service shop, decorated with tinsel-and-cloth children on little cardboard sleds, multicoloured globes and bulbs. Her hair and face, under the delicate peak of the fox-fur hat, turned abruptly crimson from the purple tinfoil of the vestment of some Santa Claus ruling on his throne between bottles and canned goods. In the hallway, when I took her in my arms, she asked me if I wanted to come up to her room. We walked in together. The television was on in the living room, a Temp 6, one of the first sets to be sold around here, and her grand-parents and aunt were watching it, wrapped in blankets and the magic light of the palpitating screen. I bade them good evening and, led by Gina, we went into her room. It was so familiar! Many times I dreamed about this room, so tall, with its upright piano and its dresser painted vaguely in the Renaissance style, the glass icons on the walls, the terracotta stove painted with beautiful blue pictures, the scarlet satin drapes faded by the passage of time. Free of our heavy coats, we sat on the narrow, quilted sofa mantled with fanci-ful pillows. She disappeared for a few minutes and returned in jeans and a thin yellow blouse that brought into relief her beautiful breasts, not large but round, with the nipples visible through the cotton. She brought me green walnut jam and fig wine in an oddly shaped crystal glass. The light fell over us, pallid and flushed and slightly dulled by the candelabra's icicles. We talked about all sorts of trifles until the wine was gone, and then we sat quietly, staring at each other and swallowing the void. A sense of tension grew between us and became unbearable. She gave up first, falling back-wards on the plush pillows. Drunkenly, I embraced her, I lifted her blouse and glued my cheeks against the bare breasts with their tiny copper coins. We clutched each other close for a long time, until I unfastened the jeans' metal button and pulled the zipper. The clam-our awoke us. We had gone too far: the grandparents were only metres away and the door was made of frosted glass. Gina zipped up her jeans, and abruptly her face darkened. Her eyes burst with tears, and soon she started to sob convulsively. I held her in my arms, I squeezed her in order to stifle her sobs: I knew why she was crying. Gina wiped her eyes and took my cheeks between her palms. With a tortured expression, she looked into my eyes and said, nearly screaming at me: 'I don't love Silviu any more. Do you understand? I don't love him at all any more, he disgusts me. Let's laugh at him, do you want to?' And, abruptly, she tore off her blouse and unzipped her jeans again, until a few sparkling curls sprung out over the top of her tiny panties. We embraced again, but this time she convulsed with an urge for profanation that made her forget everything. I pulled away despite her grip and put on my jacket. I looked in the mirror and put myself together. My hair was wet and dishevelled. I combed it with a few quick strokes. Gina stood up as well, put on her blouse, and leaned on my shoulder with her dishevelled ringlets. We stared in the glimmering mirror. My eyes shone violet above the sharp cheekbones, while hers, amber, mirrored lighter than the coffee-toned reddish light. I remember our contracted and inexpressive faces, like masks of ecstasy, and the way they shone next to each other out of the mirror's crystal. We gazed at them for a time in motionless silence, and then she smiled – that bitter, phantasmal smile of hers – and pointed her index finger at the mirror. But the image inside the mirror's frame did not repeat this gesture. The hand in the mirror leaned on my shoulder, while the real one ferried its finger with its nail, polished in a transparent and sparkling glaze, brushed my forehead directly on the cold glass, coasting down along the line of the nose, insisting on a short rest along the lips, then tracing with deliberate leisure the path of the neck, to pause finally on the chest. A streak of light steam sectioned my face now, the tiny drops quivering a crimson hue. The phantom hand, simultaneously real, headed now for Gina's mirror brow, paused with finger pointed at the eyebrows, then descended towards the lips that went on smiling strangely, all-knowingly. The finger took a rest between Gina's breasts, then departed from the glass, stained now with a line of steam. The hand then rose and pressed with open palm in between our heads in the mirror. The dissolved seal of a palm of reddish steam persisted on the glass. Then, Gina's hand alighted on my shoulder, identifying again with its reflected image. There was no longer any difference between us, the mirrored and the real. With faltering steps, she returned to the sofa, installed a silk tasseled pillow under her head, and in a few minutes was asleep. She is the only being I know who sleeps with open eyes. The fixed stare, contrasting with the motions of her breathing chest, gives her the aspect of being in coma, of a soul that sees, hears, senses its death. I leaned over Gina and stared in her eyes, their pupils enormously dilated, framed only by a thin honey ring. But, instead of seeing *my* face in her obscured pupils, I saw *hers*!

I wasn't able to take my fountain pen with me, and consequently I had to ask for a ballpoint. And, to aggravate things, they gave me a red one that stains instead of writing. My hands are now a mess. In any case, it is a godsend that I am allowed to go on writing. They probably hope to learn something from these pages that I demanded to take with me. I am certain they wrote 'graphomania' somewhere, and they're thrilled to take advantage of this discovery. In fact, I have nothing against giving them the manuscript. Ultimately, somebody has to read it and they will understand, better than anyone, whatever it is that could be understood. I ask myself how long it has been since I last wrote. I don't know any longer whether it is Tuesday or Wednesday, August or September. But looking out the ward's window, I judge it to be the timid start of autumn. I take a daily walk through the courtyard, and more than once I've picked up a dead leaf. Waves of gossamer float between the white buildings, and the sick women shake it furiously out of their hair. As for me, I leave it there, it is only in the scarlet light of evening that scatters on the glossy walls of the ward that I brush it out. I believe then that it must be halfway through September. The sky is a deep blue, and it is cool despite the yellow light that trickles everywhere.

The white bedside table I write on is made of sheet metal. In the next bed lies Elisabeta, blonde and dirty. Now she spreads her playing cards on the bedsheets. The cards will make her crazy. She dealt them for me too; no one escapes. She has an old set – Austrian, she says – whose figures' eyes have been pricked with a needle in order for the predictions to come true. First, she spread the cards out like fans, then arranged in rows and pictures, and, just as she was about to point to one with her finger and say, 'This is you,' she suddenly froze. I stared at the card that Elisabeta continued to point at with gaping eyes. It was a jack, but the lower side of the card was not the same jack turned upside down, but a superb queen of clubs, with a jasmine flower between her fingers. I quickly shuffled the cards, but Elisabeta went into convulsions. After the crisis was over, we quickly went together over every single card in the pack but couldn't find the ambiguous image. Elisabeta is very affectionate with me, clings to my every move, ready to satisfy all my whims, if I had any whims. But she is so dirty and her bloodshot epileptic eyes frighten me. She suggested a few times that we join our beds. I told her to control herself. I wouldn't want us to end up like Mira and Altamira, who sleep together and clasp each other tight all night long. It's very romantic when you consider that Mira's fingers and toes are deformed, turning in each and every direction, so that she can barely pick up a glass, while Altamira (Paula nicknamed her that; her real name is Ştefania) is in fact perfectly normal and without any defects, except for one evening when she went to sleep for sixteen days in a row and when she woke up, on her own, she behaved as though nothing unusual had happened. The doctor visits us every morning, stops in front of each of the ten beds, and talks with us. He sits on the edge of my bed and stares into my eyes. Sometimes I forget to cover my chest, and this does not escape him. He stares then at the pile of pages on my nightstand. He promises not to take them away till I'm finished. Otherwise, it is evident I have nothing to say to him, or to anyone else. In fact, I am not the only one in the ward who writes. By the window is Lavinia's bed (Laviţa, as she likes to call herself). She scribbles feverishly, eight hours a day, love letters to a certain Doru. She spaces the text widely between the lines on the pink, orange, powder-blue and violet pages, leaving room enough for her coloured-pencil drawings. Her tongue is out like a little child, and she always draws flowers and wide-eyed princesses with noses made up of two dots, little doves and hearts. Even the envelopes she puts her letters in resemble automobiles painted by pop artists. The bedsheets, too, right after they are changed, are transformed into letters to Doru. She writes on the linen with a brown pencil, sketching alphabetical characters ten centimetres long and filling the white space with her childishly coloured drawings. Her bed is curious and quaint, the way she sleeps wrapped up in the pages of a giant letter. Next to her is Paula, a well-behaved girl with good sense during the day, but whom we hate because she ruins our sleep. Each and every night, Paula talks to her mother in her sleep. She screams, she tosses, she remembers how she behaved when she was a child. The two of them lived together in a basement apartment, a woman without a husband and her little girl, Paula, who had to endure all of her mother's hysterics and who prevented her, more than once, from slashing her wrists with a razor blade. And, last night, Paula was delirious, Mira and Altamira's bed squeaked the entire night, the ward's nurses kept opening the doors so that the hallway's light charged at my eyes. The sleepless night now has made me frantic, which in turn makes me want to write. I resume my manuscript, taking advantage of my colleagues' repose, while they are reading or filing their nails.

A few days ago, while telling the story about Gina's opened sleeping eyes, in which I saw her own face reflected rather than my own, I relived that moment of frozen fright. I felt the need to see once again, to *know* once again, and once again not to understand. I got up from the desk and in despair tore away the sheet covering the mirror. I looked. Then, I began to scream. I snatched from the desk the celluloid mandarin statuette and hurled it to the ground. When the old folks rushed into the room (Maricu and Tanicu, and then Penelopa, all livid, dribbling spittle on their chins from fright), they found me rolling on the floor, dragging all the rugs after me, wrapping myself in the purple drapes, which I had torn from the windows. The books on the shelves and the tiny statuettes on the upright piano were now scattered on the ground. The more they tried to caress and calm me down, the more agitated I became, tears streaming down my face and dripping on the hardwood floor. My mind became blank, and I sensed, as though in a dream, two men dressed in white lifting and carrying me to the ambulance waiting outside in the street. The way to the hospital, no more than ten minutes, seemed to me, I don't know why, extremely long. Since I have been here, her old folks have been visiting me everyday, bringing me jars of boiled rice with milk and cinnamon, oranges and lemonade. Her mother came by, too, with her husband. Her mother resembles her down to the tiniest details but is endowed with a bigger dose of blathering frivolity: a bird brain, ready at any moment to tell amusing tales. The fact that they brought me to the women's ward disturbed me at first but I got used to it fairly quickly. I am a little leery of the passivity with which I am beginning to accept the situation, but I suspect *it is what I am expected to feel* rather than what I actually feel (what I actually feel is a desire to laugh to spite my tears, everything seems to me a carnival, a comic farce). They put me here between Elisabeta and a wildly uncontrollable old woman with facial paresis. Aunt Laura's mouth dips on one side all the way down to her chin, and she can only blink with one eye. She closes the other one with her finger when she goes to sleep. A strand of saliva streams endlessly from the dipped corner of her mouth. Otherwise, she is stridently made up like an old coquette, speaks with no one and spends her days sitting up with her eyes fixed into a pocket mirror and smiling with half a mouth. Her violet hair fans out like a diaphanous spider web on the pillow. It took me several days to get used to the surroundings, which at the beginning inhibited me completely. I soon realized they had taken me to the neurology ward. The girls have all sorts of neuroses, pareses and hysterias. I told myself, we are in a kind of a limbo, illuminated to the point of transparency by the autumnal gold outside.

I walked out of Gina's room feeling dizzy, incapable of thought. It was dark in the hallway of the apartment, the old folks had long gone to bed, while the television in the corner was swallowed by the penumbra. The only glimmer, metallic and lustrous, Rembrandt-like, came from the edge of a large copper tray on a small table. I stepped out into the street and, though it was nearly midnight, I walked all the way home through the apocalyptic snow, painfully pushed to the side by the snowploughs. In their blinding, blue headlights, the snow seemed to fall incessantly, as though to bury the entire world. My gloves were wet and soft, frozen crusts permeated my fingers. While passing by illuminated windows with motionless mannequins on skis wearing the latest fashions in sweaters and jackets, I saw in the red-and-green fluorescent light an entwined couple heading towards me. From their book bags, I gathered they were students. Once they got closer, I was amazed at the girl's resemblance to Gina: the same springy walk on interminable heels, the same fur coat. Her fox hat with the reddish glow was also the same as Gina's. I felt I was really losing my mind when it became clear that it was actually Gina heading towards me, her hand in the boy's pocket and laughing convulsively. I took a close look at him once we were practically face to face with each other. He had long and pallid features, eyes deep in their sockets and a barely burgeoning moustache, like an auburn shadow underneath his lanky nostrils. We stared for an instant into each other's eyes before they went on, towards Gina's street: the young man was me.

From that day on, I went over to Gina's place often. For a while, she seemed to have forgotten Silviu. Winter slipped away from us in the madness of her room, where she was different each time, where an emotional nuance different from any I had lived before revealed itself to me each time I caressed her, taking me further each time. One evening, she brought from another room some twenty-odd old dresses, left by her grandmother and great-grandmother, yellow as saffron, with shawls hung with silk tassels and belts embroidered with gold thread. She put on diamond earrings and twirling like a whirligig, while we drank a kind of cocktail made of oranges and Havana Club, modelled for me every single one of those dresses. Thus arrayed, with a peasant scarf shrouding her head, she looked like a Russian doll – or, as I saw her then, Grushenka in *The Brothers Karamazov*. In another dress whose waist ended at the breasts, a gorgeously designed décolletage, and a large hat whose faded blue ribbon clasped the chin, Gina resembled Adèle H. But she looked best as a Russian, because of her cunning smile and her sweet eyes lacking sweetness, sweet in a kind of cerebral mode. We were already very dizzy when she hid behind the wardrobe's door in order to put on a slip her mother had brought her from Paris. The slip was black and shiny, with silk lace. It was very short, revealing her G-string, also of black silk. This sensual vestment contrasted with her innocence, her goodness, her childlike face. I took her in my arms and stretched her out on the floor. We began to make out, gripped by a hopeless fury. Huffing, clutching my shoulders with all her strength, she sighed in my ear: 'Andrei, no, it's not possible now, but I swear, I *swear* Andrei, I will be yours . . .' I had lost my head completely, but I think I was even more afraid than she was. The erotic act seemed to me a distant rite, one in which I couldn't believe I would ever participate. I was afraid instinct was not enough, that I wouldn't know what to do, how to do it . . . I suffered, in an amplified way, from the complex my lack of experience gave me, I felt I should be the one who *knows*. This seemed to be an obstacle that could take Gina away from me. Later, I considered that if I had had then even the smallest amorous experience, Gina would have been mine, and maybe (maybe!) would have stayed mine forever. But, now, we were wasting our encounters in that room full of glass icons, in fearful exasperation.

At school, we were good friends, we were together all the time. We sat at the same desk, and everyone knew about our relationship. It is possible that they gossiped about us, because Gina's girlfriends instinctively hated her, and, while they respected me, they thought of me as some poor unlucky monster who had just ended up in bad company, something that was going to even further ruin me. Yes, they viewed me with pity and horror, as if to say: wake up now, you unlucky fool! In the hallway Gina, holding my arm, touchingly tiny in her school pinafore, would tell me about her labyrinthine dreams, with multicoloured butterflies sailing through marble temples, or would show off by asking me to go and get her a pretzel. Many times, I saw in her translucent eyes, hiding in half-shadow, so much sadness that I would become sad too, feeling that my entire life was built on sand, that everything that connected us was an illusion. Then, I wouldn't speak a word the whole day and she, squeaking and pulling at me ('Hey, Andrei, don't be like that . . . '), would try to make me laugh. Or she would draw on my notebook a little flower, under which she inscribed in a fraction of a second: GINA. And our story continued, despite the feeling that began to haunt me at that time, that I wouldn't be able to keep her and it would be best to separate right then and there, because it would be much worse later. Each time I noticed that she was bored or in a bad mood, each time she sent me home when we arrived at her gate in the evening, I would sense that everything was finished, that she had found herself another boyfriend, that she wanted to get rid of me. But she always came back, despite my behaviour, many times violent (for no reason at all, I wouldn't speak with her an entire day, until she came to me with her eyes filled with tears, while at other times, out of the suicidal impulse to end it all very quickly, I would tell her directly to leave me alone), and I believe even now that during that period at the end of the trimester she felt for me very deeply.

But during the first days of the spring break, we didn't see each other at all. The winter weather began to abate, and the icicles were melting under a glowing blue sky. The snow melted in a few days, and the pavement on Ştefan cel Mare began to show up from under the layer of muddy dirt. I stood by the window entire afternoons, looking out on the city and thinking of her. When I called, she told me she was sick with the flu; then, as the days passed, her grandmother answered the phone and wouldn't let me talk to her, telling me that Gina couldn't get out of bed or that she was taking a bath and would call me in an hour. But the evenings came and went, and Gina didn't call. It was odd, though, that at the time I did not doubt her. I was used to her being honest with me. What hurt me most was that I saw slipping away from me the chance of spending the New Year's Eve celebration with her, at some friends' place where we had been invited. I saw her over and over again in my imagination, toasting champagne with me in the trembling candle-light, and then kissing at midnight ... I secretly ordered a custom-made three-piece suit, my first, and I was proud of how I looked in it. I didn't know how to dance, but my sister taught me a few steps, and in my moments of enthusiasm I thought I could actually cut the mustard. I was getting ready to be a new man, to show her I had changed, that I could be a 'man of the world', not just a library rat.

Because during that period, through Gina's influence, I began to open my eyes to the world around me and became progressively more aware of what a drab and anachronistic life I was leading. I ogled for hours massive fashion magazines with heavy and shiny pages full of images of elegant women. I wondered if there were indeed men who enjoyed the lips and the flesh of those women, if there were such interiors of velvet and walnut where such couples sipped their J&B and made love. I wanted a motorcycle like Silviu, an AKAI component system with cylindrical metal cases like my classmates, I wanted the easy and beautiful life I intuited was to be Gina's lot. I started to suffer because of my looks, which seemed to me pitiful, because of my lack of money, because I couldn't take Gina to a bar in the center of Bucharest, because I couldn't take her on a trip to the mountains. But, primarily, I hated my unkempt dreamer mentality, which I knew would always prevent me from living the life I wished for. I felt a pang in my heart each time Gina mentioned her skiing winters or her never-ending games of canasta (she had even begun learning bridge and was wasting her nights at bridge clubs, or at least that's what her grandmother told me on the phone), because I knew the mirage of those snobbish distractions irremediably distanced her from me. I couldn't read a book without identifying the characters with me or with her. I read, for instance, *The Last Night of Love* . . . and *Dania's Games*. Both these books informed me, more, they demonstrated with near mathematical precision, that she would not stay with me, that she would eventually leave me, drawn by the life she was fit for and in which the only place I could assume was a mere amusing memory of her youth. (I could almost hear her, imagining an encounter with her after a number of years: 'How embarrassing you were, darling . . . ') Still, I wanted to try, if not actually to live, at least to mimic this way of life, because the fear of losing her was more powerful than my own ways, more powerful than the need to preserve my own personality. I would have liked to adapt myself to her from the bottom of my heart, to let myself be shaped by her, to let her 'take me in hand' and turn me into a 'man of the world'. Because of this, I thought of the New Year's Eve celebration as a departure point in my journey towards becoming the kind of man she desired.

When I called Gina again on December 29th, as I did every evening, her grandfather told me that she had left Bucharest to go to some relatives who had invited her to spend New Year's Eve with them. I knew she had no relatives outside Bucharest, so either she was staying in Bucharest or had gone to a mountain resort with someone else. Gina would toast champagne and kiss someone else under the candles' quivering light. Not even after hanging up could I believe it, could I imagine that it was possible. I stayed home for New Year's Eve. My parents didn't prepare anything special: a litre of wine, no more. About nine o'clock, they turned on the television and remained frozen in front of it. My sister had been invited to spend the New Year with some friends, so that the house seemed even colder and more drab than usual. At midnight, we turned off the lights and, against the bluish figures on television, we kissed and drank the cheap wine from the state-owned store. Then, I dressed and went out for some fresh air. I couldn't control myself and thought only of her during the moment after the last second of the outgoing year and continued thinking of her as I walked along Ştefan cel Mare, dark and frozen and drably lit by the orange lights, like a passage to inferno. I turned the corner to Circus Alley. The snowfall was light, but the snow on the ground was high, almost all the way up to the knees; you were practically swimming in it. The white cedars and the vines growing at the corners of the alley were barely standing, their branches curving under the weight of the snow. It could have been Siberia, if not for the flicker of hundreds of multicoloured rectangles, glittering in the fog: the windows of the four-storey buildings that lined up all the way to the fog-hidden Circus dome. I stared through the windows like the fabled poor boy in a socially conscious story: the majestic firs were studded with tiny coloured stars, glittering with Christmas toys and candies, sophisticated globes and tinsel. I saw the green-and-red strobe of a light show coupled with the music of a vibrating amplifier. I saw a cigarette butt, red and phosphorescent, falling from a dark balcony. With tears in my eyes I was talking to her, hoping that she would hear me, the same way I spoke at other times to Lili. I was speaking in a loud voice, blowing steam into the ice-scented air. I pushed forwards through the snow-covered firs, and, after finding my way through the snow-covered firs, and an assortment of tangled alleys, I arrived at the slope leading to the lake, where the fog was even thicker. Here and there, a bulb broke up its over-whelming presence. Soon, I began to make out the willows surrounding the frozen lake's oval. I took a step on the ice covered with soft snow. I stretched out my hand into the heavy fog. I could barely see the hand. I walked ahead for a while, taking small steps on the lake's ice; then, flooded by a gush of pain, I curled up and with gloved hands began to sweep away the layer of snow on top of the smooth, black ice. Silence permeated the dead planet. You couldn't see more than two metres ahead of you. I was alone in the midst of the frozen world. Spellbound by that new and mysterious world, I forgot about everything, even Gina. Gazing deep under the ice, I saw, tangled in the weeds, a drowned child. He was blond, and his face was green as emerald. I didn't get a chance to look at him very long because suddenly I heard a tiny staccato sound. I started to sweat and felt my heart dissolving into my chest. I froze and trained my eyes towards the place where the noise came from. It was the sound of footsteps, the clickety-clack of a woman's heels on the crystalline ice. I knew that the snow around the Circus dome had been cleared for skating, so I assumed the person walk-ing towards me was coming from there. After a while, the clickety-clack stopped, replaced by an almost imperceptible hollow noise. The fog suddenly began to take on a bit of colour, a hint of coffee brown, pale at first, then more accentuated. A few metres away I discerned the indefinite movement of a body. When it was able to make me out, it paused, hesitated, then came out of the fog and headed towards me. Even at one step away from me, smoke and steamy mist still whirled around it. It was a dark-haired woman, somewhere around thirty, with heavy eyeliner and a shiny black crayon line accenting the eyes. She wore a hooded fur coat and ashen boots. We stared at each other like two beings from other realms. Never before did the separation of humanity into men and women seem more odd to me. She was a woman, and she seemed monstrous, a harbinger of death. She was not made like me. There was no possible communication between us, as though we were each made of other matter and breathed a different admixture of gases. She stared at me with a completely impenetrable look on her face, as though she wanted to express a novel feeling, something unknown to me. I knew that she wanted to tell me something, but words in that silence would have been more than indecent. Suddenly, she began to cry in an odious, unbecoming way, howling and sobbing like a child. Quaking with tears, she threw herself on my shoulder. Embarrassed, I guided her face towards mine: it was contorted, while the make-up ran all the way down to her lips, along the tracks left by her fingers rubbing her face. I wiped her face with my handkerchief, while she, sighing and moaning, held on to my arm with all her strength. I dragged her to the shore, where she stopped abruptly and forced my face towards hers. She stared into my eyes. She was concentrating, as though she wanted to pierce my brain and leave there her terrible message. But nothing got through. I couldn't understand anything except that maybe she, too, was an abandoned woman who, just like me, had gone out into the winter. I left her at Circus Alley and, frozen stiff, went home.

During the three weeks of that winter break, there was no sign of Gina. She never called me. Pride didn't allow me to make the first move. In the evenings, I suffered like a dog, but mornings weren't so bad. I would go out into the city, visit the Students' Club, play pingpong, go to art shows. I read a lot, seven to eight hours a day, and filled my journal with delirious fragments of verses and notes about my reading in which I inserted dream fragments and short phrases about Gina. I dreamed about her nearly every night. There was something insane in my (inexplicable) tranquillity in regard to her. I could not believe that she wouldn't return to me. I wrote, I think, on January 10:

'Life directed towards exterior. It is only with great difficulty that I find again the path leading to the centre, to myself. A volatile prose, doubled by the sensation of incapacity, of indolence, emotive crises unleashed across an indifferent background, diffused focus.

'I am reading *Thanatos* by Biberi and *The Dream* by Popoviciu. Just finished *Orlando* by Virginia Woolf.

'From time to time I remember Gina. She's gone, and there's no knowing if she will come back to us. Maybe tomorrow, maybe never. My feelings towards her, no longer those of love, have now turned to tender sympathy striated by resentment. I reached the good old reasonable conclusion: I couldn't manage it, and, if by some absurd turn we begin again our love story, it would end the same way. I prefer to be next to her in poems, in dreams, in memories, where her image is aesthetic and inoffensive. If I thought there was another chance that she could love me, I would take it, but it is absurd. It is true, though, that without her I am nothing.

'I dreamed about her last night. I was at her house, in that great hallway leading to all the rooms. I don't think there was anyone else there, a dark reddish air floated in the room, the twilight of a deliquescing sadness. On the wall, a gigantic door, at least five metres tall, scarlet and filled with age. I was sitting on the ledge of a window and searching the street for Gina, who was late. Outside, it was just as sad: the same red air, through which the trams floated as in a fog. The peeling door obsessed me. When I realized that Gina wasn't coming, I went home. I got there, unlocked the door: to my surprise, I was still in the same hallway, and on the wall before me was the same immense door, of flaking scarlet.'

I tracked my feelings with great care: I was happy and at the same suffered if I noticed that my passion for Gina was weakening. In the mornings, I wanted to continue loving her, had forgotten all that she had done; I only kept in mind her image from our pleasant times. But evenings, under the weight of physiological suffering, driven insane by the throbbing of my heart, by the intense pain that constricted my conscience, I decided that it would have been best if I had never known her. I wanted death, my definitive disappearance from my own brain. Still, even that idea made me suffer – because I couldn't imagine how I could survive without at least thinking about her. I awaited the start of school and the inevitable encounter; I asked myself what had become of her. Because at night I couldn't sleep, I stood between the window and the drapes and, gazing at the moon in the clear sky, endlessly imagined our encounter.

The first day of the second trimester was a dramatic one for me. Gina didn't show up for the first hour, and I believed that perhaps she would never show up. Though I was agitated, I joined the circle of boys with their jokes and never-ending banter about records. With a hundred and a half you could buy any Indian record. Crocodile-toothed Mera, odious looking but sharply dressed, was selling two Rolling Stones and one Santana. Cotton brought with him a boxed set inscribed *King Size,* containing three George Harrison records. On the cover there was a photograph of a man, possibly Harrison himself, with a beard down to his chest and surrounded by monstrous dwarfs. Cotton was selling this 'triple', as he called it, for four hundred. He never forgot to mention, every single time he made the offer, that the first disc contained 'My Sweet Lord', magic words that lit everyone's eyes. But the most sensational record ever came from one of the great music connoisseurs, Radu G., a student with an Armenian face and thick eyebrows, who looked like a painting by the famous Baba: he showed up with a brilliantly lacquered red album, with a photograph of hundreds of characters arranged in gregarious formations, on top of which were pasted four young men in an assortment of old tasseled uniforms. Man oh man, everyone exclaimed, *Sgt. Pepper's*! And then, like madmen, they began mimicking the musical group. Some straddled their legs as far as they could, bent their knees, leaned backwards, strumming imaginary guitar strings with the left hand while picking at them with the right, emitting strange sounds with their mouths, in imitation of the guitar's wah-wah. Others beat on their desks with a deafening rhythm. They all participated in those moments of exalted pantomime. They all knew the words they were singing, entire records by heart, note by note, so that if one of them suddenly began a few measures from another song, they all followed immediately with extraordinary glee. When, years later, I saw the film *Blowup,* the imaginary tennis match from the concluding sequence seemed to me less successful than the deeply lived collective mimicking of that imaginary rock group. In fact, Radu G. and Mera had their own electric guitars and were getting ready to form a band. Now, during the break, they were talking about a certain kind of 'wah-wah' pedal, which they wanted to adapt to Radu's solo guitar. The chemistry teacher interrupted our discussion, to which I listened with much envy and renewed conviction that I was good for nothing, that I would never understand life. Light as a mouse and with a huge smile on her face, Gina snuck in, almost at the same time as the teacher. She was so amused that one of her misshapen teeth showed between her lips, giving her a malicious air, like that of a charming little witch. In her ultramarine pinafore, with a tiny gold chain showing through the collar of her blue blouse, she seemed even smaller, almost like a sparrow. She plunged to my desk, flung a 'bonjour' at me, and began to take out books from her book bag. I didn't say anything back, but neither was I able to pay attention to the teacher. She sat up straight, affecting an air of femininity and grinning like a spoiled child who knew she had done something wrong. It drove me crazy that she behaved normally, as though we were merely two desk partners, as though nothing had happened between us. During breaks she asked me what subject we were studying the following lesson, then blended in with the rest of the girls huddled about the heater and bantered cheerfully. Soon, you could hear her loud and crackly voice, which sounded like she was talking to deaf old people, chattering about lace and ruffs and fashions.

Since his parents weren't home, Mera asked a few of us over after school. Besides me, he invited Manea – a coarse, unrefined boy, who was the son of a waiter and nicknamed Little Tiger by the English teacher, because of his red-orange hair and feline aspect – Radu G. and Mera's girlfriend, Molina – about whom everyone sang Creedence Clearwater Revival's 'Molina, where are you going to?' – The Dead and his girlfriend, Sanda – nicknamed Calceola Sandalina after the foraminifer. But Sanda (Sanda was her last name) was good friends with Gina; thus, while actually not invited, Gina came along with us. In any case, the gang was thrilled, because they sensed that something was not all right between Gina and me and hoped to witness a scene. I stayed as far away as I could from her and forced myself to engage in a discussion with the boys, especially since they were speaking about films, which I knew a lot about. I had seen Antonioni's *The Eclipse,* and I was excited about the scene where Monica Vitti and Alain Delon kissed through a glass window. We had just stepped out on the boulevard and picked up a couple of bottles of vodka from the supermarket. The girls, laughing and screaming out loud, had managed to rattle the sales-lady. They were delightful and flirtatious, they loved to exhibit their teeth and gums, to act silly and flash their tongues. We turned on to a side alley with cars parked on the sidewalks and eventually arrived at Mera's home. He lived in a stylish apartment, with wood and aluminum furniture and chandeliers of ground, yellowish glass. The library occupied an entire wall and, on an especially designed shelf, there was a superb Japanese record player with tiny metal discs at the edge of the turntable and a multitude of shiny dials and lights. We sat wherever we could, trying not to dis-turb the delicately wrought vases and other odd objects on the coffee table and the trays: a daguerreotype, a pince-nez with fold-ing lenses, a Russian doll . . . The boys headed for the disc section of the library, containing at least two hundred pieces: classical – in large elegant boxes – and rock – torn and pieced back together with yellowish Scotch tape. Mera brought some crackers, put on some unbearably violent music, and turned the volume to maximum. We hit the vodka. It was almost necessary to scream in order to hear each other. Despite this, I caught from time to time fragments of Gina's stories from the other corner of the room. She and San-dalina had nestled together, and Gina was telling her about her New Year's celebration. She was laughing and, despite the excite-ment, she was constantly affecting the air of a vamp. She had gone with him to two different places that night; they had kissed on the way; and danced madly, until they fell on the floor . . . I was trying with all my might to hear what she was saying, though everything I heard was making me sick; I felt that I could no longer stand up, that I could no longer bear it. I was constantly pouring vodka into my glass. Suddenly, I lost control, and while others started to dance, I fixed my glare on Gina – who was pretending to ignore me – with ever increasing insistence. I think I must have been staring at her like a madman, because I noticed Sanda's frightened face just before I lost my lucidity. All I have now of the rest of the party are sensa-tions rather than memories. They told me later that I was staggering and spilling my vodka, complaining to the boys about how Gina was treating me, and calling her all sorts of names; then, they said, I walked up to her, took her hands and rattled deliriously for fifteen minutes about how much I loved her. 'You repeated continually like a madman: "You are my everything, you are my everything!" You were paler than The Dead. We couldn't get through to you. You attacked poor Gina, I don't mean "poor", the damn bitch, but she was trying to calm you down, except you weren't listening, it seemed that all that mattered was to humiliate yourself before her, at some point you were rubbing your face against her knees . . .' 'Man, you were a mess, there was nothing I could do, if I hadn't been drunk I would have tried to knock some sense into you, but there was no way, man.' 'After Gina left (you didn't even know when she left, you were staring after her with a dumbfounded look on your face, you actually looked kind of cool), and after everyone left, we were together in the kitchen and you brought me a cup of coffee on a tray, your eyes were nearly closed, I'm surprised you didn't trip. I helped you put your coat on. You looked like you were sobering up a bit, otherwise I wouldn't have let you go.' I recall now how I went out into the frozen January air, how I waited at the trolley station, and how, when it arrived, I fell in the snow trying to grab the trolley's safety rail. Happily, there was no one home. I threw myself on the bed, still in my school uniform, and fell asleep. I woke up in the dark and at first I was scared. Then, I remembered Gina. In a reverie that lasted an hour, listening absent-mindedly to the trams on Ştefan cel Mare, I imagined in great detail Gina's New Year's Eve till I felt I would suffocate. I washed my face and then, looking out the window, promised myself that under no circumstance would I behave like that again. Why should I destroy myself like that, for whom? . . . I found my journal and wrote with crooked letters and many corrections: 'Disappointed by Gina, by the impossibility of our being together. She doesn't want it, she freezes all affection and replaces it with affectation. She is an inferior being, you can't demand that she surpass this vapid and egotistical condition of hers, of an irresponsible demi-mondairie. I suspect that the disdain and the hatred are reciprocal. This is a jungle.' I was expecting her phone call – after all, she left me in a pitiful state – but no one called me that evening. The next morning, I wondered how I would ever go to school again, how would I ever confront Mera's sarcasm, Little Tiger's ironic comments, Sanda's allusive looks. I didn't even want to think of her. But everyone behaved absolutely fine, despite the fact that everyone already knew about the embarrassing events at Mera's. Still, no one mocked me; on the contrary, they treated me with extra courtesy and consideration. The girls especially lavished more compassion on me than ever; all of them had their issues with Gina. My friend Loretta Bedighian, the most intelligent girl in our class, talked to me every single day for a few days in the hallway, when we happened to be on duty together, monitoring the entrance. She told me that everything Gina did was for the sake of spectacle, that she liked everyone to focus on her, that, wherever she was, she just had to be the centre of attention. It was strange that everyone could see her frivolous aspect. Even then, when I was against her, I felt I couldn't be in agreement with what was in fact a defamation of Gina. I knew how charming, how kind and even how intelligent she could be at times; I knew that, despite the perennial vacuous remarks, she could sometimes come up with a stunning reply; I knew how obsessed by death she was, and by old age. Certainly, I suffered and hated her because she belonged to someone else (I wondered if she was still with Silviu or had met someone new), but that made her seem even more complex in my eyes. Even though I changed desks, even though I was determined to have nothing to do with her any more, our connection was never broken. After a few days, Gina telephoned me. I couldn't believe it when I heard her voice (in which I suspected the guilty snicker). I hung up on her, but the next day she tried to approach me during each and every break. She smiled, the slut, with her little flat nose and bat snout, uncannily beautiful, with the lightly curled hair the colour of oak. She would nestle next to me without saying a word, just staring at me, and then, with feigned shyness or fear, would grasp a finger or hair strand. I would instantly go somewhere else, but couldn't help smiling when I saw her approaching. 'What a scorpion I am!' she would whisper. After about a week we were speaking again but avoided being close. I was walking her home again, we spent hours in her room, even kissed sometimes, but absent-mindedly and without a sense of participation. She showed me picture albums from her childhood – she was an unusually sweet little girl, appeared somewhat retro, perhaps because of the yellowing photos – or she projected slides on the wall, which were also photos, but in colour. Why did she look so sad in all of them? Even when she laughed from her heart, even when she was happy, she radiated sadness. No, Gina wasn't merely a demimondaine, as I had written in my journal. She had been poorly raised. She was given everything she wanted, but she remained a restless being, predisposed, beyond appearances, to suffering and unfulfillment. One of the slides that she showed me on the wall of her darkened room (I was sitting in semi-obscurity, my cheek glued to hers) showcased her in the courtyard to the Village Museum, where she often went, her grandfather being a specialist in folklore. Surprised in a 'medium shot', dressed in a light-green suit, with emerald clip-on earrings, Gina stared frankly at us. Perhaps it was the life size of the image on the wall, under the violet arrangement of icons on the glass, that inspired my unexpected gesture: I stood up from the sofa and leaned against the wall. Gina's image was now projected against my face, and our faces merged. With her eyes sparkling in the dark, next to the slide-projector's bulb, Gina mused that perhaps that was what our child would look like. Then, she took out the slide and left me stranded in the middle of the blinding rectangle of light.

I told her many times that I loved her, but it never made her happy, so I finally lost the courage to tell her any more. I lost any sense of initiative I ever had. I had to do what Gina wanted, unconditionally. She was the one who got the theatre tickets, she was the one who proposed we go to the movies; and if we went into a pastry shop or, with the coming of spring, stopped at a bistro, she never allowed me to pay for both of us. She always said no to anything that I suggested, even the most normal things. Sometimes, we even saw each other on Sundays, but only when she felt like it. If I proposed something for the following Sunday, she would initially agree, but then I could be certain to receive a phone call Saturday night cancelling our meeting. Certainly, at times I couldn't bear any more of this dependence that she imposed on me and became violent. I would even leave her in the middle of the street; I would tell her the most insulting words in order to end the misery that was accumulating between us. During those moments, however, Gina, who had been cold and contemptuous until then, began to cry, to tell me that she didn't want us to split up, that she liked me more than anyone else. I wasn't able to resist this emotional pressure and gave in each time with a feeling of guilt. But then, the same cycle resumed, and the contempt and ennui she showed me became once again the essential ingredient of our relationship. It was all the more depressing because I had been waiting for spring as a sort of rebirth from the winter's inferno. We left our heavy coats behind and, under the brilliant and humid sun, caught by the whirlwind of raw smells, even the leprosy of the shops on Venera Street and the bathroom-yellow of the Silvestru school seemed to take on the enchantment of a new and clean world. From the courtyards, you could hear the clatter of hooves, and the shiny granite of the pavement began to reflect, albeit distortedly, the blue of the sky. In place of the winter gloom through which I had walked Gina home, we wended our way now through the dense crepuscule with its heavy scent of grass and old limestone, with purple windows and bluish cornices. And now, when Gina flaunted her femininity on Sundays, arrayed in her delicate blouses and checked skirts held together by a large safety pin with a striated stone, now, when we walked together along our familiar routes on Pitar Moş Street, Ştefan cel Mare Boulevard and Cosmonaut Plaza, and just when I was beginning to feel capable of forgetting and starting from the beginning again, she would become cold, unrecognizably so. Her indifference was becoming the normal routine. Only after a few drinks did she become more affectionate, adding insult to injury. In April, I wrote in my diary: 'I find fewer things worth writing about. Last night in the rain, with Gina annoyed with me – her familiar façade of a carefree vamp – we haunted all the crowded bars (how does she know them so well: Let's go to the Union, let's go to Capşa, let's go to the Spanish Salon . . . ?), we waited half an hour at the Continental only to be told we couldn't have drinks without dinner (Gina knocking over the salt shaker and me reproaching her), then at Muntenia, dark sweet beer, music, me prattling about everything, progressively more agitated, her making faces, her eyes roaming over those characters hunched over the tables full of glasses, bottles, lighters, their fingers holding cigarettes, then again through the rain, she more temperate now under the umbrella, holding my arm with both hands, baby-talking, and then in the hallway ("Never change your love"), and then, next to each other, in the back, on the steps of the stairs, speaking exquisitely, seriously about love, then, the punch in the solar plexus, unexpectedly: "You know, I am in love . . ." and me believing at first, believing against belief and hoping against hope that she is referring to me, but after a moment: "Today, I drank to our divorce, OK? I know who the future will be . . ." To which, though I knew she was serious, I tried to answer jokingly. I took her face in my palms. She had that air of somnolent cunning: *je m'en fiche.* I stared into her eyes, concentrating harder than ever before. I forced her to remain in that position for a few whole minutes.'

Before the catastrophe, I remember only one event, when during spring break, we saw each other one more time. We were to meet at the Garden of the Icons in the morning. The air was cold and the sky extremely blue between the still bare trees. She was dressed with a coloured wool poncho over her jeans that covered the tips of her shoes. We sat on a bench on the sidewalk separating the park from Pictor Verona Street. There was no one in the park, only an older woman in the distance with a coffee-coloured dog wearing a vest and traipsing after her. I held my arm around Gina's shoulder, and she, kind and sensitive, knew these were to be the last moments of an ultimately beautiful relationship and savoured its melancholy end. I spoke to her quietly. I told her once again I couldn't give her up, that I loved her very much. She told me that we could remain friends, that friendship is a beautiful feeling, more beautiful than love, and so on. That she was not happy, that she felt she was in grave danger. 'I think he only wants to have fun with me. He likes to play around with women.' And I sensed that she really lived the panic she manifested when she told me this. We sat for a few moments staring absent-mindedly towards the posters of the Bulandra theatre, towards the dog that ran between the black trees, until she asked me to kiss her. Because of the lipstick, her lips tasted like perfume. I asked her while I caressed her not to tell me anything more about Silviu. She interrupted me and started to laugh between the tears: 'Silviu? You are a little behind the times. His name is Şerban . . . Here he is.' And breaking away from me – so utterly amused that she forgot to act sensitively – she extracted from underneath her blouse a medallion on a golden chain and popped it open with her nail, revealing a tiny black-and-white photo of a thin young man with short blonde hair. It was the first time I saw proof that she had a boyfriend. Until then, though rationally I knew it all the time, I had expected that she was making it up in order to make me jealous. Only now did I see myself marginalized in her world, insignificant, and I couldn't prevent myself from showing my revolt, my humiliation and pain. I tried to insult her, to hurt her feelings, until both of us stood up and left in different directions. I burst into tears at the trolley station by the church, not giving a damn who was watching me. I cried silently in the trolley, the tears spilling directly on to my jacket, and at home in front of my mother I had an actual attack of hysteria. I threw myself on the floor in the hallway and, dragging the rug with me, I cried like a child, waving my arms in desperate fury. My mother tried to calm me down, cursing that 'good-for-nothing Gina who brought my boy to such a state . . .' Only after half an hour was I able to sit quietly in a chair, but I couldn't eat anything. I felt that my only choice was to destroy myself, that there was no reason for me to go on living. I could barely breathe. After about an hour, she called me. She asked me to forgive her, which made me feel better. But this time I had absolutely no hope. On the contrary, I knew that it was absolutely necessary to forget her, otherwise I would not survive. I think that night I dreamed again of the infinite park, with misty, crepuscular alleys intersecting into the horizon, with the giant monument, larger than this world and made of ancestral brick. I made my way up to the cupola on the spiral stairway with the broken steps and walked again on the slabs of marble, infinitesimal under the cupola full of echoes and shadows. I felt endlessly alone in that monstrous dough-like amplification of my flesh; I could see the circular window getting closer and closer, like a purple sun at the top of the cupola. Crouching, I kept on growing, until I felt with my elbows and hips, with the top of my head, the soft and elastic walls of the vault. And abruptly, with a grunt and a rending scream, I penetrated the vault's window with my head. Sitting on a crust of ice that reflected the stars, I made my way on the surface of an infinite mirror, on the world's glass edge. The frost roared around me, then whirled towards the stars until they, too, were bandaged in thin layers of ice and frozen needles. But the solitude was even more penetrating than the cold. A silhouette tore itself from the fog and began advancing towards me, stepping on the mirror's sheen with naked soles. It was a woman, but her image in the mirror below was a man. She came close to me and took my face between her palms. She looked deep into my eyes, as though her life depended on what she had to tell me. I was trying to help her, to understand her, I emptied my brain to make room for her to get inside. I knew there was nothing to hope for, because she was a woman and consequently I would never be able to understand her.

The weather has gotten worse. Last night, I couldn't sleep because of the thunder and lightning. We don't even have drapes over the windows. When the entire room filled with that electric, palpitating blue, followed by that blast that nearly excoriated your bones, all the girls began to scream so loud that the night nurse on duty showed up and stayed with us, telling stories and singing, like in *The Sound of Music*. Mira and Altamira held each other tight and, cheek to cheek, stared around with frightened eyes like baby monkeys, while Laviṭa, in her multicoloured bed with the sheets pulled over her head, howled like a hyena. On the bedsheets she had drawn a postage stamp, about half a metre in length, with the perforations perfectly lined up, and with a picture of the wooden church from the Village Museum. And, of course, Elisabeta, whose condition is getting worse by the day, found it necessary to fall again and started to foam at the mouth and shake like a madwoman. The nurse had to turn on the lights, put a pillow under her head and press a hand over her mouth and nose, holding her tight for about thirty seconds until the convulsions abated. And this morning, when the nurse came in with the medicine cart, Elisabeta swallowed her tranquilizers with hollow eyes and propped herself up on the pillows. They didn't give her breakfast, which awakened our suspicions, and when the doctor came in, together with two nurses – one of them carrying a nickel-plated metal box – we understood they were getting ready to subject Elisabeta to that horrible process we knew about only from stories: lumbar puncture. Nothing frightened the girls more than these words. Paula and Maia – the latter a woman of about fifty who had been in the ward the longest and suffered from enuresis and noctur-nal ambulatory automatism – told us about a sick woman whose spinal cord was punctured right before their very eyes and whose lower body became paralyzed. They said that if they ever blew air into your brain in order to conduct an encephalogram, you would end up with such headaches that, until they sucked back out all the air, you were sorry you ever had a head on your shoulders. It made us gawk with horror and fascination at the martyrdom of Elisabeta, who was all drugged up and had no idea what was happening to her. A nurse removed her pyjamas, leaving her sitting up with her naked breasts on the white metal bed, then, pressing her chin into the chest and bending her spine, grabbed hold of her shoulders and nape. The vertebrae, like some lustrous knots of skin, and the elong-ated ribs broke into view from under the yellowish skin, which made you think of an ungraceful, masculine back. The target was just below the halfway point down the spine. The doctor palpated it with a rapid motion, and the nurse dabbed it with a piece of cotton doused, I think, in iodine. Then, from under the slice of medical gauze in the sterilized case, she extracted a long thin syringe with the plunger drawn all the way back, to which she attached a long needle, thick as a crocheting pin, with the tip slashed at an oblique angle. It seemed strange, but I did not see any trace of sadism on the faces of those who were getting ready to conduct torture, who were performing with an inhuman coldness. In all the paintings of mar-tyrs and saints, with their bodies crammed with arrows shot from a short distance, with breasts severed and then placed upon golden platters, with heads carried under the armpit of the decapitated body, with intestines extracted from the belly and spun around on a giant spindle, with virgins sawed in half from head to waist, the headsmen are portrayed as hideous, emaciated, leering at the sight of the suffering. They have sores, leprosy, astigmatism, fingers without nails: it is clear which side they are on. But now – look at Elisabeta, unsightly, epileptic, unwashed, in the hands of learned and delicate beings in white coats, nonetheless manipulating the devil's tools in a manner that provokes panic and suffering. I never believed that dentists, surgeons and others of that ilk torture you for your own good: all pain is bad, whether physical or moral, bad and humiliating. The burlier nurse, with greenish shadows under her white coat suggesting the slip, grabbed the syringe, aimed the needle towards that point between the vertebrae that glittered like spit on account of the iodine and, heaving, stabbed the needle into the skin. She paused for an instant, then stabbed again, until a tiny crack was heard. Elisabeta moaned in an odd, nearly sensual way, and then began to sigh. The nurse quickly detached the needle from the syringe at the very moment when golden drops – the spinal fluid – gushed out from its wide end; they collected it inside a gleamingly clean test tube. The girl huffed and moaned louder and louder until, with an effort, the needle came out, and then she howled with a raucous voice. They kept her balled up for a few more minutes, with a piece of cotton pressed over the needle stab; then, they put her pyjamas back on and slowly stretched her out on her back. Her head had to be kept still for at least twenty-four hours. Most of the women were ill and turned their heads; Laviţa hid under her bed-sheets and cried her heart out. Only I and the lady with the facial paresis saw everything: I twisting my locks with a nervous finger, she, her face frozen in a harlequin expression, smiling with one half of her face, weeping with the other, blinking the single eye. That was my entertainment for the night and morning . . .

The doctor came by my bed a moment ago and asked if I was done with my writing. Oh, Lord, no, not yet. What do these pages, spread out over the sheets and the night table, contain? Are they her work or mine? Can I still discern what is hers and what is mine? Again, I am afraid. Lost in the landscape of her brain, stepping upon uncertain terrains, through mother-of-pearl and pinkish zones, submerged in the valleys of her circumvolutions, in her vestibular precipices. Plunged into narrow paths along the obscure forest of her prosencephalon, mirroring myself in the waters of the epiphysis (but looking at whom?), crossing above the memory *bolgias* howling in the melted pitch, writhing under rains of fire flakes, rising, purified, in the mesencephalon full of reptiles and fanged birds, lost there in the arborescent ferns. And upwards, exploring the ecstatic states of the six layers of the neocortex, painted with Gina's portrait, deformed like a foetus over the hemispheres: flattened forehead, mouth with thick lips and enormous tongue, minuscule body, but hands with grotesquely fanned fingers the size of the entire body. And everywhere the conclave of worms, of insects, of reptiles, of mammalians, the gala-gatherings of Ramapithecines, Australopithecines, Pithecanthropes, then the Cro-Magnons, the Romans, the Celts, the Dacians, the Slavs, the Tartars, the great-grandparents, the grandparents (Maricu and Tanicu), the parents, the relatives, the friends, myself meeting with myself in her brain, but no Virgil, no Beatrice, not any sort of redemption, no climbing to the stars. I roam through the labyrinths of her mind, I pull the levers that roll her eyes, push on the pedals that cause her knees to bend. I stare at my thin fingers, my new fingers, the nail polish already peeling. It is with them that I have been holding my ballpoint pen. Therefore – who is the writer?

I don't have much longer to go. I will be finished in a few days. And then, because I have less shame than Lavița, I will leave this pile of pages on the night table. Let anyone read them, let them imagine what they will. Let them find any motivation they wish, let them interpret in any way they wish this mirror cover, this text, this texture, this textile. This rag, successful only when nothing can be seen through it. I wish neither to weave it endlessly nor to unravel at night what I weave by day; on the contrary, I begin now to take things even further, to enter the dragon's lair or the lair of Kafka's insect or Rilke's terrifying angel (I am certain, one way or another he will hold me close to his heart). But to write, in conclusion, that after our separation, following the ugly scene in the Garden of the Icons, Gina and I didn't talk for at least three weeks, maybe even an entire month. It was a dark period for me, and I don't know how I managed to come out of it. I wasn't able to read any more, to study during that period when my high school finals were coming up, and especially my entrance exams for the university. I had lost my self-possession, I didn't know how to go on living. I couldn't even walk by myself any more like I did before, as a remedy for loneliness, couldn't play ping-pong or go to the movies. A few of my closer classmates (I didn't have any real friends) felt the need to help and attempted to shake me out of my erotopathia. She was becoming progressively opaque in my eyes, as if she had developed an indecipherable mother-of-pearl crust. She didn't even pay any attention to me at school. After the first weeks of the spring trimester, I moved away from our desk without getting any reaction from her. She was greatly changed, as if she had aged by a few years. Her bearing had acquired a new kind of pride and defiance. She exhibited confidence, she finally appeared to know what she wanted, she was mature and strong. She didn't put on airs any more when she spoke with her friends, but instead enunciated everything in a kind of declaratory conviction, which according to her was a sign of experience. She was a woman, she had no time any more for questioning herself, for self-contemplation, she *knew*. Because of this high style she had adopted, she probably didn't notice me any more; she had made the jump and was among the powerful, while I was still yawning with the spasmodic jaws of adolescence's standing water. If I had had the strength to go on, it is possible that after high school, going my separate way, I would have succeeded in forgetting her, even though I couldn't imagine – I can't imagine it now – what the world might be like without Gina. Unfortunately, I wasn't able to forget her, and one night I wrote her a letter. I wrote her sixteen pages and dropped the letter myself in her apartment hallway's mailbox. I hadn't been in that hallway with its steps of white stone for a long time. Our route, Venera Street, where the leprous shops were being dismantled, Calea

Moşilor, which was also under construction, then Eminescu Street, Calea Toamnei, Victoriei Street, on which I walked her home in winter and returned with my hands in my pockets, seemed to me a living zone of a psychic nature, different from the anonymous streets of Bucharest's spider web. Because that's where the spider herself lay in ambush, and the strands still preserved the vibration of the hairy limbs and the warmth of the spherical belly. I knew it wasn't wise to write to her, but it was an action that sprang from a subliminal, affective logic, all the more powerful. I did what the situation necessitated. It was not a lachrymose letter; the tone was melancholy but dry, restrained, sometimes lightly cynical. I don't remember any of it now, but generally I explained how sorry I was we couldn't stay together and how much I wanted to penetrate her brain, her nerves, her veins, all the cells of her body, to understand, finally, who she was, to be able, finally, to communicate totally with her. She called me on the phone late in the evening, two days later; she was extremely excited. She told me she read my 'love letter'. 'If only you knew how to take me, if you knew how to play me a little . . . You meant very much to me, but I had no choice, you didn't have any know-how . . . But now I would do anything for you, ask me ANYTHING . . .' I told her I didn't want anything from her and that the letter had nothing to do with her, it concerned only me, I wasn't even interested in her reading it. I was shaking while talking on the phone, but I managed to maintain my cool in spite of it, because now, now I knew her.

Everything happened the next day (I don't even want to remember the date, there is no sense to it, it has become absurd since then to speak of time). Thinking intently about it now, I realize that, beginning with that morning, when I was awakened by an unbearable sun, something was not in order. My mother had washed the curtains and drapes that mantled the triple, panoramic window of my room, which was now traversed in all directions by the sunrise's watery rays, luminous as an apotheosis. I couldn't even open my eyes at first from all that light; I lingered for a few minutes in the peat bogs, gaseous wallows, the carnivorous sundew of the tangled dreams of dawn. I slithered for a time on the humid slide, clothed in a reddish mucus marred by transparently bluish excrescences; I swam with dolphin motions through a gelatinous liquid that densified sporadically in finger-like golden shapes, shoulder blades, vertebrae, lips, cranial plates, the forearm's veins and arteries, the lymphatic system, the structuring of the kidneys, everything flashing blindingly and dissolving at the instant of coagulation. A pavilion of ears, an orbicular muscle, four acuminate roots sticking out of a molar, a contorted face howling like the hereafter. I was floating in that phantomatic fluid, through the slithery corridor, until I was discharged into the open, and in the gelatin-filled chamber, in the very centre, I spotted the crepuscular solar disc, leisurely twisting like the bloody yellow of an egg. I hurled myself headfirst, traversing its membrane and plunging into an immense and unspeakable radiance . . .

In the afternoon, at school, she sought me out. It had been so long since we 'conversed', as she called it, that I saw almost no relationship between the real her, a girl of eighteen, and the way she appeared in my own mythology, an immense woman, without precise contours, without an objective reality, a field of forces rather that controlled my inner world. In a sense I had forgotten her – all the time calling her, thoughtlessly, soundlessly, *she* – I had forgotten the amusing Gina, the grinning Gina, a girl among other girls in the twelfth grade. During the breaks, we discussed trifles, and after the second hour, we sat together again at the same desk.

During history, we started to write verses, 'You one, me one,' and we were having so much fun that we almost got thrown out. But it was an armistice; I had no illusions, I only wanted to verify, like Kierkegaard, if the act of repetition was possible. And my very own Regine Olsen appeared to allow me to believe it, certainly only for the sake of playing the game. In the evening (the light persisted now, and the still blue of the sky did not refract even a drop of pink in the clouds' alabaster), I walked her home along the tranquil, echoing streets of our route, my heart increasingly heavier. Here and there, a small deserted plaza opened out into a bed of flowers or a tiny church in its centre. A little girl in a blue dress was bouncing a striped, multicoloured ball against a wall; she paused and stared at us as we progressed along the forged-iron spiked fences. I had no longer hoped to enter her room again, with the two rows of glass icons all around, with the upright piano draped in moisture, the painted dresser and the glossy scarlet drapes mantling the narrow window reaching up to the ceiling. Even now, with summer around the corner – standing next to the cold terracotta stove – it felt like the air in that room was perennially stifling, that the space itself was pliant and contracted around us both. At times, we felt like twins clustered together inside a hallucinatory uterus without exit, twins whose birth was refused from their very incipience. In fact, both Gina and I were Gemini, born in June, only a few days apart. I searched through numerous horoscopes, both the popular sort and those aspiring to scientific pretensions, and all of them were in agreement in one aspect: no love connection could last between twins, who are sufficient unto themselves and need a powerful zodiac sign, Scorpio or Taurus, to wrench them out of their narcissism. But, that evening, I thought nothing about the astrological implications of my relationship with Gina. She was sitting again next to me on the sofa, eating green walnut jam in a saucer with her minuscule silver spoon, urging me as before to sip the cinnamon-spiced wine from the crystal beaker. The act of repetition was possible: Gina was once again the pampered little girl, with yellow eyes and glossy complexion, whose lips cast only a chaste happiness. We talked till dark, I twirling her hair on my finger, she talking and laughing, playing with the fingers of my left hand. It was as if all of my presences in this room, from autumn till now, were superimposed over each other in successive layers of thick, polychrome lacquer, so that our world became, for me at least, more and more real but touching the hallucination's reality beyond the real. Each moment with her was *all* moments with her, each thing I looked at superimposed itself upon all my memories of it, until I could no longer identify the real objects from the hundreds of superimpositions. Her voice superimposed itself over her previous voice, superimposing itself in turn on the voice before that time, and in turn on the voice before. I didn't know any more whether it was autumn or spring, if it was the second or twenty-second time I had showed up in her room. I knew no longer how many times I left her sitting there on the sofa with fanciful pillows, how many times I caressed her breasts and rubbed my fingers against her back with its barely discernible shoulder blades under her warm, dry, slippery skin, under which you could feel an elastic layer of flesh, how many times I pulled on her blouse or pushed her checkered skirt into the centre, crumpling it into layering creases. When I pushed the fingers of my right hand under the elastic of her underpants, plunging them into the rough and curly hair . . . But she sat up, took my cheeks into her palms, and said with that contracted and imperious expression that she wanted to do everything with me. 'This time I want to, do you understand? But not here. Come with me, I will show you something.' Still embracing, we stood up, and Gina showed me a scarlet door with a cast-iron handle, between the wardrobe and the upright piano, which I didn't remember having noticed until then. Gina opened it, and we entered a narrow corridor with humid walls, irregular and grotto-like. Though Gina closed the door behind her, it didn't get completely dark despite the lack of a light source. We could easily make out colours and contours, and I could see Gina's silhouette walking two paces ahead of me as easily as in daylight. Each strand of her hair radiated a golden glow. She reached behind her with her hand in order for me to catch hold of her index finger, and we advanced this way along the narrow passage. I never asked myself where the corridor went; I allowed myself to be led by a strange fascination. From time to time, we descended a few steps that had been rudely cut in the wet rock. I began to feel the cold, a draft that billowed our hair and gave us goose bumps. The ground was becoming increasingly sticky, and in the puddles you could see all sorts of debris and leavings: plastic cups that once contained ice cream, mangled matchboxes, bologna peels in waxed paper, pads of filthy cotton. At a turn of the corridor, I spotted two tiny red balls held together with an elastic, the kind of thing girls use to bind their hair. As the corridor became more tortuous – the walls oozing with streams irrigating the pallid lichen flowers and scorched moss out of which, as we rushed by, emerged groups of oversized ticks – the residue multiplied: strands of coloured wool, photographs torn to bits, tram tickets, rag-doll arms, entire lengths of toilet paper. A toy cube with a turkey tail drawn on one of its faces and a cow udder on another. Torn guitar strings, rusty and unravelling. From time to time, Gina turned towards me with a sensual and self-satisfied grin. The air became denser, and through the water that now came up to our ankles swam the blind *Proteus anguinus* with transparent skin and tiny human arms. We could hear the sound of the traffic above us, the rattle of the trams and the gunning engines fading off in the distance. Here and there, some concrete casing, growing out of Bucharest's foundations into our corridor, spilled out an assemblage of twisted wires. At times, the corridor bifurcated, and then even Gina seemed puzzled, turning towards me with perplexed eyes. But then she smiled triumphantly, pointing a few metres distant towards the floor of one of the twin corridors, a lump of pink chewing gum or half a slice of cheese pâté, wrapped in the fuzz of decomposition. We followed that course, plunging further and further under the city that floated like a cloud above our heads. After wading up to our knees through water congested with larvae that fastened to our knees, we clambered up a few steps and our path became straighter and drier. Holding on to Gina's finger, just like I held on to Marcela's skirt in my childhood when we pretended to be trains, we traversed the last portion of the corridor, which rose upwards at a gentle slope, at the end of which you could make out a scarlet door, larger than the one in Gina's room. Before opening it, Gina paused and propped herself with her back against the humid wood. I embraced her, and we burst, nearly tumbling, into the darkness beyond the door.

Large surfaces of greenish glass flickered pallidly; behind them, the obscurity seemed to coagulate in indistinct forms. Gina closed the door and felt the wall on the right, where she found an electric panel. She pulled on a small handle in the shape of a fork and gradually, though you couldn't spot the light source, light began to inundate the place. Little by little, everything that we saw acquired shape and colour, became more and more alive and precise, as though each point of space was its own source of light. Soon, that entire row of chambers with their succession of display windows became visible as though bathed in the powerful light of neon. I knew this place so well! When I was a child, and even later, I visited it numerous times; it always seemed to be the most fascinating of places, the centre of the world's enigma. I never lingered in the basement much, as I was always in a rush to get to the animals and the birds upstairs, the gigantic skeletons and the cave full of bats. The pallid cadavers preserved in the jars of alcohol, the stuffed beings with glass eyeballs, some with visible seams, this whole necropolis of the Antipa Museum was to me a morsel of dreams inside the banal core of the cosmos. It seemed very natural during those moments that Gina's room would communicate with the Antipa Museum. But, in fact, the enchantment engendered by this surprise was so great that, though I continued to hold on to Gina's finger and smile at her, I had nearly forgotten about her. We were alone in the entire museum, we could experience it as no one had ever done before! She pulled at my finger impatiently, but all the while we roamed through the museum I couldn't help but pause to view avidly all the things that were exhibited. In the first room, on the shelves of the black display windows or on the tables protected with glass, pieces of solid matter, clumps and mineral plates flickered in all possible colours. I saw sylvanite, reddish cinnabar, galena and mica sphalerite in concave boulders, bismuth, yellow sulphur like bits of sugar cubes over which someone had urinated, striated gneiss, sandstone. Special areas were dedicated to semi-precious stones with matte surfaces or glistening like water: translucent green adventurine, the way it was represented in Piri Reis's map of the China Seas, thousand-coloured agates, from glassy brown to glassy red, from glassy blue to glassy orange, azure chalcedony, tiger's-eye quartz, which causes death within one year to whomever glances at it, Mokka stone of an unknown colour and without name, sardonyx, heliotrope, also named jasper, malachite the colour of poison, serpentine and prasopal, somber colleagues emanating loneliness. Thousands of times larger, formed (by whom?) inside gigantic subterranean bubbles, lying now on the thick glass, were the quartz geodes and the violet hedgehogs of the geodes of amethyst. The precious stones, polished, well-behaved, falsified, seemed like some anodyne and domesticated individuals next to the divinities of the *mundus subterraneus,* revealed by the science of Athanasius Kirchner. Opal, sapphire, turquoise, beryl and tourmaline attempted to compete with great imitation diamonds made of cheap glass: the Great Mogul, the large and the small Koh-i-noor, the fascinating Moonstone (nicknamed the Stewart diamond), the immense Cullinan diamond, larger than a tennis ball, the South Stone. I saw Gina's face reflected in all the window displays. She began to play along, and we tried to spot the most unusual stones. I put my arm around her waist and would sometimes catch her earlobe lightly with my lips, but she would tug me onwards through this taxonomic paradise. We quickly traversed obscure corridors opening out in dioramas with tiny windows, disclosing, through grossly painted molds, life in the Cambrian, the Silurian, the Devonian (only a few subaquatic forms, difficult to identify, an ilk of mollusks inside a conical but untwisted shell, with tentacles emerging out of the jaws, then a sort of corncob of an unnatural yellow, latched to the ocean floor by thin peduncles), the Carboniferous, the Permian, the Triassic, the Jurassic, the Cretaceous, with its ludicrous reptiles (Gina was shaking from laughter while staring at the 'great' *Tyrannosaurus rex*, about fifteen centimetres tall), the Miocene, the Pliocene, the Quaternary, (snowed-in mammoths across apocalyptic landscapes, beside which the Antarctic is mere child's play). In the corridor displaying fossils, Gina was up to no good: she unscrewed a nut holding in place the knee of the giant moose whose skeleton was dominated by yellow horns, mouldy and looking like plaster; she clambered up to the cupola of the carapaceous mammal and attempted to open the window behind which, like a kind of skeletal ostrich, was the diornis. Two fossilized eggs rested next to its claws in the sand. The display's window glided open, and Gina lifted in her arms, barely able to hold it, an egg the size of a rugby ball. I rushed to grab it in my arms and put it back in its place, but as she turned her back and was squeaking like a mouse, I bumped into her hand and the egg tumbled to the cement slabs with a dull thud of stone. The egg cracked, and while we rolled it back on the sand, we spotted a thin trickle of dark blood. We slid the window shut and ran. Starry-eyed and laughing, we finally paused before the dioramas featuring primitive men, black, naked and hunched over around a dry branch fire. Though they were naked, the attributes of the Neanderthal or Cro-Magnon men were almost completely missing, while the women could boast of profound endowment in the realm of mammary gear hanging from their thin chests. Matriarchy was not difficult to understand. The basement ended with an artificial cave, wrought in wax, with mummified bats strung up from the walls. At a turn, we stopped and kissed. In the clear lake, full of reverberations, water dripped from a stalactite with a metal pipe inside it. We walked up to the first floor. The entire space was brightly illuminated. Through the entrance's narrow slits, the night glistened with the blue glow of a trolley. I thought that perhaps the light of the museum must be visible to the world outside through all the windows, but Gina dragged me on as though there were a pre-established route and a timetable she had in mind from which we must not stray.

We penetrated the great madness of the invertebrates. Room after room of windows displaying monsters. Devils and angels of pallid meat were preserved in jars of alcohol. I thought of Michaux: 'Is it nausea that is coming or death?' Gina shivered. In fact, the first row of windows preserved a few rather graceful samples: tubular *Spongiae* like white lace or like the agitated leaves of algae or like a glass, a chalice rather, a Grail of sponge standing on a foot half a metre in height. The coelenterates displayed medusas in flattened jars, hallucinatory beings, greenish veils over rose veils over blue veils, then corals: *Corallium rubrum*, in tiny crooked trees of stone, sheeny, like plastic, the sea fan, like a lumbering branch full of blood and partly azure, the white and spherical madrepores, like lumps of salt. We advanced then to the worms, and Gina pretended to vomit, though some were particularly beautiful: purple or the colour of amber, with innumerable folds and undulations. The mollusks boasted of their giant octopus, pallid and disgusting in its jar, thick as a sewer pipe; next to it was the nautilus with its orange shell, striated with black, with its cluster of tentacles shooting out of its very eyes. And then came the innumerable insectariums we inspected as we passed, each causing us all sorts of exclamations, as if we were reviewing the uncanny fauna of another planet. How were all those hideous forms of matter possible? First the termites, teeming in their meter-long spherical lair, then the wasps, some long as a finger and black, the golden Vespa crabo, the hornet, the cicada, like unsightly flies, and the praying mantises who eat their husbands. Gina, enchanted, paused before the exotic butterflies which so often made a showing in her dreams (and I too have been dreaming of them since that time, the giant, multicoloured butterflies), and she pointed to some specimens with wings larger than the human palm; they were an electric azure or pallid, silky yellow, ending in a sparrow tail or a cobra head: worms with somnolent wings, some fluffy as velvet, others translucent as glass. Gina opened an insectarium and pulled out the largest butterfly along with its needle – I remember it was called *Polyphemus* – and fitted it to her chest. She then turned for me to admire her. On her left breast, which it covered completely, the butterfly slowly began to flap it wings and to push with its limbs into Gina's blouse in order to free itself from the needle. The giant beetles, shaped like seeds but weighing a quarter kilogram, and displaying all sorts of horns and mandibles, did not pique our interest. On the other hand, we could not tear ourselves away from the window that displayed, with their pincers outstretched and in utter monstrosity – the spiders. It is odd that these faces of horror never appeared in the medieval paintings about the temptation of Saint Anthony, about the journey to Inferno or the embodiment of the Devil in the centre of Hell. Compared to it, the horned and hoofed Devil is ludicrous. And their names in the procession of their jars: all of them suggesting, in wise Latin, horror, convulsion. Some were thick, with powerful bodies and short legs, with visible claws, others with extended hooks, red as if dipped in blood. Some were thin and dry, like the tarantulas, with pallid and black bellies, with sinister crosses or purple patches, like the sting of a syringe; others spherical, with their hair-like legs ten times the size of their bodies. Among them, the bird-hunting spider, the size of a large frog, black and hairy like a grotesque sex, was the embodiment of horror itself. Gina could hardly tear her eyes away from that body with its protracting chelicerae. She fanned out the fingers of her left hand and glued them to the cold glass of the window, superimposing them over the claws of the spider. The steamed contour of her hand remained on the glass.

The scorpions were easier to stomach. They were identical, from the imperial sizes to the ones that fit inside a matchbox: amber-like, semi-transparent, with a greenish-black stripe apparent through the opal crust: the path of the poison traversing the tail's segments and arriving at the tip of the stinger. The large-sized claws, like the crab's inoffensive ones, provoked no horror. As though we had lingered too long to study the spiders and were suddenly late, we left quickly and only briefly perused the crustaceans (a rabbit-sized lobster, the red crawfish in a jar), the myriapods, the scolopenders; we paused a bit to admire the starfish, ophiuroids with long and tangled arms and five-cornered stars that looked like coral and were now appropriated by death's pallor. I was paying more attention to Gina, refracted in the greenish windows. She looked increasingly uncanny, transfigured. Her smiles became more stereotypical, like a kind of promise; they were insinuations which I didn't completely understand. She towed me on by my finger and at times, while I lingered excessively, huddled close to my shoulder and pulled or pushed until she dislodged me. How wonderful it was to roam through the fish chamber, full of artificially painted fish with torn skin! The sharks, the narwhal with the two-metre-long tooth, from which the legend of the unicorn came, the sea devil of rhomboid shape measuring four metres diagonally, like a dragon with black skin, too large for window display and placed on top of it. And then, inside a multitude of glass cylinders filled with a bluish soup, rotted the pale fishes with bulging eyes: the balloon fish, the porcupine fish, the moon fish, the sea sparrow with bird wings lined with orange striations. The salamanders and the frogs – from the tree frog to the toad with human eyes and the giant black frog of Titicaca that weighed a kilogram – the innumerable reptiles: the tuatara, the water monitor, the chameleon (bereft of the fabled colours), all seemed to have come out of the pages of the treatises on demonology, from *Maleus Maleficarum*. Poison fermented inside those nightmare beings. Gina dashed towards the glass containers where, coiled around tree trunks, awaited the python and the anaconda. She opened the container and, with a gesture that surprised me, she glued her cheek to the thick and scaly length of the giant snakes. She took the triangular head of the anaconda between her palms and stared at it with concentration. Though made of glass, the reptile's clear red eyes were fascinating. This time it was me who had to pull Gina away through the soft-bellied venomous snakes and the procumbent crocodiles sprawled out on wooden pedestals. The gharial exhibited its long thin snout, reminiscent of the duck's bill, and its sawteeth. Red as coral and sporting wide, black rings, the Surucucu snake coiled in the window next to the famished cobra and the rattlesnakes – horned and hornless. The turtles, sitting close to the reptile room's exit, were the most presentable beings in that Inferno. The soup turtle, the elephant turtle, the sea turtle amused us slightly in their geriatric melancholy, but Gina scowled because, being affixed to ledges, she couldn't ride them.

There were only a few mammals of the primitive kind in the small rooms along the first floor extending out of the reptile corridor: the flying dogs of Java with wings of black and glossy skin, as though buffed with shoe polish, held up by tiny pneumatic bones and claws shooting out of the shoulders; the ubiquitous marsupials: kangaroos, like truncated cones, much smaller than I believed, wolves endowed with the marsupial pouch and other exotic Australians. The leering beaver, ready to imprint the Masonic triangle in your palm if you shook its paw, the anthill (without Dalí and Buñuel) and the porcupine, more rodent than pork, all contorting their mugs and displaying their artificially retouched seams and sutures in the window on the left. In the right window paraded the cylindrical ilk of the moles, the rats, the mole-rats, and the hedgehogs feeding on earthworms and milky pupae. And through the Caudine Forks of those dubious ancestors, you could gain entrance to the chambers of the true mammals, in glass cages, grouped in pairs like in Noah's Ark and gravitating around gigantic skeletons: the rosy-yellow, walrus-like curving tusks of the deinotherium, the smaller, dark, purplish ones of the mastodon. Gina ran, leaving behind a trail of wolves, otters, leopards, snow leopards, antelopes, boars, giraffes, hippopotami, badgers, polar bears, seals, lions, bisons, wart hogs, wildcats with dappled fur the colour of the earth or of the snow, or furless, with skins thicker than three fingers, all of them frozen in full motion on their stumpy or graceful paws, all with friendly features or misanthropic jaws or fearful or perplexed expressions, some smaller than a ball, others reaching to the ceiling, some with camouflage patches and stripes or merely monotone, all with eyes of glass, with a somewhat innocent look, a cascade of glass buttons. She settled herself underneath the deinotherium. Only two metres above our heads were the curved yellowish ribs, the spine's stumpy bones, the large skull bigger than our two bodies put together. Between the monster's legs, thick as poles, we could see the rods and screws that kept it all together. The giant with clay legs. She didn't have to say anything, it was telepathy that we thought about attacking it at the same time. I still ask myself, among many other things, what caused us this obsession to destroy it. We worked at it for about half an hour, loosening nuts, pulling out screws and crossbars, until the old skeleton tumbled to its knees. There was nothing else we wanted. Triumphant, we clambered along the vertebral column to the top of the skull like Indian elephant riders and settled there on the hard, smooth bone, gazing with contempt at the dead creatures around us. I thought for a second that they emitted a rumble of revolt, as though the fur of all the hundreds of species suddenly bristled up in apprehension. There was nothing left to do here. Wending our way past the diorama exhibiting a sea elephant and a seal in an Arctic landscape, we climbed the steps to the next floor under the watch of all sorts of horns and craniums. Here, in the square chamber around the deinotherium room, the air was full of birds. They all turned their round eyes to look at the velvety butterfly pinned to Gina's chest, whose soft wings were still beating. Otherwise, they were completely motionless, each one on its own wooden pedestal. Gazing at the narrow beaks, those painted crows whose stuffing was coming out through the cracks, or the thick and stumpy beaks belonging to the toucans, or the rhinoceros bird's, formed like a needle, or the ones of the bumblebee-sized hummingbirds, I thought of the line from the Dimov poem: 'The toucan manes and hilarious lares'. The feathers, too, were stale, discoloured: what had been a Prussian blue or emerald green in a peacock's tail, fox-rust in the pheasant's, what had once been the rainbow in the feathers of parrots or birds of paradise had now turned to brownish ash, or had been stridently retouched, and you had the impression you were watching those wedding pictures with colour added in pencil or the beguilingly blush cheeks of the consumptive. Clearly, we didn't like them, so we entered the glorious path of anthropogenesis, represented by a few narrow corridors with displays and dioramas parading monkeys, from the tiny macaque and guenon, ambling after oranges with their coiling tails, the human faces with cat bodies, to the flying lemurs and the howling mandrills, the red-butted monkeys (visibly painted and plastered), the baboons, ancestors of the Pygmies, with prolonged rump-like noses. Gina, of course, was supremely amused. She separated a baby chimpanzee with comically threatening features from its mother's arms and swayed it to her chest, caressing its helmet of hair. Further on, she patted a large gorilla on the shoulder like an old friend, an odiously ugly male with the brutal face of a habitual criminal. She stood before him and hit him in the chest with her fist: 'Tarzan.' Then she struck her own chest: 'Jane.' And again: 'Tarzan. Jane. Tarzan. Jane.' I was laughing noiselessly, as I usually do, nearly choking. The red orangutan, on the other hand, with long paws like Popeye the Sailor Man, had a face like a melancholy white clown, hopelessly in love with a Colombina fated for the arms of another. After that, we didn't feel like laughing any more.

We broke into a circular room that attempted to present the process of ontogenesis by drawing parallels between fish, reptiles, birds, mammals and finally humans. On the mounts submerged in alcohol, you could view the evolution of an embryo from the phases barely visible with the naked eye – the morula, the blastula, the gastrula – to the differentiation of the organs. In their evolution, the embryos passed through archaic phases, developed gills, reptilian characteristics, atavistic formations that later became reabsorbed, a veritable metempsychosis, the wheel of karma, the incessant cycle of existence. On a wall hung a sectioned cast revealing the position of the foetus in the womb of a pregnant woman. I recalled the atrocities of the Tartar wars: babies wrenched alive from the mothers' bellies. Further on, distributed in a sequence on a shelf on the wall, were tens of jars containing malformed foetuses: macrocephalic or acephalic, infants with a single central eye, with a single nostril above the lips, with three legs, one of which had no foot, with minuscule, armless palms emerging directly from the shoulders like tiny wings. How uncanny they looked, wrinkled and pale or mollusk-yellow, with their distended skin drooping on their bones! What slothful stares in their eyes shrouded by flaking lids! They seemed wise and in no small measure satisfied that they didn't get their turn at living. They catalogued between frogs and geniuses, impossible to face in their cynical carnality. Dangling their umbilical cords in the nauseating liquid, their gaze seemed to pin us, they seemed to take us in. Gina perused them, not with horror like me, but with a kind of placid resignation, as though contemplating a piece of ugly furniture in the house where you've lived all your life and which you'd never think of exchanging. We crossed that chamber, examining each abortive creature separately. As she had done with the snake, Gina glued her palms to the curved walls of one of the jars and, with painful concentration, she stared deeply into the eyes of the pallid gnome. Finally, through a narrow door that I had not noticed, we entered a garret-like room the size of Raskolnikov's 'wardrobe', with peeling posters on the walls, an old sofa that occupied more than half the space and a tiny bookshelf. I remember some of the ragged volumes: *The Tibetan Book of the Dead*, Nerval's *Daughters of Fire*, Dostoyevsky's *Netochka Nezvanova* and a book of Blake's engravings, with plates from *The Book of Urizen*. One of the plates had been torn out and attached with thumbtacks to the wooden door: it depicted a kneeling woman, seen from the back, looking into a fountain. Above her scintillated a gigantic black sun. We sat on the sofa, and Gina pulled from under the bed a shoebox filled with all sorts of knick-knacks: Christmas tree ornaments, dolls with crunched heads, old photos, used tickets and postcards, a rusty syringe, a stethoscope. 'When I was very, very small, I discovered the way to this place. I would bring everything here that made me happy, everything I liked: my dolls, gifts from relatives, I would bring my cookies here so I could eat them in peace. I don't think I missed a single night when I didn't roam through the museum, alone amidst all my animals. This is how I imagined the old man's daughter from Penelope's tales, roaming among the ridiculous dragons. I know them all, they are all in the grips of bewitchment, as I am too. But most of all I like this little room, deep, deep, deep in the middle of it all. This is where I feel that I am really myself.' While she spoke, Gina, now long transfigured, became another, a strange sorceress, a priestess with ecstatically joined hands. I took her in my arms and put her down on the sofa. We made love, for the first time in our lives. It is not out of modesty, which has no place in these pages, that I speak little about those gestures, those sensations, but simply because I didn't for one moment have the consciousness of what was happening to me. Though completely naked but more alive than ever, she seemed now to possess an infinite contour that lacked reality. She was, in succession, a mouth on whose lips the skin had faded, a small breast, waves of hair scattered on a pillow, agitated breath. When I entered, the mosaic of all those impressions melted and seemed to ooze, soft as plasticine and of the same colour, and smelling almost like linseed. I suddenly had a sense of the All. It was like a pale light, a kind of tension without limits, an intuition without communication. We spent a moment in suspension and then, like lizards in the morning, shook off the stupor and returned to our limited life.

I woke up transformed, transferred into Gina. It is impossible to postpone the description, the experience of having lived through that moment, indescribable and unlikely for anyone to have lived through. I lay on my back and looked at myself in the pupils of the diffuse being leaning over me: I saw Gina's face there, slightly deformed by the eye's sphericity. When the cone of my consciousness quieted a little, I became aware that the being above me had my features and was staring at me with unceasing terror. I looked at my body, which was the body of the woman I loved: I had her arms, her breasts, her hair, her hips, her legs. I had her skin and her bones and on my lips the ether taste of her rouge. One ear glittered with her emerald earring; I spotted the other earring amidst our crumpled clothes on the bed. And she was me, the long and lanky male frame, bones showing through the skinny chest, narrow hips, the sex like a worm between the hairy thighs and, especially, my face, my eyes, my elongated jaws, my moustache above sensual and suffering lips. It was me hovering above myself, in a way that I had never seen myself, not even in dreams, as though I had come out of my body after death and was contemplating myself from all angles. If she had changed into a rhinoceros or an insect, it would not have been so shocking. Horrified, we stared at each other for a long time without speaking or touching each other. We were too tired and dumbfounded to even think. We dressed mechanically, mixing up our clothes, having to exchange them a few times. Our gestures were uncertain, our movements stuttered, the hand fumbled in its grasping. We looked at one another like beings from another world, whose functioning depended on an entirely different chemistry, biology, psychology. Suddenly, the person in front of me fell on the bed and began to weep violently, sobbing and moaning, pounding the pillow with clenched fists and shaking all over like someone possessed. But out of those outbursts of wailing, another sound became distinguishable. It came from beyond the wooden door and resembled rustling an admixture of soft sounds: ripples, crackles, a soft clatter like that of brushes or maracas. Hearing this, the one next to me (I speak this way because I can't call that person 'he') became silent, then, with a perplexed expression grabbed my hand and dragged me with an unsuspected force out of the room. Stepping forwards, the heel of my shoe pierced the giant butterfly, ragged wings still softly fluttering on the floor.

That muffled jungle sound intensified with each passing instant. Bursting out into the foetus chamber, we saw them opening their eyes wide and making bizarre gestures in their greenish jars. One of them managed to clamber on top of the cylinder's edge and was getting ready to jump to the ground, dragging after it an umbilical cord half a metre long. I would have been paralyzed with horror had not Andrei yanked me quickly out of the room. An exhausting race followed. The halls were awakening. The display windows began to move, snouts yawned, eyes rolled. The birds began to caw and clatter, to beat their wings in order to escape from the branches to which they were nailed, and stirred the suffocating dust, smelling of paint and seaweed. We ran down the stairs followed by the piercing yell of the peacocks and sped through the first-floor halls.

The deinotherium's skeleton, bones the size of tree trunks, made enormous efforts to stand again, filling the surrounding space with trepidations. All around, inside the glass cages, the animals, herbivores and carnivores, began to stretch, as after a long sleep. The leopards undulated their tails and snarled, the wildebeest pounded its hoof, the giraffe raised its spotted neck. In the 'Life in the Antarctic' diorama, the sea elephant bared its fangs, three times the size of the walrus's, and roared, its walls of fat shaking under the gloss of the skin. We ran desperately as we heard the windows shatter behind us. We scampered to the basement, making our way through a swarming of frightening proportions. The air was braided with multicoloured butterflies, cicadas, scarabs, bats, flying dogs. A flying fish escaped from its jar and pierced the hall like an arrow, bashing its head into a wall. The gigantic bugs, the praying mantises, the spiders and scorpions, were teeming on the ground, forming a live carpet of horror. The worms were creeping along with the cobras, the python began to unfurl its rings from the tree trunk, while the rattlesnake tinkled threats with its tail. All these beings seemed a little dizzy at first but were returning quickly to life. With slothful hearts, the medusas pulsated in their pure alcohol, while the heavy fish tossed about till they overturned the cylindrical jars and now were pounding their wet tails against slabs of concrete, yawning from their toothy jaws. Huffing, we finally arrived back where we started: the minerals were casting coloured shadows on the walls. We found the light lever and turned on the electricity but there was no trace of the scarlet door leading to the subterranean corridor! We fingered the walls, nearly weeping from desperation, without finding anything. The only way out was the museum gate. If it was locked, we would be lost. We turned around, confronting the waves of insects which were now alert and aggressive. It was clear that they were not merely swarming at random but were proceeding against us: the scorpions thrust their tail-stingers into the leather of our shoes, the butterflies dashed against our faces to make us dizzy, red ants were crawling all over our feet and legs. The animals on the first floor, roaring and bellowing, snorting and squeaking and barking, were heading towards us like a wall of sharp fangs and horns. We were banished. We barely found the museum's gate. It seemed like an eternity till we pried it open and burst out into the cool night air. When we slammed it shut behind us, we heard, like an earthquake, the wave of animals, birds, reptiles, insects dashing against the heavy bolted gate. We ran down the main entrance's steps. Victory Square, feebly lit by a few orange streetlights, was deserted. Only very far off in the distance could you spot a cop, walking the tedium of his beat. We took each other's hands and looked into each other's eyes for the last time. There was no need to talk. We knew that everything was lost, that from now on we were each on our own. We left for the homes to which our new feet and bodies took us. We would never know what we had to do except by doing it.

That is everything. I know nothing new about Gina. Who she is now, how she is surviving. I don't know, and I don't want to know. I don't recognize any longer in this alien body the girl who was my obsession and madness for the duration of a year, maybe the last one of my life. To attempt to continue living under these conditions seems absurd. I protected my consciousness from seeing her body by covering the mirrors with the beguiling texture of sheets. But I can't protect myself from her self, which ambushes me on the far more perfidious paths of the psyche. The monster has me, he crept up on top of me and clenches me tight in his paws. I fuse with him like the damned in the thieves' infernal *bolgia*. Even these thoughts, I ask myself, are they mine or hers? Where does this sweetness that coats so many of the pages of my confession come from? This pathetic style, which goes against my nature? Could they not be the beast's venoms, the juice trickling out of his gums? It was a mistake to begin this writing, to raise this curtain, to act in this psychodrama, with the peanut gallery and box seats all empty. Whom did I write this comedy for? Are you, now, next to me? Can you, now, help me?

Unfortunately, next to me now, staring languorously over my shoulder, is only Lavița, who is waiting for her bedsheets to be changed. While waiting, she keeps on composing her love letters, with her diverse coloured-ink pens, directly on to her body, which she has covered everywhere she could reach with naive letters and drawings. Now she is writing on her chest, with green ink: *Please write me back,* and next to it she scrawls a girl's head with brown hair, blue eyes and red lips. That's how it is. In any case, it will be necessary to get out of here, where I am doing nothing but endlessly postponing the fight with the beast. My obsession does not allow itself to be exorcised, writing this I do not become myself again, and I don't want, O Lord, I don't want to remain like this. That's why I postpone any decision until I return to the world. There I will decide what I will do and, especially, how I will do it. These pages, lying in a heap on the night table, are a greater failure than what I am recounting. I will burn them this very evening. I decided not to leave them any more in the care of the doctor or anyone else, because if they read them they would never let me out of here, or I might even end up in worse places. I will simulate – with disgust – normality; I will be a well-behaved little Gina, ready to make her grandparents happy, having returned to normal thoughts after a bout of hysteria.

Why am I continuing to write these lines, if I know that I will destroy everything? Why am I composing, look, one letter, and, then again, another? Isn't it maybe to barter for another mouthful of air, and one more after that?

No, it must be ended, finally. All right. I am finished.

You wrench the wardrobe's mirror door out of its hinges and fling it to the floor. A muffled clatter informs you the mirror has cracked, falling face down on the floor from which you had removed the rug. The rolled-up rug lies on the sofa, over the fanciful pillows of velvet and orange silk. You drag the upright piano on its casters to the middle of the room and lean the Persian rug against it. Heaving horribly, you lift the sofa on its side and prop it as well against the glossy piano. It fits perfectly between the bronze candleholders soldered to the piano's top. You pause to catch your breath and wipe your dusty hands over the yellow blouse covering your breasts. You go to the window. Venera Street blinks weakly, with the pavement's stones gleaming purplish sparks under the autumn's laden twilight. The willow with a long branch tapping against the marquee palpitates in the gentle breath of wind. An orange cat spotted with dark rust dozes at the crossing of two branches. You leave the window open, but pull shut the scarlet damask drapes. A reddish penumbra permeates the room. A ray of light, piercing through the drapes, collides with the burnished corner of the library, supporting the metal crucifix that glows abruptly with a white flame. You begin to remove the books from the library and arrange them, with a specific goal in mind, on the floor around the piano and the sofa. You take the great Baltrusaitis from its cardboard box and read the dedication: '*To Gina, with love, to remember that under the obscene rococo of our world and flesh, our bones are Gothic and our spirit is Gothic. Andrei, Feb. 197–*' You leaf through the great poet's pages, so full of chimeras. You place the book on the floor next to the others. You suddenly mimic a maddened rock guitarist, leaning back and clutching the guitar's neck with your left hand. '*Into the fiiiire!*' you scream, and begin to laugh. The so-called bookshelf was nothing but a black-lacquered structure and, without the books, easy to push towards the middle of the room. But you get easily tired and have to take long pauses each time you move a piece of furniture. Fortunately, there isn't much left in the room, which now appears taller, the candelabra hanging from the ceiling seeming to hoist the clinking crystal icicles to a greater height. Now, you grab the large armchair, marvellously wrapped in satin with greenish flowers on a pale pink background. You turn it upside down and prop it against the sofa, securing it with the rug's lightly crinkled corner. You open wide the bureau's doors, on which the Renaissance scene was painted, with the beautiful inscription above it in Latin characters: AMOR OMNIA VINCIT. You twist them out of their hinges and fling them negligently on the parquet. Inside, on the shelves smelling of sandalwood, are numerous tiny polychrome bottles, matte or transparent, fashioned out of sparkling crystal or modelled out of soft glass. Yellowish liquids, or greenish like poison, flutter their light sails inside. You take one in your fingers. You read the golden, sophisticated calligraphy on the label: *Soir de Paris*. You stand and, holding it in your fist like a grenade, smash it abruptly against the parquet. The ginger perfume explodes in hundreds of shards, leaving a wet spot whose drops scurry out in all directions. The sensual smell fills up the room. One by one, each bottle shares the same fate. You read the designations: *Sensation, Fidji, Magie Noire,* then dash them with all your might against the floor, covering your eyes with the left hand to avoid the splinters. You pause and save from destruction the last two or three bottles and a jar of blue medicinal alcohol that you find in a separate compartment; instead you drain their contents over the piled up furniture in the middle of the room, murmuring 'Pour on the carpet powerful perfumes/Bring me roses to drape all over you' and laughing hysterically. You step over the puddles of French perfume, crush with your wooden soles jars of cream and tubes of tawny beige foundation. A voluptuous vertigo overtakes your already weary body. You feel like going to sleep, like Huysmans' Des Esseintes, in his artificial paradise. But you know there will be enough time for sleep. Stepping up on a stool, you take down from the walls, one by one, the marvellous glass icons, with their worlds, red like blood, the golden and azure St. George on his winged horse with a human face, piercing with his lance the ridiculous green reptile, fierce only because of the two or three frail tongues of fire shooting out of its mouth. A skeletal Jesus showing off the wound in his ribs, from which a twisted grapevine, loaded with clusters of grapes and thin stems coiling like corkscrews, creeps heavenwards. The Mother of God sleeping under a purplish quilt, watched over by angels with wings and golden nimbi. Lazarus, wrapped up in bandages like a mummy, sitting up on his elbows in the grave's greenish box, while Jesus points to a rolled parchment displaying, probably, the motto: 'Get up and walk!' The Archangel Gabriel, in armour, his lance propped up against his shoulder, also bearing the same sort of parchment. Each icon, detached from the wall, leaves behind it a pale rectangle dressed in palpitating strands of spider webs. The putrefied wood of the frames, with thousands of tiny insect-drilled cavities. You lower the first tier of icons and then the second, totalling about fifteen or sixteen. You step down, nearly falling off the stool. The air is almost impossible to breathe. You laugh like an idiot, with large tears gushing out of your ether-irritated eyes. After waiting a while with your back to the wall, you start to arrange the icons between the books, around the furniture. Everything is beginning to look like it's supposed to.

The wardrobe is last. Shaking, you plunge your hands up to the shoulders into the shelves and begin to drag out entire armfuls of lingerie, blouses, T-shirts, checked trousers, skirts of various materials, shiny and rustling slips, discothèque vests, whole boxes filled with cosmetics and socks – yellow, striped, scarlet – a few pairs of blue jeans, some imported and not yet worn, others already faded, ethereal dresses of retted linen, black headwraps with golden coins. You place them on top of the piano, smoothing them with your hands until, amidst the taller furniture, it all begins to look like an inviting, polychrome sleeping nest of delicious softness. Then, from the wardrobe's other partition you pull out a multitude of hangers holding evening dresses, some of them old and scrupulously embroidered and thick as brocade, others of light silk, then a few vests and fur hats. There is a white sheepskin coat, with black and red ornaments, overcoats – citrus yellow and a cream-coloured one, another of fox fur that Gina never wore at school – and three long and fluffy jackets, all hooded. Underneath, you find a few of her innumerable pairs of shoes, certainly the ones she loved most: minuscule, of patent leather, some with tiny metal studs. You empty everything and spread it all over the unusual edifice in the middle of the room, anywhere that you can fit it. You give up the thought of dragging the wardrobe into the pile; you are not able any longer, especially now with this infinite somnolence creeping in your bones.

Everything is ready. The room looks as if it was prepared for painting. You laugh hysterically as you drag yourself along the naked walls, marvelling at the echo of your laughter in the devastated room. You can hardly stand. You grab the yellow dress, the heavy one with pleats and folds, and pull it over your head. Absentmindedly, you bind the laces at the neck and the wrists. You stroke your breasts and hips, caress your long locks falling over your shoulders while staring into the void. You head for the large terracotta fireplace and extract from behind it the can that you prepared beforehand. You sprinkle the entire pile of furniture and clothes, and then, keeping your head turned to avoid breathing in vapours from the brownish-yellow liquid, you pour it on your dress. 'This is all,' you shout, 'it's all, it's everything!' You feel like vomiting, and actually do in a corner of the room. But you manage to maintain your lucidity for a little while longer. You crumple a newspaper you pick up from the floor, and you clamber, squeezing underneath the rolled-up carpet on top of the piano, sheltering yourself in the thick layer of perfumed clothes. You ignite with the lighter the crumpled newspaper and throw it below, between the piano and the sofa. You hear the crackle of the flames, turn around on your stomach, plunging your cheeks into the waves of intoxicating cloth.

You fall asleep instantly.

REM

Cortázar, a copy of García Márquez in tatters (*Innocent Eréndira*, the large edition), *The Saragosa Manuscript*, in a stiff, scarlet cardboard binding, about a metre's length of *The 20th Century Novel*, and much longer and multihued rows of *The Library for All* and *The Universe* volumes; glossy books in black and white published by The Library of Art (I instantly spy *The Wisdom of Forms* by Sendrail, Brion's *Fantastic Art* and all sorts of other texts that prattle on about the Gothic style, about Mannerism, the Baroque, the Rococo and modern art, whose origin can be found in any case in the Gothic, Mannerist, Baroque, or Rococo styles). The shelf bulges under the weight of the abundantly lacquered art books resting at an angle, the size of a drawing board and smelling of chemicals. One volume alone faces out. On the cover you can see a kind of wooden trailer with doors wide open amidst a landscape of reddish buildings with archways and battlements melting into unending perspectives. It appears to be twilight but not very late. The shadow of a little girl rolling a hoop lengthens out on the macadam. You can see only the spine of the other books, with the painters' names in clear white: Tintoretto, Guardi, Da Vinci, Degas, Harunobu, Pontormo, Mantegna. Most of the other shelves are taken up by poetry: the striped and dappled collection of *The Most Beautiful Poems* (how well coffee brown goes with Eliot, strident green with American poetry, brick with Yannis Ritsos! You couldn't imagine it any other way), the *Orpheus* collection, with covers like blotting paper, ashen blue (here, let us remember the good Dylan Thomas – 'as I was young and easy under the apple boughs . . . '), finally the square-shaped yet not lacking in aesthetic sense *Poesis* collection, with the sombre black of Wallace Stevens and the deep green of Rimbaud. An entire wall of books, all the way up to the ceiling, resting on almost invisible shelves. A harmonious jumble, a cosmos. Are you a philosopher? You'll find yourself there, in your cream-coloured toga, with an azure blue rectangle on the book's spine where your name and what you wrote are inscribed. An essayist? You'll find yourself there, between Petros Haris and Camus, and you will don the black garb. Are you a political theorist, a nuclear expert, biologist with somewhat original ideas, sociologist, anthropologist? You belong in *Contemporary Ideas*. You have the right to choose your colour, from lemon yellow to pansy purple. Are you something undefined, an obscure novelist or perhaps an all too well-known pedagogue? Separate volumes, with all the advantages and disadvantages. Are you a construction engineer, expert in the strength of materials, boilermaker, mathematician? We regret, but the lady who lives in this studio apartment will never buy your books.

A minuscule studio apartment, situated somewhere towards the outskirts of the capital. You get there after changing a number of buses and then walking along a tangle of narrow ashen streets. The walls along the building's stairs are painted a pale green and reek of garbage. An asparagus plant, completely withered, in a flower-pot resting on forged iron legs, a peeling picture of the Voroneț Monastery, an oleander in a wooden box teeming with tiny kitchen bugs, these are the kinds of things you see along the hallways at the end of the long rows of numbered doors, which you can only imagine as terribly thin. A building of studio apartments, Comfort Level 3. Her room, however, is tidy and cozy. Under the endless shelves (I spot now a few voluminous and heavy treatises on oncology, a book about adenopathy, another with an aggressive purple title: *Leukaemia*) rests a double sofa, covered by a wide, reddish bedspread that appears to be very warm. It makes sense. Heat doesn't travel very well to the city's peripheries. The floor is made of sandstone slabs, a couple of ashen rabbit furs thrown over it. You barely have enough room to walk past the sofa. Still, a tiny coffee table – on top of which lie a basket of apples and an ashtray – has been squeezed into that narrow space. Under the coffee table there are newspapers and magazines, especially *The Morning Star, Horizon* – and, underneath, a yellowed issue of *Literary Romania*. Near the window, to the left, a niche with a sink and the rudimentary idea of a kitchen table. Immediately next to the entrance, the bathroom, fitted with a toilet bowl and a shower. On the neatly painted walls, a few tapestries in muted hues: a sunset, a little girl next to a goose and a woman reading a letter by the window (more than likely after Vermeer). Of course, she embroidered them herself when she was a girl.

There is no one presently in the room, but I feel her coming. The thread that connects me to all those buses that she takes, with impossible-to-remember numbers (three hundred sixty what? One hundred twenty what?), to the streets she walks on bordered by schools and shops, is vibrating. I extend my transparent paws through the room. I am quivering from the eagerness of expectation. I lie in wait at the window, then swiftly jump to the door. I squeeze through the books, leaving out only my hooks, dripping with venom. I crepitate through the bathroom, rummage through the pots and pans in the tiny kitchen. It is the old hunger, the old vigil that never ends. On an armchair, situated at the head of the bed by the door, a folder fastened together with strings. Next, a mini television set, with a screen the size of a postcard and a long, nickel-plated antenna. It leans to one side. I untie the folder's laces, I need to make the time go faster. It's an astrological reading, photocopied on thick sheets of paper. The signs of the zodiac are represented through faded and sophisticated symbols. I begin to read at random about men born under the sign of the Twins but I get bored quickly and lace the folder's strings back. I look around and my eyes fall on a pile of records sitting on a tiny shelf. I remove a record. On the cover, I see a large colour photograph of a young man holding on to the twisted horns of an immense woolly ram. I hear steps in the hallway, a key turns in the lock and she walks in.

Her fox fur smells of snow. She still has ice needles stuck to her eyebrows and her wool cap, which is lined with fox as well, is white with snow. She stomps her feet, shod in short boots, with her knitted leggings tight on her legs. She takes off her gloves, then her fur coat, hip length. Her sweater is the same colour as her leggings: dark brown. She tears off her coloured scarf with delicate Turkish designs and unzips her boots. I take a better look in order to describe her to you. She seems to be about thirty-five. Her face is not beautiful; it is a rather odd face. Because of the cold outside, her cheeks are now red but at other times they are pale as death. And there are times when they are pink, like the plaster girls in window displays, because she uses an unusual foundation, a candy pink that contrasts with the rather severe character of the face. At this moment, her eyes are pencilled with excessive black and lengthened with a smeary line. If it weren't for the visible trace of a moustache, her mouth could be considered beautiful. With her high cheekbones, her short hair arching above the ears, the somewhat stiff neck, not lacking a kind of useless majesty, she recalls a Byzantine figure from a scrupulously painted religious mosaic. She won't sit still for a moment, otherwise my description would have turned out better. But I think I mentioned the essentials. She is pulling off her sweater over her head, I can now make out her body: it is unusually beautiful, nearly adolescent. Only her chin, almost double, and a thin wave of weight at the hips infringes upon the grace of this body. If you're not too picky, it's perfect for putting one's arms around. Around her neck she wears a thin chain with a tiny cross, which has now shifted to the back, between the shoulder blades, while on her fingers – somewhat dry and peeling – a multitude of turquoise rings, the colour of her zodiac sign. She now sits on her wide bedspread and takes off her leggings, revealing her stockings, the colour of coffee with cream. She pulls over her head a black stretch sweater, under which you could spot a cotton blouse. She stands and rummages through a minuscule drawer, which I too have the chance to observe. It is an occasion to admire once more the graceful silhouette, like that of a seventeen-year-old girl. She removes the towel and goes into the bathroom, on whose door there is a whitish-yellow stick-on picture of a child on a potty. You can hear, after a while, the sound of the shower; it will not last long, because, I suspect – listening to Svetlana growl and grunt – there is no hot water. Yes, Svetlana is her name, which, in the first place does not suit her at all, and besides it sounds bizarre, not at all what I need.

Most people call her Nana: but as either they have not read Zola, or simply just don't care, everything returns to normal.

I fidget around the room. I am getting more and more restless. My paws, my claws, my transparent belly fill up the room whose glimmer fades in the winter twilight. The sound of the shower has long stopped, but she is still in the bathroom. You can hear from time to time the sound of a bottle being placed on a shelf, then other muted vibrations, hard to decipher, the faucet and the brushing of teeth. I am losing my patience. I squeeze underneath the door and look at me now, a few centimetres from her. She is naked from the waist up and, with her hair all ruffled up and painted in that artificial black like the Douanier Rousseau, she shows, at last, her age. Her face, without make-up, but which she is now beginning to paint again, has something masculine in it, and something Asiatic. The breasts – marvellous! – are the youngest part of her body. The tiny cross has caught in one of the nipples and glitters on the muscle's warm pillow. She has spent so much time fidgeting about, drying her hair with the fan, brushing it in the dirty mirror with the fallen screw in the corner, that, look, it is already five to six and he will arrive any time now. I distinguish on her face, underneath the apricot dust of the make-up, a pallor that doesn't become the natural nuance of her features, I would call it a psychic pallor. She is a little bit ill; you can see she is in a state of shock. She should be excited, even happy, but something visceral, or something in her brain, makes her feel uneasy. Her lips are stiff and sad. Like in the Eminescu poem: 'Your meretricious smile/braided on your coral lips'. Lips of a melancholy Asian, melancholy Creole, melancholy idol.

She is now out of the bathroom and begins to dress. I find it uninteresting; as a matter of fact, I am in a time bind, so I abandon the apartment and gush out of the building – hideous, translucent, my hairy paws occupying the entire sidewalk, creeping along the snow of the dark and muddy alleys. I see few passers-by strolling through the late twilight, but he is not among them. I keep on, find the boulevard and begin stalking every single red and awkward, scarab-like bus that comes along, making its way through the snowbanks, stained all the way up to the windows by splashes of brown snow. I finally sense him in one of the buses and jump on it while it is still in motion, landing in the middle of the jam-packed old ladies, students, workers: there he is, standing almost on one leg next to the driver and gripping with gloved hand the safety bar laminated in ashen plastic. I try to guess his age: I would say he is about twenty-four. He's tall enough, with unusually long locks of blonde hair shooting out of his fur cap. The golden tufts of beard and moustache barely coarsen his childlike face. The crudity of the lines of his mouth and chin are by no means malicious, they are dark, melancholy. There is something in him that makes you think that if you gave him the choice to save either a baby in swaddling clothes or a painting by Giorgione from a building on fire, he would, without hesitation, save the painting. In reality, it is possible he is nothing but a punk kid, washed out and mentally disoriented, who for the last few days has shacked up with a woman eleven years older than him. I anxiously make my way underneath his skin, slip in through his capillaries, swim in his blood, through the progressively widening arteries, through the islets of red blood cells and white hedgehogs of the white blood cells, with their thousands of tiny fingers, till I reach, creeping along the marl and alluvial deposits of the world, the immense brain's delta, where, retracting my claws, I settle at my ease. With each metre the bus travels towards the room where Nana waits, my hunger grows, my insatiable appetite approaches its apogee.

Dammit, this worthless cow didn't have anything better to do except get on the bus with her stupid basket, which she just had to prop up against my legs. Good thing there are only two more stops. It's really too far, going to see her in this cold weather, these miserable conditions, why does she have to live all the way at the end of the earth? It just isn't my style to get sick just to come off as the fearless hero. And, again, it just isn't good for me that Nana seems to have fallen in love with me, complications like that are the last thing I need. Still, there is something interesting about her, her age perhaps – which makes me feel ashamed before her, makes me feel guilty, makes me turn red – something I kind of like. An older lover, it must be every young boy's dream. But it is different with me. She interests me less as an initiator in eroticism. What I am interested in is her soul, the thoughts and memories of a woman who is ripe, a real woman. The high school girls, the college girls too, are for the most part no more than conceited girleens who veil themselves in the amber light of their eyes and a sort of brainless nonconformism. They have no past, no ability to become conscious, they're no more than discothèque appendages whose eroticism, whatever there is of it, is purely social and aesthetic; they do no more than irritate the imagination like unripe fruit. Most of them never ripen: their charm wanes, and they become part of the multitude of good wives, with a genuine vocation for normality. Engineers, sailors, accountants – they end up with the *crème de la crème* of the tigresses that undulate their flesh under the stroboscope's flames, under the patchwork of lights emitted by the globe with the tiny mirrors.

. . . The young man thus cogitating, shutting one eye, then the other, gets off the bus in the darkness of the Dămăroaia neighbourhood and sets off on a leisurely stroll towards the weakly lit squares of the apartment blocks. Listening to me carrying on about girls, you might think that I am talking about grapes that are too sour for me – and you would be right. In fact, to be honest, I never really had too much to do with those sculptural kinds of girls, the kinds who really know how to dress. I had my first woman at twenty-two, she was an old crone, already twenty-nine. After that, I only met girls rarely, just every once in a while. But it's always a problem with these dizzy adolescent babes, those chicks who always leave you, always leave you and keep on leaving you. I wasted my time for entire months with one of them. I've had it with them. I've never really had a chance to actually live with a woman. Nana is for me an unexpected opportunity: I can stay at her place the entire night, something I've never done before, not with anyone. This is the fourth, maybe fifth time I'm sleeping over, ever since I met her at that stupid party at Şerban's. Nana is his cousin, she was hanging around in the kitchen. It was easy. *I once had a girl, or should I say she once had me. She showed me her room, isn't it good? Norwegian wood . . .* But, as I was saying, it's no good that she lives so far away, it's no good that you can't go out with her, show her off to the world. If you go to the movies, to a play, people might think she's your mother, but what about your friends? They'd make fun of you, for sure. Sure, call me an asshole, but that's just how it is. I am taking advantage of the situation, that's just how it is. I just hope we can both take advantage of this situation for a while, without problems, without heavy entanglements. At times, I imagine her as Ingrid Bergman in *Goodbye Again,* leaning over the stair's gigantic balustrade and shouting after me – Anthony Perkins – now long gone: 'But I am old, I am old, I am old.' It's that perspective which worries me most, all I have to do is imagine her as a tiny animal, innocently victimized, and I am torn apart by pity. I don't think I could ever leave anyone if I knew she was suffering on my account, whoever she may be, no matter what she may look like. I just hope everything turns out all right.

At least the hallway is warmer and the snowflakes don't get in your eyes. I walk up these miserable stairs. Why the hell does it always stink like a crematorium? Finally, her bluish-purple door with the eyehole. I knock and you answer, and as always you surprise me, because I expect, with uncertain discomfort, to see your face, and you, as always, leave me open-mouthed, you look wonderful, your smile lifts your cheekbones, while the line of your eyebrows is far less circumflex and authoritarian than I expected. Your head sits straight and proud, its bearing, slightly virile, gives you that sense of ambiguity that fascinates me. You help me take off my thick overcoat traced with snow at the joints, and I am left in my red crewneck sweater. I sit down on the bed with the red bedspread; the camouflage is perfect. I am slightly nervous because no woman has ever made herself up for me like you have, Nana. I see in you a mixture of tenderness, affection and timidity that gives me courage. There is also something else, if I look carefully. I caress your hair and ask if you are sad. It is not sadness that I see, it is something else, but that's what you're supposed to ask. You hesitate a little, then begin to tell me. You have an unpleasant voice, the voice of a pedantic professor with a fastidious concern for language. You speak as though you were reading from a book. But already I know you. After an hour or two, you will drop this artificial dignity and loosen up like a kitten. That's when I like you best. But it's a while till bedtime. We will sit stiffly and discuss literature. You tell me that you were returning from work (even now I don't know very well what you do for a living, something having to do with numbers, numbers and numbers again, some institute with many initials), waiting in the snow at the bus stop. It happened an hour and a half ago, maybe two hours. You could barely look in the direction from which the bus was supposed to arrive, the gusts of snow were blinding you. A stray dog with its tail between its legs was crossing the street in the falling twilight. The people waiting with you at the bus stop were also watching it. Its yellowish fur was matted with snow, and the fur strands behind its legs were shooting out in layers of icicles. Its snout was black, and its eyes were searching the eyes of the passers-by. It was fidgeting restlessly, but drifting mostly towards the middle of the street. It seemed stiff from the cold. And, suddenly, a car screeched out of the darkness and smashed head-on into it, with a sound like a heavy object falling on a drum: thud! Incredible, how loud that dog could yelp! It was neither really a yelp nor a bark, not even a howl, it was pure pain, erupting out of a piece of flesh. It was a 'nondog' shriek, just like you would say 'nonhuman' howl. The car disappeared, but the dog remained in the middle of the street, circling rapidly around its tail, yelping just as loud as before, and crawling on its front paws. Its hind legs were paralyzed, inert. It shrieked continuously until another car, coming from the same direction, ran over it again. The dog was caught underneath the car till it got spit out from the back and landed with its belly facing upwards. The animal's shriek while it was under the car (no more than a second) surpassed the limit of the bearable. The women hid their faces in their palms, one of them propped her head against a tree, the men were yelling at the car. The little dog crawled to the sidewalk and stretched out on its belly near a fence. No sound was coming out of it any more, but every once in a while its black snout yawned. The bus arrived right away, and you almost got sick, squeezed tightly in the crowd. I believe you, I get the shakes just hearing you talk about it. I take your hand and look at your turquoise ring. I like to be considerate with you; I am really impossible with the others. You stand and take from your purse a golden bag of coffee rattling with beans. Austrian coffee, there are some who say it's the best, others who say it's the worst. You put it in the grinder, lock the transparent plastic top and, while the little engine begins to vibrate, you hold your palm over it. I place my palm over yours. I put my arm around you, I can't help if I am not behaving. I know we have the whole night ahead of us, I know that you must proceed gradually, otherwise it may turn out to be a hurtful and distasteful experience, but I am afraid I don't have enough experience to know how to wait. When I am with you, I feel so attracted to you, I feel like abandoning the conversation (and, in any case, my mind is empty right now) and taking you in my arms. If I really tried – you too are lost now in your own world – you would lift your hand and the coffee would scatter all over the apartment. I restrain myself, and while the water boils we talk about what we've been reading lately. You are reading an obscure book, you bought it just for the title, you take it to work with you in your purse. Its title is *Depths,* and you couldn't imagine it to be anything other than profound. Certainly, it is about the unsoundable depths of a woman. I mention, sarcastically, that authors who speak about those depths usually don't have the necessary tools to sound them. I finished, in fact swallowed, two books you lent me last week. *Nine Stories* by Salinger (all were excellent, but I loved 'The Laughing Man' best because I also had a friend when I was a boy who told me all sorts of marvellous things. His name was Mugurel, and once he told me there was more than one Hitler. In each episode, one of our soldiers killed a Hitler) and *Nuncle* by John Wain, not all that great, but at times – as you say – deep.

Coffee; let it be for you and me. We sip it from your cups, the ones with the blue stripes. I am beginning to shake a bit, I have no patience. Because once again you torment me with all your zodiac stuff, only to look at it makes my hair stand on end. You insist on finding out all about the useless details. How I will do in business, in love, what sort of intelligence do I have, what diseases to avoid. Good Lord, a woman is capable of driving you out of your brain for an entire night. Of course, all this time is not spent in vain, I stroke you with both my hands. With the only result that at times your voice cracks, at others you pause and close your eyes. You lose your place, but you don't give up. In the end, you reach no conclusion.

You recognize me in some of the zodiac's diagnostics, but others don't fit me at all. You finally give it up and we begin to make the bed. Then, we take off our clothes (as always, you change in the bathroom and appear, chastely, in the nightgown with scarlet flowers and, to my renewed disappointment, with nothing underneath). I am already under the immense bedspread when you get in, and you instantly glue yourself to me.

Here, dear reader, I am afraid that, without wishing to, I must disappoint you. Namely – having now exited Vali's boiling brain (I had forgotten to mention the name of the blond young man with the golden beard), perched up as I am on the highest shelf of the library and rubbing my belly against *The Black Museum* of Mandiargues – I will tell you nothing, describe nothing of what is going on in the rectangular bed, on top of which I see him now fully, his forms, his craters, his eruptions in relief. Awkwardly, I wave my paws, which now hang all the way down to the chandelier. I see my victim punctured, paralyzed, incapable of any kind of resistance. Still alive, memory still intact and gelatinous and perfect for swallowing. At the night's end, this woman with her face now contracting from pleasure (or paralyzed from suffering) will be nothing but a dried-up shell, swaying in my glimmering net. But I don't like to talk about the technical aspect of the capture and stabbing. I assume you are familiar with those aspects from your own experience. I can suggest, now that you are looking at these lines, that you close your eyes for five minutes and recall to mind the details of the most beautiful (or the last) night of love you experienced.

Open your eyes now. Everything is in order. If I don't take up the task of displaying the two beautiful nudes – and I am not going to do it because story hour is here – nothing will offend, hypocritical reader, your moral commandments. She is now lying in the inevitably conventional position: head on his chest, his arm around her shoulder. I hasten to install myself again in his left parietal lobe, where the tiniest lesion causes aphasia, agraphia, alexia.

When you pass your palm over the glass screen of your television set – the moment the show is over, and you turn off your set – you feel in your fingers thousands of tiny tingles and hear electrical crackles, all unexpectedly violent. But if you pass your palm a second time over the smooth surface, you feel no tension: the screen has become inert. That is how I caress you now, Nana. Your breasts, your shoulder muscles – they tell me nothing, they're like the chair or the coarse surface of your bedsheets. At the same time your mind, your nature, your deeper being rises to the surface out of the intensely blue water of the ocean, like an island already fitted with forests, animals, birds, flowers, dragonflies. No longer a woman, you are now Woman. We start to chat. We will chat till eight in the morning. Each time we spend the night together, we never sleep. I tell you stories from movies, I tell you jokes, then I go on to amorous confessions. I love it that you know how to listen, that you always pay attention, though not always well disposed towards what I say. Last time we saw each other (five nights ago), I began telling you my stupid story about Maria, 'Bloody Mary', as you choose to call her when you're annoyed. Now, you're just dying to know if I actually ended up going to her birthday party. This whole affair is humiliating for me to talk about. If I had not met you, I don't know what I would have done. I met Bloody Mary a little over a year before, and she fell in love with me right away. She knew me from the university, she read my stories in magazines and considered me, as she always insisted on calling me, a great something or other. I never took her seriously. She was a bulldozer of a girl, puffy, with rings around her eyes, and gorgeous black hair. Crazy as a loon. When she was happy, she became an entire melodrama: she sang and screamed in the middle of the street, she held me tight in her arms, nearly breaking my bones, she bit my cheek till she drew blood. After our dates I came home full of bruises. She collected all sorts of trifles that would remind her of our first days together: beer bottle labels from the first beers we drank together, the dry lilies I gave her, a tiny toothpick with a figurine on one end from the first dinner she made for me from a cookbook, a half-burnt ornate candle that reminded her of an evening we spent in the light of its flame, a triangular sample of plaid cloth from a tailored suit she wore the first time we went to the Athénée Palace and so on. She attached all of them with Scotch tape on an M-shaped cardboard panel, which she gave to me as a birthday present. She got easily excited, looked grotesque in her pinks and greens. Her passionate aspiration to a different world than the one that she came from was touching. She was frightening with her insane attraction for me. We walked entire nights through the streets of the city. But her total lack of taste, the exuberant kitsch of her preferences (which leaned towards popular music of inferior quality and cheap melodramas), her lack of tact (as, for instance, when she screamed 'Hello everybody!' in a hospital room, thinking she was cheering up the patients) drove me out of my mind, so that, after three or four months, I told her, cynically, I didn't care for her any more and wanted to break up. I left her that evening to return home all by herself (she lived way the hell out in the slums of Berceni), and at three A.M. her mother called me to say she wasn't home yet. I got scared, imagined all sorts of things. I was so agitated that towards morning I prayed, like an idiot: 'Lord, let me never be a writer, but let her be okay. Please, don't let anything happen to her . . .' I could offer no more. She came home at five A.M. She had walked the streets. (Here you make a face full of fake pity for me. I understand just how much this story rankles you. You are jealous of Maria. You tell me: 'You are incredibly naive, Vali. Do you really think she walked the streets all night long?' I explain to you that in fact that was Maria's nature, but you continue to insinuate that she actually spent the night with someone else. But why would she lie to me about being a virgin? No, Maria was not just a virgin, she was virginal, the stuff old maids are made of, in her own natural way, like a child. I have no doubts about that. She lied to me about many things, but in this I am certain she told the truth. So, save the sarcasm, you don't know her.) Then, we didn't see each other for a long time. We ran into each other by chance on the street in the autumn, in October. We chatted a little, then went our own way. I got home feeling, to my shock, disturbed. To my surprise, I felt for the first time that I cared about her, that I missed her. Next day, I went to the university. I waited for her to finish her classes and found myself asking her to marry me. I was very happy, thought this was already a done deed, because I knew she loved me and was convinced that nothing had changed and it had always been up to me to make the first move. But she didn't say yes, though she could barely take the next step. I had already begun imagining a happy family life with Bloody Mary. A couple of days later, we met in the park next to her apartment building. I had brought her a gigantic, juicy pear. She kept biting into it as she was screaming and acting up. Well, we need to see about this, we need to talk about that . . . Maybe in two years . . . Of course, during that time the little bulldog was to remain untouched, the Immaculate Conception herself, because she wanted to be worthy of her wreath and all that other stuff. And me, thinking I would make her happy with my proposal . . . I left her in a fury. I told her that only a mental retard would accept those conditions. For a few months I would call her, from time to time, when my conscience bothered me. I imagined the poor girl really wanted to be with me again, but was afraid of me, was frightened of how I behaved. A few times, she invited me over and acted like a bitch. It was the middle of winter and she had her windows open, was doing house chores and wearing a scarf on her head. She spoke sarcastically and sent me off in less than a half an hour, even though it had taken me a whole hour to get to her place. The cake she served me was sour; I think she put lemon juice in the dough just to upset me. It was clear she was paying me back, that she was mocking me; each time I left I was furious and determined to end it with her forever. But, once home, I would soften up, I wasn't capable of accepting the evidence: she had found another man and didn't want to have anything to do with me. I could tell from her allusions, something about this individual, some stupid sailor who brought her size 58 jeans for her imperial behind, who gave her a shiny cassette player to listen to Frank Sinatra and Cleopatra Melidoneanu; he would show up at her place from time to time, and they would laugh at the poor writer who had asked for her hand. During the summer, Mary softened up some, came over and let me take off her clothes. To stay on top of her was equivalent to a rodeo performance: she would jerk right and left like a mustang. A day later, though, she didn't know me any more: Her mate was back from South America, and she was very proud. After a month, her oarsman was off again, and she would come over or have me over at her place and once again she would cry on my shoulder till she broke my heart: that I would never know how much she loved me, etc, etc. When she cried, she became red as a beetroot, looked like the wife of an onion-smelling Transylvanian peasant; her eyes would spill out torrents of tears, and she was absolutely ridiculous. But I was still hoping that the story with the cargo ship mate was a fabrication in order to make me want her; I was still hoping she loved me and I would turn into a languishing, sentimental fool. But as soon as the ship was back from the Antilles and Popeye showed up with his two-bit necklace, she started spilling over with sarcasm again. I persisted in this madness for over a year, it's unbelievable. *Amour-propre*, that engine of paranoia, is capable of completely negating reality, of inventing a marionette play in which you always take on the role of the prince who shows up with the silver slipper, while Cinderella is waiting for you, always keeping the stableboy at bay, smelling of dung certainly, but never out of reach. Here I get to the part where *the story continues*. You want to know (and how alert your face becomes, that Oriental face, so bizarre, with its humid hair glueing itself to my collarbone) if I went to her birthday – to which she invited me unexpectedly after a month of the cold shoulder treatment. Yes, I went. I went, dammit . . . I sneaked away after an hour, it's true, in a state of absolute perplexity. I didn't know whether to laugh or cry. Sailor Boy was somewhere in the Philippines, but, on the other hand, the bulldog girl's house was filled with all sorts of sharp dudes, all of them friends of his, with delicious nicknames: Lamb, Rat, Slimy. Out of sympathy, I told Slimy my name was Rhymey. It didn't go with very well with him. He was the hard type, didn't even bother to look at me when he shook my hand. I just couldn't figure out why Mary had invited me. I also couldn't figure out the reason for the transfigured aspect of the house. On the walls Mary had strung up quotes in Greek. I have no idea where she got them, but they all had something to do with the sea: *Thalassa! Thalassa! Panta Rei*, and other wonders. One of the lamps was shaped like a sailboat, with whitish sails and a bulb behind them. On the door was a hand-painted sign with the words 'Faithful Earth' written on it. I assumed they were referring to her. Behind the pull-down bed, in an oval frame covered in celluloid – a picture of a

Cypriot peasant couple, he in fez and fustanella, she in her vest and I don't know what sort of object in her hair, miserable kitsch, the sort you can find lying around in our folk-art stores. Everyone listened to Nat King Cole in reverent silence. And there's my Cinderella, the woman of my dreams, the woman I wanted to the end of my days, yakking away about cartons of contraband Kent cigarettes, cargo ships, and whether his ship would return in ten or fifteen days. Look at her becoming ecstatic over a cheap postcard with figures in relief from Valparaiso, a little girl in sweet curls and a short powder-blue skirt, like the ones on candy boxes, awaiting a handsome young man in a boat, rowing ashore with all his might. When you shifted the position of the postcard, the young man's arms waved and his sweet young thing waved back. It was humiliating, Nana, believe me, I feel humiliated even now. On the other hand, I am troubled and upset that I am here now; I would have preferred to believe I liked a girl who was worth it, even a little. It is indeed humiliating. Good Lord, I try to imagine what this wedding with her would have been like. What pandemonium, what torment. Bloody Mary with her veil and thyme and the bride's bouquet in her arms, screaming and gesticulating from all that happiness. The folk-music ensemble pounding on the cembalo, the folk dancers leaping suddenly to everyone's surprise from around the corner: hop-sha, hop-sha-sha. Shrieks of good humour, her at the head of the table with her face mired in tears, her mother with her hair twisted in a triple bun, shoving the requisite handout envelope in everyone's face. And then, towards morning, take the bulldog to bed to tackle the labour of deflowering. Now you glue your face against my belly and wrap your arms around my waist. After this story, we lie quietly for a time. I am still bitter, though much calmer than I was a few days ago. You . . . you are quiet. I don't know what you are thinking. The bulb on the ceiling illuminates violently this chimerical room: the bookshelves, the little table with the basket of apples, the tapestries. On the armchair, our clothes are piled up on top of each other. 'How thin you are, like a little girl' – you finally say. And then you add, as a non sequitur: 'Did you notice what I have on my neck?' You pull yourself up to face me: I stare at your lightly wrinkled neck. A woman's neck shows her age the most, I heard it said somewhere. Your neck is the neck of a thirty-five-year-old woman. Under the tiny pillow of flesh beneath your jaw, you have a tiny scar on one side, not a cut, rather a crease, like a plastic graft. 'I had a mole there,' you tell me. Lord, what an entrancing brown I see in your eyes. But that's the only beautiful thing about your face. A man with woman's eyes. Perhaps a woman's mouth. My appetite for you has returned. I catch your lower lip between my teeth. But you, you lock yourself behind the sternness in your face. Your mole had to be cauterized, you explain. And then you release a stream of words, tense, interrupted, as though you were sighing. You were afraid, very afraid. Two years before, during autumn, you woke up screaming from a horrible dream. You turned on the light and spotted a few drops of blood on the pillow. You touched your neck with two fingers, looked: blood. Your mole was bloody. You rushed to the hospital – oncology – first thing that morning. You knew the doctor, you had seen him before. You once thought that you had it in one breast. You had read everything on the subject and developed a tormenting phobia. You knew that if the bloody moles suddenly changed colour, turning violet, pink or pallid, it would probably be a sign. Especially when you have certain dreams. There are studies about the prophetic dreams presaging tuberculosis, cardiac arrest, cancer. 'But what did you dream then?' I ask you. You stare into the void. 'I'll tell you later.' The doctor was a little eccentric; his wife had died, the rumour was from cancer. Before you even got the results of the biopsy, he asked you to marry him. I begin to laugh. In fact, I don't like to listen to you chattering about this subject. For no other reason except that it makes it difficult, uncomfortable to make love again. Remain the sapphire island emerging from the sea. Tell me another story. Last time, you told me that you are not living, that you're only existing. I know that you lose your footing walking backwards along the corridors of your memory, you scratch and bruise yourself, but I can't imagine that you do not find a few transparent places where you can be truly yourself and not a lonely civil servant without a future. Living underneath the earth, millions of kilometres below the city's foundations, in this cube of light of a studio apartment. Talk to me about your husband.

Bravo, young man! I am beginning to like you. You wrapped her in your strands, stronger than wire. You lured her with the sweet taste of Bloody Mary, which quivers now in her stomach. You stung her right in her nervous ganglion. I can already begin sucking, I am already holding her tight between my eight legs. I thrust my fangs into her carotid artery, and I taste in my mouth the dream's flavour of grapes. How sweet you are next to each other! Begin to caress again, before she begins a new tale. Her face, which has nothing in common with the name Svetlana, gazes upwards in unposed ecstasy, her upper lip contracts, exposing the grinning teeth, she holds you as tight as she can, she loves her exterminator. This lasts for a long time, it lasts so long, dear reader, that I feel obligated to fill up your waiting time. I don't think it would be wrong to tell you a few words about Vali. His biography follows the usual track: kindergarten, elementary school, high school, university. He is in his fourth year, majoring in linguistics, and has no inclination to consider what he will do when he graduates. If someone were to say he would end up teaching at a tiny school in the capital's peripheries, Vali would look at him with pity. He would do the same if someone were to prophesy a great future for him in the realm of Romanian letters. For the moment, he lives with his parents, reads, reads and reads. His profession is to become enthusiastic. He writes a little. He will write, for instance, two years from now (I betray this little secret solely in order for you to form an idea about his potential as a beginning short-story writer), the first tale of this tome, 'The Roulette Player'. If, according to the custom of a conscientious reader, you began the book in the middle, turn back to 'The Roulette Player'. It is the best thing you could do during this interval while the two lovers make love to each other. In terms of objective time, it will last about as long. As for publishing, he has published only two or three short stories in *Amphitheatre,* and a few poems, not very good, in *Equinox.* I don't like the substances from which poetry is made: smells too much like ether, like nail polish. You have to consume your own self too much, like Nasrudin Hodja. The true prose writer consumes others.

Good Lord, I never get enough of you. We pull apart again. You stand up and go to the bathroom. You're wearing a man's shirt that hangs down to your thighs. The sound of the water in the bathroom inhibits my thoughts. You are docile, gentle in our moments of love, you do not want to impose your personality, do not initiate any movement, but respond tenderly and firmly to all of my movements. I pick up an apple from the basket and begin to chew on it. You come back to me, your shirt like a ship's sail. You turn off the light and get back in bed. Your hands are wet and frozen. I keep on gnawing the apple in the dark, and suddenly I hear you talking. Your voice replaces the objects in the room that had been so present to us till now and from which only the ashes remain.

You do not persist – and I do not hold you to it – with the story of your husband. You tell me he was an alcoholic and you left him after seven years of marriage. Seven years of bad luck. He would throw your novels and poetry books out of the window. Finally, you divorced him, about five years ago. You recall the divorce was final during this time of the year, December. The shock was too difficult for you to bear. On New Year's Eve, you felt so alone, so senseless in your one-room apartment on Ştefan cel Mare – the first place you moved to by yourself – that you went out at midnight to take a walk on Circus Alley. You went down to the lake and there, in that strange world shrouded in fog, you met an adolescent sitting on his knees and staring through the thick ice into the deep of the lake. You began to weep. Even now you shiver to recall that scene. He was gloomy, walked you back to the boulevard and left you there. Melting slowly into the fog. Just like your husband, you never saw him again.

I ask you when you made love for the first time, and I feel you smiling in the dense darkness. I touch your face with my fingers, and, indeed, you are smiling. We burst into laughter. You tell me it is absolutely without importance when and with whom you did it for the first time. But, if I had patience, you would tell me something a lot more interesting, namely how you kissed someone for the first time. 'Can you kiss any other way than to kiss someone?' – I ask you, while my hand continues to search, not hastily but with the voluptuousness of a blind man, the contours of your face. 'Certainly,' you tell me, and I feel your lips moving. You snatch with your teeth, gently, one of my fingers. Then: 'When I was small, I would kiss myself in the mirror.' Then, in a distant and colourless tone, you ask me an odd question: 'Have you ever heard of REM?' 'No, I don't think so,' I grumble, without paying much attention or taking you seriously. 'But yes, tell me how you kissed for the first time. "Tell me about Lady Enigel the Laplander/and Crypto, the Mushroom King",' I mimic the Barbu poem. And you, dear Scheherazade, begin your enrapturing tale. The emerald island rises now a few thousand metres above the waters in which it mirrors its cliffs. Only one path takes you to the top. There, a meadow spreads out, cloaked in yellow dandelions, daisies and wild snapdragons. Butterflies and dragonflies with immense, clear eyes circle above the flowers. Further on, there is a grove of young trees in bloom. You can smell the bark from here.

I will tell you about some things that happened to me during 1960 or '61, when I was still a girl, no more than twelve years old. I was living with my parents on Calea Moşilor, in one of those odd houses with a jutting second floor, two thin columns protecting the entrance, and all sorts of grotesque plaster gargoyles hanging on the walls. The balcony hung right above the entrance; at its base, a drainpipe protruded out into the yawning beak of a metal vulture, like the nozzle of a seltzer bottle. The balcony was minuscule, but during the summer it was my playpen, my almost permanent residence. I would be bouncing a large ball with orange, azure or purple-red stripes or staring for minutes on end through the iron grating overgrown with ivy at the vulture's head, whose eyes, beak with flaring nostrils and each and every tiny feather on its crest were scrupulously chiselled in the rusted metal. When, after cradling my doll and singing alone in the full sun, I would go inside the house, still preserving the sparkling reflections of the ivy in my eyes, the rooms seemed to me sombre as tombs. After dinner, I would go out again to stare at the stars. I don't know why, but it seemed to me that there were far more stars then than there are now. Also, there were many more eclipses. Each week, there was an eclipse of the sun that we viewed through a smoke-stained sliver of broken glass we had prepared in advance. Do you recall? But you were very little then . . . The snows then were much vaster, and, during the summer of that year, a comet crossed the sky with its six fanning tails melting into the ether. I was looking at it greedily from the balcony as it froze in the sky, an alabaster stain among the shiny yellow stars, with thousands upon thousands of spiny corners. From the street – still paved with cobblestones at the time and skirted by houses painted just like ours, in all sorts of pinks and fuchsias, and decorated in *calcio vecchio* with falling plaster, with windows shrouded by dusty blinds – you could hear behind them the cloying echoes of the popular songs of that time, which even today stir an idiotic nostalgia inside me: 'Through the window shines the moon / fills with light our little room . . .' If you went up to the attic and looked up through the skylight (which was in fact a kind of telescope flanked by two representatives of that coven of Gorgons that adorned Calea Moșilor, one of which was missing an arm: she would raise up into the sky an iron stump that supported the stucco), you could see the burning reds and greens of Bucharest's billboards flashing off and on at regular intervals over the surrounding roofs. There was one I recall, it's no longer there today, the colour of sapphire, resting on a building in the centre of town. When its lights went off, I would close my eyes and count to eleven. When I opened them again, I would see, at that very instant, the billboard's lights flashing on again. It threw an azure light on my cardboard doll's shiny face, a light that would disappear to make room for reddish shadows with green stains and stripes. I hid myself in the attic until I could hear my father's footsteps clomping up the stairs. His footsteps were monstrous, and an enormous statue of red flesh filled the attic door. I was very frightened of him even though he never beat me; on the contrary, he would take me in his arms and walk with me to the little round window. A very, very large head, then a smaller head, and then one even smaller (the cardboard one, with hair of brown thread belonging to my doll Zizi – the name I gave her because at the time I liked to listen to the singer Zizi Șerban on the radio) – three heads, six round eyes huddling together to look at the stars. Afterwards, we would return to our little tenement.

We went out very rarely. I had no friends, and my parents were not the outgoing type. My mother, poor thing, only went out to buy food, while my father only went to his mysterious job from which our money came. I was very happy those few times when we went out for a walk. I will never forget when my father took me to Children's Town, by the National Square, when I was four or five years old. This miniature town seemed immense to me. In the middle of it was a fir tree that reached up to the skies, adorned with coloured bulbs and garlands, cardboard boxes wrapped in golden, purple and blue foil, globes the size of a man's head, tinsel thicker than a man's arm. On top, the tree was fitted with a red five-cornered star that coloured the snow of the entire city of Bucharest with its light. Along the alleys, you would find distorting mirrors and snowmen three metres tall made of artificial snow, whose chests opened up to display complicated machinery. There were stands everywhere, selling twisted pretzels, lemonade in nicely shaped opaque bottles. There were large boxes containing bizarre shapes of coloured sugar under their cellophane tops. There were Santa Clauses made of cake, and others that were real, with children congregating around them to hear them spinning fairy tales. There were panels with pointing arrows so that you couldn't get lost as you wended your way through the tangle of labyrinths. An old elongated shack, painted in loud colours, sheltered the Goliath whale. We lined up to see it, jostling our way through the crowd: an endless cylinder, made of purple plaster, with immense fins and scaly whalebone strips in its mouth. The strips of flexible plastic that my father wore in his shirt collars were also called 'whalebones'. Gypsies peddled them on the streetcorners. But to me the most beautiful thing in Children's Town, besides the fir tree, was the rocket *Vostok*, in a life-size replica. There were stairs that took you to the top like in a tower. Up there in the cabin you could see Strelka and Belka, the two female dogs that had flown the mission, made of pleated cloth. You had to come back down right away on the other side in order to let the other children see the dogs, suspended in their complicated, multibuckled harnesses. Father told me that before them another dog, Laika, had been up in the cosmos, and that she had stayed behind on the moon. Sometimes, when the sky was clear, I would look up at the moon's smoke-stained crystal, but couldn't see anything there, no matter how hard I tried. There was even a telescope, resting on three legs, stained in all sorts of colours. Father would put a few coins in it so I could look through it. I thought that I would see the stars with the flowers and the forests and the little girls who lived there, but all I could see through the round glass were thousands of symmetrical bits of coloured glass that rearranged themselves in different images each time you turned the telescope's tube. They looked like large and sparkling snowflakes. I would leave in tears all that scattering of light and colour such as I had never seen before. We would pass by a building with a panel above it where you could read the news spelled out with thousands of bulbs, letters that paraded in a rush to the left, created by the blinking yellow lights. People, loaded with gifts, would follow for minutes on end the strolling parade of words. We returned home walking through the city under the reign of the full, gigantic moon.

We had no phone; we didn't even know then that something like that actually existed. Our visits to relatives were rare, because we would have to drop in unexpectedly, which made my mother uncomfortable. Actually, we didn't have a lot of relatives, except for my mother's brother and sister and my godmother. I would only see my Uncle Lazar very rarely, no more than once a year, because he was divorced and changed women often, which filled my mother with fury since she had been friends with his ex-wife. Even today – he is over seventy years old – Uncle Lazar keeps up with this habit, which seems to be the source of his power . . . Again, we didn't visit my godmother very much, because she was dirty. Her house, deluged by little children, always smelled of garbage and stuffy air. But I kept asking to go there (she lived in the outskirts, in Ferentari, on a noisy and twisted alley full of Gypsies, with a horrible yellow church and a public bathroom that reeked from a kilometre away), because she had a television set, a TEMP 6 with a minuscule screen, on which we could see wonderful shows like the first episodes of *Robin Hood* and children's movies like *The Enchanted Tinderbox* and *The Lead Soldier*. That's why I didn't mind the snotty kids in flowered swaddling clothes, with their stained little booties, who never tired of pulling my pigtails and nagging me in every possible way. But, most of the time, we went to see Aunt Aura. The routes we took and everything that happened on the way there were for me strange adventures, the exploration of another world. The most important things in my life occurred there, at the outskirts of Bucharest. It was there, in fact, that the only reason for which I believe I was born, for which I was *chosen*, became clear: my passage to REM. And it was there – because we were talking about it – that I was first kissed by someone . . . Later, ten years perhaps, I made love with who knows who, at the end of who knows what party, but it wasn't then that I became a woman, because I had been one for a long time, psychologically speaking.

It would so happen that from time to time Mother would come into my room and tell me we were going to Aunt Aura's. I would jump up and down from joy, quickly get into my good dress, pull on my white knee socks, clothe Zizi in her creased, light-green velvet dress which became her so well. Underneath, she wore pink satin panties and a white cambric slip: her attire was irreproachable. I would quickly run out to the balcony in the cool yellow morning air and look at the trams and speeding vehicles that rumbled below. Sometimes, I would see a horse-drawn cart, with the side panels carefully painted in blue or green and decorated with beautiful flowers or with mermaids and deer. From time to time, the horses would drop behind them steaming globs of manure smelling of smoke and horses, not at all unpleasant. It was already eleven by the time Mother was ready and we had something to eat. We would go out into the street's turmoil and walk slowly all the way to Obor. I would turn my head to stare at all the stands with cooling drinks, with all sorts of syrup and soda-water dispensers, with crème-filled crullers and pretzels. 'Get 'em salty, get 'em hot, get 'em salty, get 'em hot!' When I was very small, I would throw myself to the ground if Mother didn't buy me what I wanted and yell like a drowning cat. Some old hag would walk up and grimace fiercely at me: 'Who is this bad little girl? Let me take her away in my sack!' which made me howl even louder. The radio broadcast jingles every day, sung by a chorus of voices: 'Candy, sweet stuff, jelly, jam, chocolate, caramels and ice cream', or 'Lemo-lemo-lemonade'. After I turned seven or eight, when I began going to school, I developed a little more control, but I've always been an insatiable being. It's a wonder I didn't turn into a whale.

Obor was an enchanting place. I remember it with absolute precision even today; I can actually see it before my eyes. A simple intersection, not very large, but permeated by the Balkan air of shopkeepers and merchants you would never find anywhere today. If you came up Ştefan cel Mare, you were assailed by the assemblage of shop signs of all shapes, colours and dimensions, inscribed with beautiful calligraphy on glass or on wood or printed in the widest variety of characters. Stove repairmen, mattress-makers, tailors, glass and mirror salesmen, watch repairmen, funeral parlours (there was always a coffin lined with folds of satin leaning against the wall), a gigantic key with the YALE trademark on it, large glass clocks like those at the train station, but with painted hands with the owner's name printed on them. On the left side was a pub that always expelled a stream of blue smoke smelling of fried meat. All sorts of drunks were teeming around it, Gypsies dressed in Hungarian costumes with their women in pleated skirts trailing after them, peasants carrying ropes of garlic and half-filled sacks reeking of hemp. Across the street was the Little Red Riding Hood toy store, of which I dreamed every night. It was a magical place for me. Each time we went to Obor, I would drag my mother inside. We would go into a long room with a low ceiling and a horrible smell of petroleum. The floors were scarlet brown, and the light that filtered through the windows was insufficient. You had to make your way for a while into that empty space in order to find the counter and the shelves full of toys. I would be lost, staring at the toys of all sizes dressed up in rough pieces of cloth. Most of them were made of rags, but their heads were sculpted out of a kind of plaster that you could easily chisel and had hair made of black, yellow or brown thread. There were also rubber dolls made to look like African girls with curly hair. There were little white horses with their saddles of flame-red lacquered cloth, yellow and brown bears, mechanical birds made of tin. On the counter, you could always find five or six toys that hopped about and played the drums, little cars that took off if you rubbed them, rockets that spat sparks from their tails. Mother would usually buy me inexpensive puzzles, like those in which you reconstructed a scene from 'Snow White', 'Cinderella' or 'The Snow Princess', fitting bits of odd-shaped cardboard together. I would quickly get bored with them because I had learned to reconstruct those rectangles backwards and forwards without even paying attention to the pictures, just by following the shapes of the cardboard pieces. She would also buy me little pieces of cardboard with coloured drawings and holes in them for sewing. All you had to do was pass the needle through the tiny holes, with brown, blue, green, red or yellow thread. I would thus follow the contour of a little shepherd and his sheep, a tractor, a boy and a girl holding hands, a butterfly, each of them charmingly stylized. Leaving Little Red Riding Hood would always make me cry. A little way up the road, on Mihai Bravu Boulevard, was a huge Ferometal hardware store where you could buy sheet metal, nails, chains, but also dishes and drinking glasses with multicoloured birds pasted on them. Further on, past a tiny chamber where a fat woman mended nylon stockings, was a sinister hole where they sold cotton, hemp cloth and jute rugs. The counters were stacked with large bales of cloth, permeating the room with a powerful odour of mothballs, vegetable fibre and jute, whose sharp smell wafted out. A mirror hung on a post, and I would stare at myself in it: from the dense penumbra, a frightened little girl stared back at me, with a face deformed by the crystal's lustre. Across the street, deep in the marketplace, was the market hall, still there today. But then it seemed to me monstrously large. Inside, it was always cold. While Mother shopped from the peasants lined up behind the tiled counters, I would crane my neck to stare at the dull mosaic on the walls and the bustle on the second floor, where they sold honey. The hall opened out into the endless corridors of butcher stalls. I was fascinated by the pork carcasses severed in half, the hunks of veal suspended from almost every hook, the butchers in their blood-stained white coats who without qualms lopped with their cleavers the lambs' skulls from which they extracted the milky brains or severed thick slabs of muscle. The slaughtered sheep lay directly on the counter, skinned and with bulging eyes crisscrossed by networks of tiny veins. In order to exit the hall, we had to pass by immense barrels stinking of whey, from which unshaven men with gloomy faces lifted large chunks of feta cheese. Their arms were wet up to their elbows with the milky broth. There were no traffic lights at the Obor intersection; cars would cross the best they could; the policemen would much rather chat with the cripple who manned the precision scales or with the lottery-ticket salesman. It was a swarming mixture that smelled of leather, tobacco, rags, fresh dung, fried meat. Me and Mother, decked out in our Sunday clothes, would take the tram that barely moved forwards, the bell clanging desperately amid the horse-drawn carts and Russian-made Pobeda cars. The trams were made of wood, with multiple exterior panels, tiny windows and a single headlight in front above the metal grating. Each time the doors – thickly oiled with a dark matter that never failed to stain me – folded open with a screech, a step would roll out for you to place your foot on and climb in. But the step was so high that Mother had to lift me in her arms in order for me to grab hold of the safety rail of shiny brass. We would get on through the door at the front because it was less crowded there, so that many times we would end up right behind the conductor, who at that time didn't sit behind the window in his little metal cabin like today, but simply sat on a stool with the sponge lining showing through, next to the passengers crowding the front of the tram. I liked to see the way he twisted and rotated the nickel-plated handle ending in a metal ball, which he rattled across the golden plate, inscribed with something in German. The car was outfitted with chairs made of polished wooden slats, while from the ceiling hung oval handles for those who had ventured that far back. When the tram began to accelerate and sped along swaying on the tracks, the handles shook, knocking rhythmically against the ceiling: click-clack, click-clack, infusing you with a sensation of torpor in the twilight. If you got in through the rear door you could see a hand brake at the back of the car, a sort of nickel-plated affair held in place by a screw.

Mother would hold the handle while I swayed next to her, and this way we saw parading before us a city so beautiful, so mysterious, that our pupils could barely contain it. Mornings, the city was veiled by an aurora like cold water. Morning glories were all the rage, opening their blue cups flecked with violet veins and twining along the fences. In the afternoon, the tram got crowded. Gangs of jolly peasants wearing berets, caps and running suits, the women in skirts with printed flowers and headscarves, filled the car, laughing, shouting, and wisecracking at the ticket-taker. Sometimes, some smart ass would intone in a low voice: 'Tickets, tickets!' – which made your blood freeze even if you had your ticket. As evening fell, the tram was nearly empty, the ticket-taker slept between stops with her head leaning against her little counter, Mother dozed too in her seat, holding me in her arms, while I gazed at the purplish clouds burning above the black roofs of the houses, zigzagging in disorderly array. Thus swaying from side to side, avoiding the drunks and retreating from foul reeks or the stench of garlic, we would arrive at Verg's Barrier. The Munca movie theater stood guard there, along with the verdigrised statue of a half-naked woman growing out of the middle of the fountain and holding a pitcher dripping a thin trickle of water. A black, despondent statue, streaked with green, grasslike trails. 'Streaked with verdigris like our brother snakes/in municipal fountains', as in the Barbu poem. We would continue for a few more stops, riding by factories with tall brick chimneys, with oily gigantic equipment in the yards, freight train depots with melancholy cars, scarlet and rusting in the snow, fritter stands where they still sold dark millet beer. The streets were lined with ancient mulberry trees, twisted and full of hollows, heavy with white or indigo-black berries, always wormy at the end of summer, teaks – in whose brown sheaths seeds rattled and which spread a raw smell of sweet and of yellow – locust and linden trees. Finally, after a few more stops we got off at the Rond. There is no place today in Bucharest like the Rond. It was a round plaza, not too large, that always appeared foggy because of the dry debris of mixed, pale colours that came from the plaster of the surrounding houses. Greenish rose or violet, that dust twirled around the plaza and landed in fine streaks on your face. The concave façades of the houses were so deformed, so ridiculous, that they roused in you a macabre sort of good feeling. Plaster lions, paws propped upon large balls, guarded the entrance of a tobacco shop. Vultures with outflaring wings and griffins with knotty spines hovered over the skylights. The roofs bulged out in oval globes of tin, like Russian churches. Antique columns, some already collapsed, complex cornices, twisted monograms framed the grimy windows of the tiny shops. The fences displayed dirty words scrawled in coloured chalk. In the centre of the plaza rose the statue of a foot soldier, standing on the largest pedestal I had ever seen and crushing the surroundings with its immense height. I would have to lean my head all the way back in order to take in the entire image of the colossal soldier, with his rifle glued to the side of his leg. Even the tallest houses squatted lower than the foot of the pedestal, while his shoulders were surrounded by brick-coloured clouds. He was made entirely of stone. While I stared at him with gaping mouth, Mother went into the hovel-like shops to get a few things for her sister and my cousin Marcel. She usually bought inexpensive lavender water, in bottles shaped like tiny cars, a few boxes of Piticot chocolate or golden chocolate coins. Sometimes she bought pink doll-shaped pralines with coffee filling or other kinds of orange- and honey-filled candy. When she could find it, Mother got rock candy that came in rough, uneven chunks, but that was very rare. She always bought me a syrupy juice, very cold and with a raspberry scent. At the Rond, we caught another tram and got off at the third stop. We were now at the Dudeşti–Cioplea district. I remember how I tried to keep pace with Mother, who walked very fast. Her dress emanated a scent of starch, while the loud rouge which she used for those occasions (otherwise she never wore make-up), of the most inexpensive sort, reeked of cheap lavender. Still, I liked it because it reminded me of the perfumed smell of certain disc-shaped candies, pink in colour and with a flour-like consistency, called 'little earrings'. All this time, Zizi rested in Mother's imitation crocodile-leather purse. After many twists and turns along streets I didn't recognize, wending our way past squat yellow schools with green transoms above their windows and coffee-hued roofs, past the long lines at the cooking-gas filling station, past the seltzer bottle refill store dominated by a gigantic, blue, ever rotating wheel, we would finally arrive at Aunt Aura's street.

It was a long and straight street, with wooden fences and squat façades on both sides. If it was summer, I always recognized it because of the assemblage of paper flying kites twisted around the telegraph wires between the oily wooden poles. Many of the kites were made of blue packing paper. Others, however, were painted with water colours or even coloured with crayons; they looked like odd harlequins spanning the smoky sky. 'Look at the harlequins!' We had to walk the entire length of the street to arrive at that bare brick house, the one just before the last, not only on that street, but before the last in the city. Beyond that other crouching house buried behind the back of the garden, the weed-grown fields stretched out across the Dudeşti district. Fields, as far as your eyes could see. How odd that seemed to me at the time, a street ending in nothing, rather than leading to other streets!

The moment we touched the gate, whose spare wooden slats allowed full view of the courtyard's interior, with the abandoned truck amidst the beds of new onions, the bitter cherry and the crushed stork's bill flowers, the young oaks and the girdling roses, and, further behind, the red, square-shaped house with the tin roof, Chombe hobbled as fast as he could to greet us. I was afraid of him because when I was about three years old he bit my cheek. But he was an inoffensive old dog with rheumy eyes, his legs too short for his fat body covered with rough curly hair. His stench was stronger than any other dog's I had seen in my whole life. Chombe barked so loud while we walked towards the house on the path, with its tiny pastel flowers shooting out through the paving bricks, that Aunt Aura, in her house robe and sleeves rolled up to the elbows, would open the door before we even got there and with a wide smile of exaggerated joy invite us in.

A long corridor, always ashen, led us to the living room. While Mother and Auntie chatted, I gazed at the glass fish in the glass case, at the yellow silk-and-satin swans floating on blue lakes on the walls; but my interest was piqued primarily by the sewing machine. I would find in its drawers all sorts of patches of cloth in all colours, rags with printed flowers, bits of cherry velveteen, all of which I used to cover my doll. My cousin Marcel would join me; he would wrap a rag around Zizi's eyes or tie her hands behind her back. He would laugh as he ran from me and, when I least expected it, sneak up behind me and pull on my pigtails. He was annoying, and his face was always full of snot; still, he was a little, plump, brown-eyed darling. At times, when he suddenly felt affection for me, he ran to his room and came back with a box of Cavit 9 candies. He would give me one of the yellow lozenges, waxy and perfumed. We could just sit there, playing together in our corner under the sewing machine. He would bring out all his broken toy cars, and we paraded Zizi back and forth in the trailer. He would pretend to tip Zizi over until he actually made me cry. Or, look under her skirt. All the while, the women's conversation flew above our heads, along with Chombe's barking and the cloying melodies of Angela Moldovan: 'The grass is green, the path is long/The love we shared once is gone.' I associate my oldest memories not with the house where I was born but with that house, my aunt's. I was two years old when we celebrated New Year's Eve there. I remember it very well. There were long tables in the living room, and the bulbs were wrapped in red cellophane. Everything, everything in the house was purple. The people's faces shone with a sparkling purple. On the table, the plates and the glasses were purple. Marcel wasn't born yet, it would still be another four years. The women were adorned with all sorts of beads that imitated pearls, and the men wore loose shirts that made them seem gigantic. I gazed upwards at their faces, lost in the light of the red bulbs. They were unforgiving, horrific.

During the summer, I never stayed in the house but immediately ran outside into the courtyard, Marcel running after me. Chombe, hobbling stiffly and reeking like a rain-drenched dog, whirled around us, his red tongue flapping between his teeth. I would step carefully between the beds of vegetables and head for the truck. As long as I could remember Aunt Aura's house and courtyard, there was that blue truck without wheels slouching there in the middle of the vegetable garden, poor thing!, peeling paint and all smashed up. All curled up on the hood slept Gigi, the last representative of a cat dynasty bearing that name. I have no idea how she could stand the heated metal; you couldn't touch it with your hand. We would open the door and get inside the cabin, where the scorching heat reeked of burning rubber or hot vinyl. Marcel sat at the wheel, I in the passenger seat. When we shut the doors, the world became small and intimate; it made you want to remain there forever. The seats with torn leather from which the spongy material burst out, the dirty windshield with frozen wipers fitted with torn rubber blades, the steering wheel which Marcel always attempted to turn but snapped back once you let go, but especially that smell, which I can recall even now, transported us into a world that bore no resemblance to the real one. Marcel, of course, imagined himself driving the truck on the front lines, shooting at German soldiers and killing them by the dozens. From time to time, he pushed the pedals on the floor, which launched the bullets of the machine guns. As for me, my pushing back and forth the gear stick with the ebony ball on its end did not share in these fantasies. I imagined that I could live my whole life inside this cabin, taking care of Zizi and telling her all sorts of tales and poems. The truck's dashboard was broken and hanging to the side. A dial was suspended by two isolated wires wrapped in yellow plastic; yet another dial, its glass screen broken, bared its hands so that you could move them at will with your fingers. Only the odometer was still in its place, but had sprung out of its screws and oscillated in all directions. It was the only piece that still worked. After sitting in the cabin for about an hour, that is, until we got bored, the dial showed a new number of kilometres, a number that grew larger and larger, as though we had in fact travelled hundreds upon hundreds of kilometres. Marcel was not impressed by this detail, but I would always bring my maths notebook, where I would note the number at the start and the one that appeared before we left. Although I never noticed when the numbers changed, they were never the same. In vain I spied on the minuscule dial, till my eyes filled up with tears; it found its own time to change. When I came down from the cab, the sky was blue and turbulent, like it usually is in the country, and it seemed gigantic to me. The sun melted everything into yellow water. The shadows were black and precise. I climbed up into the truck bed and lifted up Gigi in my hands. The cat was soft as a rag, but if I put her down she stretched abruptly, her eyes still closed from sleep, arching her spine and yawning with her pink mouth, so wide that we rolled from laughter. Then, she licked herself and afterwards flung herself down on the burning hood. She only left in the evening, when she went chasing after pigeons. After we finished harassing Chombe for a while, after we opened the hood to look at the wasps nesting between the hoses and the oily fan belts, we would clamber up the bitter cherry tree that stood straight and smooth in the middle of the rose beds. From the top, we could view that entire area of the city. Behind us, the tangled alleys with peasant houses, some with antennas on their roofs, and the tin steeple, without dignity, of a tiny, distressed church. On the horizon, rising above the houses like a swimmer on the waves, we spotted the statue of the foot soldier, a frightening figure over the Rond. We had seen the film *Godzilla*, about a monster who destroys a city. That's how the soldier's statue looked, now bluish on account of distance. Turning in the opposite direction, we could see the field, like a creature stretching out all the way to the line of trees, beyond which you could see another steeple glittering in the sun.

Despite all this, the field of the Dudeşti district was not completely devoid of interest. On the contrary, right in its midst there was something that always fascinated me, ever since I had seen it the first time from the top of the bitter cherry. About a hundred and fifty metres from the end of the street, where the field began, there was, right there in the middle of the ploughed land, completely isolated and apparently inaccessible, a kind of watchtower, scarlet, bizarre and melancholy, an eccentric house built before the war for who knows what kind of an insomniac owner. It was a tower of the sturdy kind that they build in Oltenia, with powerful buttresses and firm edges, narrowing upwards to the second floor, but ending in a cylindrical and crenellated yet smaller tower. The summer's yellowish green light fell so sharply over this unexpected edifice that, when it illuminated one of the walls, turning it into a rosy pink, it darkened the other, transforming it into a dark, putrid, cherry hue. A tiny window sparkled in the middle of the tower. You couldn't see any other windows, but it is possible there were some on the other side. There wasn't even a tree, nothing to throw a shadow that you could see surrounding the watchtower, except for a shed made of grey boards a few metres off. Who could guess that this ramshackle building would become for me the centre of my life, the only place worth living for? When they return from a 'journey', heroes have the feeling that the world is devoid of colour, that they live in a black-and-white movie where nothing ever happens, that time doesn't flow any more and that real life is no more than a limb of death. I too have known that feeling, ever since I was in REM.

Going to visit Aunt Aura once every three months, I got to know a few little girls my age who lived on that street. When they heard that I was there (I made sure that Marcelino went by their court-yards to give them the news), they showed up at the gate, two or three at a time, and I ran to open it for them. They brought their dolls with cradles, and satin blankets, their toy medical kits with stethoscopes and plastic syringes, their baby blankets and rattles. We hopped up on the truck bed and improvised a kindergarten. We lectured the dolls, taught them how to behave, undressed them and dressed them again. When we got bored, we would leave them there and go to the back of the house, by the kitchen door. There was a well-burnished cement platform there, about three metres wide, maybe wider, where in the summer, under the roof's shadow, Aunt Aura would set up a table with legs in the form of an X; they played rummy and sometimes ate there. It was there also that we drew our hopscotch squares with coloured chalk in complex, labyrin-thine constructions, some in the classical shape of a man with open arms, others in the form of a snail's spirals. We drew each square's lines, whether straight, crooked, or thread-like, with chalk of differ-ent colours: extravagant pink, azure, orange, citrus-yellow . . . The numbers and names inside the squares were white or purple, cho-sen according to their beneficial or baneful predilection. I remember so well how the alabaster clouds that passed over us were reflected in the platform's burnish . . . We would sit all curled up for an entire afternoon. While one of us played hopscotch, tossing the stone inside the numbered squares, the rest of us drew houses with cur-tains in the windows, yellow fences that were nearly invisible, trees in the shape of brown rectangles shooting out branches with red apples. We drew fantastically coloured princesses with blue eyes, with pigtails and long dresses. We used pistachio-coloured chalk to draw the leaves of the roses that the princesses held in their orange fingers. The twins, Ada and Carmina, drew them monstrously, with short, stumpy legs and hands that hung down to their knees. It was even more amusing to watch them draw: they both began the same drawing at the same time and both finished it at the same time, rigorously executing the same gestures, choosing the same colours. Uncannily, their drawings mirrored each other perfectly. If one of them drew a tree on the left side of the house, the other drew it on the right. Otherwise, you couldn't find anything dissimilar in their drawings. They were very tiny, about three years younger than I, and dressed exactly alike: pinafores with a knitted hedgehog on their chests, so short that their tiny panties would show each time they moved. I liked Ada better, she was cleaner and more fun to be with; the other had a continually runny nose, and if you told her to use her handkerchief, she would get angry, grab her doll and go home. Ada would stare after her for a long time. She had brown, glistening curls and sad eyes with puffy eyelashes. She'd hang out with us a little while longer, but then run after her sister, because they couldn't bear to be separated. Carnation, the little Gypsy girl, cursed them between her teeth, because the twins would sometimes come to her gate and scream, 'Carnation-tarnation', until the whole Gypsy camp came out, foaming at the mouth with fury. The rest of the time, though, when we played at Aunt Aura's or in the field, or stared at the boys who yanked hornets from their nests with a rolled-up piece of bread on the end of string, the girls got along well. However, all of them envied Puia, the daughter of a waiter; I never saw her wearing the same dress twice. Looking at her, you thought you were part of another world, not the decaying Dudeşti–Cioplea slums. Her mother, who had a screw loose and sometimes walked around naked in the house (and once in a while, when we mustered the fortitude to go ask Puia to come out and play, she would even receive us in her Edenic attire, astonishing and frightening us with her perfumed skin, with her French-curve-drawn contour), sewed Puia's entire wardrobe and bedighted her fancifully, just like a doll, with pleats and ruffles, with dresses of pink silk, with flowered cashmeres and bed satins with bluish ripples. The girl's minuscule hands were unusually white and she painted her fingernails with blood-coloured polish. Her blonde hair was always braided in different styles, tails twisted like ram's horns over the ears, in multitudes of corn rows like African women wear, or tied like a wavy, fluttering horse's tail. Sophisticated but disproportionately large earrings, rings with wine-red stones and imitation pearl necklaces adorned her tightrope-walker silhouette. On the other hand, she had no toys and felt a vague repulsion for our soiled teddy bears or dolls spilling out their twine stuffing. No matter how much we begged her, she would never let us try on her jewellery. Her movements were glacial and phantasmic, her gestures codified in the manner of the classic ballet. The only one in our group with whom she would play was a fat girl, much fatter than normal and stupid as night, with slow movements and cold skin like a lizard. She had a beautiful name, the only beautiful thing about her: her name was Crina. But we malicious girls stripped her of this last grace and called her, of course, Whale. Whale and Puia were always together. It wasn't hard to discern the nature of the relationship between them. They participated in a delirium for two, fascinating and odious, in which Puia was the vital force that absolutely controlled the will of the other girl. Whale was Puia's public. She listened in crooked wonder to the coquette's enchanting scenarios, the tales about princesses in silver-embroidered pumps who rest on the edge of crystal pools, full of crimson and gold fish. Princesses who stroll through gardens with thousands of sweet-smelling flowers, with odd-looking fig and orange trees whose bark is scaled by green lizards. Princesses in gauzy crinolines with the consistency of frayed and precious spider webs, searching through the grass for the gem that shields one from love. Princesses in golden threads, with chalcedony and pyrite hair, straying through bitter forests, illuminated by clouds of roses. Princesses mirroring their melancholy lips in emerald-green ponds in which a unicorn sheds a tear. Princesses who fatally murder their preordained lover with poisoned sweetcakes and make a ring from a chestnut lock of his hair, which they sever with obsidian scissors. Princesses with azure and distant eyes clasping withered marjoram twigs between their pale fingers, with spherical and twitching breasts and palms without lines, abandoned by fate and fortune. Whale saw and felt everything; these tales were her daily drug. She watched the way her friend rouged her lips, the way she inked her eyelashes, the way she flecked her cheeks, in a mirror's corner, with pink powder. Puia was everything she always wanted to be. She loved her with lethargic devotion, like you loved a mother but much more. As for us, we saw Puia's problem in a completely different way: we simply called her pompous and conceited. Still, we mimicked her despite ourselves, and many times we looted our mothers' make-up cases for a piece of leftover lipstick or a stub of eyeliner and doodled our faces according to our lights. We did this especially when we went out into the field to play our favourite games, singing and dancing together and forgetting any grudges we might have borne one another. We hopped on the ploughed earth until evening, singing: 'You're a flower, you're a rose/You are as pretty as a pose.' Then we began to fool around and get silly: 'I send you from beyond the waves/A burning candle and three graves . . .' When one of us sang: 'I see three princes mounted on a steed . . . ,' another one replied back: 'What sort of gifts do you think they need?' Then all of us answered: 'One handsome brave with a broken head/Deep down in the sea, where he is dead.'

Of all the girls, my best friend was Ester. I ran into her again, about two years ago. I was walking on Magheru Boulevard, in front of the Little Garden restaurant, when a woman the size of a horse stopped me. She was shrouded in fox furs, wore a hat with a Nile-green veil and carried a lilac bouquet in fishnet-gloved hands. I didn't recognize her at first, but, after taking a better look, I recalled those features of hers, so difficult to forget, the thin, contoured lips, the aquiline nose, the triumphant, leonine gaze radiating tenderness from the distant eyes, the curved forehead. Pity she had dyed her hair black, which back then curled in ringlets like electric wires, red as flames, over her freckled back. She reminded me a little bit of Barbra Streisand. We had a cup of coffee across the street from the Italian church. It was odd, she seemed to remember absolutely nothing of that week I am going to tell you about: she had forgotten Egor, had forgotten the girls (she recalled Puia vaguely), had forgotten the large skeleton. When I brought up REM and the Queens, she changed the subject and began speaking about her impending departure to the country of her people, that strip of land next to the Mediterranean. 'I will scatter you among all the people of the earth.' We kissed, and I gave her my address before we parted. I felt faint for the rest of the evening. But at night, after roaming for whole hours along the red and foggy streets, I had the dream I told you about, and then woke up with my bleeding mole. In the dream I saw Ester, who had died and now was lying on a black table in a coffin without a cover. Red pear branches hung over the side of the rough wood of the coffin. Her face was white and calm. Even her freckles had paled. Her eyes were green and looking up at the ceiling. I was sobbing; a rending sadness overcame me as though everything that meant anything good to me was gone and I was left alone in the ashes. I was looking at her with tears in my eyes when I realized that my friend was pregnant. Underneath her dress of white lace, her bulging womb seemed to be pulsing with torpid contractions. The child was still alive in there, I told myself; perhaps he will be born. And at that very moment, Ester's womb abruptly became empty, and an amorphous form began to swim underneath the folds of her dress, ready to come out into the light. A corner of the dress jerked to the side, unveiling her thighs and legs – pure and white like ice – and revealing the long, multijointed claws with which the being groped at the surroundings. I remained frozen with fright, until a large and pallid hand suddenly clenched the edge of the jacket of the two-piece saffron suit I was wearing. I wrenched myself howling from the coffin, leaving the torn jacket in the horrific being's claws. I woke up on the wet bedsheets and turned on the light . . .

But during the time I was going to Aunt Aura's, Ester was a very smart and lively child who was always reading thick books while roasting in the sun on the old truck bed. The more she tanned, the more freckles she grew on her skin. She had freckles all over her body, on her reddish skin, and especially on her shoulders, her back, under her eyes and around her nose. At times her voice sounded a bit like bleating, and she had the tendency to sink her head between her shoulders, but those habits were compensated for by the beauty of her purplish-gold hair that cascaded down to her waist, by the green gaze of her wisely playful eyes. She drew complicated hop-scotch patterns, in the shape of snail shells, with ornate squares and menacing layouts. Tossing the stone, she would rapidly mur-mur over them uncanny words: 'ánkara-nánkara-ashtarot-zefirah-shabaot-shabaot-shabaot', and we would traverse them hopping on one foot. Woe to her who ended up in one of the ornate squares: she felt herself consumed in intensifying flames or imprisoned in a crust of ice. Poor Carnation, she screamed an entire afternoon, impris-oned in such a square and pounding her fists against the invisible walls. But those of us who paused in one of the good squares would find there an unknown flower or a colour photograph of a gulf filled with many yachts or a tiny plastic doll with real hair.

You realize that next to the monotony of home, where I didn't even have a single friend, where I roamed alone in that grave-like house, the journey to Aunt Aura's and the days I spent there seemed like miraculous events to me. The garden, the truck, Gigi and Chombe, Marcel and the girls, the unending field and the arched vault above it, blue and flecked with clans of lovely little clouds, caused those days to detach themselves from my life's pattern like playful, solitary pearls. Once a month, sometimes once every two months, for the period of a few years, Mother would tell me in the morning that we were going to Aunt Aura's. Before I begin the story itself, before I begin to tell you about the Long Ones and our game and the dreams, I want to tell you a few things about a place in the garden. Every once in a while, when I was at Aunt Aura's and the girls hadn't showed yet and Marcel was playing soccer down the street and the garden was sunny and calm, I would just sit for a while in the truck's cabin, with Zizi and Gigi (the drowsiest cat you have ever seen, opening her jaws so wide when she yawned that she could have swallowed the whole shed). When I got bored, some-thing would call me towards the courtyard's centre of horror. I would go to the kitchen and grab a large knife with a serrated edge, the kind you use to slice bread. Thus armed, I would go to the outside privy. There was no other way I would have gone in there. Sometimes, I wouldn't even go in there if I needed to; I preferred to control myself till I got home. But that minuscule shed, the size of a sentry box, made of whitewashed boards and plastered with tarred cardboard, fascinated me as much as it frightened me. You could find it in the back of the courtyard, about fifty metres behind the house, at the end of a brick alley. It looked sinister, its black profile against twilight's purple sky. Only at noon did I dare to venture in there. I opened the door, pushing aside the primitive wooden bolt, and quivered with horror: The walls were studded with spiders who were keeping vigil. Motionless, fat, spherical in their trunks and thread-like in their claws extending past the length of my fingers, spiders of all sorts, spanning all of putrefaction's hues, from viridian to chestnut to amber . . . I could tell they fixed me with their unseen eyes and together were ready to leap upon me all at once. Lying in wait for me in tortuous webs densing to a milky white, there were others, much larger than the usual scamperers on short, muscular paws. Pierced by a hooked and rusty nail were pages torn from a book with geometrical figures. The black hole that yawned out of the polished seat teemed as well with larval life. With a gesture of supreme courage, I closed the door and latched the wire hook. I stood up, lying in wait. Yellow rays of light penetrated through the door's boards, disclosing out of the penumbra hundreds of thrumming flies that droned at heightened pitch in that infernal slot. If a wasp happened to get in, the buzz became unbearable and the sensation of peril was supreme. The tiniest motion that I observed in my foes caused me to lose my composure and begin to hack at them. I slashed at the walls with my knife, severing those thread-like legs, which continued to throb even when fallen to the ground. The spiders hobbled away with waving motions, the ones studding the webs escaped with unsuspected speed to their nests up in the nooks, while I, shaking, butchered them crosswise and lengthwise until not a one of them was to be seen populating the walls. It was only then that I unlatched the hook, pushed aside the door and charged outside, with the obsessive feeling that I'd done a bad thing and would be in turn the recipient of their revenge. The same image returned insistently to my mind, especially in the evening, before going to sleep: Once the lights were off, they would all charge upon me, would get tangled in my hair; they would scamper across my arms, would attempt to invade my nostrils and mouth with their hairy legs, with their curved fangs and soft bellies. They would bandage me in their alabaster strands, and their thousandfold brotherhood would sup on my flesh from below. In order to banish that image, I would shut my eyes as tight as I could and wave my arms as though to chase it off. Despite this, I could still feel on my face, on my belly, on my chest, their horrific race. With my eyes open in the darkness, lying in wait for any sort of noise, I had the sensation that a large, heavy spider rested on the ceiling, right above my face, and that abruptly it would scamper down on a sparkling strand with fanned-out claws. I would sit up then and howl for Mother, who would rush in from the next room and turn on the light.

We usually stayed at Aunt Aura's till seven or eight in the evening, when it began getting dark. Sometimes, if Father was there and Uncle Ştefan was home (most of the time he was 'out in the field': he worked as a long-distance trucker), we would leave later, around eleven. They walked us to the gate, demonstrating an exaggerated happiness heightened by the wine they had drunk, and suddenly we found ourselves alone under the glimmering, yellow stars flooding the black street. At that time of night, the stars were the only real, concrete things in the entire world. Even my parents, between whom I shuffled along with my tired head leaning backwards, were mere shadows in the absolute dark, velvety and warm. Their eyes caught tiny reflections from the stars. All you could hear was the barking of dogs in the far distance. We waited endlessly at the trolley station until the broken-down piece of junk finally remembered to show up, after innumerable out-of-service trams or others going places we weren't going to paraded by. Father hopped in first, dragging me after him, and then finally Mother crawled up too, and we sat in those uncomfortable seats. We swayed endlessly till we got home, to the rhythmic clack of the polished wood handles, colliding right and left against the ceiling, under the lurid light of a yellowish-orange bulb. Usually, I fell asleep on my seat and woke up only when we got off at Obor. We then walked home on Calea Moșilor and finally got home to that old, paltry, familiar hallway. We shook the stellar dust off our hair and shoulders. We went to sleep.

. . . And you, Yvonne de Galais? . . . You stopped speaking and turned towards the coffee table to get an apple. While you spoke, you stared into the void. My eyes get used to the dark, and I can see your face, your shoulder and your left arm like a bluish-purple palpitation. You eat the apple, I put my arm around your shoulders, you snuggle up to me. I feel your ribs and hip next to my ribs and hip. I say nothing, like when you're walking out of the cinemathèque and it seems in bad taste to begin commenting on the film you just saw to the friend who accompanied you. You must let it simmer for a while, image by image, the consumptive blue of *The Birch Forest*, the pearl grey of *The Duellists*, the soiled red of *Illumination*, the sepia and brown of *Five Nights*. Well, yes, I like to listen to you, my poetess. I remember how I told you, at the party where we met (I was posing, of course): 'There is nothing more ridiculous in the world than being a poet.' And you answered right away, as if it were something you had thought about for a long time: 'Yes, there is: to be a poetess.' And the first time I came over, you showed me the poems you cut out of magazines, especially *The Morning Star*. Too bad you only showed them to me but didn't let me read them. You showed me as well your poetry chapbook, published by Albatros about seven years before. I have no idea what sorts of poems you write, but, on my word of honour, I would love to read them. But on that matter, you are inflexible. If I don't take the initiative to investigate on my own, I'll never know anything about your verses. You ask me if I am bored. I can't read in your voice whether you're being coquettish or worried. I take it to be coquetry and answer brutally: 'You bore me to death.' Then, I start to laugh, while you – I think – only smile, a chunk of apple filling up the cheek facing me. Go on, go on with the story, dammit. Little by little that torpor, disquieting and hurtful (but, I admit it, why not, amorous as well) that my own story about the

bulldog left me with – I think I will keep that name, the bulldog; I like it better than Bloody Mary; it fits her a lot better; you could almost see her, a bulldog – begins to dissipate, and I hope that tomorrow I will be thinking much more about REM, whatever it may be, than about that two-bit Popeye. I sort of went overboard about that lately, I admit it. Each time there was something on television about the Romanian navy, those wonderful boys carrying our country's flag towards the distant meridians, following the swaying image of the bowsprit cleaving the waves and the lowering of the anchor, I expected the seamate in question to break in the middle of the sequence with an interview about the tons of mineral cargo and the loved ones waiting back home. In his place, however, there were old captains with accountant countenances who bored me to tears. How sad, how sad that I can't, whoever you may be, however many REM you saw, however intelligent and sensitive you may be, how sad that I can't, Nana, stay with you. A few centimetres, a few years, a few more thousand coins, a few more read books, how can I put it – those are the things that separate people. I try to draw you closer to me, as close as it is possible. But our skin, which gleams unevenly in the dark (yes, *'Hiroshima mon amour'*), rejects closeness. You have nothing any longer of the woman in you. You are a map. The map of an emerald island, shooting out of the ocean. I followed with my finger along the abrupt rise of the cliffs surrounding the shoreline, the path that severs the grass flecked with flowers, and arrived at the budding grove. On the ground, everywhere you look through the thicket, you see nothing but withered orange flowers. Each branch of the tangled grove has hundreds of poisoned thorns. Amongst them, forest fruit, red and mauve berries with extremely fine skin, adorn the branches, pecked by uncanny, minuscule birds. Lucky thing that I am only spirit, made of psyche alone, because no flesh can pass through here. Even the psyche, when it leaves, if it still has the power to leave, bears upon it the black dew of nostalgia. Departing the perfumed tangle, you witness knife-edged whetstones, a desolate path leading to a cliff. At the foot of the cliff yawns a cave's mouth.

You munched the apple to its core. You sit up and place the

leftover delicately in the ashtray. The air in the room is cold as ice, so that instantly, shivering, you withdraw your arms underneath the blanket . . .

That summer, as I told you, a comet appeared in the skies. I couldn't unglue myself from the skylight. I stared at it until I couldn't stare any longer, followed its six tails fanning out into the east. Toward the end of June, Mother got very sick, perforated duodenal ulcers, and the ambulance came at night to take her away. I remember the way she turned and twisted on the stretcher, the way she screamed. It seemed to me very odd and indecent that a grown woman should cry from pain like a child. And that bed, soiled with blood . . . For two days I roamed through the house, in a state of bewilderment and hungry reverie because Father, always at the hospital, couldn't take care of me. But one very cold morning, he and I (and Zizi made three) went to Aunt Aura's. This time, she was expecting us. She had been at the hospital where Mother, still hovering between life and death after the operation, managed to ask her to take care of me for a while. So Father hurriedly stuffed in a couple of badly folded changes of clothes in a bag for me. We changed trams at the Rond, in the interlude buying a flat box of mints and another of Vinga candies for my cousin, and around ten we arrived at Aunt Aura's house. Something strange had happened since I had been there last, at the end of fall when school began. I was now nearly twelve, and when I went out in the courtyard hand in hand with Marcelino – who tortured me something terrible by telling me over and over again the story of the film *The Mongols* – everything seemed very different. It was another light, another substance that wrapped the surroundings. With Gigi around my neck like a live fox fur, I turned again, as usual, the truck door's handle. The same intimate smell, still full of voluptuousness, persisted in the cabin, but a piece about ten centimetres long was missing from the steering wheel, while the sponge stuffing underneath the seat's leather, now torn in a few new places, had been removed. One of the side windows was broken, so that minuscule world wouldn't close upon itself as it should any more. I went back into the house and occupied myself with sewing together a few patches of coloured cloth. Naked, deformed, Zizi was lying face down next to me.

The arrival of the girls, alerted meanwhile by Marcel, gave me yet another sensation: odd, painful, impossible to comprehend. It was as though I had hibernated for a while and now woke up in a world different from the one I had gone to sleep in. And what confused me the most was that the differences were not radical, but of nuance – and it was those nuances that I couldn't untangle, they were jumbled and swirled in my mind. It was difficult to discern in what way, say, Carnation was different from the dopey girl she had been before, except that she had started to smoke. Is it possible the nauseating reek of cheap tobacco could estrange her from me so much? The twins had grown taller, and you laughed from joy at seeing their simultaneous smiles, half silly, half ironic, illuminated almost to the point of beauty by their white teeth and their large amber eyes. Puia and her hypothyroid shadow dragging after her left me cold despite the rainbow-like fires that ignited from everything that she was adorned with, hairpins studded with mauve pieces of glass, gold earrings with emeralds, a cross with imitation diamonds around her neck. And, when Ester showed up, on a small, sparkling, crimson girl's bicycle – they had just appeared on the market at the time – I felt a pang in my chest, and, instead of running to embrace her, as I had always done before – and as I felt the need to – I acted distant and indifferent towards her. I wasn't capable of doing otherwise; something inside prevented me from acting natural, and this saddened me. And she too seemed to avoid me. Maybe she was also just as uncomfortable as I was, even though our eyes were seeking each other – though meeting, they quickly turned away. The twins and I were the only ones who had brought their dolls, which were named Ada and Carmina; but the rag Ada belonged to Carmina, and the adorned Carmina belonged to Ada. They were large dolls, almost as large as their mistresses. Carnation had made up her eyes to look languorous, something between a monkey and Marilyn Monroe, and she spat nonchalantly from the corner of her lips. The previous year, she had lugged along her doll too, the hideous Florina, a puppet whose eyes she had removed, but now she was staring at us with contempt. Puia never played with such things, and Whale, who had an African girl for a puppet, had obviously left her somewhere else. Zizi too was getting bored among us. Huddled in the truck bed, we spoke of films and dresses, bragging the best we could. It was amusing that Whale had sprung breasts like a grown woman. We knew we would also be growing them soon, but to see them on someone our age, especially on Whale, seemed bewildering and ridiculous. The girls began talking about naughty things, lowering their voices and giggling, so I stuffed up Zizi's ears. We began to be preoccupied with the eternal question of giving birth. We knew in general how that happened – some of us had seen our own pregnant mothers – but the details were beyond us. We knew that being girls we would also eventually bring babies into the world but couldn't imagine what exactly we needed to do to make it happen. We finally agreed that they would have to cut our bellies open and had already begun to bemoan our fate. We changed the subject and went on with our juvenile discussions, because nothing was nicer than pampering ourselves like kittens.

Towards evening, after the girls left, wending their way through the violet air full of kites hanging over the houses, I gazed at the field, now beginning to turn crimson, and saw them coming. They were two silhouettes, incredibly long and thin. From a distance, they seemed to be walking on stilts, lugubrious, frail wraiths. It was as if they had been born from the fog on the field, which was becoming progressively denser around their contours, suffusing them, as they approached, in a haze of insubstantiality. They had finally crossed the field, so I could now take a good look at them: an aged woman holding on to the arm of a young man leaning on a cane. Their height was unquestionably monstrous. They couldn't have been shorter than two metres twenty. But they were unspeakably brittle; they seemed ready to crumble with each move, like a castle made of cards. Their bones were probably thin as matchsticks, and sheathing them was nothing but skin over which their clothes – which were far too short – fluttered leisurely. Each breath of wind erased their contours. Their faces, melting in the clouds, were bluish, identical, ill-looking. Her hair was painted in an old woman's mauve, while he, her son more than likely, was an albino-blond. He was even thinner than his mother and hobbled on one foot. His calves and thighs were long, hard, and thin, like the legs of a lobster and just as slow-moving. It was becoming clear that they were heading towards our gate, behind which, frightened out of my wits, I had curled myself into a ball. When they got closer, I realized I stood no taller than their waists. I ran into the courtyard in horror because the two had stopped and were staring at me, their heads higher than the top of the gate. Chombe, choking and yelping, began to bark. I rushed into the house and threw myself into the arms of Auntie Aura, who had just opened the door. I dashed into my room – where I planned to sleep for an entire week, protected from the living room by the French doors. In the room's penumbra, I glued my face to the cold, narrow glass, adorned with flowers and arabesques in relief, like windows filled with frost. Aunt Aura had invited the Long Ones in (I later found out that was what the neighbours had nicknamed them, and that was also what I would call them) and was chatting with them, screaming and laughing according to custom. For her, politeness probably meant exteriorizing to an extreme the feelings the others might imagine you have for them. Auntie was the type to stuff you with food at the dinner table, insinuating that 'You don't like my food' if you couldn't handle another portion and threatening to take offense. The type that wouldn't let you leave the house, except after uncomfortable bargaining, after repeated returns to the hallway. Meanwhile, with lively and smiling squirrel eyes, she quizzed and grilled you and wouldn't relinquish till you blurted out stuff you'd never dream of telling anyone. The endless woman barely got in a word or two, and in a very subdued tone. I understood that this was the last fitting for a dress that Aunt Aura – who was a seamstress working from her own home – was making for the woman with mauve hair. When the ear I was listening with got cold from the glass, I would turn and glue the other against it. I knew that on the other side, in the living room, the glass was covered with curtains made of dense, pleated cloth, and I would never be discovered. After a while, the conversation faded, and I began to hear the intermittent sound of the sewing machine. I flung myself on the bed and started to read *The Commander of the Snow Fortress*.

The air had turned crimson in the room when, lifting my eyes from that pink-paged book, I burst into a howl: the long young man had slowly opened the door and now advanced like a somnambulist towards me. The top of his head touched the ceiling, and his slightly asymmetrical face, wrinkled and bleached, widened into a smile that looked like a scar from an operation. His eyes were large and colourless, edged with black, as though crayoned. When he saw me scream, all balled up in the corner of the bed, he paused and began to turn around. But he banged into Aunt Aura, who had run in and looked like a girl of seven next to him. After she hushed me, she made the introductions. Strange, after about ten minutes of conversation, the young man didn't seem so monstrous; or rather, his monstrosity appeared more benign and worthy of note, like that of a camel at the zoo. He had to come into my room because in the living room his mother was trying on the dress. He wasn't that young, about twenty, and his name was Egor. Up close, in the room's purple air, his face, spotted by several days' growth of beard, scintillated with a mass of blonde strands. His jaws were tragically prominent, the nose long and straight, with visible cartilage, and his pale eyes were of a greenish hue under desiccated skin. He was friendly towards me from the very beginning, as soon as we were left alone in the room. It was clear he was used to people's frightened reaction when they first met him, but he knew how to make himself at least tolerable. Swaying leisurely back and forth, he sat on the chair next to me like a large, airy insect. He told me in lowered tones that he lived with his mother in the watchtower in the middle of the field, the one I had seen when I crawled up the bitter cherry. When I opened my mouth for the first time to tell him I knew his house, he became lively, as though I had given him a beautiful gift. And, without even an introduction, he began telling me a strange story: 'My people are of Georgian descent,' he said. 'My great-grandfather came to Walachia during the reign of Hangerliu, a ruler who was slightly demented. He traded Indian satin on the Danube port of Giurgiu. When the Danube froze, its crust the thickness of a pistachio shell – you could actually see through it the salmon and the carp at the bottom – he would cross to the other side with all his

merchandise and set up a stall on an old golden caïque, long ship-
wrecked on the shore. His wares caught the eyes of the Turks, Serbs,
Albanians, Bulgarians and even Tartar traders who got trapped by
the waves of thick and heavy silks. The Venetian and the Italian
ambassadors bought from him too, thanks be to God, even though
they had their own silks, embroidered with great mastery at that. It
is told in our family that this ancestor was sliced open by the pasha
of Giurgiu himself, with his very own dagger, after the cruel ban-
ishment of Hangerliu, who in order to save his head had managed to
send word to his uncle in Thessalonica through a silk merchant,
asking for two hundred and fifty purses of gold to offer as tribute to
the Turk who had come as a messenger. My great-grandfather first
sent his family to a safe place with relatives at Silistra, and then,
with one faithful servant only, fled in the night across the Danube's
ice with the horses' hooves wrapped in hemp. But, out of the darkness, the pasha's horsemen suddenly sprang out with drawn
yatagans and sliced them up by the reeds on the shore. For fifty
years afterwards, his descendants roamed through Bulgaria and
Serbian Transylvania and even wended their way as far as Germany,
trading in glass trinkets, as far as I know. My mother, my sister and
I are descended from a grandson of that merchant, who went as far
as the Adriatic and, once there, boarded a ship sailing to Morocco
loaded with crystals and returning with cinnamon. From there,
from the Berber coast, he travelled down to Ghana where the yellowish ivory comes from and whose coast was haunted by a fly,
blue-winged and transparent as glass, whose bite was infectious.
From the sting of this fly, the sailors' bones grew long, their hands
and feet distended, their noses and ears protracted. Ever since then,
our entire family has grown thin bones that fracture at the blowing
of the wind. But we also received a gift from the sting of this fly, a
priceless gift, about which I will tell you later. The sailor, the Indian-
silk merchant's grandson contaminated by that bone disease,
became a monk at the age of fifty-eight and died around 1850 in a
monastery on the isle of Samos, which was governed at the time by
Ion Ghica Bey. The sailor's four sons became soldiers of some
renown in the Greek army. Macri Iani, who gave himself up of his

own good will to Ghica Bey, was one of the better known of the six hundred pirates who plundered the archipelago, from Léros to Smyrna. He died of tuberculosis in prison. When rigor mortis set in, he measured, it is said, two metres eighty. The twins in the middle, who had taken on the Greek names of Spiro and Zotalis, opened a tavern in Cyprus. Getting rich on some shady business, they began to squabble with each other and, in 1880, Zotalis stabbed Spiro, took his wife and his riches, exchanged everything into gold and jewellery, and ran away to America. Those all too tall and frail individuals must still be roaming around somewhere in the Midwest, which is where our family received news of them for the last time at the turn of the century. We have practically lost all contact with that branch of the family. We are direct descendants of the sailor's youngest son, who returned to Giurgiu, where his great-grandfather had eaten too much fish, from need rather than appetite. 1877 caught him in Bosnia, where he kept a delicatessen in a village of Macedonian Aromanians, that mysterious people whose language so resembles ours. The delicatessen was taken away from him, and Marcos ended up as a company cook in the Grivița stronghold, under fire at the time from the Russians and the Romanians. A shell hit his cauldrons, and he was taken prisoner by the Romanians; he lost a leg in the Giurgiu lazaretto. Having recovered after six months of agony, with four splinters in his right lung, Marcos did not go back across the Danube but managed well for himself in the kingdom of Romania, getting another tavern started in Chirnogi, near Oltenița. It was a good location, and business grew accordingly; The Gimp became so renowned that even as late as 1937 you could find a beer hall in Oltenița also with that name but with no connection to Marcos, who had been long buried. He managed to stash away a pretty penny and left the tavern in the charge of a nephew on his wife's side (a yellow-haired Romanian girl whose daguerreotype we still have) and, despite his wooden leg, he leased property which he diligently subleased, and ended up leasing and subleasing as many as eleven estates. He died in 1906, and his sons, already in the elite cavalry, became officers and fought in the First World War. Actually, only one of them, Dumitru, got to fight. Mihai died of typhoid fever before he got to the front. Dumitru is our grandfather. When he stopped growing at the age of nineteen, he already measured two metres forty-eight, the tallest in our family. After the end of the war, he moved to Bucharest and got involved with gambling, champagne and French girls, the kind that put up shingle in luxury hotels, and in a few months he turned to dust everything that was left over from Marcos. He roamed the taverns for a while, hitting the skids and going progressively to the dogs, until he disappeared from the city and faded from everyone's memory. He returned in 1923, with the Circus Vittorio, one of the three great circuses that travelled the country. The largest, Sidoli, distinguished itself by its gigantic tent made of white and azure strips of silk, the tops adorned with flags in the shape of lemon leaves. The second largest was Le Magnifique, belonging to the Borzoff Brothers, boasting of renowned tightrope walkers and of Tudoriţa the Contortionist, who was able to bend backwards and grasp in her teeth a rose that rested at her heels. Both of those great circuses flaunted their fierce or odd animals, but only Vittorio, whose bright amber cupola made camp from time to time at Bucharest's peripheries, could boast of the only genuine pair of superb griffin-like syruses in this boreal hemisphere. My grandfather made his appearance with the very first show on the way back from a tour of Poland and Lithuania. He was introduced as the tallest man on earth and made his grave and silent entrance into the arena costumed in an ample cashmere mantle of sky blue. He was surrounded by hideous crooked-legged midgets with heads the size of barrels, who juggled oranges and tumbled in the dung-filled sand. He was a great sensation. When the drums rattled and Dumitru (baptized Signor Firelli) tossed off his mantle with a royal gesture, he would be costumed in a pair of minuscule trunks alone, revealing his body, thin as a fakir's and unbelievably long, tattooed from neck to toe with the strangest images that only dreams could bring. The inks and coloured dusts that had been implanted in his skin needle prick by needle prick transformed him into a live chronicle of the world – what had been, what was, what would be. His tattoos seemed to circulate under the skin and admix their contours. During one show, if you studied him carefully through your binoculars, you could spot a rain of stars in blood-coloured ink on his right shoulder; the next day you would find the same thing on his belly, but this time in green ink. The parrot with a diamond on its forehead that adorned his shoulder blades today would ascend to his neck and chin tomorrow, while the day after, it floated phantasmically above Signor Firelli's head, only to unravel later like steam in the air. My grandmother was a young Finn, employed by the circus as a cook. Sleeping night after night in the show horses' stables with him, she soon discovered her gift of prophesying the future in the ever-shifting tangle of drawings on Dumitru's skin. One August evening, when a huge number of spectators had gathered underneath the circus tent, there materialized in the middle of the jungle of frantic tattoos, crafted as if in sapphire, three letters, REM, blanketing his entire chest like a prevision. While tracing with her finger the bewitched contour of those three letters, my grandmother Soile, who had already given birth to my mother in 1921 and had left her at Chirnogi in the care of Marcos', widow, began laughing and crying, screaming and rolling in the arena's dust, until, propping herself up on the scruff of her neck and her ankles, she arched her spine so drastically that even Tudorița from Le Magnifique would have envied her. That was the year when Don Vittorio Carra, the circus proprietor, went bankrupt. Soile died at the Dudu monastery, diagnosed with hysterical dementia, while Dumitru ended his circus career a few months later. After appearing in the winter at Brăila among fire-breathers, sword-swallowers and chain-girdled musclemen in leopard skins in the greatest of shows, he was torn apart in full view of the audience by the pair of syruses, who abruptly leaped upon him. The legendary animals, endowed with a dragon's snout and tail, a lion's paws and bat's wings, had perhaps seen in the ever shifting tattoos on my grandfather's yellow skin something that provoked their ferocity. I have somewhere at home a folder with newspaper clippings, presenting "Signor Firelli, the tallest man in the world". One picture shows him next to Gogea Mitu, the Romanian prizefighter who measured well over two meters, but who looks like a pygmy next to my grandfather. I think they even organized a boxing match between them, which eventually never took place. From this strange man my mother inherited two unexpected things: a family chronicle (of which I just gave you the short version) and a stamp collection. Dumitru's chronicle goes far deeper than my story. It begins with some muddled events that occurred in a monastery in Tibet in the thirteenth century. An apprentice monk left the monastery, and his descendants journeyed to Kashmir, traded in Bukhara and Tashkent, wended their way on the carpet road to Iran, arrived in Georgia, where they settled for about ninety years and where the merchant from Hangerliu's time began his journey . . . You see, it is as though my people were a kind of finger that slowly strays, hesitating along a path laid out on a map, seeking something whose existence it knows about, but without it being transmitted other than through the blood. Until my mother, who discovered REM, they were not even conscious of their search. They simply lived their lives, which instinctively always led them west. Mother married very early, in 1936, when she was fifteen and only one metre ninety. Father was a head shorter than she was and probably married her for her stamp collection, whose value, I think, is enormous. I don't recall him very well. He was a fervent stamp collector, from somewhere near Braşov, whose name was Augustin Bach. These are my childhood memories: Two crazy people turning one black page after another, albums spotted with tiny coloured squares. My sister was born in '37, and I followed in '40. Because of the bombing raids during the war, we moved to the country till '45, where Father died of diphtheria in the hospital where he worked as a male nurse. Returning from the country, from the district of Dudeşti, where we had stayed at an acquaintance of my mother's – my mother in mourning vestments, my sister and I dead tired and crammed in the back of a horse-drawn cart – we passed by the shed that you may have seen, the one next to our watchtower, which was built, certainly, later. It was a shed situated, God knows why, in the middle of a field. While Mother was looking at it, she became ill. We stopped the cart and she climbed down. She walked around the shed many times, touched it apprehensively with her fingers, wiggled the rudimentary lock with infinite delicacy, and finally fell to her knees on the muddy earth, as one does before a temple. She wouldn't budge. The peasant manning the cart was barely able to get her to move. We the children were frightened out of our minds and wailed and wept. But the next day, Mother made her decision: she sold a single stamp from her collection and used the money to build the watch-tower. The construction was finished in '47, when we moved here. My sister stayed with us until four years ago, when she married a carpenter. She has a boy who is three, very precocious. My mother and I live alone, selling a stamp from time to time to cover our expenses.'

Only when Egor finished speaking and a few seconds of ear-piercing silence followed did I realize how entranced I had been. I had not even noticed the room get so dark that all I could see were a few glossy surfaces: the alabaster lip of a drinking glass on the table, the purplish eyes of the Long One, the round corners of the furnace. The slash of the door's opaque glass abruptly flashed a soiled yellow: Aunt Aura had turned on the light in the next room. She trilled in her clamorous and penetrating voice: We were to admire Madam Bach, bedecked in her fantastic blue dress printed with branches of cherries in bloom. I was dwarfed by the scarecrows who filled the living room with leisurely gestures. We walked them to the gate under the starry sky and through the chirping of crickets. Madam Bach went ahead while Egor bowed deeply before me and murmured the invitation to visit him the next afternoon at the watchtower. 'You know how to listen,' he said. 'But it all depends on if you know how to dream.' And he placed in my palm a tiny object, cold and well polished. 'Put it under your pillow and tell me what you've dreamed at night.' He walked off towards the street's end where the sky was bluer and the comet, ecstatic spider, fanned out its tails among the stars. I went in the house and stared at the object that Egor had given me. It was a pink mother-of-pearl shell in the form of a Japanese fan, with a mul-titude of wave-like, superimposed layers. The exterior was striated and darker in colour, while the interior, smooth and slippery, was white as a fish's belly. There, inside the concave interior, someone had scratched with a sharp point an outline: an open circle with hun-dreds of crossing paths inside, like a network of intestines. I killed some time till it was time for bed next to Aunt Aura, who was busy picking up the lint that had scattered all over the house. Marcel came back from playing, filthy as a pig, and escaped punishment only because I was there. After dinner we ate a Mentine, a chocolate disc with white puffy filling that tasted of peppermint, and then Auntie made my bed. I put the shell under the pillow and went to sleep. Only in the morning did I remember Zizi, whom I had forgotten for the first time since I'd had her and who had slept on the hardwood floor under the table.

That night, I dreamed of a forest. A greenish-golden forest, sparkling like the sun in the after-rain air. A morning forest, filled with dew, buzzing with tiny golden flies purling amidst billions of transparent leaves. I roamed through that forest swallowed by the smells of redwood, of tannin, of mould, through the tall, young trunks, supple and arching towards the sun in a single motion, stalks of emerald and gold, and yet so alive! Through the vast vault of the branches, eyes opened out to the blue skies. I felt it was from there that the bird whistles that banished the silence came from ... Hedgehogs flitted, weasels fulgurated through the hundreds of paths that crossed the forest. In the clearings, stinging nettles and violet bellflowers and cuckoo-pints made bowers for the chaotic bustle of the ladybugs. The forest seemed to me, a little girl lost among its paths, the only possible reality. I couldn't remember anything else. And I didn't feel I was lost. Enchanted by the colours of the butterflies, by the fragrance of the raspberries that stained my cheeks, I skipped along gleefully, at times dropping down on my belly to sip the cozy water of some crystalline spring. That was my world, from which I would never wish to part. Underneath a mud-smirched leaf, I found a snail with a broken shell. Between two trees a cross spider stretched its net, laced with drops of water. A desiccated branch scratched my bare arm. I wasn't looking for the way out, the paths were not leading anywhere, going towards somewhere else, everything was the pure joy of strolling through the Marvellous.

At eight in the morning, Carnation yelled my name from the gate with her guttural voice. I drank my milk quickly and came out. My conscience tormented me because of poor Zizi; to compensate, I had now dressed her up in her best change of clothes. But talking with the girls, who all finally showed up by nine, I forgot about her again. I told them about Egor and his stories, at which, unexpectedly, they seemed to take offence and mumbled out of the corners of their mouths: 'Leave him to the Devil, that stupid idiot of a beanpole,' or something of that sort. But as I was still very excited, they finally told me that he had told that same story to each and every one of them the first time they met him, all those crazy tales about his ancestors and that old shed that contained who knows what sort of stupid old thing. 'Little John', as they called him, had given them all in turn the shell with the scratches, and they had all slept with it one night under the pillow. But they hadn't dreamed what they were supposed to dream and the Long One had looked at them the next day with contempt. 'Lunatics, both him and his mother!' Listening to them, I got scared he would despise me as well: did I or did I not dream the true dream? Will I disappoint the gigantic and frail young man who looked at me with such dolorous hope before he left? In any case, until that time I had never had such a live dream, such a real one. We began to draw with coloured chalk. The girls sketched Egor in the most distorted fashion: either banging his head against the tip of the grinning moon or grabbing with an endless arm, green as gall, or scarlet, a multicornered star. In exchange, I sketched the shell he gave me with pink chalk. We got bored of drawing very quickly and all at once decided (I don't remember who the first was to come up with the idea) to play Queens. The game was not difficult: each one of us would be queen for a day. Because there were seven of us, the game would last seven days. Each day, the respective queen would receive a colour, an object, a flower, and her very own place. The queen would have to improvise an entertainment out of those, a beautiful game in which the others would participate as her subjects. The most enthusiastic was Ester, whose face turned so red from pleasure that her freckles nearly disappeared. Certainly, this way we would not get bored for one instant for the entire week. Ester proposed we draw lots. We instantly started to erase with a wet rag all the drawings on the ground and to chalk out a circle for each of the seven days. We drew the largest with violet chalk; then we drew another inside it with indigo chalk; the next one was blue, then green, then yellow, orange, leaving the centre circle no larger than the diameter of a ball, which we shaded with red. Once we were done, the girls scattered and rushed to their houses to get flowers and objects. I was left alone, all curled up, my fingers full of chalk and Chombe breathing in my nose. I felt very sad, just as I had ever since I arrived the day before. I had no idea what was wrong with me: the brick house, the well cared for courtyard with the beds of young onions, the tomato trellis, the blue truck frying in the sun with the perennial Gigi yawning on the hood, everything seeming illuminated by a dolorous, visceral, black sun, like when you feel you will lose something forever. I was looking at the bitter cherry, rising tall over all the other trees in the courtyard and hanging heavy from the resin. The memory of the watchtower and the night before with Egor swaying like a hypnotic cobra before me caused my heart to tighten. I went to the gate and gazed down the street: the tails of the kites tangled in the telegraph wires fluttered disconsolately in the yellow air, while a turtledove resting on the pole ogled them with a lone eye. I was waiting for Ester, was asking myself what role I would grant her when I was queen, but especially I was thinking how well it would become her to sit on the throne, holding in her hand the flower she would get when we drew lots. I wanted this flower to be a red rose and even decided to suggest it: maybe she would even draw the rose. I went into the house and began to fashion a crown of golden paper. Aunt Aura, who found out about our game, brought me multicoloured strips of velveteen, leftover shreds of Indian silk and crepe de Chine. And she also gave me a few sheets of coloured, glossy paper, from which my cousin scissored out apples, pears, and cucumbers for his kindergarten crafts shop. The girls filed in one by one, and soon the room turned into a bustling work station. We fashioned chains of coloured paper, made necklaces, lace and bracelets from whatever we could lay our hands on, and from a kitchen chair we improvised, with the help of a few pillows and a bedsheet, a veritable throne, canopy and all, worthy of a queen.

Wielding the scissors with an unearthly grace, Puia cut out of the golden paper a unicorn and a lion, which we glued, face to face, on the throne's back. After we collected the leftovers from the floor, we got hold of one of Uncle Ştefan's old hats and began the task of drawing lots. We wrote on pieces of paper all the colours of the rainbow (we matched each colour – as in a little fantasy – to its opposite one in the spectrum; for example, we wrote the word 'red' and matched it with violet, 'orange' with indigo, and so on, except for 'green', which we matched with the colour green) and put the pieces of paper in the hat. We were very nervous, because the day we picked would determine the day we would get to be queen, and each one of us was anxious to be the first on the throne. Eventually, this is how the drawing of the lots turned out: Orange went to lucky Whale – who for a while wasn't even aware of her good luck to be queen that very day. But, on the other hand, we consoled ourselves that the first day you barely have time to realize how lucky you are, and then, all of a sudden, you are already no longer queen. It is much better to be queen later, to learn from the others' mistakes, to have time to think about what you want to do when your turn comes. Ada got the indigo, Carmine the blue. It couldn't have been otherwise, these two colours being so close to each other. Green, the middle colour, fell to Puia, and it suited her perfectly, because of the green clarity, somewhat perverse, of her eyes. Ester ended up with a random, ill-suited yellow. She grimaced when she read it: it was clear that only red would have suited her, she would have been the Red Queen from head to toe, but that's just the way it turned out. Yellow was the only colour that she couldn't stand. Everything seemed to go against my poor friend. And that was only the beginning. Carnation got orange – a Gypsy colour if ever there was one – which made us burst out laughing. But the little wild thing was enchanted: it was the most lively and glistening of colours for her. With a voice that came out as if she had rinsed her throat with kerosene (which made absolute sense, because we always saw her waiting in line to fill up the gas can and then dragging it home in a crooked little metal cart the colour of rust), she told us that she knew exactly what she was going to wear, because one of her cousins was a garbage collector and had a 'cool' orange vest with fringes; she was thinking of spiriting it away for this occasion. I didn't even open up my piece of paper. I was to be the last queen, and my colour was red. I felt like a usurper and, if it were permitted, I would have exchanged colours with Ester. I felt no relationship to red, even my name, Svetlana, suggests a very pallid greenish-blue.

After the excitement over the selection of colours subsided, after we had finally calmed down over the sequence of queens, we used the hat again for the secret object each one of us brought from home. I knew only mine: I had appropriated a broken thermometer from the sewing machine's drawer, with the frozen mercury displaying 36 degrees. The hat was passed from one hand to the next, and then we pulled out the objects one by one and lined them up on the table. They were: a ring, a toy watch, a doll the size of a finger in a crimson voile skirt, an unusually large wishbone from an old chicken, a transparent ballpoint pen, one of the first to appear on the market around here, a pearl with a hole in it and my thermometer. We wrote their names on pieces of paper and drew them from the hat. I got the ring, Ester the thermometer, Whale the wishbone, Puia the ballpoint pen, Ada the watch, Carmina the pearl, Carnation the doll. We looked at our objects as though they were strange creatures. We had no idea what we would do with them. But, with the exception of Whale, the first day's queen (who ended up with that inexplicable wishbone, a bone fork you couldn't figure out what to do with even if you thought about it a thousand times, because it was evident that to break it in the customary way was not permitted), the rest of us had time to think. We hadn't brought real flowers, because they would have withered by the time our game ended, but each one of us thought of a flower and wrote its name on a piece of paper. Whale drew the morning-glory, Ada the zinnia, Carmina the carnation (we laughed a lot about this), Puia the portulaca, the dahlia for Ester, the snapdragon for Carnation, and for me – lucky me! – the king of flowers, the rose. I didn't feel worthy of being such a queen. In order to get down to work, all we had to do was select the locations where our games would take place. After some dispute,

we parcelled out our domain in seven sections: my room, the courtyard, the street, the field, Egor's watchtower, the truck and a ruined
building behind our courtyard where a school used to be, which is
why we called it the old school. In order for us not to know everything beforehand, we decided to draw lots for the places where we
would play the game each morning: the respective queen would
draw from the hat the piece of paper indicating her location. For
now, Whale, leering from her jowls that made you think of little
butt cheeks, shoved her pink-stained fingers into the hat and came
up with the field. We all grumbled our distaste: it was the first day
and we had to spend our time on plowed land. We hated it because
certain boys usually went there to play and loved to terrorize us,
threatening to put the maggots they caught in our hair. On the
other hand it was good, because none of the rest of us would end up
being queen on the field. Ours would be the more noble locations.
The most coveted place was the courtyard, where you had room
enough to stretch out and the space was both open and protected, so
that no passers-by would be snooping and gawking at us.

Now that everything about our game was in place, we sat and
looked at one another smiling. How could we foresee that this was
not in fact our game, in the same way that chess is not the pawn's or
the knight's or the queen's game? No, at that time we could not discern the Chess Players gravely leaning over our world. Carmina ran
to get a morning-glory from the hedge of the twins' house while we
began to adorn our first queen. We dressed her in an old violet house
robe belonging to Aunt Aura, one in which she barely fit. We suspended chains of violet paper from her hair, we placed the little
golden crown on her head, and around her neck we hung a string of
beads the size of fists. We brought out our adorned chair and placed
it in the middle of the chalk circles. Whale ruled there like a Magda-
lenian Venus, imposing on account of her proportions, but always
seeking Puia, whose help she was imploring with frightened eyes.
After we displayed our reverence before her, we handed her the
morning-glory and the wishbone. Whale dodged them at first with
an awkward gesture, but finally accepted them. We all felt it necessary to regard her with disdain, even in her curious hypostasis as

queen. She put the morning-glory on her chest, shoving the end in the blouse's bodice. She twirled the wishbone several times between her hefty fingers until she ended up grasping it by the wide bits at the end of the fork, one hand on each of the horns. The free end from which the bifurcation began, where the two horns joined together, started to move, very gently, up and down. We all huddled around the throne, gazing at this seemingly intelligent, unforeseen motion of the wishbone. Whale's mouth gaped open as she stared at her hands. The flexible two-branched bone began twisting visibly, ready to drop from her hands. When Puia approached, the wishbone wrenched itself away and fell at the girl's feet, who stared at it with cold eyes (nothing ever fazed Puia), picked it up and gave it back to the queen. 'It's pulling me forwards,' said the queen, and we could see now the long bones in her hand lurching forwards, millimetre by millimetre. 'Go after it,' Ester told her. Whale rose from the throne and, holding her arms pointed forwards as though aiming at a target, gave herself to the will of the wishbone. It dragged her like a dog on a leash. We followed after the hefty girl bedecked in mauve like a scarecrow. It was almost one o'clock in the afternoon, and a shimmering silence ruled the world under the tranquil skies, which would be kind to us for the rest of the week. The wishbone was dragging the queen towards the gate, and so all of us followed her on the deserted street. We veered to the left in the direction of the field. We could barely keep up with Whale, who marched forwards in ridiculously long strides, rattling her bulk with every step on the irregular, rough pavement. Strands of grass grew around the cobblestones. We passed the last house, and the field unfurled before us, stretching all the way to the horizon. Far off in the middle, we could see the melancholy watchtower, with a flaring windowpane in the tower, and next to it, like a scabby frog, the shed where I knew the REM resided. The wishbone forced us to make our way directly over the ploughed land, or rather over the fallow field, sprinkled with thistles, weeds and here and there a few timid cornflowers. There were maggot holes everywhere. Propped up on their long runner's legs, the green and powerful ground spiders that had ventured far from their holes retreated at our passage back into their lairs. We would have liked to follow them into those mysterious catacombs, but were stopped by a phantasm that made us quiver: the spider lunging like lightning and slashing at our eyes. Up above in the skies, the pale clouds were drifting and, like a good omen, looked as though they had been painted. I was walking now shoulder to shoulder with the blimp, who was staring cross-eyed at the tip of the wishbone. We had advanced about fifty paces into the field. Ada and Carmina had woven little crowns out of asters and cornflowers, looking cloyingly silly with their smiles and twin dresses, when suddenly Whale stopped. Nothing was pulling her forwards any more. The wishbone remained suspended for a moment, then slowly, like a clock's minute hand, began to point towards the ground. Whale screamed and dropped it as though it burnt her, and the bone glued itself to the ground like a magnet. We all stared at each other. We knew that there was something there under the earth. Two of us sat on our haunches and began to scrape the broken-up soil with our fingers, but it was pointless. As lunchtime was approaching and we had to go home, we decided to return at four with a shovel or spade. We even saw ourselves standing before a case of coins or an ancient helmet or something similar to the hen with golden chicks from our fourth-grade history books. Or a diamond the size of a turkey egg, that 'precious stone, one alone, one alone, precious stone' we sang about in our games. We kowtowed to our queen for about fifteen minutes, but the numbskull wouldn't give us any orders or commands; she just stood there staring with gaping mouth and bulging chin, crown tilted towards one ear, so that you just felt sorry for her. She looked like a kitchen maid dressed up like a queen. We finally scattered to our homes, but not before we marked the place with a dry branch adorned with a strip of mauve satin. I went into the courtyard and sat down on the empty throne, abandoned in the middle of the coloured circles. I was void of any thought. I would have preferred that Ester said at least one word to me rather than find God knows what precious stone. I wasn't even sure I wanted that. The truth was I didn't know what I wanted, perhaps I wanted not to suffer so much, I wanted everything to stop being so endlessly painful. Aunt Aura was busy with a client, but after a while Marcelino showed up, and we ate together. From the very beginning, he started to pry, to ask about our game and especially about the throne. He wanted to erase our circles and draw a Ceaika limousine instead; fortunately, I knew how to handle him. As soon as he finished eating, he grabbed his box with the button soccer game and went to meet with his buddies. My poor auntie didn't have much time to take care of him, busy as she was making dresses all the time. Father wouldn't be coming to see me till the day after, when it was visiting day at the hospital. He was going to take me to see Mother. But I didn't feel much love for either of them.

Around three o'clock, the girls showed up, dragging a few shovels after them. It was a dog-day afternoon and the violet rag hung limply on top of the stick like a scarecrow. We tore it off and began digging, but not before we convinced ourselves there was no one watching us. Many of the neighbourhood boys had gone to the country for the summer, while others were playing soccer till nightfall a few streets over, so we had all day to ourselves on the field. We dug awkwardly, our tongues out, and only after we managed to whittle out a narrow hole, about sixty centimetres deep, did we hit a root-punctured board. An enlarged bloodshot chrysalis was glued to it. Carnation hacked at it with the blinding edge of the spade, and it leaked a repulsive milk. We widened the hole a bit till we were able to loosen the board; it opened out into a tunnel with steps that descended down into the deep of the earth. The lair exhaled a cool draft that blew our hair out into the skies. Down, all the way at the bottom, you could spot a streak of bluish light. We agreed – because we all were dying of fright – that the queen should be the first to go down. Whale, however, was so slow in reacting that I suspect she didn't feel any fear till later on that evening. She was disoriented and staring at Puia, who was nodding in the direction of the tunnel. She sat on her butt, put her feet on the first step and disappeared into the dark, getting all dirty and tearing the chains of glittering paper around her neck. You could barely see the top of her head hesitating in the dense shadow. The tunnel fell at an oblique angle like basement steps and after about ten metres appeared to become horizontal, because the top of Whale's head, with its bluish streaks, dissolved completely after about a minute. We waited for a while and then followed, one by one. If someone saw us, they would believe it was a hallucination: young witches, extravagantly bedecked, vanishing amidst sulphur smoke into the earth for who knows what kind of scatological encounter with the Great Goat. The steps were made of solid rock and opened out into a corridor that sloped at a barely discernible angle. It was odd that, as we proceeded along the narrow corridor, the bluish, unearthly light became surprisingly brighter despite the lack of an apparent source. After turning a number of corners, we arrived at a gigantic hall.

In that ultramarine aura that spilled out of nowhere and permeated the entire hall, the soles of its feet facing us, its arms lying next to the ribs and pelvis, a giant human skeleton reclined before us. We stared at it with gaping mouths, unable to believe what we were seeing. We advanced towards it, some of us to its right, the others to the left, taking its measurements with our steps and staring at its mountainous kneecaps, its endless thighbones, the spinal column like an antediluvian reptile, the ribs the size of an old ship's, joined together by the triangular and lace-like sternum. Beyond the collarbone and the shoulder blades, on the other side of the neck's seven vertebrae, the skull leered with the air of the one who laughed last. Each molar was as large as one of our fists. The cranial vault measured about a metre and a half, and on its ivory surface we could see the zigzagging of the bone sutures. The entire skeleton from head to foot measured forty of my steps, which meant it was nearly twenty metres long. I recalled that sensation of the unnatural, of the artificial, of painted plaster, which I felt when I saw the Goliath whale with Father when we went to Children's Town. In comparison to that sorry sight, the skeleton we discovered in the oval grotto was entirely credible; we had seen cattle and bird bones before and knew what a real skeleton should look like. Credible, but with the exception of its extravagant size. The grotto surrounding it was oval, as if it had been built for it alone. At first, we were awestruck, but after a while we got tired of treating it with respect and began to scale its bones, wiggle its fingers; eventually, we all huddled inside its thoracic cage. We sat there about fifteen minutes in order to rest, and then we began to chatter about all sorts of things. The skeleton seemed to us like a child inside its mother's belly. Except that a little child couldn't lie there in an erect position, it wouldn't fit. It would need to curl up. We began to wonder how it was possible that the bones actually took shape there inside the belly. The twins couldn't believe that the two of them had spent so much time all curled up together inside their mother. 'Nine months?' 'Nine months!' Carnation screamed defiantly, though no one contradicted her. 'What if,' asked the green-eyed and icy Puia indifferently, who up till then had taken no interest in our conversation, 'what if we were in fact in the lair of a gigantic earth spider who had eaten the man inside whose skeleton we are and who perhaps had been a god?' It was as if all of a sudden we could actually see it, hairy and agile, running towards us with its eight interminable claws, seizing each and every one of us and injecting us with its poison. We dashed off, stepping all over each other on the way to the stairs, from where we stared back in fright: Puia was still there next to the skeleton, where she had tied a strip of violet velveteen to its left pinky's phalanx. We relaxed. There was no spider, and the skeleton was ours, we conquered it, and our flag, our current queen's flag, was hoisted on its edifice.

Our game had begun well, and the girls, content, went home. We were to reconvene the next morning, under the rulership of Ada, the indigo queen. We would rendezvous at the skeleton at ten in the morning. Each of us, before descending, had to make sure not to be seen. Because Rolando, as we had baptized the skeleton after the name of a blond boy on our street whom the girls liked, had to remain ours alone. I went home quickly, washed, and changed into a nice dress (Sarita Montiel, the beautiful Spanish chanteuse, was singing on the radio) and left with Marcel, who had promised to go with me to the watchtower of the Long Ones. Auntie let us go on condition we came back while it was still light outside, eight o'clock at the latest. Marcelino was happy; he was hoping that Egor would show him stunning toys or tell him pirate tales the way he always did when he came to see Aunt Aura with his mother. My cousin had never been to the watchtower but knew the path, so we left hand in hand, laughing and chatting, walking along the barely visible trail along whose margin grew solitary brambles. We took a left by the last house with the uneven back wall, dim and ashen, and set out over the field. A warm summer evening's wind blew in from the skirt of the forest, barely visible on the line of the horizon. Bathed in the late afternoon light, the clouds were the colour of roses, and locusts, grasshoppers and tiny field flies of all sorts drew capricious circles in the air. I liked my cousin very much, with his blondish brown hair and hands crossed behind him, walking a few steps ahead of me in his shorts and light blue shirt with elephants. We were getting closer to the house with the little tower, a completely unreal object in the surrounding landscape. A few years ago, when I saw Wajda's *Ashes and Diamonds*, I was unexpectedly thrilled to see that shot with the olive Renaissance chair sitting in the middle of the dusty field. The Long Ones' watchtower presented the same kind of impossibility. Only when we got very close did I realize how large it was. Looking up at the old mouldy walls, you had the impression of a line that aspired towards infinity. In reality, the watchtower was not more than fifteen metres in height, although it had, judging from the windows on the opposite side, no more than two floors. But above them rose the tower, not round as it seemed from a distance, but octagonal. We walked around the fenceless building, without any trees around it, without even a dog cage: only fallow ground sprinkled with wild flowers. About ten metres off was the shed, covered with tarred cardboard that appeared completely rotted. A lock, red from rust, was hanging on the door. We knocked on the door and Egor's deformed figure, pallid as though painted in oil, appeared at the second-floor window. But it was Madam Bach who opened the door and saw us inside.

The rooms were tall, narrow as wardrobes. Brass candelabra of faded crystal hung from the ceiling. We walked through three rooms, all exactly alike: there was barely enough space for a tiny round table and a few chairs, but the ceiling was so high that even Madam Bach seemed like a little girl under it. When Egor entered, hesitating in front of the stairs, the last room became unbearably crammed. Because his mother was in the middle of ironing, using a coal-heated flat iron – though the new electric ones had just appeared on the market – and because in any case we had been invited by Egor, who was now wearing a cherry robe through whose opening slit we could glimpse his hairless, bony chest, we all four mounted up the wooden stairs that spiralled once around an ice-cold pole. Up there, it was marvellous. Even today I would give anything to live in such a round room with the four arched windows. The hardwood floor smelled of wax. A minuscule Persian rug, worn down to the point of being transparent but filled with wonderful arabesques, covered a patch of flooring. 'Original white Bukhara rug, three centuries old,' Egor told us. He had put his immense palm on top of Marcel's head as though taking an apple from a dish. A chest of drawers, as old as the rug and encrusted with yellow ivory intarsia, and a sofa were the only pieces of furniture in the room. We sat on the sofa and waited for a few moments, just us, the children. Egor returned with a chair. Behind him followed Madam Bach with a plate of chocolate cookies. Egor sat on the chair and began to pull out of his pockets an army of lead soldiers, decorously painted with red and blue enamel, a bronze cannon ornamented with acanthus leaves and a tiny leather-handled stiletto, which he left in Marcel's care. During the time I spoke with Egor, Marcel led one battle after another on the precious rug.

In the beginning, the discussion didn't go anywhere. Egor put his questions with great concentration, with a look difficult to define, and I replied with short and timid answers. Yes, I liked it here at Aunt Aura's. I had to stay at least one week, because Mother . . . Then we were both quiet, and I took the shell-fan out of my pocket and handed it to him. I told him what I had dreamed, fearing that it was too little, but the giant suddenly rose, reaching almost all the way up to the rainbow-like icicles on the ceiling, lifted his bony arms and exclaimed with his unpleasant voice: 'Thank God!' I began to laugh. I felt proud to have passed this test, which I felt was to be so important in my life. I was waiting for him to reveal something essential, to introduce me to the enigma that consumed his bones, his cartilage, his flesh and the hours of his life. But he merely handed the shell back to me and told me to do the same thing the following night. 'The dreams will connect with each other, if *you are*, and they alone will lead you to REM. There is no other path.' 'But what is there?' I asked impatiently and somewhat irritated at his insistence to shove REM down my throat. 'There,' he replied, looking out the window toward the horizon that had become veiled by reddish clouds, 'there is *everything*.' We were silent. The air in the room took on the golden hue of tea. Marcelino knocked the rigid soldiers against one another, crawling on his knees under the curved-legged chest with the stiletto in his fist, making cannon noises and wailing at times like dying soldiers, at others like vanquishing ones. 'How much I would love to be a woman!' said Egor suddenly. 'You are lucky to be a woman. We men, we're not good for anything. We're always looking to find what in fact we will never know. We destroy our lives far from others, only in order to satisfy our limitless madness. The true human being is the woman. We are merely modified beings, crippled. Just because we cannot bring the world out from inside our bellies, we agonize to get it out of our heads. Woman lives, man writes.' After which, with an unexpected smile, Egor continued: 'If only they carved my name on my grave I would have no need to live.' I know now it was a quote, but at the time I was shocked by the gap between its content and the nearly humorous tone that he used to express it. I didn't know how to reply, although I felt a light emotion flowing through my nerves. It was already dark outside, so I ate another cookie and stood up to go. Marcel didn't want to leave, he would have liked to play all night, but finally he had to forsake his lead soldiers. We said goodbye to our hosts and I promised Egor to come by again the next evening, 'Only for five minutes,' in order to tell him about what I had dreamed. Their silhouettes, long and undulating like streaks of violet smoke, the way they gazed after us from the watchtower's doorstep, he leaning on his walking stick and holding his mother's waist with an odd gesture, with their motionless faces lost in the heights, made me recall something so intensely that I had to turn my head. I felt in my palm Marcel's tiny hand. For no particular reason, I brought it to my lips and kissed it while we walked off along the narrow trail, minuscule under the flaming sky. Fortunately, the boy was still preoccupied with his games at the watchtower to notice. The cold wind, blowing in red gusts, tainted the flowers of the field with purple.

That night, I saw myself again in the forest. It was morning again, an eternal, blinding morning. From the hundreds of crisscrossing paths, I chose the one which I had determined I could take without turning away from my course. The gigantic trees were adorned with tinder half-moons. Stems shouldering crumpled leaves on their tips shot out, pallid as reptile tails, from under the pieces of bark on the ground. Here and there, a whitish worm hung on the end of a nearly invisible filament. It twisted and turned in the green air beneath the foliage. I hopped and danced along my trail, when suddenly a fallen tree trunk barred my way. My heart sank. For a moment, I stood there disconcerted: The trunk was as wide as I was tall and appeared completely rotted. A swarm of carnivorous ants armed with claws streamed out through a crack in its bark. I couldn't walk around it, as I had promised myself not to turn away from my path, and my heart wouldn't let me turn back. I sat on a log and began to cry. And the tears of dreams are far more heartrending than those of reality. A hideous centipede, the length of my palm, crept by my feet while I wiped my tears with the lap of my dress. I stood and, without knowing what I was doing, I grabbed a piece of the cracked bark and pulled at it. It was rotten and light as cork. Underneath, I found the corpse of a blackbird being devoured by ants. A live and aggressive red mass teemed over the bird's body. I grabbed it by the tip of a wing and tossed it, ants and all, a few metres away from me. Soon the ants abandoned the trunk; all that was left were burrowing woodworms digging parallel canals into the loose, spongy trunk. All the voracious insects followed after the blackbird's corpse. Then I clambered atop the fallen tree. I mounted it like a horse, feeling the rough bark underneath me. My tears dried up, and I felt happy. I carefully let myself down and went on my way again.

I woke up early, and after I washed myself I went into the kitchen, where Aunt Aura spread out a sticky layer of dough on the clean oilcloth sprinkled with flour. I pulled a chair and watched her make doughnuts. She shaped them with the round edge of a drinking glass and spread them on the hot pan, where they sizzled until they became red and crunchy. I liked to drop the odd-shaped bits in the pan, all the triangles and curves that were left after moulding the perfect circles. After frying, the fluffy shapes resembled dogs, deer, dragons, which I then rolled in powdered vanilla sugar. I would then pamper myself by eating their heads or a leg. Meanwhile, Auntie Aura told me about the time when Mother brought me there when I was a year and a half old, 'tinier than a dougnut hole.' She would line the wooden tub with bedsheets, and they rocked it till I fell asleep. When I cried, they tried to frighten me: 'If you don't straighten up, the doughnut monster is gonna gobble you up. Listen to him coming . . .' But I was far from being scared. I would just widen my eyes and bring a finger to my lips: 'Shhh! Listen to the doughnut monster!' while Mother and her sister would roll with laughter. I filled up on doughnuts so much that I didn't need to eat anything else. I grabbed Zizi and went out into the yard. It was already ten, and I had to keep the appointment with Rolando. Chombe, an omnivorous dog, was munching on some stuffed pepper leftovers next to the chicken coops. Gigi was keeping an eye on the dirty dove's nest that hung high on a pole in the neighbours' yard; lazy as she was, she could still leap up in the air and even catch a dove from time to time. Of course, the neighbours would complain. Aunt Aura would then catch the cat and beat her on the head. Gigi endured stoically, shut her eyes tight and glued her ears to the back of her head. When she finally got away from her martyrdom, she began washing herself, rubbing her head with her paws, licking her chops and staring at us through her nearly shut lids. I liked Gigi a lot, even though, despite her cleaning habits, she was not a model of virtue. I went out in the street and sauntered over the fields. I quickly found the hole we had camouflaged the best we could and descended the steps to the gigantic blue chamber. The gigantic skeleton filled up the space. Its hipbones were wide, a little too wide for a man. But the shoulders – next to the collarbone, which was almost as thick as my legs – and the triangular shoulder blades were large and gracefully joined. No one was there yet. I was alone, like an animal in a cage, sitting on the vertebrae between the ivory ribs. That's why my heart skipped a beat when I heard a deep voice booming out of the cranium: 'Whooo are yooou, straaange girrrl, and whaaat are yooou looking fooor here?' But I sighed with relief when I saw Carnation's inky head popping out with a wide grin from one of the cranium's eye sockets, spitting sunflower seeds all over the place in the Gypsy fashion. I joined her by crawling into Rolando's skull through the hole at the bottom of the socket. The interior was smooth and clean as a celluloid doll's. Though we were a bit crowded, Carnation and I fit very well inside; there was even enough room for another girl. Clashing against the skull's shiny, furrowed walls, each word sounded sharper, more concrete, nearly material. I remember one moment when the Gypsy girl asked herself: 'Why the hell don't we got no savarins here, oh mama, how I'd gobble 'em . . .' and the word 'savarins,' polarized by the bone wall's echoes, became so thick that for each one of us the well-known form of the cake, leaking with red jam and whipped cream on top, doused in syrup and aromas, coagulated right before our eyes. But unfortunately, they had a gelatinous consistency, and when we grabbed them they dribbled through our fingers, breaking apart in the air. We were still swallowing the void when the twins showed up, whom we scared so badly that they were ready to run back up the stairs. Fifteen minutes later, everyone had showed up and we were looking at Ada, the day's queen, with completely different eyes. She was dressed up in a little indigo skirt and a blouse of dark mauve. We would now adorn her with all the attributes of royalty. But, first, Ada picked from Carmine's fists the ticket that would reveal the place where she would reign. She ended up with the most coveted place, the courtyard. When she read her ticket she began to hop between Rolando's ribs so hard that the skeleton began rocking like a ship. We left the grotto and settled in the yard. We sat Ada down on the throne and bedecked her with all the trinkets we could find. In her left hand, she held like a sceptre the iron statue of an Indian warrior. From her chest hung her flower, the yellowish-orange zinnia. I brought her from the house the watch that she was to use in the game. It was a tiny lady's watch with a red-lacquered band, golden dial and hands like black needles. It had no movement; it was just a toy designed to learn how to tell time. The hands could be moved by pressing on a button. We put it on her wrist. The ritual of investiture being completed, we bowed deeply before our new queen. We were curious to learn what our commands would be, each of us wondering what she would do if in her place. After staring at her watch hundreds of times in order to buy time, after sending us to get miscellaneous things for her and ordering us to make all kinds of funny faces, Ada finally made her decision. I think she invented the game on the spot, because I didn't recall us playing it before. She commanded us to draw lines, two metres apart, across the width of the brick alley that led to the back of the yard. There were seven white lines. They represented, the queen explained, the ages of man divided into decades. That is why we wrote the number 10 next to the first line, 20 next to the second, and so forth, all the way to 70. Following the order of our colours, each one of us would have to cross the alley and, as we stepped over each line, mime the respective age. We didn't think it was a wonderful idea, but it would do for starters. We concluded that old age was easy to mime, but thirty or forty might be baffling. Still, a command was a command and had to be obeyed, so Whale, still wearing the now withered morning glory of the day before on her chest, stepped over the 10 line – she was already eleven – and started off with small sporadic steps across the alley. In order to time her, as we had heard was the custom in a competition, Ada, while sitting on her throne, glanced at her watch. She belted out a short scream of surprise because the hands of the watch had disappeared. Could they have fallen off? It seemed impossible. Only when she popped open the crystal did Ada understand what was taking place: she poked her finger inside but pulled it back instantly, staring in fright at a drop of blood. The watch's hands were still there, but they revolved so fast that you couldn't see them. The drop of blood, shiny and purple, spread out into the weft of her dress, forming a scarlet stain on her lap. We would have continued to wonder at the mysteriously animated watch had we not suddenly noticed what was going on with Whale, waddling like a somnambulist along the brick-paved trail. She was very close to the third line, and at first we thought she was playing at being mature in a disturbingly truthful manner. But it wasn't merely miming: Whale had grown tall, her hips and breasts had become heavier, her hair lighter. She was now indeed worthy of her nickname: a totemic female, round as planet Jupiter and just as massive. Her clothes were changing shape during her journey, the hem of her skirt rose or fell, her shoe heels were thin at times, stumpy at others. Halfway through the third section, a thick golden wedding band began to shine on her finger, and when she stepped over the fourth line her hair started to turn grey. She was much wider than she was tall. She had developed a triple chin, and her breasts hung down to her belly-button. We walked alongside her on the edge of the alley, but she stared ahead with an absent look. She had grown a sparse moustache, and thick strands of hair shot out of her chin. A little before reaching the fifth line, Whale collapsed within herself. We drew back, mad with fear. In a matter of seconds, all that remained were a few bone fragments, wrapped in rotted rags: an earth-hued maxillary, a thigh-bone, a few ribs . . . They became dust and turned to impalpable matter, nothing. We were about to howl but suddenly Whale materialized next to us, outside the borders of the accursed alley. And seeing how she was staring at us, in utter perplexity, we understood that she didn't know anything and that she must never know. It was now Ada's turn, who took the watch off and left it on the throne. And instead of being frightened, we suddenly got very curious: we wanted to know how the other girls would look when they aged and died. Because the idea of death itself didn't faze us, it was like watching a movie, and we saw everything as an odd hallucination whose truth we would never think to take seriously. When Ada headed towards the first line, Carmina ran after her and took her hand. They couldn't imagine going on this journey except together. It was against the rules we had established but, since the queen was implicated and because we didn't want to separate the twins, we allowed them to begin at the same time, shoulder to shoulder, in their little white dresses spotted with tiny red polka dots, with the same glassy, coffee-brown hair fluttering behind them, the same idiotic-charming grin on their identical faces. Their clothes changed right after their first step, while they – dissimilar enough to those who knew them closely – were impossible to tell apart. They were a double organism united by the same metabolism, they were Siamese twins sewed together by their interlaced hands, Carminada or Adacarmina stepping forwards with identical steps, their hair fluttering simultaneously, blown by the same yellow breath of air. Approaching the second line, they became two young women in green and white, wearing emerald snake bracelets around their wrists, smiling with raw, full lips. You could imagine them under their clothes encased up to their necks in nylon stockings with seams at the back, each body a warm and sensual thigh. At forty, they were stout women with proud bosoms and high shoulders, veritable mares in delicate black-leather shoes, red turtleneck lamé dresses. Their chests sparkled with identical broaches – spiders with opal bodies and platinum legs. They didn't reach the fifth line either. Abruptly, one of them dissipated in the wind so quickly that for several moments the skeleton remained standing in its high heels, silk rags suspended from it. The hair fluttered for a time atop the skull, then turned to ash. The fingernails fell to the ground, twisting in the air like the petals of a red rose. The other twin hadn't yet had time to react and, as her sister's skeleton sagged, turned to dirt and disappeared, she stared at it in bewilderment. She fell to her knees and spread out on the ground, one hip joint sticking out. She froze into place, became white and turned to stone. She looked like a statue, like a lava cast from Pompeii. Her nose then broke into pieces, her arms shattered, her trunk fractured in segments, only slivers and shards remained, which pulverized into chalk dust: the wind blew it away towards the back of the yard. But Ada and Carmina were now next to us again, in their usual clothes. Ada put the golden crown back on her head and the watch around her wrist. Puia was next, cold as ice water, fascinating as the viper's transparent eye, but, above all – indifferent, absent-minded. Lightly clattering her pendants and her earrings, she traversed the seven intervals at a steady pace, unchanged, always identical to herself. Crossing the seventy-year line, she was the same child, beautiful and without equal. Her image dissolved into the backyard fence and melted into the horizon under the beguiling clouds. In their passage, Ester and Carnation took on the traits of their races. Ester grew large and red, with her piles of furs and sophisticated hats, and after fifty she became monstrously fat. Her teeth lost their gums and became horse-like between her Asiatic lips and a mole showed up next to her nostrils. When she crossed the seventh line, she became a disgusting corpse. Carnation, on the other hand, dwindled and darkened in her green headscarf with red figures, in her male jacket and creased red skirt dotted with blue and orange flowers, her pitch-black bare feet. At fifty, she was an old hag in a ragged trench coat with torn pockets. She had one hand in a cast tied around the neck with filthy bandage gauze, and she waddled along on bowed legs, a hunchback crow. She croaked before sixty. But there they were again, next to us, quaking and trembling as though they had retained something incommunicable but which revealed itself only through the language of sweat and shivers. Not one of them knew what had happened to her own self along the brick alley.

I also prepared myself for the great departure. I asked myself whether I would lose consciousness, whether it would be like in a dream or heavy sleep, or death. Many times, alone in my bedroom on Calea Moşilor, during crimson afternoons when I should have been sleeping, I fought with all my might to remember anything, be it the most insignificant thing, that had happened to me before I came into this world. The world has been around for millions of years. What had I been doing during that time? To believe that I hadn't felt anything or that I hadn't lived seemed impossible. When I stepped over the first chalk line, I felt suddenly as though I was coming out of myself. Before that, I had been scattered inside the thin body of a little girl, crammed between the intestines, the arteries and the lungs, twisted around the spine's marrow, sunk into the fingers and the thighs. Now I was leaking out through a craggy surfaced tunnel, elastic and gelatinous. The tunnel's walls were rushing backwards at infinite speed. I felt far-reaching and pure. Hurtling headfirst out of the tunnel, ectoplasmic and gleaming with happiness, I forged through the night on a trail as wide as the distance between stars. Having arrived at a barrier – which was inside me rather than out – I saw a fantastic aurora approaching me from the unthinkable places on the other side, in which every gleam was a world, in which every point of light was a god. It seemed like an ecstatic explosion of the cosmos, an apocalypse and genesis mixed in equal proportions. Everything drew me towards the light on the other side of the light. However, I couldn't go beyond the barrier ('Not yet,' I heard a voice within me), and I turned back. I was again among my girlfriends, in my aunt's courtyard under the summer's opulent skies. I didn't recover till evening. Before the simplicity and power of that world into which I had almost gone, the forms of the present world (the darkly transparent leaves of the bitter cherry, its ruby fruit with softly wet flesh, the truck with the peeling blue paint on its hood, the kites levitating over the field and nearly colliding with the turtledoves, each brick embraced by the spider webs on the house's façade, each greying hair in Chombe's thistle-filled fur, his jaws and snout like humid rubber, Ester's face – Ester to whom I hadn't yet spoken) seemed to me superfluous, distant, like the world of tropical corals, with warm waters, parrotfish, sea stars, sea sponges and madrepores. So that, even before REM, the world became strange for me. Certainly, I was tempted to find out what had actually happened, what the other girls saw, how I looked at each age (I am certain that between the third and fourth lines I looked as I do now), and especially I wanted to know the end. But I knew that no one would tell me. That was the rule of the game.

We finished at two, I slept in the afternoon, I played a little with Marcel, and in the evening we took off for the watchtower. Egor was standing in the doorway, and we only stayed long enough for me to tell him the dream of the night before. He seemed tired; he said he had 'worked' the entire day. But, propped up on his cane, he listened to me carefully. How frail he was! A breath of wind could make him sway. When I finished, he told me it seemed that I was the one. So far, so good. 'You see, in order to get there, you must either be from Tibet and have lived seven hundred years ago, or to dream the seven dreams of my shell. It is like the code of a bank vault. You found the first two numbers. Maybe you have been chosen to find the rest. Dream carefully, don't rush. Trust yourself.' We returned quickly over the deserted field. Halfway home, we ran into an accordion player. With his brown hat pulled over his eyes, he had the look of a bandit from *Pinocchio*. The accordion was hitched to his back with scarlet straps, and he carried in his arms a gigantic bouquet of wild flowers, camomiles, winged brooms and snapdragons. After he passed, I turned my head but quickly turned it back, because he had also turned his to stare at us, his look as puzzled as mine. The trail led only to the watchtower. What could this man be looking for there? I couldn't imagine the Long Ones as lovers of Gypsy music. After all, they had a radio, an old but good one.

The third night I dreamed that I went farther into the woods. I had left the log behind; the pleasant trail snaked and twisted before me. Sunbeams fell through the branches on the oily bodies of the centipedes. Squirrels leaped from one branch to another. Soon, as I ran filling my lungs with the green air, I came to a meandering brook whose glassy, ashen-blue water sussurated between the grassy banks. My path ended at the shore but continued on the other side of the brook. I paused in the shore's grass, wet from the spray. Deep in the water, alabaster trout slithered to and fro. Looking to the right, about fifteen metres off, I saw a wooden footbridge covered with moss. But something else was more attractive to me. I took off my little dress and stepped voluptuously into the icy water. I immersed myself up to my neck, feeling with my toes the silt, fine as thick water, mixing with thin strands of aquatic grass. Seized by an agonizing pleasure, I plunged under the murky surface with my eyes wide open. The water caressed my arms' muscles, pressed on my belly and drew the contour of my spine with pieces of ice. I sat there curled in a ball underneath the silt curtain and I would have stayed there forever, like an insect caught in a drop of resin, if I had not remembered about my trail. I came out with water streaming from my hair onto my skin and walked to the other shore, where I had tossed my clothes. I dried myself, my arms raised to the green-blue-yellow-transparent-sonorous morning sun. The bird trills sketched in thin lines gigantic, arching vaults in the silence of the forest. I continued on my way, tiny and pure and a little ashamed, on the trail between the trees.

Father came that day. I heard his voice before I was fully awake. I lifted Zizi from the floor and held her tight to my chest. I don't know why I was always afraid of him. It is true that sometimes his face turned red and he shouted with that voice full of anger belonging to men, that voice that makes your entrails curl, like the wolf's howl or the profound growl of the tiger. Though he never beat me, Father was always the Beast for me, capable of tearing me to pieces someday. I was most afraid when he kissed me. He kissed me passionately, all over my face, scratching me something terrible with his unshaved beard. He never imagined that I didn't love him. Actually, I never loved anyone besides Zizi, and even Zizi was the target of my cruel wrath when she didn't study diligently or give the right answers when I tested her on the ivy-covered balcony before the blackboard improvised from an old servants' entrance door. So, that morning I dressed especially nice, with my little Sunday dress ironed by Auntie Aura and my white kneesocks, and hand in hand with Father headed for the hospital. I believe I would have died of sadness if I had thought we would never return. Even so, I woke up snivelling in the tram that rattled along Mihai Bravu Boulevard. We got off at the Colentina Hospital, where everything was at the same time so real and so indifferent that I felt I was dreaming. Old chestnuts rose in the courtyard between the pavilions with sunny verandas that reminded you of mastless galleons. On the benches beneath the trees sat patients in cherry-red and dark-blue gowns. Some of them were complete wrecks with green faces, while others, especially the girls with shiny and curly hair, looked so good that you wondered what they were doing in a hospital. Speaking with the patients and walking to and fro were the visitors, people in street clothes who, like Father and me, had dressed better than usual for the occasion. Mother was not in the courtyard; she couldn't get out of bed. A dark-haired doctor in a white short-sleeved shirt followed by a group of nurses rushed from one pavilion to another. We went up a flight of cement stairs, mournful and unconcerned, spiralling along the institutional-green walls. We went through a large glass door that opened out into an endless corridor, painted the same institutional green. Then, we opened countless other doors that opened out into other taciturn corridors. I was always expecting each door to lead to Mother's room, but we were always turning corners, going up and down along the twisting corridors. From time to time, the door to a numbered room would open and I saw a glazed sink and a toilet or a closet full of dirty brooms, filthy mops and boxes of sodium bicarbonate. I also spotted closets stacked with shelves of tagged pyjamas. Finally, when I got so dizzy I thought we'd never get out and end up leaving our bones along the walls of some corridor, we opened one last door. The room we entered was very large, the size of the room underneath the earth where we found Rolando. The thirty or so beds made of pipe tubing and lined up along the windows were filled with female patients, young and old alike, some just lying there or sleeping, others talking to one another across the night tables with flowers sticking out of drinking glasses. There were a few visitors sitting on the edge of the beds. A man in a train conductor's uniform and a little boy about my age with one shoulder raised higher than the other had come to visit a woman with a lemon-yellow face. We headed towards Mother's bed. I was a little emotional. Mother began to weep tears of joy when she saw us. She was sitting up halfway with her elbows on the pillows. I kissed her, and her skin was wet. Her hair was so thin that it was sticking to the skin of her skull. She didn't look good and had lost lots of weight. We spent about fifteen minutes with her. I told her I liked it at Auntie Aura's. 'But don't you miss home?' 'Yes, I do,' I said, looking at her neighbour, who was pouring water from a glass carafe into a pot of fuchsias. When I turned my eyes from the fragile flowers with scarlet petals and cyclamen hearts, my mother's face looked whitish, like plastic or wax. She had lost blood, but most of all she had been in such pain that she never recovered. For many years afterwards, during my entire adolescence, she put us all through hell with the new habit she picked up after the unfortunate ulcer: she felt the need to see her own blood. She pricked her skin or cut herself every day and, when we attempted to take away all sharp objects, she would bite herself in order to cause a tiny pearl of blood to spurt out, which then she watched for minutes on end, finally happy and at ease. This imperious need would suddenly gain control over her wherever she happened to be, on the street, in a store, out visiting friends. She would then grab the needle she always kept handy and skilfully stick it into her skin. Later, she developed the need to see a whole stream of her own blood, and then she would cut herself dangerously deep with a knife. Eventually, she had to be hospitalized, though physically she was perfectly healthy. During the days when she didn't succeed in procuring for herself, through a quintillion methods of subterfuge, that unique satisfaction, her face darkened and melancholy's great Omega appeared between her eyebrows. But that time at the hospital, Father and I, sitting on the edge of her bed, could not suspect what awaited us. We kissed her and then left quietly, finding ourselves suddenly outside in the afternoon's soft and blistering sun.

Back at Auntie Aura's, the girls were waiting for me, a little tired from their games. They couldn't really play Queens without me there. They had decided to delay the crowning of Carmine until the afternoon, and until then they played Countries with a striped rubber ball. Then they changed to Slaps and Three Princes on Horses. They played One-Two-Three to the wall and Ant-Walk, Lion-Walk, Fairy-Walk. After I told them about Mama, we scattered, and I ate lunch with Auntie Aura, Father and Marcel. Under the table – we ate outside – Gigi and Chombe shared the leftovers. There was a melody on the radio that I recalled for days to come: 'Ada-Kaleh, Ada-Kaleh . . .' I played for a little while with my cousin in the house and then went out in the courtyard around four. Carmina was dressed up entirely in sky blue: she wore a short-sleeved linen blouse, a pleated skirt she had borrowed from Ester (which is why it was a little too large for her) and a pair of ashen-blue tights. On her finger, she wore a ring studded with turquoise, more than likely imitation, and braided cornflowers in her hair. She looked like a real fairy, the way she sat on her decked throne. Behind her ear, she wore a carnation flecked with white spots which she'd got from our garden – because she had pulled her hair to the side, so that her right ear and entire neck all the way to the ringlets on her nape seemed open and pure, as in a painting. We handed her the pierced pearl, her object, which she grasped between her index finger and thumb. From my uncle's hat she drew the piece of paper with the place where she'd rule. It was the street, perhaps the most flavourless of all places. Indeed, there was absolutely nothing you could do there. The street was long, silent and sad. Looking at it, you could feel how insignificant was the corner of the world it was a part of. Maybe that's what a street looked like in a tiny, godforsaken provincial town, or some back alley in a South American city, or a lonely dusty trail in Kansas. The kites, fluttering in many colours with their corrugated paper tails tangled in the telegraph wires, magnified the sense of the street's desperate loneliness. Weeds and minuscule red flowers grew between the pavement's stones. The withered sun was hanging high up above it, far-off where the street narrowed towards the city. A blue shadow leaked from an emergency vehicle parked about a hundred metres down from us. There we stood in the middle of the deserted street, awaiting the queen's commands. Carmina, with the golden crown plopped on top of her head, stared attentively at her mother-of-pearl bead. The wishbone and the watch proved to be filled with great powers. What could the bead in Carmina's fingers do? It seemed like it could do nothing; after fifteen minutes, we began to try to invent something. Finally, however, the blue queen figured out its secret: you had to look through the pearl's hole. Through the tiny sliver of light, you could see an uncanny city. As she began describing it to us, we found ourselves suddenly walking through a strange metropolis.

It was an ashen world full of astonishing buildings, as in an etching. There was no one in the whole city. The buildings, placed irregularly and forming choking streets and triangular plazas, were made of rough-hewn polygonal stones and dotted with glimmering transparent windows. Rotating doors were still in motion, as if it hadn't been long since someone had come out of the enigmatic palaces. Up on the cornices, there were allegorical statues depicting Envy and Slavery. Behind the curtainless windows (because everything there was made of ashen stone and glass) were stuffed owls the size of grown adults. Stuffed parrots leaned over and peered at us from the edge of the walls, astounding us with the purple and green of their wings, with the azure of their long tail feathers. The glass eyes of the birds interfered with the demented architecture. As you turned the corner, always other plazas, other perspectives, other cyclopic hard-edge constructions rose abruptly or in steps before your eyes, ending in cupolas of ash, speckled with the eyes of sky-lights, opening out towards the melancholy-toned fog that was the sky. In the plazas, statues balled up from the cold, provoked questions without answers. One of them displayed a kneeling child. Finally, we went though a gate. Its poles were guarded by two Beasts. Not tigers, not lions or hyenas, bears or reptiles or ghosts, but Beasts. We traversed a nearly infinite, foggy square. In the middle rose a building with metal reinforcements, with a violet-blue glass cupola. Something throbbed inside the cupola, something that looked like the feetus of a fish as it emerges out of its egg. We climbed a monumental stairway, rough-surfaced like granite, and went through a rotating door. The inside chamber was immense. The thin nerves of the vault looked like the ribs of a gigantic thorax. The light fell in violet stripes through the cupola where that hideous, translucent something throbbed in slow motion. The mosaic marble of the concrete floor curved like the earth. As we paused in the middle of the chamber, we all had the same thought: *to give birth to a human being.* Whale stood first in front of everyone (the way we huddled there together in chat chamber, minuscule as ants) and spoke her desire, touching with her lips the bead's mother-of-pearl skin. And then, nearly touching the cold vault with its skull, at first transparent as glass, then milky as a white emulsion leaking out of a thin vial, finally yellowish as ivory, a skeleton resembling the one in our grotto, resembling Rolando, rose right before us. However, standing on its feet, creaking under its own weight, it was far more imposing. Its grin beneath the vault seemed like a defiance addressed to the unseen stars. Next, Ada stepped forwards, glued the pearl to her cheek and uttered her wish. Over the bones, over the spinal apophyses, like red, striated leeches, the interlacing warp and weft of muscles began to take shape, sewn in solid alabaster tendons, forming rings around the mouth and eyes, triangular stripes between the ribs, powerful discs on the chest, vigorous cylinders on the arms and thighs. Before us stood a skinless man, sadder than death. Carmina asked for blood, and that muscular flesh was suddenly woven with violet and red ropes, the threads of the veins, arteries and capillaries, and the room began to vibrate soundlessly with the powerful resonance of the heart. Puia asked for the nerves and the senses, and the man opened his eyes, his blue eyes. The yellowish nerves, in their medullary sheaths, snaked along the still visible flesh. Ester kissed the pearl, and the man was encased in bronze skin and became beautiful as a god. His hair, golden and curling, grew on his skull. Was he complete? Carnation asked for his sex, and all of us were forced to look down, as though blinded by the light. There was something between the thighs, where we had almost nothing. A fog of golden hair palpitated on the chest, while the cheeks waved in goldenreddish reflections. Finally, I walked forwards towards his feet (the tip of my head was no higher than his ankle), and I asked that a soul be given to him. His chest was suddenly adorned with two white round breasts with rosy tips, and curly hair fell in golden vines to the hips. A rose bloomed between his fingers.

We left him there under the vault, in order for him to go on with his fantastic life by himself, and went out into the deserted city. Coloured birds, larger than us, spied on us from the windows. Otherwise, the city was ashen grey, like all cities that inhabit a pearl. When we got tired of roaming through the stone city, Carmina put the pearl's hole to her eye and saw our street. She began to describe it with such precision that soon we found ourselves again on the stones of our sidewalk, surrounded by squatty greenish and pink houses and by poles blackened by tar. The sun was setting and the sky surrounding it took on an indigo colour, while across from it on the other side of the sky you could see the moon, steamy and blue. Our shadows lengthened hideously on the field, like filiform insects. Carmine's day had come to an end.

In the light of the approaching twilight, the bricks of our house glittered like rubies. The house seemed to suck the light around it, causing the air to appear withered and brown. A window facing the sunset burned yellow, like burning salt. When it was time to say goodbye, I did what I had wanted to do from the very start (which seemed to me a suicidal gesture): I approached Ester and asked her to stay with me for a little while. From the gate, we watched the others as they trailed off towards their own homes. Against the darkening background of the fields, the face of the red-headed girl appeared the colour of ivory. The whites of her eyes reflected the orange sun in sparks of light. In the corner of one of the eyes, I saw a tiny vein, like a strand of bluish wool. We stared at each other for a long time, without saying anything – she melancholy and grave, I feeling suffocated, lost. When she took my hand, her palm was wet with emotion. I felt, I can finally say it now, that I loved her, that I wanted to hold her in my arms, that I never wanted to go home. I walked her home, hand in hand. All we said before we separated was, 'See you.' I returned home by myself, dizzy. I saw and continued seeing the entire evening before my eyes (or behind them), Ester's reddish-orange flesh, her full cheeks, her last smile that gave her that bitter, exotic expression of African women. I was no more than twenty steps from the gate when an overly made-up woman walked by, swaying her hips in a ridiculous manner underneath an impossible skirt. Her arms were full of yellow tulips. Despite the fact that I was feeling so nostalgic, so happily unhappy, I stared in astonishment after her mare hips, while she, leaving behind her a beetlelike black shadow, walked off into the distance towards the watchtower. Far off into the distance, you could see on the same trail two other bluish silhouettes. I walked into the house and went directly to my room. I threw myself on the bed. I lay there for about an hour, not thinking of anything, not being present. I lay there face down, without caring that I was getting my best skirt, the skirt I wore to visit Mother and which I didn't want to take off, all wrinkled up. I put one hand underneath the pillow and listened without hearing to the obsessive clickety-clack of the sewing machine in the next room. It was already dark in the room when Auntie Aura called me to dinner.

After dinner, I went to sleep and dreamed of a drinking glass. You could only see one part of its lip, sparkling in a sorrel bush. Because I was back on my trail in the forest without limits. I picked up the glass and looked at it carefully. It gave me a disturbing feeling. I saw it as an obstacle on my path. I was upset that it halted my aimless pursuit, but

I kept looking at it, entranced. It wasn't actually a real glass, rather a cup made from the most translucent of crystal, with a delicate foot and its oval shape lengthening into a pure curve. A fissure, extending from the lip to the widening base, was proof of its fragility. It was a condemned glass. It would soon be splinters. In it, there still was (through what miracle?) a tiny remnant of ruby wine, thick as red honey. I stared for a long time in fascination at the undulating purple shadow the glass cast on the ground amidst the branches. I hesitated, wondering whether to drink the wine or not. Finally, with a guilty feeling, I swallowed a drop. The rest I tossed in a tiny stream on the ground. When I looked again at the cup, I shuddered: at the bottom lay a large and heavy drowned spider. I smashed the glass against a trunk, sat on my haunches and began to cry. There inside the dream, I felt a loneliness without exit, without hope . . .

I woke up in the middle of the night and realized I was in love. Why did I have to love Ester? For many years, she had been just another girl like Puia or Carmina or Carnation. And now I couldn't wait till I saw her again. I was confused and disoriented, because the world didn't believe that the love I felt was possible. People talked about love between a boy and a girl, between a man and a woman, but I never heard anyone speak about two women in love. It was more than certain, I thought, that I would never be able to marry Ester when I grew up. This upset me, because I felt that my love would extend forwards into the future. What would happen when we separated, was it possible I would never see her again? I walked slowly out of the room in my pyjamas with little rabbits, crossed the tar-black hallway on tiptoe and opened the front door. I was suddenly greeted by the hundreds of thousands of stars fanning out across the sky, burning and gleaming in all colours. Between them, descending across the vault, the great alabaster comet fluttered its tresses, foretelling cataclysms, floods, fires, disasters. Below the stars, very far below on my street, which looked now like the bottom of a river, other lights moved, undulating oddly. Stepping with my bare soles on the alley's bricks between the shrubs and the roses, I walked to the gate. Carrying flashlights, lanterns or candles in their hands, in small groups or alone, revealed in all their aspects by the chiaroscuro that enveloped them, hundreds of beings were heading for the fields: silent women, dark and enigmatic, hobbling old men leaning forwards on bent knees, children with primitive jaws and dragonfly eyes, unshaven men with caps pulled over their faces, carrying newspaper-wrapped packages tied together with a string. They held bouquets of flowers in their hands. Bewitched, I hugged the gate's pole and stared at the procession melting together on the path to the watchtower, shining now like a star. My eyes were sleepy, and I could barely keep them open. I would have liked to walk through the warm night and join the procession, but my feet drew me back towards the cool sheets of the bed. I went back in the house and curled between them. Underneath the pillow, my hand caressed the tiny pink shell from which the dreams had sprung.

The next day, Auntie Aura woke me up at ten. I was dead tired and begged her to let me sleep. Then, I recalled with great joy that our game of Queens (the most beautiful we had ever played) would continue with the fourth day, when the beautiful green queen would be Puia, the portulaca queen. I was even happier to recall that in the evening I would visit Egor again. This time, I would tell him two dreams at once, and I was certain I was on the right path. What had taken place the night before at the watchtower? Who could those people with flowers in their hands be? Maybe I would find out that evening. I ate and went out in the yard dressed in a Tyrolean skirt. Carnation, always the first to arrive, was swinging on our gate in her red skirt, which she had inherited from her mother and which had been worn by a few sisters before her, and slippers with pompons. She had that laughter of Indian women, as though she were cringing from something unpleasant, but at the same time voluptuous, vicious, false. We began to prepare the throne for the new occupant, to cover it with leaves and green branches. We refreshed the colours of the seven circles with chalk. The twins showed up next, carefree for having already discharged their duties and happy everything had ended well for them. Again, they were dressed alike, in white pinafores with a tiny duck in front. Ester trailed in next, her head lowered, and smiled at me discreetly with her sweet eyes. I smiled back at her. Everything was ready, except for Whale and Puia, who were more than an hour late. When we finally saw them, we understood why.

Puia looked fabulous. If an eleven-year-old girl could look like the Queen of Sheba, Semiramis, and Cleopatra all wrapped in one, then she was it. She had piled up her hair on top of her head and woven it into a spiral cone, around which twined viper-like a green velvet ribbon. The oval temples, the tiny pink ears, weighted down by earrings studded with a mesh of copper and sapphire, the thoroughly plucked eyebrows, the curving eyelashes measuring nearly three centimetres in length, the oval cheeks and raised cheekbones, the lips too perfectly full to be beautiful but from which you couldn't tear your eyes away, the neck's white skin with its harmonious muscles, the nape's hollow, the few twining curls spotting the absolutely bare back, everything seemed unreal, as if painted by a great Renaissance master. Her eyes were not made to see with but to decorate her face with their watery agates. There were four rows of pearls around her bare neck (certainly artificial, like everything else she had on, but what did that matter to us?). In minuscule fulgurations of light, each mother-of-pearl-like bead refracted our garden, the house, and the flower beds. Her dress, hanging down to her ankles, displayed an unbelievable extravagance. It was of a brutal green and shimmering yellow, opening up at the front in a triangle reaching down to the waist. The two strips that covered her minuscule breasts wedded at the nape in a bountiful bow. Her arms rattled with enamelled bracelets studded with imitation diamonds, while her fingers, tapering in pearly fingernails, flared with rings flickering with lizard-green beads, transparent as the waters of the seas, the waters of the *China* seas. Huffing and puffing behind her, underneath a turban and waving a fan, Whale bore her rings of fat with the dignity of an Aunt Mame.

I myself tore a gorgeous portulaca for Puia, the colour of carmine, from the edge of the alley in our yard. I wanted to put it on her chest, but Whale wouldn't even let me get close to her. She was jealous of our glances but happy at the same time: Puia was far above the rest us, she was a goddess of love and death. Whale took the flower and, after hesitating a bit, kneeled and sewed it in between the folds of the dress, four fingers above the ankle. Puia wore high heels made of snakeskin. She sat on the throne and drew from the famous hat a piece of paper: it had the word 'truck' written on it. Then, she received her object: that strange ballpoint pen, which to us – accustomed as we were to the boring pens we used at school – was an object of wonder. Through its perfectly transparent plastic body, cut in hexagonal sections, you could see the inky paste inside, still unused. The tip was made of a coppery metal, gripping in its end a tiny yellowish ball. The cap was made of an ultramarine plastic. We walked towards the place that was to be Puia's lot. Meanwhile, we adorned our nails in many colours, using torn flower petals which we glued with saliva. We waved our new claws through the air with such ferociousness that Gigi, perennially asleep on the hood of the truck in the tropical sun, bristled up and began to shake. We hopped on the truck bed – managing with much ado to hoist up Whale as well – and sat on the peeling edge. We stared up at the sky reflecting the garden's green and awaited Puia's commands. The green queen held the ballpoint pen between her fingers and said nothing. She was staring straight ahead, without listening to our whispers – because we had begun to play telephone. Puia had unscrewed the pen's cap and was now removing the ink tube. She finally pulled it out and showed us the transparent tube. We were going to use it, she told us, to blow soap bubbles. It was marvellous. I rushed home and brought back some corrugated glass bowls with carved flowers, in which we dissolved the soap for our bluish solution. We looked for straws and tubular stalks and, returning to the truck, went to work. Soon, the multiplication of rainbow globules swallowed us along with the truck, then wafted in the wind towards the vegetable beds. The fine skin of the bubbles stretched softly in convex sparkling landscapes. In the speckled admixture of colours, a kind of mauve predominated, leaning towards brick and orange. You can see the same colour in the morning in the dewdrop that glimmers in the sun. Whale dipped the ballpoint's tube in the bowl, filled up her cheeks like a trumpet player and caused a large and oval balloon to appear at the other end; it unglued itself with difficulty and, instead of rising up with the wind, fell slowly to the wooden floor of the truck bed, where it remained motionless. It was a quivering glass ball. When the quivering stopped, Whale touched it with her finger and said in shock: 'It's hard!' She put her palms around it and tried to lift it, but couldn't. The balloon was heavy as lead. We watched it in silence while it began to steam as if from inside, becoming opaque until it appeared coated in plaster. After a few minutes, we had before us an egg, reminiscent of prehistoric reptile eggs and which Whale, in order to be able to recognize it later, marked with a tiny violet star. The tube was then handed to Ada, who succeeded in creating an egg similar to the first one, at the end of the same metamorphosis. She drew on its rough surface a tiny indigo star. An hour later, the truck's wooden floor curved under the weight of seven eggs, the size of our heads and marked with the seven colours. We caressed them and tried to hatch them by curling up over them. We even lifted Chombe into the truck and tossed him over the eggs, but the dog suddenly heard an infinitesimal sound that frightened him so badly that he yelped and leaped out of the truck bed and didn't stop till he got to his cage behind the house. As for us, we could barely hear the tiny crackle; instead, we saw right before us how the shell of the egg marked with green began to display a zigzag-shaped break. We jumped out of the truck and hid behind the rosebushes. It was from there that we heard clearly the eggshell exploding into shards. From the truck rose the figure of a unicorn with large, beautiful eyes – the eyes of a woman – and a spiralling horn. Gracefully, she leaped out of the truck and galloped slightly towards the back of the yard. She leaped over the rotted fence and disappeared into the field. The space, deprived now of that presence, remained painfully empty. But soon we preferred it so, because the second egg, Carnation's, shattered to produce a giant caterpillar. Crawling away, it left behind it a trail of slobber, like a green jelly. Large blobs of mucilaginous ooze flecked its long brush-like body. It was blue with yellow stains, while its head, tar-black and eyeless, bore powerful mandibles, also black, and very sharp. It dragged the front part of its body on two childlike hands, and its tail was covered with folds, like a fish with a veil. It disappeared quickly, digging a hole in the ground. Only its pink tail fluttered for a time like marine algae between the tomato trellises. Two eggs cracked at the same time, certainly the twins'. Two beings germinated from them, long and forlorn, the colour of ancient mother-of-pearl. Through their transparent flesh, you could see their bones like an alabaster steam. You could see the hearts pumping blood through the arteries, like rosé wine. You could see their kidneys, like two diamond lumps. Each one of them had a single arm, a single eye and a single dove-like wing with white feathers that hung to the ankles. When they noticed each other, they embraced passionately and thus fused flew off, rowing energetically with their giant wings. They vanished quickly, melting off into the blue sky. Whale's egg bore a crab, red as blood, with two long eyelashed orbs at the end of the lateral hornlets. Underneath the eyes, the mandibles and the maxillae, minuscule hooks and pliers moved about as though searching for food. The most articulated pliers tore at the air in slow motion. It rolled with difficulty over the truck's panelling and took off, running sideways on its thin legs and disappearing in the weeds behind the garden. The most hideous spectre came out of Ester's egg. It was the skeleton of a horse mounted by the skeleton of a rider. Pieces of putrid meat, strips of skin and dried tendons hung on their yellow bones. With snarling teeth, eyes leaking out on the cheeks, ribs visible through the rags that hung suspended on them, an equestrian statue of desperation ruled the middle of the truck. A rusty lance with a bloody tip and a standard sewn with golden wire were swaying in the horseman's hands. Light as a feather, they leaped out of the truck and headed for the fence facing the street, which they jumped over so leisurely that their flight seemed endless. For a long time we heard, slowly fading off into endlessness, the clack of the horseshoes down the street and a neighing that came from another world . . . When this creature vanished, we waited in vain for the last egg to break, mine. But it never broke. Ever since then, I've taken it with me wherever I've gone. It is proof (where in fact proof is not needed) that everything I lived then was real, that that world from Dudești–Cioplea was no childhood phantasm. In fact, you yourself noticed,

I think, that, while men always will remain more or less children, women try to hide their childhood, as if it were something shameful or malefic . . . Here, let me show it to you.

You get up and turn on the light. I feel a live, burning pain in my pupils. I poke my head out of the sheets and see you as if in a sea of flames that flares out over the entire room. Suddenly, everything seems phantasmically real. Another world. The shelves bulging with books, our clothes tossed randomly all over the room, the basket on the table where only two apples remain, the ashtray in which a few apple cores are now slowly turning black, the coffee grinder, you looking for something under the armchair on top of which the mini TV set has flipped over, your nude flesh turning a pale yellow-pink-gold and forcing me to consider just how wide women's hips seem from the back – everything speaks, then turns to silence in surfaces of light. Surfaces of light, I tell myself in a daze, there's our world. Your short hair is ruffled. Your face is old, your neck soft as doeskin and you have a double chin. I am disgusted with you, but I smile at you mechanically, and you smile back, with very little hope. An old crone. With beautiful breasts, true, but for what reason? There is no love left in me, and your story makes me sleepy. Dawn is almost here, Nana, keep going. You return to the bed with a shoebox. You open it and under a layer of cotton you find a large egg, the size of an ostrich egg, with a rough, yellowed surface. The light bulb casts a blue shadow over it. There is a red, amorphous stain on it where you drew your little star. I take it into my hands and weigh it carefully. It is heavy, massive. The shell is slightly warm, as though someone were sleeping inside. You put it on the table and leave it there, on the striped napkin, where I see a few breadcrumbs casting tiny coloured shadows. You turn off the light. Outside, the sky is no longer black. The objects in the room have now turned dark blue, and the walls are almost light. Your voice resounds in my ears, your voice which for a while now is sound no longer, but a string of images. I feel drained after this unsleeping night; I feel as if all my internal organs were composed of rubber and hydrochloric acid. I almost don't

notice when you take up the thread of your tale once again. Your tale
has the temperature of my body, I plunge into it, isolate my senses,
leave myself prey to the illusion. I head for the cave's mouth in the
emerald isle. Around the narrow opening grows a bony bramble
patch, as rough as wires, glimmering in the mauve of the flowers
creeping behind the thorns. I enter the stone corridor that leads to
your deeps. Translucent larvae glide along the walls. Thousands of
ocelli ogle from the low ceiling. In the stream, you will find the sight-
less *Proteus anguinus*, the one with the baby hands. And there, in the
centre, wrapped in night as in a silk cocoon, I find You, the way no one
knows you, you with jaws filled with crooked and curved fangs, you
with dilated nostrils, tossing out sheets of fire, you with your scales of
devouring jade, with demon's wings, with anaconda tail. You wrapped
in your sulphur stench, you between skulls and bones . . . You in your
female silence, in your speechlessness, in violence and fear.

In the evening I took Marcelino's tiny hand again and, happy beyond
measure, we headed for the watchtower. Though I had missed only
a single day, the day before when I didn't go to see Egor, I felt as if I
had wasted an entire week, no, an entire year, as if I hadn't gone to
see him for all eternity. I missed Egor; I even missed his mother.
When we went in, we couldn't believe what we saw: The house was
filled with flowers. All the bottles, glasses, cups, not to mention the
vases, from those made of crystal or Chinese porcelain to the cheap
earthen ones, had been removed from the cupboards and filled with
flowers. There were flowers on the sideboards, on the edge of the
fireplace, on the poles of the oak banister of the inner stairs, on the
footstools and even on the wooden floor. There wasn't a room in
the house where you could rest because of the flowers. On the top
floor, in Egor's room, you felt you were suffocating: there were
white and red lilies, fully open and spilling out pollen from their
stamens; there were yellow roses, piles of capdragons, alder flowers,
bluish camomiles on tangled stalks. There were blooming cacti
and other twisted flowers, blue and red, poking out their sticky
tongues, orchids whose names I didn't know and saw then for the
first time. A sundew flower of unearthly beauty swam in a pot filled

with muddy dirt; its corolla of fine needles ending in drops of transparent liquid flared out in the room's penumbra. 'It's a carnivorous plant,' the Long One told us and sat down in his usual chair. He touched the bristly disc with his finger, the size of my forearm: the bristles shot out as though on command and then, one after another, curled around the finger, gluing their sticky beads around Egor's fingernail. 'If I left my finger there, they would eat it to the bone in a jiffy.' It was a spider plant, a bewitching spider. I told Egor the dream with the water and the one with the glass, and he approved, nodding lightly but without being as enthusiastic as he had been at the beginning. He knew now. I was, without a doubt, the chosen one, I would penetrate REM. 'Look, all these flowers are for you. People came to bring them from everywhere, to wish you, through me, success. They have been waiting for you for a long time, they come every year, they look at my mother and me as REM's priests. But they all know that none of them could ever gain access to REM. Because REM, the only one in this world, was made only for the one who dreams the dreams, that is, only for you.' Egor told me that people from all over the world knew about the existence of this Exit – as he sometimes called REM – and they were connected to each other through the revelation of the secret and the vow to keep it. 'REM is, in a sense, like this sundew flower, a sort of trap set everywhere and endowed with infinite patience, a place of passage that waits for many years to be discovered and then many more years until it is found by the being who can penetrate it. There are secret handwritten books about REM, and there are a few parallel sects that recognize REM but have contrasting ideas regarding its significance. Some maintain that REM is an infinite machine, a colossal brain that regulates and coordinates, after a certain plan and for a certain purpose, all the dreams of all living beings, from the unconceivable dreams of the amoeba and the colchicum to the dreams of all people. The dream, according to them, is the true reality, in which the will of the divinity hidden in REM reveals itself. Others see in REM a kind of a kaleidoscope in which you can read all at once the entire universe, with all of the details of each moment of its development, from genesis to apocalypse. Not long ago, I read a book in Spanish where REM was perceived the same way but called *El Aleph*. Some are convinced that there is only one REM, others say that there is one for each human being – these people even made up a form of writing in which the signs are placed in such a way that anyone can find the way to his or her REM, if they could only read the signs. But what the truth is, whether REM is Redemption or Damnation, only you can find out.' Egor spoke to me with a voice softer than usual and his unsightly acromegalic face made me think of an emaciated mask. 'I am horribly tired. I didn't sleep at all last night, and today I wrote too long. But there was no other way. I was so far behind.' I asked him what he wrote, and he answered me genuinely but with a grimace of disgust: 'Literature. I am a writer, not that I wish to be one.' I told him I thought it was a worthy occupation, and in order to show him that I understood I asked him, using words I had heard before, if he wished to become a great writer. I was expecting him to smile, the way adults do when children meddle in grown-up matters, but Egor, paler than usual, with the transparent-green cartilages of his nose, with his dull eyes, answered me immediately, as if he had asked the question himself. He was speaking, in any case, both literally and figuratively, and far beyond the understanding of a twelve-year-old girl. 'A great writer is no more than a writer. The difference is not radical, it is only of nuance. All the high jumpers can make it over, say, the two-metre mark. But only one can jump two metres and five centimetres: he is the great athlete. No, it's not worth it trying to become merely some poor great writer, some mere unfortunate genius. Take the best books ever written. You're lucky if they are a little better than the mediocre ones. Fundamentally, they're all books, nothing else. Reading them will give you a somewhat more intense aesthetic pleasure. Like coffee with a little more sugar. You will abandon them after thirty pages to make a sandwich or go to the bathroom. You will read them concurrently with some detective novel. After a few thousand years, they will be nothing but dust. Under those conditions, it is humiliating, it is insignificant to suggest that you, a mere human, a being who was given the mad chance of existing and reflecting upon the world, may get to become a genius. It is as if you were to give up everything and return to the forest. There are possibilities in each human being besides which the ambition of being the greatest writer of all time in the entire world is simply disgraceful because of its facileness. Because, what miracle can be of any consequence next to the miracle of being alive and of knowing you are alive? The distance from us to the richest man in the world, the most powerful, the most talented is like the distance from a billion to a billion and one, even less. No, I don't wish to reach the point of being a great writer, I want to reach *The All*. I dream incessantly of a creator who, through his art, can actually influence the life of all beings, and then the life of the entire universe, to the most distant stars, to the end of space and time. And then to substitute himself for the universe, to become the World itself. Only in such a way can a man, an artist, fulfill his purpose. The rest is literature, a collection of tricks, well or not so well mastered, tar-scrawled pieces of paper that no one gives a damn about, no matter how filled with genius those lines of engraved signs may be, those lines that sooner or later will no longer be understood.' He uttered his words passionately but with a bitter expression. Then, in the golden evening, he stopped speaking for a long time. On all fours, Marcel was building a castle out of play blocks on the floor. He had just placed a blue pyramid on top. I was picking up fluff from the lap of my dress. I was thinking of Ester: while we had waited in the rosebushes, frightened of the phantasms produced by our eggs, we held hands, caressing inside our palms with our fingers, and then glued ourselves lightly to one another. I felt her red hair touching my cheek, tangling in my eyelashes. When we looked, for no more than a moment, in each other's eyes, I felt myself suddenly full of sweat. Egor was speaking again: 'But most people – or let us say, most writers – will never reach *The All*. They will never even become geniuses. They will never become anything. I . . . I am one of them. But at least I know this and try to express this powerlessness through everything I write. I know that nothing can be said, that no one expects you to say anything, but that you *must* say it. I know you must somehow go against the injustice of being human and being unable to reach *The All*. I do all that's within my power. Look . . .' he stood up from his yellow veneered chair, stepped over the cube castle and opened wide the two bewitchingly adorned doors of the wardrobe. It was much roomier in there than I had suspected. A reddish wood with a pleasant smell lined its interior. It was filled with a few thick layers of writing paper, stacked on top of each other. He stabbed his fingers into them, managing to scatter them all over the room; I saw then that they were covered with an even and oddly inexpressive script. It was only when I tried to read a few lines of the Long One's work that I understood the immense horror that they contained: Egor had written, covering many thousands of pages with ant-like patience and tenacity, one word alone, incessantly repeated hundreds of times on each page in a succession without beginning or end. The word was *no*. 'I have been doing this for sixteen years and I have barely written fifteen thousand pages. Sometimes I write eight hours a day, but other days I can barely write a line. This will make you laugh, but sometimes I founder and, though it may seem to you that it is easy to write as I do, I have known crises that nearly caused me to give up writing. I know the fear of sterility and the one where you can't keep up with yourself. Because I don't write mechanically. I want that every single *no*, and I mean *every single one of them*, to be thought and felt from the depth of its marrow. To be lived with all my nerves, with all my flesh. Don't think it is simple. Sometimes, I meditate an entire week till I can add one more word. I want my work to be perfect, to represent me completely.' I didn't understand anything. Sometimes I was looking at Egor, sometimes at the sheets of paper that the twilight turned into a mother-of-pearl pink. I tried to pick up all the papers from the floor, but the Long One, taller than ever (he had stood up and was looking out the window), wouldn't let me. We went downstairs, said goodbye to Mrs Bach; in her fanciful house robe, crowded between flowers, she was listening to a sad love song on the radio, sung in a ridiculous nasal voice: 'What should I write you, now that you are gone?' and we were again on the trail in the middle of the field, leaving behind us Egor's smoke silhouette. As I walked slowly, hand in hand with my cousin, I was suddenly invaded by a wave of sadness.

That night I dreamed of a key that someone lost in the woods. I had just walked down a narrow valley strewn with a few scattered beech trees; dappled streaks of brilliant white and yellow light were quilting the black earth between their thin silent trunks. The blinding sun broke through the branches, shaken by a green breath of wind. The peeling bark dispersed a bitter aroma of tannin essence. A fog that was not made of steam but of longing and nostalgia spilled out in the chill of the eternal morning. I had spotted the gleaming of the key from afar and left the path in order to get to it. I kneeled and picked it up. The wine I had sipped in the previous dream, admixed with the spider venom, had made me dizzy, put me in state of exaltation that I could barely control. It was a golden key, twice the size of my palm. In the hollow left on the ground, a fleshy earthworm snaked leisurely, contracting a few times before melting into the earth. I wiped the key carefully with the hem of my skirt. Its end was club-shaped, excessively adorned with golden loops and branches. The key stem, thick and scintillating, reflected my deformed face and the surrounding trees. Dreamily, I touched the tiny plate with three equal teeth at the opposite end of the key. Then, I kissed it and shoved it carelessly in my pocket. I started to run along the path taking me deeper and deeper to the bottom of the valley, where it was getting cooler and cooler. I could hardly wait to use the key. I didn't care whether it was Pleasure or Terror waiting for me behind the door.

The next morning we met in Rolando's grotto. We now hopped on him without fear, shook him while we swung back and forth hanging from his sternum, broke into his cranium through the round eye sockets and, quivering, glued ourselves to the cold, smooth bones of the spinal cord. We decked him with ribbons like a Christmas tree and crowned his fingers with rings of flowers. Ester, who was to be queen that day, refused stubbornly to dress in yellow. It's true, it would have made her look ridiculous. In exchange, she brought – I had no idea where she borrowed it – a tiny umbrella made of yellow lace such as we had never seen before and a folding fan behind which she hid the lower part of her face; she also narrowed her eyes in the style of the Japanese girls, with a cheek glued to her raised shoulder. She made me crazy with love, the little red devil! On the bosom of her white starched blouse she had pinned an orange dahlia. We waited for Puia again for over an hour, but she didn't show up. No one, not even Whale, knew where she was. Finally, we left the grotto and walked over to Auntie Aura's courtyard. Ester sat on the throne, and we placed the golden crown over her copper wire curls. There were only three pieces of paper left in the hat indicating our places: the old school, the watch-tower and my room. Ester, unlucky as usual, drew the narrowest place, the most deficient: the room. At the time, I wasn't aware of the truth my consequent connection to REM revealed to me with the force of evidence and which I will never forget: the narrower the action's or the play's or thought's space, the larger the rest of the world, that is, the World. And it is always worth it to constrain yourself, even reducing yourself to nonexistence, in order to increase the wonder of the world. Ester's object turned out to be my thermometer. Puia still hadn't showed up and we began to get worried. Without us all there, the game was meaningless, so we decided to pay her a visit. We went out into the street and for the first time since we played Queens – because it was already eleven – we ran into passers-by or people who had come out into their yards. The busybody housewives gawked at us and gesticulated – after all, we looked like a bizarre parade in our strange outfits. The boys our age and even the toddlers, dirty as the devil, threw little rocks and made weird faces at us. This Calvary, however, lasted no longer than five minutes, till we arrived at the green hedge with silvery tin flowers – the epitome of elegance at the time – behind which there was an odd house with a glass veranda. We were a bit embarrassed as we rang the bell, because we knew very well her mother's ways. But now this woman, built only with curves, was dressed relatively decently, in a shiny blue robe adorned with twisted chrysanthe-mums. It was in fact a kimono, but at the time I didn't know it was called that. Without a word, she let us in the large, sandstone hall-way whose walls were adorned with tin-and-wire art depicting peacocks and windmills. She motioned to us to go into Puia's room, after she told us in a kittenish tone that her little girl was not feeling well. We entered all at once into Puia's room and froze. This enchanting child lay on her bed, with her face turned to the wall. The bedsheets were pulled to the side, and her pink thin body, drowning in her ruffled tresses, was endowed with a harmony of lines that was unimaginable for a mature woman. The most stunning thing to us was that between her round thighs Puia was smooth as a puppet. There wasn't even a trace of sex, which gave her a surplus of unnatural beauty. Puia was no more than an animated marionette, the plaything of a grown-up child, her mother. When she turned her face towards us and saw us, she covered herself with the sheets and sat up. She explained to us absent-mindedly that she was ill. She was happy, however, that we showed up and didn't want to ruin our game. So that if we wanted to play there, in her room, she would go along with it. After we thought about it for a while, we convinced ourselves that Puia's room, since it was after all still a room, would do just fine. We were already there. Why not play the game instead of giving everything up? Especially now that Puia's illness gave Ester a chance to use the thermometer . . . So we sat down, some of us on Puia's bed, others on the carpet, and waited for Ester to give the commands. Ester stared at the thermometer, whose thin mercury strand rested on 36 degrees. With amusing seriousness, she inserted it into Puia's armpit. We all sat around the little girl like doctors at the side of a moribund princess. Suddenly, we began to perceive the change. When we first came in, we saw, through the curtained windows, the crown of a sour cherry – fruit still green – and the eaves with the gutter and drainpipe. When we lifted our eyes from the thermometer, all these had disappeared. Only the sky, blue as turquoise and tinged with alabaster clouds, was contained inside the window frame's rectangle. We felt at the same time a strange rising motion; we felt it in our organs, in our entire bodies. Later, I felt the same oppressive sensation the first time I took an elevator. Screaming, we rushed to the window. Underneath, hundreds of metres below our feet, we saw Bucharest stretching out before us, tortuous as a labyrinth, drowning in a vortex of dust. The tallest buildings – the Telephone Palace with its tangle of ashen metal crisscrossing the roof, the Fire Watchtower with its prismatic windows, the Victoria shopping complex, the old buildings on Magheru Boulevard and far on the horizon, blue and intimidating in the middle of green pastures, the Scînteria newspaper building – were all wrapped in a variety of fogs, mother-of-pearl, yellowish, pale pink. Bucharest like a spider web, on the strands of which crawled the trams with their ringing bells and the trucks with their trailers. Bucharest full of scaffoldings and cranes, hospitals and post offices and the tiny newspaper stands. With gray lakes shaped like stomachs, opening out into each other. With parks and blackened bronze statues, a population of minuscule inky humans, progressively smaller as we rose. With workers' districts, like cakes you are averse to eating. Bucharest with railroad yards stacked with bundles of lumber, clusters of coal and piles of pipes, structures of rusty pumps, splinters and magnets. With train stations bedecked with round clocks and steam locomotives, train stations that always reek of coal, garlic and crude oil, train stations leaking out mounted rails that disappear under viaducts and gangplanks, and, inevitably, 'under the Grant bridge', where the soccer stadium is. Bucharest with its lumber warehouses and, coiled-wire factories and slaughter houses and the reeking Stela soap factory, with the Donca Simo textile mills, with its Julius Fucik, Olga Bancic, Ilie Pintilie streets, with the Vasile Roaită power plants. Bucharest with its men in white shirts and slicked-back hair. With soccer stadiums invaded by young workers with emaciated faces under their grey workers' caps, shouting and standing when a soccer player, slicked-back hair as well and shorts down to his knees in the Moscow Dynamo team style, kicks the leather ball into the torn net. Bucharest resounding with songs whose purpose is to mobilize the people: 'Dear laggard Comrade Marin,/with you in charge we'll never win'; and the celebrated: 'Cranes of laughing silver in the sun/noble cranes at the break of dawn but also the nostalgic: 'Hand in hand/me and you/let's roam the city/through and through', the Bucharest of the Do-Re-Mi Trio, of The Rabid Lamb, of Love Below Zero, of the artists Ciubotărașu and Giugaru and Silvia Popovici. Bucharest of evening classes . . .

As we rose at great speed, the city became smaller and foggier.

Soon, our eyes could take in much vaster spaces. Blue and green stretches, yellow rectangles crisscrossed by rivulets, cotton clouds enfolding other cities no bigger than our palms. In order not to get dizzy, we returned to Puia's bed. Absent-mindedly, Ester pulled the thermometer from Puia's armpit and checked it, twisting it at the required angle. Its mercury displayed 37 degrees. At the same time, the contents of the room disappeared in a brief explosion. The walls too disappeared, along with the ceiling, and we were suddenly surrounded by an ocean of frozen air, by a mountain, by the colour of sapphire. We were sitting atop a giant elephant's back, made of stone and sculpted on the peak of an immense mountain, white as milk. The mountain was in fact a peak of quartz, sharp as a razor, peppered with tufts of juniper creeping over a few small plateaus under our feet. Hallucinatory, inaccessible, the mountain with the elephant on top rose over a flat world, reflecting itself through air transparent as bluish glass. The ivory tusks and the raised trunk gave the elephant a warlike, regal appearance. Huddled together and holding each other's hands around the bed where Puia was still resting, we couldn't get enough of contemplating the world. Because from this peak, despite the distance, we could see with absolute clarity everything on earth that we wished to see. We were looking at a village surrounded by olive trees and spotted an old church with its metal-plated belfry and a curled-up cat sleeping on the burning metal and a flea venturing for an instant out of the cat's eyebrow, fidgeting next to the ear where the cat's hair was ashen and scarce, then disppearing in the head's fur. And, somewhere else, we saw an open-air bowling alley and could even make out the tiny strands of tobacco trickling out of the pipe hammered against the brown wall by a red-faced kibitzing barman in an apron. We saw a child peeing in a hazelnut grove in the middle of a field of flowers rising taller than him. We saw a rainbow arching over a tractor factory and a factory girl with a headscarf staring at the light, through a window made of tiny glass squares, something resembling a spark plug. We saw a line of peasants with scythes in rumpled and sweaty shirts marching with long steps across the field, the blades sparkling in the sun. One of them was shirtless, and on his red shoulder blades with twisty hairs we saw a monstrous wart. We saw ships frozen on emerald seas leaving behind an alabaster streak of foam just as frozen. Sitting on a hatchway, two sailors were darning their cotton socks. We saw polar rabbits dropping their pellets on the porous snow and a kangaroo with black and wet nostrils sniffing the bark of a eucalyptus tree. Puia's forehead began to burn, radiating a reddish heat. Ester looked at the thermometer again, whose mercury now displayed 38 degrees. And, from the rough back of the elephant, we saw a hand with black fingernails tossing a screw nut into a blind man's hat and an accountant with a razor scraping a number from an accounting book. We saw a priest fondling the hip of one of his parishioners, a magpie resting on the edge of a pram and staring at the suckling babe, a woman rouging her lips. We saw a judge leering at the accused and an army surgeon wrenching a horse's tooth with a pair of pliers. We saw an alembic spanning the length of entire kilometres, a forest of pipes leaking one drop of liquor. We saw a dam splintering at a zigzag and thick torrents of toadstool-infested waters inundating the rice paddies. We saw an old man decapitating a locust. And when the thermometer's mercury reached 39 degrees, we saw a priest beating an old woman and a house whose roof was patched in newspapers and a hearse dripping a trace of blood and a guitarist torn by a Gila monster. We saw a fly fighting for its life in a spider web and a sick man smiling at a butterfly. We saw a man lost in a power plant and a scientist harnessed to a wheelbarrow and a wolf sighing sadly. And a girl giving in, in a kitchen in the country, and a film playing backward and a ladybug walking on a scratched disc. And when the thermometer's mercury reached 40 degrees and Puia became translucent as a fingernail against the light, we saw three men hanging from a willow and a thousand sheep sacrificed on the shore of a lagoon and a peasant eating dog kidneys with feta cheese. And a cyclotron invaded by bedbugs and a hat with its feather stripped and two trusting blue eyes belonging to a leper. And a thermonuclear mushroom and a tanning vat of spider leather and an adolescent confronting his parents. And a fire consuming a warehouse and a sea of people with cut-off tongues and a chapel under the roof of a mouth, right between the molars. And the sharks instituting a brotherhood. And, when the thermometer's mercury reached 41 degrees we saw one race oppressing all the other races, an army fighting a buffalo, a lance point drawing a petunia. A wounded man disappearing into an ice hole, a blood wave sweeping municipalities, a magic square on an actor's brow. We saw a tyrant flushing a throne, a mangy dog vomiting diamonds, a corpse standing up, a doctor ripping out his eyes. And open graves and the rattling dead in camouflage gear on top of tanks, turning the machine gun handles on gunboats. Bone armies blasting their bazookas, lobbing explosives over cities from mortars, Molotov cocktails, bedsheets. The field marshals of carnage and destruction crossing rivers on horseback. Barrels of oil burning in food stores. Archives of films in flames. Necrotic salesmen, milkmaids with shingles. Populations on crutches, men with broken eardrums. The trumpets in power. Viruses under the standards. Cathedrals in ruin, cardinals in blue, skeletons everywhere. Heart illnesses called to arms. Cancer as the only source of energy. Dried-up rivers and Death, the ruthless star, putting the newborn to sword. And a cherrywood cross hoisted on Everest and Celsius nailed to it with a crown of thorns on his head. And the Earth under his bloody soles stained with seven-degree burns. And when the thermometer's mercury displayed 42 degrees, we saw the deity of Earthquakes dancing over Eurasia, the deity of Frost swallowing the Poles, the deity of Deluge crushing Japan under its heels. And the dark deity of the Deeps, Nife the Avenger, suddenly made his lava voice heard, hurling the earth's crust in the air and drying up the ocean. And the Marianas and the Eleven Thousand Maidens and all the hurricanes with female names scampering with skirts in flames, with singed hair, with bare breasts, tripping over capital domes. And rivers of wolfram and streams of iridium and fjords of chromium and lagoons of strontium and cascades of platinum and brooks of cadmium and seas of copper and gulfs of zinc and oceans of iron boiled together with their blinding flora and fauna. And the seasons underneath a rain of stars, underneath a hail of meteorites. And we saw the Sun melting together with the Earth and fumigating the eclipses. And the thermometer exploded, and the mercury fell like a tear in the chasm below us. And then we saw how the stars shrivel, how space contracts and how the inter-active forces, weaker and stronger, the gravitational forces and the electromagnetic forces sit down for a game of poker and throw dice made of hypercubes. How time practises a ruinous ipseity. How the world becomes the size of an apple, a cherry, an electron, and finally disappears, unmade. And when there was nothing any longer around us, not even darkness, not even nothingness, we suddenly saw with our peripheral sight a luminous point. When it came closer, we recognized with a shout of joy: It was our dear child, the great male with female breasts, with his hair falling in blonde curls down to his hips, with his blue eyes. He was coming closer and closer to us. He was much larger than the mountain we were on. The closer he got, the better we could make out his fea-tures, and soon we could see nothing but his face of light, then only his eye, which suddenly became the sheltering sky, blue and spot-ted with little clouds, and we were staring at it through the window in Puia's room. Our sick friend sat up and smiled. Ester, the strange yellow queen, was still holding the thermometer in her hand, and through the window we could once again see the sour cherry and the eaves of the neighbouring house. The thermometer's mercury was back to 36 degrees, as in the beginning. We remained with Puia a little longer; she promised she would stay in bed like a good little girl so that she could get well and join us the next day. Then, we all went home for dinner. I walked with Ester. We were happy the game had turned out well once again. She removed her little crown, shook her red wire hair and we were now walking together hand in hand under the tropical sun. We were soft as cats. We were both yawning, sticking out our tongues and laughing. We smiled one more time at each other when we got to her gate, and when I turned around I felt a jolt in my heart. For the first time, I had the sensation that soon everything would end, that the good times would be gone forever.

The sadness wouldn't leave me. It grew during the afternoon, became acute, sweet, unbearable. I traipsed aimlessly about the deserted garden, tore off a tomato and bit into it or hugged the trunk of the bitter cherry, thinking of Ester. I walked along the narrow path between the vegetable beds to the truck and hopped up into the boiling cabin. I was twisting the wheel and pushing the brakes and suddenly burst into tears. I hopped off the truck, wrapped Gigi around my neck, and strolled to the back of the courtyard, next to the rotted fence drowning in weeds. I went back into the house where it was cool and stood for a time in the empty hallway, long and narrow, weakly lit by the dull glass of the windows. Leaning on the window sill, I counted again and again the petals of a flower whose name I didn't know. It was quiet, and the light was grey. I pulled myself together. And again in my room, again in bed, under the sheets, with my face to the wall . . . I cried the entire day all the way into the evening, I couldn't control myself. When Auntie Aura came, I pretended to be asleep. I cried especially when I saw Zizi, poor thing, forgotten for entire days under the table, with her beautiful dress saturated with dust, with her thread hair so tangled it made her look like a spectre. I remembered the love with which I had changed her clothes, her underwear and her slip and everything else she wore, and now I had abandoned her like a stepmother who maltreats her child. I held her tight to my chest and began wailing once again.

Towards evening, I washed my face, gathered Marcelino from the streets, where he was busy playing a game of leapfrog, and we took off together to the watchtower. Madam Bach let us in, but we almost got scared when we heard the screams from the second floor. 'Egor is with a friend,' the Elongated Woman told us, pointing upstairs. I was surprised, because I had thought of Egor as an individual of absolute solitude; I couldn't imagine what a friend of his would look like. When we opened the door, the screams intensified abruptly. The screamer was, of course, the guest, a young man of Egor's age, but who was no taller than his waist. He was very dark and wore his hair parted to one side, very unusual for that time. I couldn't understand his name, but he seemed to be a student. He paused for an instant when Egor introduced us and then began to shout louder. I didn't understand a thing of what they were talking about but now I realize it must have been politics.

East, West, Russians, Americans, Congo . . . the atomic bomb . . . the Cold War . . . Khrushchev . . . Gheorghiu-Dej, our president at the time . . . Algeria . . . Vietnam . . . The student returned again and again to the same fixed idea: 'We're headed towards catastrophe, sir! The arms race, sir! Growing hatred, sir! Suspicion, paranoia! The apocalypse is nearly here, my friend! They all want the bomb, they all proliferate their own propaganda, they all spread lies, sir! Public opinion! FBI! KGB! It's going to be a hecatomb! It's going to be a nightmare, don't you understand?' And so on for a half an hour, while Egor listened gravely. When the student was finally silent from pure exhaustion, Egor stood and extracted from the chest of drawers a large photo album, bound in scarlet silk printed with roses. He opened it and began to leaf through it. The thick pages full of yellowed pictures alternated with thin, nearly transparent leaves, filigreed with ingenious arabesques. The pictures showed smiling women with odd hairdos and arms around each other's shoulders, dressed ostentatiously in national costumes, children in sailor suits, groups dressed in clothes from the previous century, men with endless moustaches and top hats, ladies with long dresses, large bows ending in bustles, and hats tied under the chin with ribbons, military men with swords hanging from their waists or leaning on their bayoneted rifles, boarding-school girls forcing their cheeks to dimple, their curls hanging in tresses next to their ears, tubercular young men playing the cello. 'You're speaking of the atomic bomb? Of mass destruction? This is what I say. Look at this album with old photographs from the last century. It contains my answer to all the problems in the world, all the problems of history. Look at all these people, these girls, the children in these pictures. They're all dead today, all of them, to a person. There is not one survivor among the millions of humans born a hundred and fifty years ago. What nuclear weapon can compare to this, exterminating time, time that takes no prisoners? What are conflicts, what is the struggle for power compared to the meticulous, calm, even gentle victory of time against everyone? Bombs, wars, earthquakes, disease, floods are all superfluous, all they do is recklessly rush the work of time; they are glances tossed into the near future, like indiscreetly raising the curtain's corner.' To this the student began again to vociferate in a foul-mouthed manner, without taking into consideration that children were present in the room. He accused Egor of being already dead, that all that was left for him to do, if you were to believe his philosophy, was to wrap his head in a shroud and abandon the terrain. In the end he left, slamming the door without saying goodbye. Egor laughed gently and then turned to us. 'Let the world see to its own problems, and let us see to the world's,' he said, and then asked how the dreams were going. I told him, and he said, again, that everything would turn out well. 'I can see from everything that's happening to you that even if you were to deviate a little from the geometric, symmetrical model that I am familiar with, it should be welcomed. Projects never correspond exactly to their realization. An action (or, to speak about my profession, a work of art) cannot be symmetrical except in death, like a city born on a drawing board. In the same way that a spider under the influence of a drug does not sew a perfect net but one with chaotically placed loops and holes, the creator of our world (and imitating him, the writer) deforms matter, disturbs it under the influence of the demented wind of inspiration. The laws, the schemes, the threads remain the same, but lengthened, crooked. The lacework comes alive.' And then: 'You haven't told me any more about your game of Queens, that's not very nice of you. But I know this game better than you, and I will tell you that everything in it has significance and that your dreams and your games, braided with one another, form your spider net, sewn by you not in order to catch something in it but to be caught in it. Because we are merely flies that secrete their own net, while the spider is the same for everyone. It visits each one of us only once, but only at the right moment, when the net is finished and strong enough to support your weight. And you alone, out of all the beings of this world, will be able to wrestle yourself out of your own net for one moment, only you are given this chance. And as for me . . . my net has only a single strand, long and straight. You must travel on it as well. Because I am Guide and Guardian here, at the edge of the world.' I listened to him, fascinated as always. I tried my best to keep in mind every one of his words. The sunset outside transformed him into a giant red insect. I was looking at the prayer rug, so worn out that in spots you could see the filling. Woollen strands of many colours were blended inextricably in it, forming complicated arabesques. I remembered that during the first day, when he told me about his ancestors, he spoke to me about a wonderful gift that his people had gained along with the bite of the fly with blue wings on the shores of Africa. He had promised to tell me about it some day. But everything in this prismatic room of Egor's in the watchtower seemed now, as evening fell, to take on such a solemn note, so distant and so sad, that I couldn't find it in me to disturb the silence. And still, a few words escaped my lips, not the ones I wanted. 'Egor, I love Ester!' I said in a whisper, with emphasis. But he seemed not to hear anything. He was silent for a while, staring at Marcel's games, and then he repeated: 'Yes, Guide and Guardian.'

I tossed and turned for a long time before I fell asleep. With my hand under the pillow, I examined the concavity of the shell, sweet as silk. I felt with my fingertips the labyrinthine scratches. Eventually, I got to see them as well, there in the darkness, with the skin of my fingers, as though I were reading them with my own eyes. This attribute has remained with me until now. Many times when I return home dead tired, I throw myself on the bed and, without turning on the light, I read the newspaper with my eyes closed. The letters over which I pass the tips of my fingers appear in my mind as if lit by a small pocket flashlight. That night, I dreamed that I was walking on the trail in the middle of the woods, feeling more and more nauseated and dizzy. I was staring at the ground, and the mixture of twigs, caterpillars, dead leaves and wet mushrooms quivered before my eyes. The forest had no limits, had no sense, it was the only world one could imagine. A fox barking somewhere on top of the hill. Dew glimmering on a spider web. A blackbird trill. Cool breaths of wind. Far off in the distance, at the end of the valley, in a mixture of gold and shadows, I spotted a house. The closer I got to it, the clearer its contours became: a two-storey wooden, ramshackle cabin, rectangular like a chest, without a tapered roof, windowless. It was sinister from up close: a large shed built with boards and held together with tar. There was an open door in the middle; the trail ended at the doorstep. My shadow fell over it like the needle of a black, oscillating gauge. I stepped forwards, hesitating in front of the door. It was large and scarlet. Inside, the darkness was dense and shaded. I wasn't feeling well and propped myself with my forehead against the door. I had no place to run. There was no place in the world where I could have hidden, because my path ended here. I stepped over the threshold, and my ears began to ring from the solitude. There were long and twisted hallways, full of dust and dirt, scattered with old furniture, shattered pianos, books in old leather bindings. There were yellowed photos in oval frames. There were bent-iron beds and chamber pots eaten by dust. There were faded clothes in the wardrobes with broken mirrors: a swarm of gray and beige butterflies flew out of the collars and the pleats, scattering their wing dust. There was a large candelabrum that had fallen from the ceiling and an icon broken in two. A large, thick buzzard shot out buzzing from a corner and circled the room, incessantly searching every corner. I made my way fearfully through that old junk and found the first steps of a stairway that led to the top floor. I climbed the stairs slowly, making a thumping noise with my feet. In the nooks and crannies, the spiders, giant and motionless, watched from their dense nets. After walking along some corridors on the second floor, I found a locked door with a blunt handle made of brass grown over with verdigris, under which I could see the indecent keyhole. The tension, that fear I felt, that desire, that *evil* had all reached their peak inside me. I stared at my gold key. I was certain it would fit. And at that very moment, I awoke, in a bad mood, feeling uneasy and frustrated.

The sixth day was like a veritable vacation. It was eleven and Carnation, whose turn it was to be queen, still hadn't shown up, so we all went to her house. There were about fifteen souls living under one roof not much higher than a metre and a half. Three or four tiny brats were galloping around by the gate, the youngest sporting their bare butts, the others wrapped merely in grime-blackened undershirts. All across their fence, you could see the outline of palms dipped in whitewash, while the courtyard was strewn with heaps of old metal: chains, cooking stoves, drainpipes and corner-shaped pipes from old heating stoves. A fleabag of a bitch with tits like the legendary she-wolf from Dorobanti was chomping on something stuck between some crumpled newspapers. A few Gypsy girls and a Gypsy boy in school uniforms were sitting on the doorstep, spitting out sunflower-seed shells. The boy wore his hair in a pointed hairdo like the edge of an ax, slicked with sunflower oil and probably sugar. We found out that Carnation 'is with her mama, out hunting for empty bottles' and wouldn't be back till evening. After we thought about it for a while, we decided to postpone our game of Queens till evening or even the next day and just play our usual games until then. And so for the rest of the day we drew, played hopscotch and clambered up the bitter cherry, amused ourselves with London Bridge and red rover. In the afternoon, Ester and I went out in the fields together among the wild flowers, at first holding hands and then holding each other by the waist. We picked bouquets of flowers, which we gave to one another as gifts. And we put flowers in each others' hair. You boys will never understand . . . We sang to each other all the songs we knew, and as evening fell the songs became progressively more melancholy. Ester's hair, which I caressed with so much love, turned dark red, the colour of the bitter cherry. We were both very happy. We wondered what life would have been like if we hadn't met. We talked about books and films, and I was amazed at how smart she was. She had finished reading a book, thick as brick, named *The Deemons* (that's how she accented it) and told me about the poor clubfooted girl. Her name was Liza, and she lived in a fairy tale. 'But the name Svetlana is even more beautiful than Liza.' Then, we went home to Auntie Aura and gave her all the flowers. We sat down and chatted. Auntie was crazy about us. She too would have liked a girl but ended up with that 'badly behaved boy' (she said it because she knew Marcel was hiding under the table and could hear her). Around seven in the evening, the girls began to show up. Carnation was fifteen minutes late, but to our amusement she kept her word: she had borrowed her cousin's orange vest (he was one of those men with rubber kneepads who hoist up manhole covers on the street, sniff inside, and then fit them back afterwards with a knock of the hammer) and was very proud of her looks. She proposed that we play the game at night, in order to make it more interesting. At ten sharp, we would meet in front of the twins' house, which was located on the corner of the street that led to the old school. Because that was the place that Carnation had pulled out of the hat; now, I could be sure that the next day I would be the queen at the watchtower. After dinner, I went to my room. Auntie Aura went to bed early, because she had spent the whole day at her sewing machine. I didn't even undress, but sat comfortably on the bed with *The Commander of the Snow Fortress* on my knees and began to leaf through the yellow and beautifully illustrated pages. I had no patience for reading, I was thinking of hundreds of things at the same time, each of the six days that I had spent at Auntie Aura's was shuffling around in my memory (and even deeper, down there where feelings are born) with all the others, spawning a marvellous and at the same time painful image. I was physically agitated, infused with a muted sensation of unease. It followed me in my dreams, and now it manifested itself in my reality. When my eyes fell on Zizi, I had a kind of presentiment. I picked her up from the floor, shook the dust off, then spoke to her tenderly for a long time and promised her I would never neglect her again from that day on. Especially now that Carnation's object was a doll. I wanted Zizi to see our game, so I thought it would be a good idea to take her with me. How could I have known that my doll would participate in the game in such a savage way? Sometimes, I cry even now to think of that horrific night. But it seems that was its fate . . .

At a quarter to ten, I went out the gate, slowly, with Zizi in my arms. I hadn't even noticed that the moon was full. The sky was bright with the light of the stars. Dropping across the vault, the white comet with its six tails, so easy to make out, looked like a newborn kid goat grazing a pasture strewn with yellow flowers. When had the moon grown so big? It spanned a quarter of the sky with its glimmering disc. I walked down the silent street, alone under the rain of the stars. The twins were already waiting at the corner. Puia appeared next, with her lightly tinkling earrings. Whale arrived with Ester (they had run into each other on the way). Finally, Carnation showed up too. She was wearing the orange vest. Around her forehead she had tied a schoolgirl's ribbon, from which she had pinned a huge snapdragon that stood at rigid attention like a nobleman's feather. She wore a tight flowered dress, as was the fashion in those years, but badly tailored and not conforming to the shape of her waist, while on her feet she wore the traditional Gypsy slippers, red and lacquered and fitted with a rabbit pompon. She had braided the black shine of her tresses into two thick pigtails. In the half-shadow, her face, which was actually beautiful, looked primitive as a wooden idol. Slowly and fearfully, we all headed for a dark building, taller than all the rest and standing out against the starry sky at the end of the street that intersected ours at a perpendicular. It was an old ruined building, with partially collapsed walls and floors with fungus-eaten woodwork falling at an angle. The window frames were missing, so that the windows looked like amorphous holes in the peeling walls. The sloping roof had lost its tiles and was filled with large black gaps. I had been there before, during the day. I had walked with Puia through the empty classrooms, with mutilated benches and old blackboards resting on three legs only, all forgotten in a corner. Some of the blackboards retained the writing of the past years, fractions and additions scrawled in white chalk. The walls were stained with yellow rectangles where the posters of 'Domestic Animals', and 'Let's Get to Know Our Country' and multicolour maps were once hanging. A heap of crushed glass mixed with rods and tin discs was all that remained of the chemistry lab. An uncertain straw-filled animal was abandoned in the natural science room. It lay on the floor, its seams torn in many places, with a glass eye rolled to the side. There was also a broken cast, representing an ear section. We also found, strewn across the classrooms, torn pages from a spelling primer and from a music book, and tests corrected with red ink. The children who had studied there were now adults; they had passed into another species, into another world. They would never return. We found the entrance with difficulty in the dark, and we crept in like cats. Carnation flipped on her flashlight and moved its beam along the walls. The main-floor corridor was endless. The flashlight's beam couldn't reach to the other side. The dirty mosaic underneath us produced reverberations. We entered a classroom where a few benches and a hobbling teacher's desk still remained. A corner of the wall had collapsed and a cool wave wafted in from the outside. Some sort of grass had grown through the bricks on top of the ruins. Carnation sat on a bench, and we adorned her with the golden crown, a few ribbons and bows, and other trifles. She looked frightening, lit as she was from below by the flashlight's beam. I handed her the doll to use for the game. She snapped it from me and, growling, pretended to swallow it. Then, she tossed it away, towards the giant moon that shone through the cracks. It wasn't a good sign. A chill descended upon us and made us shiver, because we were wearing only our summer dresses and thin blouses. Sharp squeaks suddenly intruded and frightened us and, when we spotted flying shadows contoured against the windows' bluish air, we realized they were bats. A few slithered into the room, silently fluttering, circling rapidly around us and shrieking with piercing sounds at the edge of hearing. We started to scream and put our hands on top of our heads, because we knew that bats clamp on to your hair and you can't tear them away. They whizzed by our ears with their leathern wings. Soon, they swarmed the classroom's air, now teeming with them. We ran from one corner to the other, frightened out of our heads. Profiled against the moon, they came in flocks, we could clearly see their diabolical silhouettes, with toothy wings and rat ears. Suddenly, Carnation came up with an idea that saved us: to make a fire. Screaming and dodging, we quickly collected from the floor dirty notebooks, round bits of wooden pointers, splinters from the teacher's chair, until we piled in the middle of the room a heap of junk which the Gypsy girl set on fire with the matchstick she perennially carried with her. Blinding flames of saffron and purple rose in crackles, spreading suddenly around them a palpitating light, reddening the walls and painting our faces in the liveliest colours. Our screams were now of joy, of triumph. The bats, confused, couldn't find their way any more, collided with one another, flew through the black smoke that rose towards the ceiling, singed themselves in the happy flames. A few had fallen to the floor and crawled on their wings, shrieking excruciatingly and twisting their miniaturized heads with uncanny speed. Some disappeared in the dense darkness of the corners. The fire warmed us and intoxicated us, and we stared at it, hypnotized. It scorched our cheeks and eyelashes. We were dizzy from the smell of wood and the smoke. Our world was now small and mysterious: a sphere of agitated light and warmth. We tossed into the fire everything we could find, simply for the pleasure of seeing new tongues of flame shooting out to the ceiling, breaking apart or braiding with other flames, spitting sparks. 'Fire, fire!' we screamed like madwomen. I don't remember who it was that stood up and began to shake and twist all over the place. Suddenly, all of us began to dance, jumping from one foot to the other, singing and clapping our hands. We waved our hands through the air like witches, wove ourselves into a hora around the fire and hopped till we got dizzy, jumped in place with closed eyes and arms wide. We had the feeling of absolute freedom, a thirst for . . . what? – we didn't know, but we had in us a longing, a lust. We scowled and showed our fangs, we roared gutturally trying to imitate Carnation who, standing on the teacher's desk, was frozen like an idol and howled at the moon like a bitch. Her little crown had rolled off, and the snapdragon hung to the side, broken. We attempted to jump through the flames, and many times we almost caught on fire. The hems of our skirts smelled scorched.

When we got tired of all that playing around the pyre, we constituted ourselves into the Great Tribunal. It was headed, of course, by Carnation, the orange queen, and we, the others, were her aides, judges and executioners. It was the puppet who was to appear before us. Because the tiny doll couldn't be found, I myself picked up Zizi from one of the benches and offered her as the accused. The game had bewitched and entranced me and, in any case, I was so dizzy and oppressed by an evil feeling inside that I didn't realize my vile deed till the next day. But then I cried in vain. With her hands twisted behind her and tied together with a piece of thread, Zizi stood before us, supported by the wall behind her. We scowled at her and flicked our claws to scratch her. Sullenly, Carnation ordered us to utter our accusations. For every accusation, the fire would shoot out violently while Zizi looked as though she recoiled, her hair standing on end. The first one to step forwards and make an accusation was Whale, who pointed with her finger at Zizi and shouted: 'You are small, you are a freak, you don't deserve to live any more.' Ada spoke with a silky and perfidious voice: 'You can't read, you can't write, you can't count. You barely know your name. Death to you!' Carmina leered: 'You're filled with sawdust and wool. Shame on you! Let's finish her off, once and for all!' Puia whispered from where she stood, lost in that same cold dream from which she never awakened: 'You are ugly. You are a sloppy dresser. Who would ever marry you? No, doll, it's better like this . . .' Carnation flung ruthlessly over her shoulder: 'You are so stupid you would set your own clothes on fire. You'd better write your last will and testament, you're history.' I murmured: 'That's what they want, Zizi. I don't matter now. Don't ruin our game, Zizi. For us it's only a game, and you're too small and limp to understand.' Ester, with her voice that always seemed to be asking a question, nasalizing entrancingly, added her own straws to the fire: 'You have no life, that's why you have to die. You don't exist, that's why you have to disappear.' Zizi's fate was sealed; there was no escape. Carnation uttered the sentence: 'The Black Tribunal sentences her to die by hanging and by burning on the pyre.' We rushed to carry out the sentence, because we were afraid that Zizi, who was still dumbfounded and hadn't yet had a chance to comprehend her miserable situation, would start to sob, which might cause us to have a change of heart. We found two boards that had been glued together at a right angle, which we thrust into the cracked floorboard of the classroom. We got the rope from the string at the back of a poster showcasing the rape plant. In a silence in which you could only hear the crackle of the flames, we stripped Zizi of all her clothes – which I had sewn myself with so much dedication – and we threw them, one by one, into the fire. Her little dress rose instantly to the ceiling, like a butterfly of flames and ashes. Naked, Zizi looked pitiful: it was an amorphous body of rag with a badly sewn plaster head on top. She was dirty and grey. Her arms and legs were cylindrical and looked like plasticine. We strung her up in the noose and watched her sway, casting a sharp black shadow on the floorboards. We began to play again around her, but this time it was a sullen rattle of a dance, tiring and without mirth. We scattered throughout the classroom and returned with pieces of paper, sticks and pencil shavings, so that a small pyramidal pyre rose under the feet of the suspended puppet. Carnation lit it with a piece of wood from the great fire, and we watched with dilated eyes the first yellowish blades gluing themselves to the body of the puppet, the arms and legs beginning to burn like torches, a thick smoke emanating from the body. In a few seconds, Zizi disappeared inside a shroud of fire. The string caught on fire too and broke, and the puppet tumbled into the pyre, where she burned for a long time, until turning into a sheet of ash. Only her head remained, turning black and resting like a dirty orb in the middle of the flames. Her hair of thread had carbonized long before. Suddenly, like a forcefully slammed door, the two fires burst into an explosion of sparks and went out. Not even the embers were still aglow. Everything was ashes and smoke. The dilapidated room was filled with a stinging smoke, difficult to breathe. Through the collapsed corner of the wall, you could see the quarter moon, turning the sky around it blue. Everything had unravelled, and we found ourselves now, in the middle of the night, in a ruined building: a bunch of frightened little girls. From their corners, the bats came alive anew and began to blast their wings through the air. The ones outside heard them and came charging in through the windows. We took off, running for our lives, screaming along the corridors, pursued by the hordes of winged mice that now really slammed into our faces and strove to rend our clothes. The corridors multiplied, and we couldn't find our exit. Carnation's flashlight beamed along the lichen-covered walls. When we opened one of the innumerable doors at random, we found ourselves abruptly outside, under the magical light of the moon and stars. We sprinted down the black street, still pursued by the bats that swarmed around us all the way to the corner of our street. We didn't stop till we got to our own houses. Hobbling and growling, Chombe chased me till he recognized me, and then he immediately became calm again. I stole into my room, completely dizzy, incapable of any thought, with a horrible fatigue in my bones. I didn't care about anything any more, I didn't even care then whether I would ever enter REM; the thought of dreaming that night was unbearable to me. Everything hurt me, everything oppressed me. I took the shell from under the pillow and put it on the table.

I slept a heavy, black sleep until ten in the morning, when my aunt woke me up. I had guests. The twins and Whale had come over to console me for my sad story with Zizi and to honour me: I was to be the last queen. I remembered then everything that had happened the night before and had an actual attack of hysteria. I howled and rolled on the floor, slapping my face with my palms, driving my nails into my arms. Shouting at the girls, I threw them out. Frightened, Aunt Aura rushed in, and I screamed at her as well. After an hour, I finally calmed down and began to laugh through the tears at the jokes my aunt was telling me to put me at ease. I told her that I lost Zizi, with whom I had slept in my bed since I was five, but that it had happened yesterday afternoon. After I washed my burning cheeks, I ate and began to think about what to wear. I didn't have a lot of alternatives: I had only brought with me a single red blouse (brick-coloured, actually) and a pair of kneesocks with a red stripe. But I put on my white skirt, for lack of something better, and tied a long silk scarf printed with cherry flowers on my head. I fussed and fidgeted a bit in front of the slightly sloping mirror and then went out to get a rose. I severed a stem full of thorns with a knife. The rose was tiny and had barely bloomed, but a few purple petals had unfurled and opened out, so you could see the others, curled up and wet with dew. I decided to hold it in my hand. I would have fastened it to my chest, but my blouse was also red. I went out in the sun and found all the girls huddling on the small cement platform, on which you could still see the seven circles around the throne. I sat on the bedecked chair and Puia placed the tin-foil crown on my head. They wrapped me in long garlands of shiny paper, red as fire, braided carnations in my hair and put ruby rings on my fingers. I was handed my object, a ring that appeared to be gold. I wasn't feeling like myself. I had sensed that I wasn't up to it, that the day would end in failure. I knew I wasn't beautiful, that red didn't become me. I squeezed the ring on my finger, and we took off towards the watchtower, the place where we had decided I was to be queen. I was thinking that I would go to see Egor after the game. I was going to tell him that I had failed the dream, that I was no longer worthy of going There. We walked across the field and decided to drop in for a few minutes on Rolando. The same bluish light was refracted on the walls, but when we saw 'our friend' – as we had begun to call him – we were struck dumb: It was as if a few thousand years had passed. The giant skeleton had turned into a pile of dirt. The bones of the pelvis still stood out, albeit broken, from the dirty dust, next to cranium bits, quartered maxillaries, vertebrae remains. Time had whistled through it with unbeliev-able speed and fury. We emerged downcast from this ossuary and continued our sojourn through the field towards the watchtower that now rose under the shimmering sky. Blue flower thistles scratched our feet in their canvas sandals. Big-bellied bees paused in their flight on the lips of snapdragons, opened them and pushed in. They rummaged inside, and then emerged with their backs yel-lowed with pollen. They flew on, suspending tiny sacks from their invisible wings.

Egor was home, up in his room. He was watching us from his window and waved his hand. We waved back, most of us smil-ing sweetly and, of course, ironically. The twins bowed and then burst into laughter. There was enough of a beaten path between the watchtower and the shed, so we could play at our heart's con-tent. Now was the time. In a few minutes, I had to come up with an interesting game. The responsibility for the game was mine. I turned and twisted the ring on my finger. What could I do with it? Nothing came to my mind. I tried to stare through it the way Carmina did with her pearl, but nothing came of it. In the vaulted sky, the sun burned like thunder. I stared at its circle of melted metal until, shifting my eyes, I couldn't see anything but violet and purple stains. I looked up then at Egor's window, but the curtains were drawn. I decided: we would play wedding. The ring would be a wedding ring. I would be the groom, and the bride would be chosen by drawing lots. It is true that we never played that game before, but the girls showed themselves from the very beginning happy to play. It was a game you could keep playing without getting bored. Suddenly, there was a commotion, as if it were a real wedding. As usual, we had brought with us paper, pencils and scissors. First, we cut out six pieces of paper on which I would have to write the names of my six friends, in order to find out who would be the bride. Here I cheated, but I couldn't have done otherwise. I wrote Ester on all the pieces of paper. I folded them, and Carnation drew a single piece from my fist. I quickly tore up the others and threw them away. If they had asked for them I would have died of shame. I had taken a risk but won. Ester would be my bride. She couldn't have turned any redder, but it became her. They all fussed around her in order to gussy her up, while I, having been left alone, didn't find anything better to do than try on my uncle's hat, which I had brought with me along with a few other things. I pulled my hair together under it. I tied a ribbon of green cloth around my neck like a kind of bow tie, and I asked Ada to draw a moustache under my nose with a piece of coal I picked up from the ground. Ada broke the piece of coal in two, gave her sister a half, and both of them drew, symmetrically and simultaneously, two arching handles of a very convincing moustache. There was nothing else to be done. They adorned Ester with a veil of white gauze that came down to her chin. They wanted to put on her all sorts of jewellery they had brought with them, but Ester refused. She kept no rings on her fingers. By chance, the dress she had put on that day was white (with a bluish hem), so that in her simplicity she seemed like a veritable bride in miniature, a red-haired curly bride, with a graceful and noble aquiline nose. For the bridal bouquet, the girls gathered an armful of wild flowers from the field: dandelions, camomile, cornflowers . . . The others divided their roles among themselves. Ada and Whale would be the groom's parents, Carmina and Puia the bride's and Carnation the priest who married us. In order to fulfill this role, she fashioned from a black rag a beard that reached all the way to the ground. You couldn't look at her without suddenly being infected by irrepressible mirth. We decided that the 'altar' would be set right in front of the shed's scarlet and dusty door. The bride and the groom were to walk along the alley that led from the watchtower to the shed, and there, in front of the door, the priest would be waiting with the rings. Along with my brass ring another ring that would serve as Ester's wedding band suddenly showed up, probably made of silver and without a stone. Everything was ready. We formed the wedding procession next to the watchtower. Ester looked into my eyes for an instant and then took my arm with a timid, partially playful gesture, holding the bouquet of flowers to her chest with her other hand. You could hardly see her features through the carefully arrayed veil over her face. I watched her though the corners of my eyes while we advanced with tiny steps towards the altar. Solemnly, the other girls followed us in groups of two. As I walked, I felt overwhelmed by powerful feelings by a suffering and a sadness that I didn't understand, mixed with a dark happiness, bitter and unbearable. I knew that soon everything would be over, that soon the charm of those days (that world) would disappear as if it had never been. Ester's arm, which I held so tight under mine, would no longer be there. The Great Games were ending. We arrived, halted before Carnation, staring only ahead. The shed's door had rotted almost completely. The large rusty lock hung like a seal. Egor's words flashed through my mind, that REM must be behind that door. This idea seemed to me more absurd than ever. Carnation mumbled something very quickly, probably in the Gypsy language, holding her hands out like a book, scowling and pulling at her beard. The solemn moment finally came when she asked each of us if we wanted to get married. Quietly, we both answered yes. The rings were then put on our fingers, and we were declared man and wife, while the girls could hardly contain their giggles. It was now time to kiss the bride. But I couldn't. The girls were shouting at us that we absolutely had to, that it was the custom, and were pushing us together. Finally, having lost any control of myself, I took Ester by the shoulders, lifted her veil, and kissed her lightly on the lips. I don't remember, as I told you, when I made love for the first time, but I will never forget how I kissed Ester . . .

We played for a while, we were congratulated by all, but we couldn't go on, neither I nor the bride, we couldn't handle it any longer. About a quarter of an hour later, we removed our matrimonial array, wiped off my moustache and were getting ready to go home for lunch. I stayed behind to speak with Egor. I walked up to his room. I told him I hadn't dreamed anything the night before, and he was disconcerted. 'Still, it is not yet a disaster. You look disturbed. You're only a step away, what the hell, you're closer than ever. One single dream, think of me, of us, of all those who know about the Entrance. Look at the flowers they brought you a few days ago.' But those flowers had withered. 'One single dream, Svetlana, and you will get to a place where no one has ever been, you will know what no one has ever known, you will know, FINALLY, The Truth.' As he spoke, Egor was becoming increasingly agitated. He was terribly afraid. If I failed, it meant he had lived for nothing. He would be like a eunuch, getting old while guarding the door to a harem that wasn't his and that he had nothing to do with. His entire fantastic genealogy would prove to be futile. It would take another few hundred years till a successor of Egor's, just as long and filiform, found another little girl who would conscientiously take on the dreaming of the dreams. I reassured him that I would go to sleep, but Egor seemed at that moment so distant, so unreal. My REM had been the kiss I had given to Ester. In that moment I had the All. 'Tell me, Egor, what is this marvellous gift that your ancestors received from the African fly?' I asked him the question without curiosity, staring out the window at the sunny field. Puzzled, Egor looked at me and after a moment he answered: 'Oh yes, put your hand here.' He opened a shirt button so that I could touch with my fingers the top of his chest. It was a soft spot, like a layer of fat. 'It's the thymus,' he said. 'The childhood gland. It usually disappears during adolescence, but mine will last all my life. I will remain a child all my life, that's the gift. This soft place on my chest helped me to get to know you, to understand your game, to keep vigil over your dreams. Yes, the bite of that uncanny insect preserves the thymus. Through it, you penetrate the dream and become a citizen of the dream.' I left Egor with difficulty that afternoon, as though I knew I would never see him again. I looked at him as he stood in his doorstep, where he had escorted me: a melancholy monster from another world, frighteningly frail, a sad and desiccated giant spider, slowly waving at me. I turned my head back towards him many times as I made my way home on the trail. He was always there, standing motionless in the doorway. I turned the corner and the watchtower with its glimmering window disappeared.

At home, I ate quickly, putting up stoically with Marcel's pestering and Auntie's questions and attentions (which I didn't answer out of distraction rather than stubbornness). My aunt, poor thing, would bring her sewing with her even to the table, stitching a skirt's hem or some other thing, tearing the thread with her teeth in between taking bites of bread. I went to sleep, curled up under the sheets, with the shell, so wonderfully sweet to the touch, under the pillow. I was on fire, my head was spinning, my senses seemed inside out. I turned and twisted, wrapping myself up in the sheets until I fell into a state of dark delirium, a sleep filled with dream fragments, spoken more than seen. I was talked about by someone outside of me; I existed only for the period of time that this someone uttered the indecipherable words, the hieratical mutterings. And those words were by no means abstractions, the language was by no means merely a language: some of the words were gelatinous, others wet or frozen, and others still burned like acid. All in all, that speech was a bizarre world, which I perceived with something other than the senses, which I lived with something other than the body and the flesh. I was tortured, martyred by that language that dreamed me. I opened my eyes after a while (how long I couldn't tell) and sat up. I was still dizzy but could distinguish the golden colours of the afternoon. The thought flashed that I still needed to get to REM. I even had the feeling that I was late, as though a precise indication had been given me (when?) regarding the second when I needed to be there. I got out of bed and ran out of the room. The ashen corridor leading to the front door seemed unendingly long. When I opened the door, I was abruptly startled by the splendor of the garden, exploding in millions of colours: red and blue flowers shooting out of gigantic calyxes and burning like flames, vegetables with leaves green as bile, everything brilliant in the blinding sun spanning half the sky. The truck had been literally consumed by the sun: the paint peelings had caught on fire and smoked in the monstrous light of the tomatoes. I went out through the gate, and soon I was running across the field on the trail to the watchtower. I crossed the distance as though in a single step, and abruptly I was facing the dilapidated shed where REM was located. Without hesitating a second, I took out the golden key and planted it in the rusty lock. As I had expected, it fit perfectly and turned voluptuously, as though it were turning in butter. I tossed the lock away, and for an instant I propped my head against the scarlet door. I cracked it open and went in.

I found myself in a medium-sized room whose walls were painted in a soothing cream yellow. A green rug with a design of black-and-white rhomboids was spread on the hardwood floor. The furniture was modest: a plain bedroom made up of a few pieces veneered with a yellowish wood. I stood on the doorstep and looked at a wardrobe standing against the wall next to the door. There were two suitcases on top of the wardrobe, made of imitation leather, one orange, the other black. There was a guitar sitting on the orange suitcase, with its neck pointing towards the interior of the room. A postcard was glued to one of the wardrobe's doors, depicting – I realize now – an illuminated cathedral at night. A large recamier was leaning against the wall on my right; it was crammed with piles of all sorts of books, some of them very thick, like dictionaries. The bed was unmade, heaped with crumpled sheets. A raised corner revealed the blue upholstery. The entire wall before me was occupied by a panoramic, triple window revealing a row of apartment buildings beyond the wide street. The window was decked out with a white curtain hung from a yellow cornice girdled with brown margins and drapes with green stripes and yellow carnations on a pale background. A lean armchair with spongy upholstery garnished with red Turkish designs leaned against the window wall. Randomly tossed on top of it were two green baby pillows, a brown sweater and a yellow plush towel. But most interesting was the wall to my left. Glued to it, next to the door, was a make-up table with a mirror. A metallic tube with a white plastic cap was lying in a corner of the table (later on, I realized this was a spray can). Next to the make-up table, in the middle of the wall, was another table, underneath a watercolour painting done in imitation-Japanese style: two birds sitting on bamboo branches and looking at each other, with the appropriate ideograms trimming the margins. At that table – loaded with books, white sheets of paper, thick notebooks, files, another metallic tube, a roll the colour of honey (which I now know was a roll of Scotch tape), a wrist watch, some letters, a beaker filled with coloured crayons and some tests corrected with red ink – at that table sat a young man pounding on a typewriter. I had seen typewriters once or twice before when I went with Mama to the notary, but those were black and metal and made a deafening noise. The one I was looking at now was much smaller and made of shiny bluish plastic, and on a tiny metal plate on the left was inscribed in black letters the brand name 'Erika'. The young man had popped off the typewriter's top – coloured a darker blue – so that now you could easily see the two black spools, the metallic type bar in the middle from which the letters fanned out in order to strike the paper on the platen, and the bicolour ribbon, red and black, that hopped rapidly at each strike of the fingers on the white letters of the keyboard. You could find those typewriters a few years ago on the market. The young man was not in fact so young. He must have been about thirty. But his frail silhouette, his narrow and triangular face, his long, light-brown hair that fell over his ears in unruly locks, made him look no older than twenty-five. In any case for me, the one I was then, there was no great difference between twenty and thirty. For me, the young man was an adult. I closed the door behind me and took a few timid steps, until I stood next to his shoulder. He was engrossed in his typing, his fingers sought the letters on the keyboard, which seemed to fascinate him, but he didn't type by far as quickly as the typists at the notary. His dark-brown eyes were adorned with long and dense lashes. The eyebrows arched above them. His nose was straight and with long nostrils, and his cheeks yellow, sunken. A sparse moustache was framed, like two parentheses, by two wrinkles that might have betrayed an inclination to excessive laughter had they not been at the same time bitter and skeptical. His mouth was fleshy, simultaneously sensual and austere; it might have been the mouth of a lanky saint, in ceaseless struggle with temptations and especially with the diabolical temptation of not being tempted. A lightly asymmetrical mouth above a firm albeit narrow chin. His face had little to show on the outside. To the left of the typewriter, just underneath the carriage that kept shifting with jerky motions, I saw a pile of typewritten pages. The first page bore the title 'REM'. There were many of them, at least one hundred, but for the moment I was only interested in the young man. He didn't pay any attention to me, even though it wasn't possible for him not to see me coming in, at least from the corner of his eyes. He was there in the flesh, with his burgundy sweater, dark-green velour trousers and cream-coloured socks on his feet. I remember him in the most insignificant details. For instance, he wasn't shaven and didn't wear a wedding ring on his finger. His fingernails were trimmed short. I gathered all the courage I was capable of to touch his shoulder. Then, he paused. He turned his face towards me (our faces, as he was sitting in his chair, were at the same height) and smiled as if he had been waiting for me. When he smiled, he looked childlike and almost cute. He lifted his left hand and caressed my hair. Then, he picked up the pile of typewritten pages, put them on the bed and indicated I should read them. I was too dizzy and disturbed to read the entire manuscript and, in any case, it would have taken me a few days to finish it. At the beginning, I didn't understand anything; it was a kind of convoluted story. I skipped about twenty pages, and suddenly I was in awe. It was my story, it was about me. About going with Mother to Auntie Aura's and with Father to Children's Town, about travelling by tram and how it swayed, about Chombe and how he bit my cheek once, about how I made little dresses for Zizi. Then, it was about my friends, about Carnation and Puia and Whale and Ada and Carmina and Ester, all of them represented exactly as they were in reality. He had written about Egor and Madam Bach, about their ancestors, about the shell that emanated dreams. He wrote about our game of Queens and what happened to us while we played during the week I stayed at Auntie Aura's. He wrote that I finally entered REM and found the young man working at his typewriter and that he caressed my hair and gave me this story to read. I got frightened. I dropped the pages and turned again towards the young man. He was looking at me as well and smiled again. Then, he showed me a calendar on the wall, the popular sort, with jokes and advice for housewives on the back. I didn't understand, so he stood, tore the page off, folded it and placed it in my hand. Then, he leaned again over his typewriter. I headed towards the sorrowful door. On the inside, the door was yellowish in colour, with a tiny curtain draped over the sliver of an opaque glass window. A large poster with white margins depicting an engraving in dark tones was pinned to the curtain. The right side, containing more than half of the engraving, was submerged in the warm and suffocating darkness of a baldachin bed. On a confusion of pillows and embroidered eiderdowns wallowed the body, white as a fish's belly, disgusting in its obscenity, almost crippled, of a woman with her shirt raised above her waist. The nude had a heavy quality to it, it was impossibly twisted, and the woman's face betrayed a primitive sensuality. Her left hand clenched the coat of a short-statured young man, occupying, in full light, the centre of the engraving's left side. He was leaning towards the opposite side of the bed, his hands appeared to protect him from a phantasm, his face expressed a mixture of suffering, shame and humiliation, a struggle with himself rather than with the woman who attempted to hold on to him but would only be left with his coat. A long strip was torn off from the lower part of the engraving, so that all that remained from an apparently longer inscription were the first three letters, in beautiful calligraphy: REM. I opened the door and left.

When did darkness fall? I couldn't make out anything, I couldn't see the watchtower or the surrounding field. Instead, I felt a squeaking wooden floor under my feet. After a few steps, I tripped on something and fell. When my eyes got used to the dark, I saw that

I was in a tortuous corridor, against whose walls were leaning old pieces of furniture, old metal bed panels, gigantic ceramic vases, broken and cracked, upright pianos with missing keys. As I rushed ahead, feeling more and more certain of my path, a horde of beige and ashen butterflies burst in on me from everywhere, fluttering on the lone light-rays. I descended a stairway shrouded in spider webs and plunged into interminable corridors. It smelled like bathrooms and chlorine, and the air was an unhealthy blackish-green. Suddenly, turning a corner, I saw a door ajar and rushed out in the full morning light. I found myself in the ceaseless forest, without beginning or end, dipped in gold and dappled by shadows, set on fire by the song of unknown birds. The sun burned my eyes. I stared at the sky and saw how the wind caused the transparent leaves to tremble and the young branches to sway. Then I knew I was dreaming, but this thought didn't stop me from feeling happy, from breathing the air that smelled of broken bark, of sap, of earth full of torn roots. I wanted to run back to my path, to pause at the place where I first found the key, where I broke the glass, where I crossed the brook, where I leaped over the log, to regress back into the zone from which I appeared, from where my journey began. I knew, though, that my return wasn't possible. It was finished. I needed, O Lord, to wake up. I let myself fall to the ground and began to toss about, to strike my face with my palms. And suddenly, I woke up for real.

I was back in my room, in my twilight-reddened bed. I had slept about four hours, and I still wasn't feeling very well. I lay there for a long time staring up at the ceiling, dappled by red stripes that had oozed in through the window curtains. I had cramps and felt a desiccated, wooden pain below my belly. I couldn't think of anything, but, when I closed my eyes, I saw under my lids clear images from the endless day that had now passed: the watchtower, the girls dressed for the wedding in the full midday sun, Ester's face . . . A few minutes passed till I realized I was clenching something in my right fist. I thought for a moment it was the shell, but the shell was in its place underneath the pillow. I didn't have enough courage to open my fist, but when I finally decided to do it, I saw that it was a folded piece of paper. Suddenly, I recalled the calendar sheet that young man from REM had given me. I unfolded it. It was dated May 3rd 198–. On the back, printed in tiny letters, there was an article about the history of stamp collecting. I still have that piece of paper. Very soon, there will be tens of thousands of identical pieces of paper; it is very possible that year's calendars are already printed. Thus, my proof will soon lose any credibility. Only then, looking at that page, still curled up in the humid bed, did I understand a part of REM's infinite presence. It hadn't all been a dream, and it hadn't all been reality. I was given a page from a calendar that would come out more than twenty years later. This I knew, and it was something that should have horrified me. When I regained my composure, I heard from the other side of the French door the murmur of a voice I knew. I got out of bed and glued my ear to the coarse surface of the opaque glass. Auntie Aura was saying: 'I think she's getting better, Costele. As you know, I'm busy working all day, I can't look after her all the time. She's been wandering around all week, she's lost some weight. I don't know what's happening to her. I think she misses home, I see her crying a lot . . . Now, I don't want you to think that . . . She can stay here for as long as Viorica is in the hospital, but . . .' And Father answered: 'I appreciate it, Aurelia, but I think I'd better take her home, I am taking some time off from work . . . In any case, I haven't been paying as much attention to her lately. I need to take her to the movies, museums, to the park . . . She's become kind of wild, all by herself here.' I froze, as if the two of them had crashed through the door to take me away by force. After a few minutes, I heard them heading for my room. I threw myself on the bed, and pretended to be asleep. They sat on the edge of the bed, and Auntie Aura, caressing my hair, whispered to me to wake up. I opened my eyes, sat up, kissed Papa, and suddenly, very unlike me, shouted at him: 'Papa, I don't want to leave, I want to stay some more. Please, please!' They didn't contradict me, they were very sweet to me. While I was changing my clothes, I looked at Papa from the corner of my eyes. I was sorry for him: his hair had turned almost completely grey, and his face, which before looked ruddy and healthy, was now wrinkled and desolate.

He was unshaven and looked like a man who had no one to take care of him. Together with Marcel, we sat outside under the light of a bulb and had dinner. It was night. Towards the back of the court-yard, the moonlit night was even bluer than before. Gigi crawled between our feet, with her tail stiff up in the air, and at times stood on her hind paws and gawked at the plates. I patted her head absent-mindedly. I put a piece of food on the side of the chair just to see her claw it away. Farther off, Chombe was gobbling from his dish. Thousands of flies, moths and aphids circled around the blinding bulb. Papa paused from time to time to tell me what films were playing in the city. Tomorrow was the last day to see *The Sorcerer's Apprentice,* about which Ester had told me so much. There were also *The Crystal Palace* and the first episodes of *The Phantoms of Spessart.* And, there was a surprise waiting for me if I wanted to go home that evening. I didn't say anything, I ate and stared at the flies, at their sharp twists and turns around the bulb, at their disappearance into the darkness and re-emergence into the light. Finally, I decided to go back home for one day only; I would then return the day after. Papa agreed, and after we prattled some more in the cool air, I got dressed and packed my suitcase. I was so sad I didn't even notice that Auntie Aura had already put all my clothes in a bag. I took with me the things which were dearest to me: I wrapped the egg in leftover bits of cloth and put it in the shoebox together with the shell and the calendar page. Auntie walked us to the gate with her ceaseless ear-to-ear smile, with her gestures of exaggerated ami-ability. Papa and I ambled down the street hand in hand under the sparkling stars. I was looking up only at them and tripped from time to time because of it. The stars were very far away. They didn't care about anything on earth. I looked for the six-tailed comet for a long time and found it only with difficulty. You could barely see it, like a pale cloud at the edge of the sky. The next night, I looked for it in vain through our skylight on Calea Moșilor. We plunged into a tangle of dark streets, weakly lit by drab bulbs, until we hit the high-way where every once in a while a lone truck or tram rattled by. We waited at the station for a long time, and then we swayed along next to a sleeping ticket-taker through the phantasmic city. Because of the orange light in the tram, I couldn't see anything out of the window except the reflections of our earth-coloured faces and the seats made of shiny yellow slats. We finally got home, and I went to sleep. I twisted and turned the entire night in a benumbed half-awake state, dreamed in senseless fragments, sweated until the sheets got soaked, moaned in my sleep.

That night I had my first period.

Certainly, once at home, the magic was gone. Mother left the hospital about three weeks later, and then, about three weeks after that, school started. Sometime in October, Auntie Aura came by with Uncle Ştefan and Marcel and our families had a fight, I still don't know why. So we never went back there again. Around 1970, their street was torn down and new apartment buildings were built instead, extending beyond the street, halfway to the watchtower. I went there one day in July, a few years ago. I found my way with difficulty through the identical four-storey buildings, standing only a short metre from one another, with their balconies scattered with hanging multicoloured clothes and the concrete stairways teeming with little children in undershirts, but I finally found the place where my aunt's house had stood. The name of the street had remained the same, after some corporal who had distinguished himself in some war or another. I walked down to the end of the street, which still ended at the edge of the field, despite its currently more urban aspect. But the watchtower was no longer there. It was as if it had never been. Beyond the apartment buildings were ploughed fields as far as the eye could see, all the way to the edge of the forest towards the Dudeşti district. But in the middle of the field, still standing, was REM! The old shed had endured the test of time. My heart stopped when I saw it. Even though I had new shoes on, I started walking over the fallow land until I got to the door I knew so well. The lock was on the door but not fastened; it was just hanging there on its shackle, porous and rusty. I opened the door and peered inside. Underneath the spider webs, heavy and full of teeming insects, you could see in the half-shadow a series of old tools: adzes, shovels, strange pieces of sheet metal, an anvil, twisted metal bars, chisels, all of them covered with brick-coloured rust. A squashed bucket was filled with solidified plaster. I left right away, overtaken by fatigue, by a feeling of uselessness. I remember Egor's words: '. . . exterminating time, time that takes no prisoners . . .'

And now I've told you my 'all too beautiful story'. It took me many years, I needed to mature, to become almost an old woman, to begin to understand what REM really is: that REM is not to be found there, inside the shed, but outside; that in fact *we are REM*, you and I and my story with all its objects and characters, with Bloody Mary and the dog that was hit by the car, that our world is fiction, that we are paper heroes, and that we were born in REM's brain, in his mind and heart, in him whom I saw. Because he himself is comprised in REM. That maybe even he, in his world which I penetrated – that being perhaps the only reason for my existence – is nothing but the product of a much vaster mind, from another world, itself fictional. And he himself, I am certain of this now, is searching feverishly for an Entrance to that superior world, because our dream, everyone's dream, is to meet the Creator, to look in the eyes the being that gave us life. But, who knows, maybe REM is nothing like what I believe him to be. Maybe he is only a feeling, the heart tightening before the ruin of all things, before everything that ever existed and will never exist again. A memory of memories. Perhaps REM is nostalgia. Or something else. Or all of those things at once. I don't know. I don't know.

It's already daylight in your one-room apartment. The ashen shroud that hooded the surface of objects has slowly evaporated, and the millions of colours belonging to the day's world have overtaken the book spines (the Cortázar, the García Márquez in tatters . . .), our clothes randomly tossed everywhere, the fur-covered floor, the coffee table with the basket filled with apple cores and a prehistoric egg, the naive tapestry on the walls. You're silent now, and suddenly things take advantage of this irresolution of yours to charge at us, to shove their fingers in our eyes. I stretch, I feel full of dregs. What the hell am I looking for, way out here in the Dămăroaia slums? Where am I going to end up, with this stupid relationship with you? I have time to think about your story now; something in me gobbled it up in a hurry, swallowed without chewing, and is awaiting better times to ruminate over it. All I want to do is go home to sleep, never see you again. You're flabby, used-up, you have circles under your eyes the size of your entire face, your hair is a mess, your complexion is marred by innumerable pores, at night you camouflage them somehow, but now . . . And it's damn cold in this room. Hey, woman, the fun is over.

Have you forgot about me, beloved reader? It is me, the narrator. It's true, I haven't showed my darling little face for a while, but that's because I have been occupied with other things. I am he who languishes now on top of the egg on the table, as though to hatch it; I am he who stirs his invisible paws (many, I have many!) through the room, fat and satisfied. Everything that took place last night between these two friends of ours (who were not so well behaved!) has been transferred into my spherical belly. Look at them shivering as they put on their clothes in a hurry. They avoid each others' eyes, have nothing more to tell each other and, even if they did, they don't figure it's worth the trouble. She smiles coldly; she sees and knows nothing. She had never told anyone before what that blockhead Vali had the fortune to hear the night before. From this, I draw the conclusion that she loves him. Tough luck! Because Vali – the instant they are out the door to the apartment building and into the snowstorm outside, she holding on to his arm, their cheeks freezing and their eyes shut tight from too much white on the trees and the alleys between the greenish buildings – tells her again what he told her before each time they left her place together: that it's over, that there is no sense to it, that it is the last time. She withdraws her hand lightly from underneath his arm, looks to the side and says nothing for a long time, then speaks with an indefinable expression: 'Do whatever you want.' They walk together to the bus station in silence, watching the snowflakes falling lightly over the white pavement. When the red bus arrives, Vali mutters a short goodbye, and in a few seconds Nana watches him as he sits down: a greenish shadow across the frozen window of the bus. Vali now becomes entirely uninteresting for me. In fact, I am so full that I couldn't bear a trip by bus. So, I return with Nana, who walks with tiny steps back to her apartment. She knows that in the evening Vali will ring the bulldog's doorbell. But she also knows that, by the end of the week, he will wait for her by the entrance to the institute, and last night will repeat itself as everything else repeats itself, from a certain age onwards, in the life of a single woman. She enters the reek of the apartment building, unlocks her dark blue door, locks it again, takes off her fur and her boots and lies down on the unmade bed. She lights a cigarette and stares at the emptiness. I get very close to her and see precisely, as in a scientific documentary film, how the teardrop takes shape in her eyes, how it grows suspended by the shiny edge of the lower eyelid, how it glides along the cheek next to the nose and tumbles like a spark on the sheets. Before she finishes her cigarette, she sits up and opens a tiny door on her bookshelf. She extracts a pile of papers thick as a palm, layered with minuscule writing. She tosses it on the bed, picks up a ballpoint pen and writes anxiously, continuing where she left off on the written page. She has been writing now for a quarter of an hour, when, thundering apocalyptically, the shell of the egg on the table cracks open revealing the rising Chimera, who fills the room with her dragon roar, her lion claws, her immense bat wings. She swells triumphantly over you, shrouds you in shadow, while you, minuscule, cowed by the cold and abruptly buckling over, continue stubbornly writing: 'no, no . . .'

Epilogue

*There is only one problem in the world . . . How does one
burst the cocoon and become a butterfly?*

THOMAS MANN

The Architect

Emil Popescu was an architect. His speciality was designing sunflower-seed oil factories, and it could be said without exaggeration that, anywhere in the country that a sunflower-seed oil factory was built during the last five or six years, you recognized the deft hand and the mind accustomed to the solving of difficult technical problems belonging to the architect Popescu. His passion for designing sunflower-seed oil factories was not new. He had desired it passionately ever since his childhood, which he spent in the giant shadow of the sunflower-seed oil factory near the bus depot and Ştefan cel Mare movie theater. It was a windowless, scarlet, brick building, tall and straight, fastened with iron bolts and shooting up at a dizzy height into a sombre gable, as though to slash the clouds. This uncanny construction, planted in the middle of a deserted courtyard, was built along the main highway the same year as the Dâmboviţa Mill. A century back, both were part of the famous Asan Mill complex. When, with the passage of years, Emil Popescu began to become interested in culture, on account of the atmosphere at the university, he could see the sunflower-seed oil factory of his childhood in virtually every building that would rise, infinite and melancholy, out of the shiny pages of a catalogue on whose cover you could read the name 'Giorgio de Chirico'. But many years had passed since then, and today the architect Emil Popescu, born in 1950 and married without children to Mrs. Elena Popescu, born Deleanu, was renowned as a specialist in his field. He had designed all the sunflower-seed oil factories in Kabul and even those next to El Aghar, this last being the most renowned in Egypt. He was deeply respected by his colleagues and loved by his subordinates,

within the limits of course of the envy inherent in any establish-
ment of employment, which leads to malicious gossip, not always
justified and in any case unethical.

The architect's family life was a happy one. He had married out of
love an appealing girl from Moldova, herself an architect specializ-
ing in milk factories and with whom he had an excellent relationship.
They lived in the Berceni district, just over the way from Mărțișor, in
a tastefully furnished three-room apartment. The fact that they had
no children, even though they had married while still at the university, made it possible for them to save. Adding up all the things
brought back by Emil from Turkey, Iran and Egypt, and by Elena
from the Soviet Union and Hungary, places they had travelled to on
account of their work – things of value on which they capitalized
profitably – the two architects managed to put in the bank sufficient
funds towards the purchase of a Dacia automobile, a longtime dream
of Elena's. The day they accomplished this dream was, as Elena put
it, almost as enchanting as the day of their wedding. Just like then,
they kissed long and leisurely and toasted a glass of wine with their
in-laws and other relatives. The automobile, the colour of cream, was
parked at an angle between the Lada belonging to Gheorghian, who
lived at Number 6, and the cherry Wartburg belonging to the photographer from the adjoining entrance, owner of the bulldog Dolly.
The Dacia had a beguiling contour, and the two architects stared at
it from their balcony from morning to evening. It glistened in the
sharp spring sun, brighter than the automobile belonging to Colonel
Boteanu from Number 2, a Citroën, which a soldier washed with a
hose every day.

Emil Popescu enrolled in a driver's training course. However,
even before completing it, he came out daily to hover about the car,
to brush it, to wipe off the mud tracks left by the children who
played behind the apartment building, but particularly to unlock
the door and sprawl out on the front seat, to stare at the dashboard
from which the steering wheel sprang entrancingly, and to inhale
into his lungs that intimate, sensual smell exhaled by the rubber and
upholstery of the vehicle. When he slammed the door shut, the
noise of the world came to a stop and the architect felt happy in that

tender and comfortable space, where everything was built in order to serve him. Not even the conjugal bed made him feel such happiness. Sometimes, Elena joined him and the two sat, enthralled, for an entire hour, like bewitched twins inside their mother's womb. It was as though they had no interest at all in putting the vehicle in motion. They would keep it like this, parked behind the apartment building, in order to savour from time to time these moments of full and genuine intimacy.

The tenants of the apartment building eventually became accustomed to the architect's supple silhouette constantly hovering about his Dacia. He always wore the same pair of shorts, the by-product of blue jeans cut off above the knee, and a printed shirt depicting, if you looked carefully, the Romanian Athenaeum with the statue of the great poet Mihail Eminescu. He was a young man of nearly inconspicuous appearance: the typical figure, you might say, of a Romanian originating from the Carpathians. Dark-brown hair, jaws giving the impression of a permanently unshaved look, prominent masticator muscles, as though always cursing between the teeth, somewhat expressionless eyes, about which you couldn't say very much except that they were black. He wore his hair closely cropped and parted to the side. He was good-looking enough to make an impression on the Czech and Polish girls on the Black Sea beaches, and they had been his speciality in his student years. He carried in his hand a tiny blue-plastic bucket filled with water and cleaning detergent, in which an orange sponge sloshed about. He circled his Dacia, scrubbing and wiping in the spring's tonic air, which impelled the buds of the acacia trees and the building's hedge to unfurl.

This was the architect Emil Popescu. All else you might say about him would be superfluous, even ridiculous. Does it matter that he smoked Cişmigiu cigarettes? That his favourite soccer team was S. C. Băcau? That he was in the habit of reading everything that appeared under the category of history's secret dossiers and especially the ones about the Gestapo and the SS? That he subscribed to the news review *The World*? That he religiously never missed an issue of the magazines *The Flame, The Week* and *Potpourri*? That when he watched a programme on television, it was always from the beginning to the end? That he did not own a reel-to-reel tape recorder, and his record player was part of his wife's dowry, which came with a few records: *Famous Tangos*, Remo Germani, *Los Para-guayos*, the short story *The Lost Letter* by Ion Luca Caragiale, poems by Ion Cristoreanu, and Tudor Arghezi, *Rigoletto*, and *Dentes*? That he fell for a divorced co-worker, but after the second time became apprehensive and stopped seeing her? That he never wore a tie? That at night, it was well understood, he dreamed only of hydraulic conduits and viaducts essential to the functioning of sunflower-seed oil factories? That every Friday he played bridge with a few of his colleagues and, it might be added, not very well? All these are trifles.

One morning during that particular spring, before leaving for work, Emil Popescu went behind the apartment building to take another look at the automobile. The night before, he had drunk an Albanian cabernet at a friend's birthday and it had made him sick. All night long, he felt palpitations in his liver, and now, in the morning, the back of his neck hurt and a sensation of nausea leaked down through his sinuses. The cool air revived him a little, even though the trash containers reeked at him with a characteristic smell. The cream-coloured automobile gleamed bleakly, geometrically, near the carpet beater, between the Lada and the Wartburg, and the windows reflected opaquely the morning sun. The architect took out the silvery key and unlocked the door. He propped his briefcase against the tyre and stepped for a second inside the car. He switched on the lights, alternating between their two phases. Then he tried the wipers and the radio inside the dashboard. A male voice spoke about the weather. The architect smiled. Everything was in order. He pressed his index finger on the disc in the centre of the steering wheel, under whose plexiglas the car's emblem stood out in relief. The tenor sound of the horn burst out, but would not stop when Emil Popescu lifted his index finger from the disc. The sound persisted, monotonously, stridently, rending the dim air of half-past six in the morning. The architect pressed desperately a number of times on the plexiglas disc, but without effect. He felt he was going mad. He dashed quickly out of the car, whose lights he had forgotten to switch off, and walked helplessly around it. After about a minute of the unbearable wail, citizens in pyjamas appeared at windows and balconies, each one shouting something at the architect, but because of the horn he couldn't make sense of what they said. The young man wished he could disappear inside the earth. He lifted the Dacia's hood and began to shake at random the yellow, black and red wires, insulated in thick plastic, arranged here and there in the form of loops. The reek of gas and the noise made his head burst. He had no idea which wires connected to the horn and became more agitated and uncomfortable from one moment to the next. Elena finally showed up too. She was in her dressing gown, and the two of them bustled about in bewildered confusion next to the monster that kept on howling without respite. A potato banged on to the hood of the Dacia and ricocheted to the side. It was hurled by someone from one of the balconies. The entire apartment building had woken up and unshaved men, women without make-up and unshowered children yelled at the unhappy owners of the Dacia. Finally, Colonel Boteanu came down behind the apartment building in his undershirt and pyjama trousers, pushed them aside without a word and, with a single gesture like that of a magician, which he performed in the obscurity of the engine, severed the sound, after which he scornfully left. With their ears still ringing, the two could at last hear what the tenants from the balconies were shouting. They were not pleasant things.

That day at work, Emil Popescu did not perform at his usual level of proficiency. Before the drafting board, staring at the plastic beaker filled with pencils from many countries, playing with the Richter compasses and the case of drafting tools, following absent-mindedly the thousands of lines on the drafting paper, the architect felt tired. His mind was still at the morning's scene. He was obsessed by the powerful and monotone sound of the horn. He began to think about all sorts of horns, from the spring-triggered ones of the bicycle, emitting a sound like that of an alarm clock, to those with a rubber bubble furnishing the old jalopies in *When Comedy Was King*. When he came home, he asked his wife, in whose eyes he didn't dare to look, for the automobile's documentation. He leafed through the shiny pages of the instruction manual, full of poorly superimposed colour photographs exhibiting the Dacia 1300 in all possible positions, read distractedly through the text filled with spelling errors, but found hardly any mention concerning the functioning of the horn. It was the customary, electromagnetic type, built at the Electrowire factory in Bucharest. Discontented, he himself didn't know why, the architect sought excuses for confrontation all evening and went to sleep on the couch in the living room. He fell asleep late, with the instruction manual on his chest.

The next day, after work, he went directly to the Electrowire factory. He knew it well: when he was a boy he used to steal magnets and brass hoops by hopping over the concrete wall, and in college he had been sent there for in-the-field training. It was actually a cooperative, where tens of female workers wrapped wires around giant spools. It reeked permanently of insulated wire and cardboard soaked in oil. The architect spoke with an elderly shop superintendent, who gave him the facts about different types of horns. When he found out that there were also musical horns, built with a series of electrical trumpets that could play a melodic phrase, Emil Popescu, without being able to explain it, felt himself filled with enthusiasm. He asked the superintendent to tell him where he might be able to find such a horn. The superintendent sent him to a young mechanic who occupied himself with affairs of that sort at the Autoservice shop in Colentina, on Nicolae Apostol Street. Emil Popescu could barely contain himself till the next day. He twisted and turned in his bed all night long, passionately dreaming about the miraculous horn. In the morning, for the first time since he began, he arrived for work two hours late. He had rushed over to the Autoservice, where the young mechanic in question offered him something close to what he was looking for: a Gordini model with six nickel-plated trumpets, which intoned the first measures of the 'Triumphal March' from *Aïda*. The young mechanic might be able to get a hold of such a horn: he knew an Italian who needed money. In about a week, he would communicate the result of his search to the architect. Of course, this being an article from a foreign country, the cost of the horn would be rather high. Emil Popescu said money was no object and even stuffed a hundred-lei bill into the pocket of the young man's overalls, because he felt the need to assure himself of certain possession of the article. He went home both happy and unhappy, horrified by the thought of having to wait an entire week, while obsessively humming the whole evening, 'Sing, sing to the glory of our country, / Today is a day we celebrate . . .'

After only a few days, the architect received the much-awaited telephone call. He rushed over to Nicolae Apostol Street. The young mechanic showed him an odd piece of machinery resembling an ebony plate; from one of its sides emerged six tiny brass trumpets, from the other a mesh of electrical cables. Plugged in, the machinery emitted the Verdian measures at a burlesque speed. A few mechanics huddled around them, joined soon by customers and even some of the students from the school next to the Autoservice, who marvelled at the odd singing object. The architect returned home accompanied by the young mechanic, who mounted the new horn under the Dacia's hood. Pressing the disc at the centre of the steering wheel, he incited a veritable wave of contradictory feelings among the groups of tenants, feelings ranging from admiration to envy and sacred fury. Elena came out as well from the apartment building's hallway. She had noticed for some time that something strange was going on with her husband, but had no idea what it was about and, consequently, how to react. When she found out just how much her husband's whim had cost them, she adopted an appropriate demeanour, one she had inherited from her mother and which manifested itself through mimicry, gesticulations and especially exaggerated language. A whole month's salary had perished on account of the Italian's contraption. But Emil Popescu had no intention of returning it, as Elena threateningly suggested; lounging in complete *dolce far niente* on the front seat's upholstery, he pressed incessantly on his horn, listening with the voluptuousness of a melomaniac to the short phrase of the famous march.

As could be expected, one day the architect became bored with the Verdi phrase and started to look for something else. One after another, Elena was horrified or disgusted by the jovial and primitive depictions of the 'Marseillaise', 'Yankee Doodle Dandy' and 'God Save the Queen' gushing out of an electrically powered musical trumpet. The expenditure wasn't so overwhelming any more, because the architect made exchanges with a series of different drivers whom he encountered God knows where. Once, Elena spotted her spouse from out of tram Number 21. Instead of being at work, he was circling around the electric clock in the centre of the Bucur Obor Plaza, listening to the way it intoned a well-known song every quarter hour. Things became tragically complicated for the brave-hearted wife, who didn't yet want to admit to herself the sad truth. The whole story with the horns lasted the better of six months, while the architect, progressively more nervous and discontented, exchanged eight of those noise-making products. The happiness of the beginning transmuted to hatred and venom. Harassed by the neighbours, who threatened him with legal action, by his bosses, who were unhappy with his lack of efficiency before the drafting board, by his wife, who gave him a domestic ultimatum, refusing to cook or wash for him or fulfill other matrimonial duties, the architect was now left without even the consolation of being able to enjoy his own passion. He had arrived too quickly at a peak that he had no hope of surpassing. He had experimented with the most modern and complex horns built in the entire world, even with the much-celebrated product made by Toyota, the one that blared out the refrain from the song 'Satisfaction' by the Rolling Stones. And it wasn't as much the banality and the limited character of the horns that infuriated Emil Popescu as the passive attitude the horn's owner had to adopt in the course of exercising his rights. That was the principal rub with all the horns now available in the trade. How was it that it didn't enter anyone's mind that the man behind the steering wheel might get sick and tired of one single finger pressing invariably upon one single button? Wouldn't he desire to collaborate with the machine, to become a creator? Perhaps he would like to compose the melody emitted by the horn, each time a different one, after the state of his soul, his talent, his taste. Wracking his brains and biting his fists during interminable nights when he barely managed to doze off for an hour or so towards morning, the architect imagined a horn that would be built on entirely novel principles. It would be provided with keys like a piano, each key connected to one of the tiny electric trumpets.

The next day, a Sunday, he paid a visit to his cousin Virgil Ciotoianu, who lived in the Almo 3 apartment building above the Bucur Obor shopping centre and whose occupation was fixing television sets. Before broaching the subject of his visit, the architect admired the photo-wallpaper adorning the living room, displaying a blood-crimson lake at twilight and a gigantic pine, black as pitch. They spoke about the new colour television sets. Finally, Popescu informed him about his plans. The repairman, after giving them some thought and unpleasantly surprised by the originality of his cousin's thinking, asked him why he didn't simply buy a piano, which he could play in his own home to his heart's content. As for the horn, it would be much better for him to hurry and get his driver's license, otherwise the car would just rust for no reason. But Emil Popescu would not give up. Patiently, he explained once more about the insufficiency of today's horns and that it was not his wish to learn how to play the piano but to improve the state of the horn, thus effecting a service to millions of automobile drivers. At length, they reached an agreement: The architect would purchase an electric organ and the repairman would install it on the car's dashboard. Of course, he explained, the car would become inoperable; the steering wheel would have to be removed, otherwise there would not be enough room for the keyboard. The architect, in agreement with all those conditions, insisted that his cousin rush over immediately to install the organ, spilling, on account of an exalted gesture, the glass of Bulgarian gin which Virgil Ciotoianu had offered him. After the architect left, the repairman phoned Madam Popescu. They spoke for a long time, in hushed tones. Their voices emanated worry.

In consequence, Elena threatened the architect with divorce – without any regrets – if he intended to destroy the automobile. He tried to explain that it was an experiment, but she did not wish to hear any explanations. Still, she didn't divorce him when their relative showed up the following Sunday with a professional case containing a soldering iron, solder, a screwdriver with attached light bulb, transistors, diodes, a roll of single-strand coated wire, special oil, thinner, electrical tape, pliers, a wire stripper, a complete set of screwdrivers and a receipt book with pencil and indigo carbon paper. The Reghin organ, already purchased by Emil Popescu from the music store Muzica, stood in the hallway of the apartment, propped up against the kitchen wall. It looked like a wooden board, veneered in a pleasant coffee gloss, from which issued forth, touchingly pure and positioned in two rows, the bright alabaster and ebony keys. It was about two o'clock in the afternoon when the two men, one palpitating with anxiety, the other bearing the aspect of an undertaker, hauled the organ downstairs and leaned it against the cream body of the Dacia 1300. The installation lasted more than three hours, but at last, a little past five o'clock, the neighbours, who had been leering out of their windows and balconies, heard the first cacophonous notes issuing out of the organ by the pressing of the awkward fingers of the architect. Happily, the sound's volume, amplified by speakers that had cost him a pile of money, could be adjusted at one's pleasure; thus, the neighbours did not become annoyed when they noticed that the architect, eccentric that he was, did not leave his keyboarded crib until long past nightfall, emitting in an undertone sound after sound, fascinated by the novelty of his occupation. At the same time, at approximately twelve metres above ground, in the apartment the two architects shared, Madam Elena Popescu, born Deleanu, wept large tears, which glued themselves to the embroidered pillow in the bedroom. She could no longer tolerate the reckless expenditure of her husband. She had had enough struggles, enough toil, enough of life itself and desperately realized that without a doubt her husband was going insane before her very eyes.

It was already three o'clock in the morning when, exhausted and hungry, the architect Popescu wobbled in through the door of the apartment. Standing in the kitchen, he guzzled down, without bothering to discriminate, whatever he found in the refrigerator.

His mind was filled with sounds. Hour after hour, he had pressed at random the black and white keys, one key at a time or several keys simultaneously, feeling like an adolescent waking up unexpectedly in the bed of his first woman. He would have liked to remain there eternally, to try out all the possibilities, pressing each of the keys, at first one at a time, then two, then three . . . A few of the sound sequences made him happy, as though he had previously known them and awaited them for a long time; the others, however, the most in fact, wounded and insulted not only his hearing, but perhaps his entire being. He sprawled out on the living room sofa and fell into a comforting sleep, for the first time in months.

Every day now, after the hours he spent at work, Emil Popescu sat in the comfortable seat of his Dacia and resumed his sounding of the horn. After a few decades, when enormous quantities of studies, monographs, commentaries, articles, diploma and doctorate dissertations – tens, even hundreds of times more voluminous than those about Dante, Shakespeare and Dostoyevsky put together – were consecrated to the architect, these few months of *sotto voce* groping on the keys of the Reghin organ would come to receive the name of his 'subterranean' or 'underground' period. From time to time, a neighbour or an old friend would come by to sweeten his solitude, taking the seat next to him and marvelling each time at the uncanny look of a car furnished with an organ instead of a dashboard and steering wheel. Without interrupting for one moment his saraband of sounds, the architect patiently explained that the fundamental function of the automobile is not, as it is commonly thought, to shorten distances, transporting a person from one place to another. That was but the secondary function, and, if you thought about it, without any real value. The nobility of the automobile lay in the sound of its horn, that is, in communicating and expressing itself. The sounding of the horn, as conceived by Emil Popescu, was the voice of the automobile, until now oppressed and throttled by man, reduced to a single animalistic and guttural sound, but from now on liberated, dignified and sovereign. We complained about the invasion of the technical, about the lack of dialogue with the machine, but we never thought about giving the machine a chance to express itself. It was not absolutely necessary that machines functioned, but it was, in point of fact, an elemental right of theirs to be able to express themselves. Having taken the explanation to that point, the architect's eyes sparkled in such a maniacal manner that the neighbour rushed his goodbyes and clambered up to his apartment, where he felt disturbed for the rest of the day, unable to decide whether to laugh or feel pity.

The 'underground' period lasted until the next spring. Once the hedge and the acacias behind the apartment building turned green, Emil Popescu turned up his speakers, so that you could hear what he played over the radius of a few metres but without disturbing the neighbors. Many of the neighbours made it their custom to walk by the architect's automobile each afternoon, fascinated by the pene-trating harmonies that began to take wing, each day more flawless than the last. During the first days of spring, the architect obsti-nately resumed the same monotonous but pleasing sequence of complete notes, each growing as though from the previous one and transmitting an odd state of ataraxia. 'Sounds kind of like Pink Floyd,' the kids in the neighbourhood would find themselves mur-muring, but quickly sensing it was a Pink Floyd 'in agony'. Indifferent to the commentaries, our hero resumed, day after day and with evident enchantment, sequences of whole notes that glis-tened mutely and profoundly. Telente, the Gypsy violinist from entrance Number 6, whose three daughters wrapped themselves in silver fox furs, possibly in homage to the incredible succession of men that trafficked through their home day and night, listened attentively to the architect's music, swearing with professional admiration under his handlebar moustache. It was a scale, he sensed that right away, but a scale he had never heard before. At the restau-rant Hora where he played, Telente sketched during a break the sequence of ten whole notes which he had heard from Emil Pope-scu. For a few seconds, the knives and the forks of the various clientele that frequented the restaurant remained frozen in the air, as if time itself had suddenly dissolved, but the fiddler, as though frightened of himself, resumed the melody he had been playing before, 'Long Ago Tango', his great success with the public. After the end of the set, Telente downed a beer with the band members, who had recently been joined by a new saxophone player; he was a quiet young man who, after graduating from the conservatory, chose not to move to the village of Argăşeni in the township of Bǎcau, where he was to be assigned the position of music teacher. But his friends from the restaurant's band still nicknamed him the Professor and took jesting pride in the fact that at least one of them could read music. That evening, he asked Telente in passing to tell him about the scale he had played after their arrangement of the Beatles song 'Something'. Telente could hardly wait to talk about the show behind his apartment building. The Professor listened to him absent-mindedly, pondering about the ironies inherent in history and remembering a passage from Eliot's 'Gerontian'. Yes, only traps, only snares and tortuous paths . . . The scale that had been the glory of Pythagoras, the celebrated musical scale comprising ten sounds, each corresponding with one of the planets (the last being the mysterious Antichthon, while the first the Sun itself) and composed to harmonize with the Rule of the Golden Mean, was now being reinvented by some maniac who played it over and over again like a scratched record. At home, in his little room measuring two metres by a little more than one, walls lined to the ceiling with frayed-cover books and a collage representing St Augustine staring at the bare breasts of a woman from God knows what dirty magazine, the Professor wrote in his journal a few notes about the matters discussed at the restaurant. But he paused halfway through a sentence, because at eleven his friend Iolanda, recently divorced and desirous of rapture, knocked on his door.

During this time, Elena, the good wife of the architect, consulted with myriads of psychiatrists, whom she brought home under different pretexts to take a look at the architect. Their opinions differed. Certainly, it was not a usual case. Most of them were inclined to speak about monomania, the type shared by stamp or cactus collectors. But who could track precisely the border between a simple hobby and a psychopathological manifestation? Was it not true that there were many examples of absurd passions that lead, under the heading of normality, to manifestations of abnormality?

Didn't everyone know somebody who threw a television set out the window during a soccer game? Weren't there cases where some retired old man living on his pension committed suicide after losing a game of backgammon? As long as her husband still managed to fulfill his duties at work and live according to the social conventions of family life, Elena would do well to be patient. Ultimately, she should not forget that she took Emil Popescu as her husband for better or worse. She could be certain that, once declared mentally insane but as long as his delirious state did not present a danger to society, the care of the architect would still fall to the hands of the family. She shouldn't rush with the divorce; she should wait a while; after all, they had already accomplished so much together, and besides, you couldn't abandon a man like a dog. Other husbands were far worse; they cheated on their wives, drank, practised sexual perversions; how many women didn't wish that their good-for-nothing husbands would sit down after dinner and play the . . . well, play something. Before the wisdom of these professional prescriptions, which found their echo in those of the family, the poor woman resigned herself to resume her waiting. It was very difficult. The architect was not the same man, nothing relating to her or to their home interested him any more. She tried for a time to sleep next to him on the bed and even intended to show tenderness, but not only did he lack any amorous desires, he was not even conscious that such things existed. Over time, he was losing the most elementary human notions. Each morning, for instance, he had to be reminded to shave.

Telente now made it a point to walk by the cream-coloured Dacia every day. Before heading for trolley Number 95, which he took to get to the city's centre, from where, in order to get to work, he took Number 88, he would listen for a few minutes to some of the architect's musical phrases. He quickly realized that the architect did not repeat the same scale incessantly but that he built tiny melodies based on it, uncontrovertibly proving that a technical evolution was actually taking place. His fingers, at first wobbling and awkward, became agile and supple, while their tips became firm as ivory. Still, the melodies had no rhythm, flowing on in whole notes only, or even in double notes, in drawn-out litanies. The adept fiddler of devilish tunes, of the Gypsy glissando and tremolo strains of the cabaret, could not swallow what Emil Popescu was producing. He retained, however, a fragment that seemed to him more melodious and accomplished than the rest, and, after closing time, played it as a curiosity for the Professor. This time the saxophone player pricked up his ears, because the melody seemed to him unbearably familiar. No, it was no longer a question of coincidence. Once every thousand years, someone, pressing the keys at random, might reproduce a musical scale composed of ten sounds, but this time it was different. Back inside his basement hole, the preoccupied Professor reviewed his notes from the conservatory regarding archaic music. He tried again a few times on his saxophone (his great frustration was the lack of an upright piano, for which, in any case, there was no room) those few phrases of the melody which, played on that barbaric and yet refined instrument, sounded novel and penetrating. Invigorated, he noted in his journal that 'the same maniac' succeeded in the bizarre performance of reinventing, note by note, through God knows what parapsychological intuition, the score of the single Orphic hymn that managed to survive from Greek antiquity. It must be, further wrote the Professor, something similar to 'speaking in tongues' or those visions men have about cities they had never visited. The very next day, he asked Telente to introduce him to the automobile organist.

The meeting between the Professor and Emil Popescu is historical. It cannot be overestimated what role the young saxophonist played in popularizing the gigantic *œuvre* and personality of the architect. From the very first notes emitted by the organ, to which he listened while sitting in the passenger seat of the automobile where he had been amiably invited, the Professor intuited what was in fact taking place: after playing the Orphic hymn a couple more times, the organist moved unexpectedly to something else. It was a new scale in his repertoire, but a scale that was thousands of years old and might have been sung on the shores of Asia Minor. After playing this minor scale a few times, Emil Popescu began improvising on its foundation. The Professor asked him a few questions and realized from the answers that the architect had no idea that he was making music. Transported, he did not cease with his theories about the diverse aspects of the man–machine communication through the sound of the horn. What he did was no more than a modulated form of horn sounding, dictated to him by his intimate relationship with the automobile. More than that you couldn't get out of him. While he paid no attention whatsoever to the Professor's attempts to speak to him about scales and melodies, his fingers contoured in the summer air a paean devoted to Apollo, in which the saxophone player recognized a composition by Onesicrates. Only towards evening did he manage to tear himself away. From that moment on, the Professor showed up every day to listen to the fantastic creations of the organist. At night, when he was not under attack by the sensual and enrapturing Iolanda, the young man read and reread his manuals of musical history, marking with a check the stage the architect had reached, attempting even to foresee the steps he would take next. Because, exhausting one after the other the successive stages of antiquity, one afternoon Emil Popescu took the saxophone player by surprise with the first sounds of a Gregorian *cantus planus* in a swell of unmistakable majesty. About that time, the neighbours began to take renewed interest in their eccentric cotenant. The old ladies in particular were positively impressed: this 'church music', although different from the one they knew, had a pleasing effect on them. For two weeks now, you could spot a group of grandmothers dozing off on their kitchen chairs next to the architect's Dacia.

For the Professor, all doubts were now gone. He also abandoned his job, left everything behind, even Iolanda, in order to be constantly with the architect. His journal, which until then contained no more than weekly notes about the books he read and impressions of concerts, in addition to a few details about his amorous affairs, now grew to *roman-fleuve* proportions. Everything was in there, in a jumble of crooked text and musical staves, marking the unlikely explosions of spirit through which Emil Popescu managed to cross from one juncture to the next, from one mental state to the next, from one set of conventions to the next, duplicating, rediscovering step by step the history of music. Of this the architect himself had no understanding. In a hopelessly entangled confusion, his scales and exercises of harmony and counterpoint concatenated late into the night air behind the apartment building, glistening here for ten minutes in a diamond-like limpid melody, plunging again there in pursuits and moody preoccupations. The seasons changed, admixing their colours, projecting their clouds over the shifting skies, but each twilight and each star-rise found the two men behind the windshield of the Dacia 1300, which was now filthy with dust to the utmost degree. Fortunately, the Professor took care to charge up the battery from time to time and to pass the sponge over the cream-coloured sheet metal, to protect it from disappearing into rust. The children playing behind the apartment building made sure to puncture holes in all four tyres of the automobile.

From time to time, Elena came by as well, sitting behind them in the back seat, not so much to listen to the sophisticated melodies of her husband – at this point, he was proceeding through the contrapuntal fury of Dunstable, Palestrina, Dufay, Ockegem, Josquin Des Prés and more particularly Orlando di Lasso, overlapping nearly alchemical chords – but because the deeply romantic appearance of the young saxophone player, why shouldn't we say it, began to attract her. She had realized for a while now that, as long as he continued to play, her husband practically left the daily world behind, blind and deaf to any exterior stimulus. No matter what she said to him, he mumbled the same text with his horn, more and more obscure, more and more delirious. So she did not hesitate to complain about her husband to the Professor, who listened to her, at first with one ear, then with both, but without understanding very much. However, when he opened his eyes, or, better said, when he lifted them up from his journal, he became instantly interested, because Elena had a pair of very nice breasts. They resembled those possessed by the girl from the photograph in his cell, the ones poor St Augustine was forced to stare at without surcease. And these breasts had not been touched for a very long time. When the saxophone player, after a few evenings of hesitation and obscure spiritual intimacy, touched her with his fingers on the cheek (he was also sitting in the back now), Elena was first to mould her barely open lips into a motion of seeking his. They made love right there, during the first chords of the 'Adagio' from the *Concerto for Violin in E Major* by Bach.

After that, the trio was constantly together. Returning from work, Elena usually found the two men already in the car. Ever since he began playing Bach – and he had now been playing Bach for the better part of one year – the neighbours had all turned into music lovers and even asked him to turn up the volume of the speakers for a few hours until evening fell.

The Professor was busy with his notes. He had already published in *Potpourri*, under the column 'Dialogue with our Readers', an essay about the musical phenomenon behind the apartment building in Berceni. He then sent an article to *The Flame*, which was published the following week, and attracted the attention of a committee in charge of cases such as this one. As the architect was becoming more and more difficult to communicate with, and as the saxophone player received the nice sum of 380 lei, he took upon himself to become his odd friend's artistic impresario. Since the music the architect played was merely harmless and perennially useful classical music, the architect became eventually known to the Radiotelevison network, so that a Sunday night or Thursday morning concert on the electronic organ became part of the usual programme. The radio station killed two birds with one stone: first, it proved that new talent emerged among our people everywhere; second, it clearly demonstrated the superior quality of the musical instruments produced at our well-known factory at Reghin.

The following year, the television station popularized the image of the architect for the first time in millions of homes across the country. The television vans pulled up in front of the apartment building under the gaze of the neighbours in their pyjamas and unrolled long blue and orange cables all the way to the back, where two cameras blinked with their green bulbs underneath the lens. The animated reporter, after speaking for a while into the cameras, attempted to penetrate the cabin of the Dacia and interview the architect. But the Professor and Elena explained that the maestro, whose incredibly long fingers danced their ballet on the mother-of-pearl keys, might not be disturbed from his trance. Eventually, the television crew had to contend with a fifteen-minute segment about Mozart, using the architect's music as background.

It was during that time that Elena discovered she was pregnant. At first, she was alarmed, but the saxophone player – who no longer played the saxophone but instead, during mornings, circulated quicksilver-like between the radio and television stations and the editorial offices of various publications, while evenings he meticulously filled his seventh or eighth journal with notes and musical staves – the Professor thus, who had already for the last few months been sleeping in the architect's house, reassured her, and the two of them decided on what had been apparent for a long time: her divorce from the architect. The process of the divorce did not drag on exceedingly long, approximately eight months. The facts were clear, and Elena's pregnant state was advancing rapidly. The outcome satisfied both parties: Elena was left with the apartment and all the furniture; Emil Popescu with the car and an allowance that she would pay him in the form of a pension and which included three meals a day and lodging for the night. Thus, the only thing that had changed for the three – soon to become four – was their social status. This unusual divorce stirred up enough controversy, and certainly everything might have stunk of promiscuity had public opinion not taken up the task of familiarizing itself with the unusual persona of the architect.

He had changed much during the few years since the fatal sounding of the stray horn of his Dacia. He had become enormously obese; though he ate nearly nothing, the skin of his face extended over his cheeks, while his eyes, coming closer and closer together, acquired a fixed look, paying attention to nothing in this world. A spider web of sparse beard strands, unusually long, twisted on his cheeks. But it was his hands that surpassed even the pathological, crossing the border into teratology. His fingers, over thirty centimetres in length, spread out like a fan comprising the entire keyboard.

Thick crisscrossing ropes of muscles hoisted the phalanges, contracting and relaxing at an incredible velocity. The tips of his fingers sped like nervous mosquito legs across the cold keys. With these monstrous hands, Emil Popescu performed entire concerts by Beethoven and Tchaikovsky in a state of constant hallucination, reinventing them without ever having heard them before. Whenever he stopped playing, his fingers, which now reached down to his knees, gave him unbearable pain, so that after only two years the architect left his job, remaining practically unfettered by any ties with customary social life. He now played without interruption, day and night. Short notices about the Romanian organist began to appear in the curiosity columns of all the great newspapers and magazines. Reporters from the *New York Herald-Tribune, Life, Strange and Astonishing Stories, Paris Match* and *Penthouse* were now teeming behind the Berceni apartment building, flashing their sophisticated cameras, recording entire video and audio cassettes with the enchanting music of the architect and his incoherent muttering. The Professor hovered around them, 'translating' the words of the organist and, at the beginning of spring, published simultaneously in Paris and London the notes he had scribbled in his journals under the title *Un Génie aux Portes de l'Orient*, or *A Man of Genius at the Gates of the Orient*. The unimaginable success of these publications among the ranks of musicians as well as those of laymen, followed immediately by others in various other tongues, hoisted Emil Popescu to the status of the 'man of the hour' in the entire world.

In the years that followed, the saxophone player, now married to Elena, travelled the world, untiringly holding one conference after another. Elena raised the child alone. Emil Popescu became the best-known Romanian artist on earth, and a Japanese firm presented him with a magnificent Mishiba synthesizer in order to open up new possibilities of expression. After a journey via airplanes and various trucks, the gigantic instrument, measuring eleven metres in length and two in height, finally reached its destination behind the apartment building. A few tenants had to give up their parking spaces, and the carpet-beater rack had to be repositioned a few metres away. A special construction, of transparent plexiglas, protected the contraption from the ravages of weather. The two Japanese specialists who had accompanied it mounted the entire installation and attempted to persuade the architect to move under the plexiglas roof. It was impossible, however, to remove him from the car. The automobile's cream-coloured body was, for Emil Popescu, just as important as the music itself. Ingenious as usual, the Japanese resorted to the only possible solution. They shifted the architect to the back seat, removed the front seat and the old keyboard of the Reghin organ, and in a few days installed the immense apparatus in its place. It was a dizzy tangle of screens, potentiometers, monitors with electronic displays, with eight extra rows of special keys, so that you could almost believe you found yourself before the controls of a spaceship. The two little men, after activating the synthesizer, attempted to enter into conversation with the celebrated musician. Their surprise and relief were indeed great when they saw that the architect handled the electronic apparatus, pressed the buttons and adjusted the frequencies as if he had spent his whole life handling such things. From the initial pressing of the keys a striking purity and richness of sound that shamed the primitive squeak of the Reghin blasted out into the regions of the air: the successive waves, soaring upwards at first, then withheld like a gigantic anguish, of Ravel's *La Valse*.

The great Mishiba could reconstruct any sound, natural or artificial. For a few years, Emil Popescu did nothing but explore incessantly the fantastic possibilities of the synthesizer. From time to time, among the most faithful renderings of natural sounds – the rustling of dry leaves, warbles of blackbirds, the gushing of river springs, inflections of feminine voices of a sweetness that dissolved one into nothingness, the turbulence of landings and takeoffs, the babbling of dolphins – the saxophone player, inasmuch as he still tarried around the Dacia behind the apartment building, had the opportunity to feverishly note pieces of a disturbing orchestration. One could hear, with a pure and simple clarity of timbre impossible to obtain in a natural manner, flutes and violas, horns and bassoons, triangles and tympani, weaving their melodic lines into filigreed melodies or glistening dissonances. The architect's paws, with tens of articulations of the fingers, sped across the hundreds of keys, adjusted the thousands of concurrent frequencies, programmed simultaneously entire orchestras. The modest speakers of the Reghin organ had been replaced by a globe of special wire, with a diameter longer than three metres and capable of emitting a quad-raphonic sound with a directed multiple echo. Along with the minor disadvantage of the demolition of the apartment building – the ten-ants had been forced out due to the pronounced state of stress – came a great advantage: most of Bucharest found itself permanently under the umbrella of sounds emitted by the architect. The ground of the now levelled apartment building was surrounded by a wall of concrete and wood. The serial music of Schoenberg and Webern agreed with the pine trees planted around its circumference, so that their needled branches soon began to distend, angling over the rusty Dacia and surrounding with coffee-coloured needles the Plex-iglas block where the enormous belly of the synthesizer player slept, next to the two Japanese specialists, who by now had begun to lose their hair. Day and night, the music bellowed and rumbled, vibrated and warbled, monopolizing the surroundings.

The saxophone player and his Elena occupied the metal and glass villa which had been built on the foundations of the previous apartment building. They lived in peace, surrounded by the power-ful smell of ozone. They began to realize they were getting old when their boy got married. The Professor was regarded as a bril-liant impresario, but after a while no one seemed to have any need of his services. He was still invited to conventions as an honourary president, but the only thing that was demanded of him was to tell and retell the circumstances of his meeting with Emil Popescu, whose popularity did not appear to follow any fashion or trend, but grew ceaselessly in an exponential manner. Listeners of all genera-tions demanded the same music, something that was sociologically inexplicable and unheard of until then. Three quarters of all cable television and videocassette markets were dedicated to the con-certs of Emil Popescu.

The crucial moment of the inauguration of the architect's melocracy came and went unnoticed by public opinion. It took place one evening when the saxophone player, returning from a conference at the new Athenaeum, found Elena, now portly and grey, listening in a trance to the music of her ex-husband. Their old agreement required that they didn't speak about him and that he was accorded no more attention than that demanded by legal obligation. Ever since she stopped feeding him, Elena seemed to have forgotten about him completely. But now, on the veranda, she was listening in ecstasy to the desperate screams of electronically simulated guitars. The Professor went into a rage. He was moved by the music as well, but this time he paid no attention to its bewitching charm. In a moment of lucidity, he saw himself: a little old man who had earned his existence like a circus master, exposing a monster of nightmares to the public curiosity. He was abruptly overwhelmed by an intense hatred for him who, a few steps off out into the night, psychically ravished his wife and reconquered her love through the power of music. He left Elena and headed for the kitchen. He grabbed a glistening loin chopper, the kind used to portion slabs of meat, and rushed towards the contours of the outmoded Dacia, flickering pallidly in the dark. The Professor glared at the sheet-metal of the body, literally eaten away by rust, the crooked rims of the erstwhile wheels, the windows without windshields. But inside, where the dashboard once was, thousands of green and blue lights glittered fantastically. They blinked rhythmically off and on, exercising a hypnotic effect upon the saxophone player. He approached the car and peered inside.

The architect was there. His deformed, naked and whitish body weighed at least four hundred kilograms; it had long burst out of its clothes and literally filled, the way the snail fills up its shell, the entire back of the car, even overflowing a little out of the windows. His head had joined his torso, his features, like finely traced lines, could barely be spotted on his fleshy face, while his eyes fused into a single eye that perused in one glance the entire complicated machinery of the command counter of the synthesizer. His elbows and his upper arms had been reabsorbed into his ribs, so that two bouquets of fingers issued directly out of his torso, each comprising an assemblage of complexly articulated twig-like filaments, which pressed incessantly on the mother-of-pearl keys. The Professor felt like vomiting, overtaken by a shiver of sacred horror before this unhuman-like being. In order to force himself not to retreat, he turned off the headlights and headed for the front door. As he pulled on it, it came off its rotted hinges and fell on the grass like a crooked splinter from a shell. He grabbed firmly the bundle of fingers and began to hack at them furiously. Blood and bits of fingers dribbled on the greasy flesh of Emil Popescu, but he appeared not to react in any way. The remaining bundle of fingers continued imperturbably to crepitate upon the keys. A weighty reek, like a room where a woman gives birth, emanated from underneath the needled branches. When the last finger fell, throbbing on the striated tyre at the feet of the architect, the saxophone player – his hatchet glittering under the powder of tiny stars – circled around the front of the automobile remains, through which the darkened engine could be partially spotted, and clasped tight in his fist the stub from which the other bundle of fingers shot out. But this time, at the very instant he was about to strike with all of his power, something astonishing occurred. Abruptly, the fingers trembled delicately over the stacking keyboard's layers, like the trepidation of the phylloxera's antennae and, out of the great sphere of metallic mesh, a few overwhelming chords dispersed into the air. It was no longer Alban Berg, and nor was it Orff, Duke Ellington or even Pink Floyd. It was nothing that had ever been heard, nothing the human mind could conceive that could ever be heard. The saxophone player froze and listened. It was a form of music not to be listened to with one's ears, but with the whole of the skin at once, a form of music that filled the canals of the veins with echoes and turned the bone structure to resonance. Like a dose of mescaline reaching the brain, the gates of the soul, or a sweet spider injecting the dissolving enzymes into the victim's flesh, that music substituted itself for the soul and, like a perfidious homunculus, took over the reins of the body in its firm hands. Then, like a sequence of azure peristaltic waves, the music leaked down to the jugulars, invaded the lymphatic canals, irrigated the fusiform packets of the muscles, appropriated, along the length of the spinal nerves, the internal organs, the hexagonal cells of the liver, the heart with its electrical embryos, the suprarenal and the great precincts of the urinal bladder, descended into the calves like a mist of twilight, and sped along the femur, tibia and fibula to the tips of the toes, replacing with a musical tangle every cell, each mitochondrion, each crumb of nucleic acid. Overwhelmed, seized by the sensation that the world was coming apart, which, it is said, may be known only by those experiencing a heart attack, the saxophone player tumbled down on the grass next to the car door. He had the impression that the great transparent leaf of the sky in which the stars were encrusted was distorting itself, that it advanced towards him, that it moulded to his body and wrapped itself tight around it like a multihued shroud. He lost consciousness.

When he awoke, it was already light, but the Dacia's palpitating shadow on the grass protected him from the sun's melted disc. He was covered with blood. The stub from which he had chopped off those gigantic fingers had already scarred, and the likeness of tiny fingernails began to bud in their place. The Professor began to weep painfully, choking and sobbing. He felt himself capable of nothing any more. The world seemed to him an inferno of ash, impossible to tolerate. He longed from the bottom of his entrails for those chords he had heard the night before. For about eight hours he suffered horribly. He felt sick, in his body and in his soul. A paranoid delirium grew under his skull, and he grabbed the meat cleaver again, determined this time to kill the architect for real. But the same ecstatic music threw him again to the ground.

He understood that the architect emitted those dolorously melodious sounds like a poisoned secretion against any aggression. It was enough only to pretend to strike him in order to hear once more the music he could no longer live without. The stronger the aggression, the stronger the music's power to take possession. Year after year, practically until the end of his life, the saxophone player viciously profited from this discovery. In order to enhance the effect of the music, he attempted, in succession, to asphyxiate, set on fire, boil, dynamite, electrocute and irradiate the architect. Each time the melodic line shifted, the sonorous and the extrasonorous volutes

swivelled in new ways, in compositions more powerful and penetrating than anything that had ever been realized by any other
composer. In those moments, the architect no longer imitated any
styles and modalities already in existence, but became a superartist
and superinterpreter. Over the decades, the entire mentality of
humanity transmuted under the overwhelming influence of the
architect. There were no more conflicts, because the only concern
of every single human being was to listen day and night to the un-
interrupted recital. The only thing anyone ever wrote was about the
architect: entire newspapers about the architect, books about the
architect. The only paintings ever painted were official portraits of
the architect, and every poem was a hymn of glory devoted to the
architect. People worked only to ensure minimal means of suste-
nance and for the maintenance of the vast network of satellites
continuously rebroadcasting the architect's music. Humans loved
one another to the music of the architect, and when they were buried, they shared the same funeral music.

The two Japanese men who took care of the great Mishiba
entered the realm of legend, and after their death two others followed; they took on the names of their predecessors. Thus, in the
course of the centuries, an entire dynasty of Japanese men came by
turns to the tiny oasis under the pine-needle branches. Pilgrims
from all over the world came to listen to the sacred music directly
from the original source. Thousands of attempts on the architect's
life were organized in order to incite the defensive reaction, that
music which was hundreds of times more profound than the ordinary. The hunger for music became monstrous; it obsessed the
minds of men to such a degree that, in a moment of collective madness, they determined, out of an irrepressible desire to dissolve into
harmony, to exterminate the architect by means of thermonuclear
rockets. The moment when the finger of the man in uniform
approached the button that would unleash the few thousands of
nuclear strikes, the music blasted like flamethrowers from all recep-
tion apparatuses, in concatenations of tonalities and unbearable
frequencies. The majority of humans were carbonized, while the
survivors became no more than accessories to the architect. Their

lives were preserved by music alone. Blood circulation, the movement of thought, the digestion of food were supported artificially by the melodic weave issuing from under the fingers of the architect. With those few million survivors acting in synchronicity like termites, the architect built a new synthesizer of unconceivable complexity, unfolding over a quarter of the planet. The monster himself grew. The body of the Dacia remained encrusted on his whitish spinal chord like a minuscule shell. His body occupied a vast surface, while his fingers, infinitely ramified, extended from his two forearms and circled all around him like a spider web. At the first touch of the billion terminal keys, the last humans turned to powder. This was no longer music – or perhaps it was the music which the Pythagoreans spoke about. No human ear was capable of hearing it, because it was no longer made up of sounds, nor of matter, but penetrated the cosmic pulsations, weaving itself into them and forcing them to transmute. Throughout millions of years, the architect modulated his melodies so that they caused the acceleration of the fusion process at the core of the stars, producing the surrounding matter, provoking the explosion of stars having now reached critical mass, forming the marvellous supernovae that shrivelled the tinier stars until they became white dwarfs, pulsars or desperate black holes through which matter disappeared into another universe. It was supernatural to be able to view how the billions of yellow stars and those glittering white or bluish crowded into the spidery levels, spinners of the galaxies. Most were double or even multiple systems, like the Pleiades or the Hyades; some, Regulus, Syrius, Rigel and Arcturus, were a few times larger than the Sun; and others, of a positive magnitude of +14 and beyond, glittered and throbbed, coagulated and exploded, receiving instantaneously the rhythmical waves from the new synthesizer. After four billion years, the sun began to dilate, comprising at first the orbit of Mercury, followed by Venus, overflowing like dough the vicinity of the Earth. The Earth, however, was no longer visible, being enclosed in its entirety in the organic mass of the architect; it was of spherical form, of solar dimensions, with two plethoric arms endowed with filaments like the arms of a medusa. The great synthesizer was now an internal element of the immense body. The moment the Sun exploded, hurling into space volatile, ether-like matter in the form of purple and violet flames, scintillating in millions of fringes, the architect began his leisurely migration towards the centre of the galaxy.

The universe was ageing; it wrinkled like a fig, its matter crumbling like rot. Even interstellar space, otherwise flexible and vaporous, brimming with methane clouds and strands of golden dust, became rigid and tough. Through it the architect now advanced, like an ever-expanding nebula, swallowing whole constellations, fluttering in the motion of electromagnetic fields, but permanently emitting, like a great wish, his own rhythms, fresh and imperative. When he reached the centre, his arms, twisted in a spiral, filled the entire space of the erstwhile galaxy. The matter of his body and his arms, having reached in the course of the migration an extreme state of rarefaction, condensed itself during a period of incommensurable time, lost its consistency and became star crumbs, which ignited suddenly in the darkened and empty universe. A young galaxy revolved now, throbbing, pulsating in place of the old one.